# BLIGHT-BRINGER

## B.D. MCATEER

GOLEM HEART
PUBLISHING

This is a work of fiction. All of the characters, organizations, and events portrayed in this novel are either products of the author's imagination or are used fictitiously.

BLIGHT-BRINGER

Cover Art by Etheric Tales
Edited by Susan at Grendel Press
Chapter Heading Ornament and Scene Breaks by shathedesigner

A Golem Heart Publishing Book
Golemheartpublishing.squarespace.com

Printed in the United States of America

For Corey, this is where our years of unhealthy imaginings begin to take their physical form.

...world, forgive us...

## Acknowledgments

To Dwight, for the only decent thing you ever said to me. You looked down at the very first drawing I ever did of an Alerez back when it was called ColdWest. "Keep it up. That could be something one day," you said. Thank you. See you in hell.

# Prologue

*I've made a mistake. I am sorry.*

The words were smeared slightly but remained enough to read legibly. It was a simple enough statement, and I had no doubt it was heartfelt. I wondered why it was written in blood. The starkness of the words, in contrast to the brightness of the pages, drew my eyes in. I was cautious not to touch the print; knowing enough about the author, it could've just as well been poison.

I closed the journal and looked down at the others in the ashes. I counted four journals, but there was no way of knowing if this was all of them.

I picked up each of the journals, partly in reverence and partly with caution, slow and methodical.

"Zephrus." Her white wings flinched. I followed my eyes to where she had been looking.

"Why does it count backward?" she asked.

"I am unsure. I've never known a bell tower to do so."

I paused to verify I hadn't been seeing things. The hands of the clock were indeed ticking in the opposite direction. It occurred to me the bells had not tolled since we arrived. Had they been disabled?

"The Clock Tower is no more," I said.

"How do you know?" Zephrus sent Shell away. The heavy mosoleth armor faded away in hexagon flakes of green light, until she was left in the limited amount of fabric she normally wore.

I placed a hand on her shoulder to stop her flying off. I couldn't let her explore this place alone.

"I said Clock Tower was gone, not that their effects on the world were. Head back to camp. Send Olu. I need his talents, I think."

"Why can you wander off, but I cannot?"

"Tell him I'll be in the belfry." I pointed up at the tower, ignoring her complaints.

She huffed passed her mask, spread her wings, and launched into the air. Sending her to retrieve Olu was more about getting her out of the city. It felt as though the particles in the air were going to stain those wings of hers. I didn't want the poor Anirlit to have to go through that. She had enough to worry about already when it came to dark omens. At any rate, I needed time to think and reflect. Olu was a chatty person, but if I asked him nicely, he would let me have my time.

The inside of the tower's adjoining structure appeared to be some sort of church once upon a time. The structure had been weakened by a large blow from above. The impact had shifted the entire structure and the pillars stood precariously. Any further change in the integrity of the church would see it as lost as its followers.

The stained glass, which once graced those in prayer, now told a different story, one devoid of hope. After a while of attempting to step over the multicolored shards, or any other possible holy symbols, I resorted to trudging through like a nonbeliever. It's not that I was impatient; I was, but there was no way around. I tried to make up for it by correcting one of the Ald'Kair statues near the altar. The other statue in the worship hall was too far gone. I ignored the obvious omen that it was the Tyrant who had risen again, not the Savior.

The clock tower's structure was just slightly more adequate than the adjoining church. I had no doubt it would carry me all the way to the top. The particles in the air were thicker here, though. More of the husk-like material crawled across surfaces indiscriminately. I adjusted my mask and checked its filter. The seal held despite my beard.

"Ah, you made it." Olu's smile bothered me sometimes, but I supposed he was a decent enough bard.

"Who does this remind you of?" I held up some of the husk pulled from one of the support beams.

"Always a pleasant conversationalist, Iter. Let me have a look."

He took the husk and shifted his fingers. The mass crumbled into sand.

"This I'm not familiar with. I'm not sure what to make of it. It seems like something you'd expect from Disiea, but the other realms are just as likely. It doesn't follow any rules I'm aware of."

"No one comes to mind?" I asked.

Olu shook his head. "I'm sorry, no."

I nodded, understanding. "Did you find anything?"

"I did." Olu is usually quite a chipper lad. His songs or conversations are enough to make any of us smile. But this time, he simply magicked a lute into his lap and tuned it idly. "A girl." He pointed with his chin. "In the holding cells, underneath the keep." The keep was plain enough in the city's sky line.

I didn't ask why he hadn't brought the girl with him. Who would've fed the child while she was confined? The city had been abandoned too long for anyone to have survived. The girl had to remind Olu of Unna. The bite of that one had never subsided. To grow past something like that, a change to some degree was required. Change was not in his nature.

"Found something too." I produced the journals. "They are probably his."

Olu's mood perked up. "Well, why didn't you say so!"

I took a seat next to him on the ledge of the belfry. Olu pushed the particles in the air from us so I felt comfortable enough to peel my mask away.

"Zephrus says you think he is long gone."

I nodded again.

"Then why are we not heading out after him?"

I watched the city below. It had looked bad before, amongst the destruction. From the tower, the city was one large grave, a parable to fallen glory.

"I believe there is still something here for us to learn. We should understand before we move on. Would you mind telling me a story?"

"Oh, most certainly. I would like to see this one myself, honestly."

Olu opened the first journal and hesitated, reading the same first words that I had.

"I guess I didn't expect a happy tale, but...anything particular we are looking for?"

I shrugged. "I don't have enough understanding of what happened here to know where to take us next. We could go after him, but the blight has been pushed back quite a bit. Does that mean he is no longer a threat? We could move on if that were so. However, if he is still as big a menace as this land remembers, we must do something. We have to figure out where he went and how to stop him."

"Any idea why the clock is ticking backward?"

"I was hoping you did."

"The mechanisms had to be changed deliberately in order to make something like that happen."

"I noticed the function of the bell had been changed as well. It won't ring, at least not yet. There are some interesting symbols on it, though. Not something you'd expect to see, let alone on a bell tower of the Breathing Church."

Olu magicked a book into his hand this time, a leathery thing that, though standard size, looked like it weighed more than despair.

"What did they look like?" Olu asked.

I opened my mouth to explain one of the symbols but realized how fruitless it would have been. I drew one in the purplish sand on the floor.

Olu flipped the pages of his book until he was satisfied and placed a finger on the page in question. He read for a long moment and then slammed the book closed with his hand along the book's spine.

"Nope. Nothing."

"Nothing?"

"Nothing."

I took the book from him and flipped through the pages. The book had enough drawings to give credence to it being an alchemy book, but he was right. Nothing. I could make out some of the symbols from the bell, but no amount of want was going to tell me what the damn book was trying to say. The only clue was the final symbol at the zenith of the clock's face, it was nowhere to be found in the book.

"Story time?" Olu smiled. Annoying. He knew I'd have to be patient now.

"Story time." I nodded settling in at the base of a pillar.

Olu's image wavered a bit and I could feel a large amount of essence pouring from him. He gingerly turned the page written in a red substance. Then he ran a single finger across the ink that lay there. We watched as the letters began to unfold.

## Of Minotaur and Men

Name day. It was *my* name day when they took me from my home, setting the end of the world in motion.

I was naive then. Back when the world was simple, and I didn't have to think so hard about the future. I couldn't fathom that Korigara, a land of ice, could somehow become coated in ash and fire. We barely acknowledged the humans, save for the traders that had business with father and in the market.

A Tréges brought me a gift once, a crisp jewel of a fruit. He called it an apple. It was the most delicious thing I'd ever tasted. The flavor forgotten for rot when I saw their colors during the raid. Our crystalline refuge cracked wide open, and they took me. I wasn't sure if anyone else suffered the same fate, but before I knew what was happening, I was alone in a cage somewhere below the ice shelf. The boar on their flag mocking me in the fire light. No flames have lit up my night sky thus ever since. Sometime later, they carted me and my cage away. I couldn't call out for help. It wouldn't have mattered anyway if I did. My small voice would not have risen over the screams.

My mind started to go numb by the time they transferred me to a larger cage with others inside, none Alerez. No food or water had been provided to me and the sun grew hotter than I should like. Though they aimed to receive a hefty price for me, these men were not caretakers. I would've killed for someone to lean on in my weakened state, but my captors and fellow cage mates kept their distance. My captors chained me up to the side of the cage before we moved on. Everyone was far more relaxed then.

After the sun had come and set again, I weaken further still. I had been saving my appetite for the large feast intended for myself and the other hatchlings before I was taken. But that feast would never come now. I and the others would never know who it was we were supposed to be. The name that was never uttered, died, suffocated with the rising smoke.

· · · ❧ ❧ ❧ ·

"Out." A bearded man demanded when we had been stopped for some time. The rest of the captives had already been moved out of the cage and the man had undone my chains, but I was not inclined to obey. The sun and malnourishment left me unable to do so.

"Out," he demanded more fervently with a slap to the bars near my face when it became apparent I would not move. At any other point in my life, the tone he used would have compelled me to obey. I didn't understand their lack of comprehension that I was too weak.

He cursed under his breath in the Oreculian tongue as he climbed in to retrieve me himself, the beads in his beard clattering. The Tréges grabbed me by the wing and dragged me out of the cage. He muttered under his breath something akin to "dumb lizard." Next, I was struggling to catch my breath after the impact with the ground.

As the bearded man pulled me across the permafrost, the heat of the land began to affect me further, making my head feel as though it were full of air. My vision swam. By the time I felt the flagstones across my back, another had joined us.

"You didn't feed him? He's a youngling. You could've killed him. Then—"

"—didn't want to get frosted—"

"—legends and idiots like you who believe in 'em—it's too damn hot for a razor—"

"Hot? I'm freezing my arse off."

"Stop wailing the both of you." There was a slight pause in realization. "You didn't bind his tail?"

With that, I felt something left in me. My tail *was* free. I wanted to fight back; I wanted to take my fate back into my own hands. Like a frost flame coming part way back to life as it died in the hearth, I moved my body. The bone fin at the end of my tail cracked apart, separating into blades, and I swung with all I had, which apparently wasn't nearly as much as I had built up in my mind. My tail swung with the vigor of a sunbathing seal. Then, also like a flame, I was out.

Sometime later, I gained a small level of consciousness. The distant sound of something wooden sliding across stone was the first thing to bring me out of my dreamless slumber. Cracking an eye open, I saw a bowl before my beak. It brought me the rest of the way back to life. Primal instinct took over and I tore into the mush in the bowl. It was a putrid mess tasting of corn and sweat. I ate it anyway. When your body still wants to live, it will force almost anything down your gullet to make that happen. I cursed between swallows. I didn't gag once, though I knew I would have at any other time. I lapped up the remnants, cleaning the bowl with my fingers and tongue.

Tears began to well up in my eyes, grateful at life, until I looked up from the bowl and took in my surroundings. A little over half a dozen sets of eyes fixated on me, on the life-confining side of a cell door, a side I shared. I found pity in some of those eyes, but some were fearful, and some malicious. I wasn't sure what to make of it, and I sat dumbfounded for longer than I'd like to admit. For a moment, just a moment, even though they were human, I wanted to take that pity. I wanted to break down and find comfort where I could; I didn't care in whose arms. I couldn't do it. These...creatures...were to blame for my current misfortune. Instead, I focused on the stares of indifference. Those faces, those at least helped me wise up.

In lieu of tears, I settled for wiping the corn shit from my face with the tatters of my seal skins. Then I found an empty space toward the end of the long bench lining the wall. I sat there, awkward but defiant. I did my best not to let it show how weak my travels had made me. I couldn't let myself feel safe here, and I couldn't show any vulnerability. Thankfully, the humans nearby inched away from where I chose to sit. I would not have to do much convincing.

I glared through the corners of my eyes in an attempt to look tough and assess my situation without appearing too concerned. The humans didn't look as diverse as the *Histories of the Empire* suggested. Surprisingly, most of the humans were Tréges by ethnicity. Only one other kind was there, a Lycion by the look of her. She almost blended into the corner of our cell for all the shadow there. Only the gleam of gold on her wrists and collarbone cut through the gloom, but not nearly so much as those eyes of hers, those eyes that bore into me. Her elegance in posture and finery seemed odd. The other humans gave her a wider birth than they gave me. She was a woman and possessed jewelry in a cell full of men, and no one would accost her? They felt safer around what they knew as a razor than one of their own? I couldn't take her stare any longer, so I opted to occupy my mind with different thoughts.

The Lycion woman's jewelry had me in mind of my own, clunky and lackluster as it was. I tried to reach my horns, but the wrist restraints pulled my hands short, tugging at the harness on my chest. Instead, I shook my head, testing the areas I could not reach. Something weighty was up there. They must have been corked or wrapped heavily. I lifted my tail that lay next to me and observed the heavy cloth and rope they had used to lock my blades into place. My wings were free, save for balls of iron and chain draped over them to keep me from flight. I'd keep the fact that I was too young to fly to myself. I wasn't pleased with how much I had been restrained, but I was grateful they hadn't decided to just lop it all off. I'd heard of such stories. Apparently, whatever the plan was for me, I was more valuable in one piece. I wrapped myself with my wings for comfort, however difficult the task.

"They couldn't be too careful after you killed that man." The woman in jewelry startled me. Her accent was rich and thick, an unexpected assortment of curt words and odd emphasis on syllables. Very different from the Tréges accents I was used to.

"What?" I asked, not understanding.

She gestured to her head as though she had horns.

"No," I said, trying to gather my thoughts. I wasn't being poached for parts. "No, I mean, killed?"

The woman shrugged. "I didn't think you had the look of a killer either, but according to the men carrying the wrapped corpse in the market..."

"They said *I* killed him?" Me, whose father didn't trust him to protect their land?

She shrugged and stared at me from her corner of the cell.

Uncharacteristically, I suddenly became quite irritated. I suppose it wasn't her fault, but for that moment, I needed someone to aim my ire at. I needed to blame someone for my fate. I understood what the woman was telling me, but I couldn't accept it. I was refusing to understand everything about my circumstances.

I gritted my teeth. "How are you called?" I bit off the 'human' at the end.

She paused and gracefully stood up. Her movements were like that of a dancer. The others in the cell shifted in their seats. The woman sat down next to me. It may have been sensually so, but at the time, I wouldn't have known.

"Navitat. You see? Nav-ee-tat." She pointed to her lips and exaggerated her pronunciation. She wasn't having it, my petulance.

"Navitat, listen."

She nodded.

"I'm sure in time I'd like you well enough, but right now, I need answers." Panic started to boil over in me.

She pulled my face away from her own via the chain on the back of my head like a dog. "I believe I have just provided an answer, razor."

"Answers are a commodity for a slave, boy." The voice that intervened came deep and intimidating without the aim to be, which made it all the more so.

I couldn't help but lean toward the bars leading to the adjoining cell despite the extra rattle in my chains. Trying to make out the source from where even the torchlight wouldn't dare go was like reaching into the mouth of a wolf den to retrieve your dropped waterskin.

*Would be better to remain thirsty,* was my decision.

Almost as soon as I decided to preserve my life, the beast blew out a great sigh. It caught me in the face and I backed away in a panic. The result was a headache, with the wall behind me keeping a bit of my scalp in remembrance.

"Dear Nybe," I hissed.

The other prisoners had themselves a laugh at my expense. Scorn colored my cheeks. The voice behind the bars overpowered the others, his only being a chuckle.

"And you, how are you called, minotaur?"

The cells went silent, the laughter dropping like a broken promise, awkward and visceral. Even the constant dripping sound decided to voice itself at another time.

I knew what I had done but didn't know just how bad that decision was at the moment. The faux pas was intentional but the price had been unknown. In the towns and villages of Orecul, only two creatures could produce an exhalation such as it had. A horse or a Materic. Since horses cannot talk, I had just used an incredibly racist slur toward one of the largest sentient species in Orecul.

There was a shift in the dark. "Well educated, aren't you, boy?"

The boards beneath us groaned as the first hoof hit the ground. No one spoke. Even Navitat seemed like she wanted distance between us. She found her original seat. Even so, the place grew stiller with each earth-cracking step. When the minotaur opened his own cell door and started down the hallway to our cell, I started wondering if I could wake myself out of this progressively worsening dream. When the door to my cell opened without so much as the rattling of keys, I was glad to lack proper hydration to void myself.

"You didn't know the whole floor was ours, did you?" He smiled. "Now that I'm getting a better look at you, boy is indeed the word that I would use. Probably scared too." He shrugged. It was like two boulders dancing to the rhythm of an earthquake. The minotaur's presence filled the room as he made his way in, all eight feet of solid muscle and bone. He had to hunch over to admit himself to the room. "But if you ever say that again," his voice was calm, though I may have managed to find the proper hydration in that moment. "I'll wear your head like a hand puppet."

With great effort, I nodded, all wide-mouthed and sweaty.

"Alright then." The minotaur straightened up and his demeanor changed instantly as though none of the previous ugliness had occurred. He shooed away the closest man sharing my bench. Then he plopped himself down next to me opposite Navitat, who had magicked herself back to my side. If he had dropped any further, I was sure the impact would have fractured the wood. A red gleam flashed around his neck.

"Leegius. You, boy?" the mino...Materic asked.

I opened my mouth and hesitated, realizing I had no real answer.

"Your name, child," Navitat persisted.

"I have no name." The memory still ripe, I hung my head. "They took me before it was spoken.

"Ah," Leegius said but left it for a moment so I could collect myself. He flailed about anxiously on the bench as though trying to find a comfortable position. The motion may have been able to go unnoticed, if the beast didn't take up so much damn space. "You are younger than your gall a moment ago would've led me to believe. My memory is a little foggy on your people. How old *are* you?"

I looked at Navitat. "To a hum—your people, maybe nine." Back to Leegius, "For yours, I am not sure."

Leegius nodded to himself. "Your people name off actions, yes? I'd say we could name you, but somehow 'Pisser' doesn't seem proper." He jested, but I couldn't help my cheeks coloring.

As uncomfortable a moment as it was, in the midst of laughter all directed at me, I was able to notice something. We were in a dire situation. Some, myself included, barely had any idea of what was going on, yet this massive presence called Leegius had us finding our smiles.

"Perhaps our new masters will give you a proper name, in time." Leegius gestured with a hand. "Or leave you in this cell to rot if you keep offing their employees." The Materic spat. A rat could've drowned in it.

"How did he die?" I asked. "The man in the courtyard." I thought that maybe Leegius liked me enough for some straight answers.

"You really don't know?" Navitat asked, incredulous.

"Or perhaps he just needs to remember?" Leegius looked down at me expectantly.

"I think I swung at someone before I passed out." It came out as more of a question.

"Lopped his foot right off." Leegius snickered to himself.

"Really?"

"No, child," Navitat interjected, regarding Leegius. "You nicked a vital artery and it was enough." She slapped Leegius's arm. "Do not fill the boy's mind with false grandeur."

"Sounded better my way, priest." Leegius shot back, but there was no heat to it. "Poor bastard bled to death. Slow as hell a way to die, though. You look pale, hatchling. Do not fret. It was a fine first kill."

I shot a look at him, ready to protest, but it died in my throat. There was no fooling someone like Leegius or my father. They just...knew.

"Where are we?" I asked, changing the subject. I glanced up at the window above us. There was no seeing through it unless Leegius let me up on his shoulders.

"A place where paths diverge."

Navitat and I glanced up at his bull head as Leegius gazed off at greener horizons like a scholar.

"Along the Southern Trade Route, child. I have not been out this way before. So, I do not know where we are."

"Wherever we are, there will be an auction. And we will find what fate has in store for us," Leegius said.

Navitat threw a thumb his way. "This one knows less than I do." She turned toward him. "Did you get into some bad mushrooms over there? Last I checked, Ligshrum did not sprout in prison cells, man."

"Is that why it is so dark in your cell?"

Navitat shot a look at me. I had missed something. Leegius, though, was flustered.

"No. My damn lantern keeps going out." Leegius pulled the nearest lantern from its hook and placed it at his feet. "I was just coming to borrow some of your light when we first met. I'll get mine up and going again and bring it right back."

"They give us a lot of freedom to move about for slaves, don't they?" I asked.

"One should accept blessings rather than question them. Brings bad omens and such to replace it," Leegius groaned.

"Nothing much to that, really." Navitat flicked her wrist out to reveal the one bit of ugly jewelry she possessed.

I checked my own to confirm. An ugly off-orange crystalline cluster lay in the wrought iron shackle.

"All that is needed to ensure our cooperation." His mood soured, Leegius made to leave.

"Leegius, wait." I held it out as much as I could manage with my bindings. "Your lamp." When the Materic reached out to take it, a perfect red gleam winked at me from around his neck again. This time, I took notice.

Leegius placed the lantern in the middle of his cell and lay on his side as if to shield the pitiful flame from a windy world.

The rest of the cell came to life as others became too bored to remain silent. Conversation broke out here and there, each person's story worse than the last. Tears fell. I passed the time listening to them, but most of the time, I sank back into my own hurt and thought about the life that had been stolen from me. I wondered if mother had survived. And where the hell father had been. That merchant had flashed that odd coin again and father was gone soon after.

"*On mission*," he would say.

He had been gone longer this time. Why? How could he not be there when we needed him? Probably the greatest warrior in the Fissure Tribes and his allegiances elsewhere had left us vulnerable.

I looked down at the dull, imperfect gem on my wrist. No more thoughts came. I just fixated there and started to shake. I glanced over to where Leegius had been lying on the other side of the bars and was greeted by the dark.

## The Price of a Life

The sun almost brought a quick end to my tale, its harsh embrace turning my skin pallid. An odd buzzing came from the trees outside of town, almost like they worshipped the heat and were attempting to summon every bit of it from Disiea. I wondered just how far north we had come. I could barely focus, but the vegetation here was vastly different from the lack of flora that surrounded Korigara.

Didn't they know that Alerez couldn't survive in this environment? We had ways to travel through Orecul safely, of course, seldom as we did. But, once again, I had been too young. That particular lesson had not been passed down to me, so instead, I fried like a fish.

Navitat and the Materic seemed unaffected until they started having to drag me along while the slave drivers led us through the streets. Leegius said something to one of the slavers, but I was unsure what. I was starting to resent my new friends just about the time that a splash of chilled water went up my nostrils. The little shite who had done it ran off, presumably to refill his bucket. After the initial shock, I was grateful and could stand a little taller, ignoring the fact that I was trying to appear smaller amongst giants. I shot my eyes around, looking for the water's source. It must have been emyon chilled or produced as it couldn't have been that cold here naturally. Instead of an essence wielder, I notice the privies. I prayed the water used to fill the buckets was close enough so that they wouldn't choose to change sources.

We, myself and fellow slaves-to-be, shuffled forward intermittently. The others were as docile as if this were simply everyday life, so I followed suit. After watching the slavers marching back and forth with their scowls and whips, I concluded keeping my head down would be the best way to avoid their lash.

Leegius's back was covered in scars from his neck down. A fresh wound stood starkly among the old, stretching from his shoulder to the small of his back. I hadn't noticed it in the cell, but in the daylight, with flies buzzing about ravenously, it was hard not to. The smell was beginning to take on a sickly-sweet nature. I turned to avoid gagging but examined it just the same. I peered closer and was almost knocked over by the next bucket of chilled water.

Leegius and the man behind me cringed out of the way as the water splashed in their direction.

"Don't know how you enjoy that, hatchling. Too cold for my kind," Leegius smirked at me as I spat up the water that had made it down my nasal cavity. I think the kid was having fun at my expense.

The town we were shuffling through wasn't much to look at. I couldn't understand how humans could live so close to one-another. There was a castle, which was interesting enough, but the smell of waste nullified any awe I could have felt toward it.

The people watched us come in. Children played and remarked about the "animal people," referring to Leegius and I, but soon lost interest and left to look at the other unique characters in the line. Soon, adults came to view us. They were obviously not buyers, but perhaps they were checking the stock for their wealthier patrons. It could be beneficial to know what was available for auction ahead of time.

With all the disgust I had for the aromas of the town, I didn't believe my sense of smell when a pleasant one drifted by on the hot wind. It was subtle, there for only a moment, and then the breeze changed.

All at once, the market came into perspective. A festival of sorts greeted us. Arguably an odd time for a slave auction, but there we were. Children ran around with streamers and ate candied everything. Dances were held under a great statue of some prosperity god. Stalls with sweet meats, pies, and exotic fruits ensured all the attendees had their fill. Preachers spoke with great blanket voices to the masses, droning on about the sharing of one's wealth to ensure wealth. There and then, I couldn't argue their reasoning. Looking up at the god with his massive ox companion, the people did indeed seem to be in an age of good fortune. What would they say of their god when their fortune came to an end?

As I turned my beak up to their god, something caught my eye. A red thing in a stall. The most bewitching fruit I had ever seen. A perfect ruby with a yellow sheen. It put me in mind of the rare fruit father's trader friend had gifted me long ago. In that moment, I realized how little the corn mush had sustained me. But this was more than that. I wanted that red orb more than I had ever wanted anything in my life. I salivated, and then another bucket of water toppled me over. Falling over may not have been *all* pretense. I saw an opportunity and grabbed what I could, tucking it away.

"Get up, lizard!" A bald slaver pulled me up roughly. "I'll not have our product looking lesser than the others. Stay up and walk straight, or I'll give you a thrashing."

I nodded meekly. He gave me an odd look before trudging off to give someone else a hard time.

"Don't bring attention to yourself, hatchling. The more they see you, the worse things will be," Leegius whispered out of the corner of his mouth.

I ignored him and threw some of what I hid from the slaver into my mouth and began to chew. Its pungent odor filled my nostrils. I wasn't worried about anyone mentioning the smell. It was earthy enough to go unnoticed.

We lined up under the god's statue and watched the dancers. Many fine men and women danced to the tunes of string and wind instruments, spinning with each other by the wrists, trading partners and trading again. All throwing scowls our way anytime they were cursed to face our direction. The audience was losing interest in the dancers, anticipating us coming on stage.

The bald-headed slaver came to the front of our line. He had found a moment to change into a finer set of clothes. The outfit wasn't of the same degree of finery as our audience, but it was still very fine compared to the rags his product wore.

"Hold!" The bald slaver shouted in my direction. I stopped chewing and a chill ran down my spine. "Easy with that, now. I can't have you making a mess of anyone else around here, myself included." He fixed his button line with a proud grin.

"Sorry, just been in a rush. It's a bit of a trip to get there and back." The boy with the bucket slowly poured the icy water over my back and set off at a slower pace, taking care not to run into anyone.

"No more chill water until we are off stage."

"Yes, father," the boy called back.

The song came to an end and the dancers gave one final bow to their partner. The audience clapped politely but with enthusiasm. Apparently, the dancers were presenting a set of new foreign styles. One of those sets were likely to start a trend at their next fancy gathering.

"Let's give our dancers another round of applause!" The announcer led the audience. "Wonderful talent, as always, from our Moon Tides dancers. It is such a wonderful sight for me during our Yaul Festival. My favorite, in fact. I can't wait to bring the Swaying Yew dance from the Ojin people to my next gathering. If you feel the same as I, pick up instructions for your favorite dance at the Moon Tides stand near Eshel's Pies stand. Which reminds me, Eshel has some new flavors this year. Be sure to see her while you are there. While on the subject of new—" The announcer beckoned the bald slaver forward. "Our very own Master Carter."

The audience applauded as the slaver stepped up to the center of the stage.

"Thank you. This season has been good to me. Grisheim and his Ox have followed me and graced my journey. For this, I offer Nybe, the Breathing Church and the Ox Head devotion four of my best." Master Carter waved forward and four humans approached, led by other slavers, two adults and two children. "These two were master craftsmen in their village. They will take their secrets of the craft and add to the prosperity of our home for all."

The adults fought to stay together as the slavers ripped them apart to take them to their new lives. They may stay in the same city, but they would not see each other again. When the mother realized how futile it was to be with her husband, she fought to stay with the children. This, too, was futile. The daughter ran toward the mother, tears streaming, but stopped short of the next slaver who approached to block her. The little boy just wept silently and watched his father and mother go. One final plea to remain with her children echoed out passed the disinterested audience. We couldn't see them any longer, but a dull crack followed and the woman's weeping ceased.

"These two," Master Carter placed a hand on the shoulders of the young children. "Will go to the lord of the land's stead, Lord Vallent. The boy is strong and brave. And the girl will grow up to be quite lovely in a few years." He gave a wink and the two children were guided away. Master Carter looked to the statue that towered over us. "Grisheim, accept these gifts that I bring for you." The audience gave a polite applause. The gesture was appreciated, but was not why everyone was there.

The slavers brought the rest of us forward to the center of the stage. "I have here before you, the most exotic finds I have ever been blessed with. Griesheim's ox, Yaul, walked alongside me many nights and days, guiding me this way and that. For some time, I wanted to curse him as it seemed we were aimless, but I kept faith, aided by a few strong drinks and my son's encouragement. Finally, the sun one morning felt different. Our haul was plenty, and it didn't stop for some time. We obtained a Derosec of the drone variant, without a connection to the Hive Mind, numerous artisans, the strongest laborers the five races of man have to offer, a priest from the Golden City deep in the Dwerian Jungle, a minotaur ready for battle and so much more! Fortune never stopped, not even on my way past Korigara, that massive glacier that remains scarcely explored, as we returned here from the south. I'll leave the details a mystery, or trade secret." He winked, and the slavers pulled me forward. "We were able to acquire an Alerez. This one is so young, he is incapable of flight. Yet he is our deadliest catch this season. Murdered a man on his first day in the city. All that is upon him is for your protection, I assure you." The crowd regarded me oddly. Small disbelieving chuckles came from the foremost rows of them. The slavers guided me back to the line and linked me back to Leegius. "We have only scratched the surface. Please come see me and my stock in the courtyard. I'll be enjoying one of Miss Eshel's pies." Master Carter smiled again and the audience laughed and applauded. He seemed well-liked and his charisma appeared effortless.

They lined us up in long rows near the food stands. Arguably a well thought out placement. The smells and food would keep everyone who approached in a good mood, even jovial. The slavers were professional and well met by prospectors. Even though Master Carter was the only one dressed expressly well, no one looked down on the others. They could have been business partners. It occurred to me they pretty much were. Slave markets seemed to be common here.

A band started to play a relaxing ambiance for the festival. A lull between acts. We weren't the only thing people wanted to see and the crowd dispersed accordingly. The foods available were the most popular attraction in the market. Miss Eshel's pies were the most popular of all. The crowd was too thick for me to see much, but the festival seemed to be citywide. Sounds in the streets had me in mind of something I heard of once. A parade, I think, is what they are called.

We stood facing each other, two lines of slaves segmented strategically to allow buyers to check all angles easily and improve traffic. No sooner were we in position, did the customers approach. All were well dressed in fine, fitted tunics. Escorted ladies watched as their servants checked us for them. The prospective buyers drew our eyes as we did theirs. Some tried to stare forward to appear more appealing. Others looked down as much as they could in hopes of being forgotten or overlooked. I did my best to pull my attention away from the fruit stands after the red orb caught my eye again. I regretted my choice as I placed more of the greenery I hid in my hand into my mouth. Whatever that orb was, I knew it must have been worlds better in flavor. I was certain it was an apple. I chewed, mixing the plants in my cheek, imagining the apple's flavor, careful to pause my jawline when someone came near.

Men and women in fine tunics moved through us. A few were less flashy in color and splendor. I took those to be buyers rather than the collectors themselves. All were hasty in their assessments, only stopping briefly to speak to their friends and partners. Most of the prospectors paid me little mind, but more than a few looked me over...thoroughly.

They would lift my lips to examine my teeth and comment about how dirty they were. They examined my beak like checking the trueness of an arrow. It was getting difficult to hide the wad of vegetation in my mouth. They pulled the corks from my horns to compare mine to their ram creatures before returning the corks. Some joked about my blueish skin; others called it beautiful or marvelous. All who stopped to examine me seemed intent on participating in the auction to be held later.

After the third sweaty man cupped my groin, my patience ran out. The woman who came up next to repeat the process stopped at my teeth as I snarled. She made a quick exit from the scene. Truth be told, I was not very intimidating, but these people didn't know what I was. The unknown is always more of a threat than the known. I was lucky she had been one of the patrons with lighter coin purses, because Master Carter stepped into view and watched her scurry away. He eyed us suspiciously and rewrapped his whip around his arm as though sending a message.

A wash of icy water flooded over me and I yelped. I had thought another's whip found my flesh. Master Carter and the slaves chuckled and he moved on. Another slaver pulled me up from the ground.

"You'll find your feet, or you'll find the lash. I'd hate to do it in front of all these fine people, but I will." This slaver was scarred up and had beads in his beard. They rattled as he pulled me up. My shoulder felt like a ligament almost tore. He stared at me expectantly, his Trégesian skin pinkened as he waited.

I felt there was some proper response he expected from me, but even if I knew it, my mouth was full of muck. If he wasn't going to whip me then, he would've if that mess were discovered. I answered with a meek nod. It seemed to satisfy him enough. He spat and trudged off to give someone else hell.

"When they come to examine you, let them do as they see fit, hatchling. It's easier that way," Leegius whispered to me. After a glance at his back, I decided he was the expert in the matter, though I wanted to fight back. My mouth was too full to respond, but I was rearing to argue.

I wasn't entirely sure what my stance would be or how I could go about it, but I was growing desperate to go on the attack. It was the child in me fighting against the reality of my place in the world contending against my lineage and parental structure. My desire to curse my circumstances every time my father struck me down. I've since learned there are ways to change these things. There are ways to beggar the odds.

I chewed my thoughts over and resentment grew in my chest. After a moment, I spat the mess into my hand. A crude, rudimentary medicine I wouldn't have offered to the least of peasants, but it would do.

"What are you doing?"

I froze and cursed myself for the fool I was. I had forgotten to check to make sure it was safe before I pulled the medicine out. Maybe he was talking to someone else. Without looking, I knew I was lying to myself.

"Lizard! What are you eating?" It was the same slaver with the beads in his beard, but this time, it was very red instead of pink. He snatched me by the wrist. "Euque! What the hell is that?" I had no words. The whip in his hand was the only thing in my world for the moment. "You eat when given permission, lizard, not when you damn well please."

The slaver stepped back and the whip unraveled. My tail shot up instinctively for the attack, but with the extra weight, I was barely able to pull it from the ground. Realizing how defenseless I was, I did the only thing I could think of. I cowered to the ground and covered my head. There was no time to tremble or cry. A heat ripped across my back. The pain registered as fire rather than leather and I arched with it. For a long time, breath worked its way out of me in silence. Then I curled back into myself, causing more pain, and screamed. The barbs of fire reached into my body and dug their nails in before they subsided to a manageable level. Even then, my body shook uncontrollably.

Leegius knelt next to me. "The shock will pass soon, hatchling." Later, I was able to understand how he guarded me from further punishment then. "They come. Master yourself if you are able. Your future pivots here."

I remembered praying to whatever Ark would hear me then. I'd never bothered with the realms of the soul before, but I was as humble as any devotee in that moment. I could not pretend I was in some bad dream any longer. This was my life now; this was my reality. The chains were not something I could will myself free of. I *was* a slave.

"What's happened? What are you doing to my merchandise!" Master Carter snatched the whip from the slaver with beads in his beard.

"He was eating, sir. I disciplined him."

"We don't..." Master Carter stopped himself and offered an apologetic smile to a wealthy-looking couple. He hushed his own voice. "You could have cost me 200 florins with that one idiot decision. This is a rare find, you fool. They go for more than the others. We use the bands on their wrists. The whips are for show. What the hell were you thinking?"

The other slaver blustered for a time until prompted further. "This lizard killed my friend, Carter, sir. He doesn't get special treatmen—"

"L...Lord Conarance?" Master Carter's attitude shifted drastically then.

I tried to do as Leegius suggested and slowly carried myself to my feet. I wanted to be more like him. I was certain Leegius had never screamed like that when he had been whipped. My reaction had embarrassed me and I sought redemption. I should have stayed down. My life as a slave may have been different then. Standing there was the single worst decision I have ever made. It was then that my eyes met the man the slavers were referring to: Conarance.

Lord Conarance wore a turquoise tunic with silver trim. Not the richest I had seen that day, but the man carried more weight and authority than anyone else. He was a smaller man. Denkian, but not a Tréges like my captors. His features were sharp and handsome by human standards, so far as I could tell. He was flanked by two large human guards, each in grand white plate armor. A blue gem inlaid in their left pauldron stood stark under a white hill, the rays of sunlight promising the dawn to come. The crowd seemed to give Conarance more space than necessary. Somehow, it didn't seem to be the guards they were avoiding.

"I...I was just disciplining the slave on proper behavior, m'lord," the slaver said, regaining his composure.

Lord Conarance smiled at him. "My good man, you are well within your authority to do so. You were merely doing your duty. Please, I would love to taste one of Miss Eshel's pies, but I'm afraid I didn't bring anyone to stand in line for me."

"Sir, forgive me, but I don't think you'd have to stand in line. A man of your stature..."

The lord gave him a long look and the slaver understood. It was a dismissal. He left without argument.

"Master Carter, may I approach your stock?"

"But of course, m'lord." He announced to the crowds next and waved them back. "I am sorry, we are now closed for a private viewing."

The other slavers escorted the patrons away with an apology and directions to where the auction would be held.

"There is something curious happening here. Will you indulge me?" Conarance approached us, awaiting no answer.

"Of...course, Lord Conarance." He turned to us and barked. "Up straight. Show some respect. You are about to be addressed by a man whose boots you're not worthy to lick."

"I cannot imagine why one would do such a thing, Master Carter," Lord Conarance said and he knelt in front of me. I was eye level with him with him on one knee. He adjusted the cape on his left shoulder to be mostly behind him. "What is your name, Alerez?"

I watched him like a feral creature, afraid someone wished to steal his last bit of bread. The pain prevented me from straightening and the shock had not yet passed.

"I'm not the one who hurt you," Lord Conarance said all gentle-like. He slicked his hair back. "No need to look at me with such hate."

"I..." I tried to speak, but I couldn't find the words. I found myself less confident about anything I may have to say. In that moment, I wasn't sure that I'd ever be again. "I have no name."

"Oh? Why not?" He pursed his lips.

I glared at the two slavers. "I was taken before one was granted to me, mister."

The lord raised a thin eyebrow at that. Not one who knows about Alerez culture then. A sudden violent feeling came over me. I saw each of these men for what they were, Humans. Conarance was close enough for me to throw my skull into his perfect, stupid face. The padding on my horns wouldn't allow them to do much damage though. It would just piss everyone off.

"You weren't eating, were you?" the man gestured to my hand, surprising me.

I had forgotten about my little project and unclenched my fingers. Amazingly, some of the mush remained despite my tight grip. I shook my head.

Lord Conarance smiled. "Show me then. What was the plan?"

I glanced at the half-dried patty glued to my fingers. "I'll need water."

"Water!" the lord demanded.

Master Carter's boy was nearby with the next bucket he had fetched for my survival. His father had held him back but now let him through. The boy, for the first time, was gentle about his delivery, all excitement gone, replaced with self-preservation. He placed the bucket before me and slinked back behind his father.

The water in the bucket sloshed, and my mouth became suddenly dry. Could I do this right now? Lord Conarance gestured for me to procced. I plunged the mixture into the crisp liquid. I pulled it up quickly to prevent it from washing away. Shaking as I worked, I used the flagstones to work the mixture harder, grinding it. Without my tools, I had to improvise. I wasn't sure I was doing the right steps either. I added a trickle of more water into the remains of the mixture and left a green stain on the flagstones.

The other slaves watched me intently. Leegius was leaning in close. His Materic brow furrowed when I turned toward him with the product like an offering.

"It's for your wound, Leegius. A poultice," I said, feeling ashamed for a reason I didn't understand.

He looked like he wanted to say something but instead turned his back to me and took a knee. I pushed my thumb into the mixture with a practiced hand and the poultice began to glow with a faint yellow sheen. I had to climb and stretch some, but I managed to plaster the green muck to Leegius's freshest wound. My work complete, I turned to the lord. His grin had morphed from amused to a mix. Somewhere between what you would present to a dear friend and a wolf's maw seemed right.

Lord Conarance stood up and straightened his cape over his left shoulder. Embroidered upon the white fabric was that same hill and sun rays, but with all seven colors that light could be broken up into. "What will that do, Alerez?"

"Stop the swelling," I said. "Or reduce it anyway and help it heal cleaner. Numb some of the pain."

"And where did you get this...thing?"

I looked around for an example, but there were none within view. "I just collected the herbs on my way here."

"Is this something you just happened to pick up, or is there more of an art here?"

"I'm an alchemist by trade...mister."

His smile twitched, then widened, deepened almost. This man had more muscles in his face than anyone had the right to. It was unsettling, demonic even.

"Minotaur," Lord Conarance's change in subject was so abrupt I hadn't realized he was done speaking with me.

Leegius stood up and turned his mass back to us. The lord's eyes barely twitched when he saw the necklace. The ruby stared back at us, gold surrounding its tear-drop shape. Judging by its size, it alone could have purchased a number of slaves here.

"Ah, yes, this one is a bit of an oddity, as you can see, m'lord," Master Carter began. He approached, hands clasped and held to his chest as though he should like to keep his fingers intact. "There was nothing we could do to remove the ruby from his neck. Unfortunately, that raises his price quite—"

"I'll take them." Lord Conarance glanced down the line. "All of them."

"All of them, m'lord?" Master Carter stumbled when he realized what Lord Conarance was suggesting.

"You have a few burley men here." The lord slapped the slaver's back. "My mistress will be pleased."

"But...but, sir, this is an auction. We were—"

Lord Conarance didn't hear the man. He strolled off and spoke over his shoulder. "I will be expecting them at the estate within the season. Oh, and I know the appropriate price for the glacier-razor. Just mind that."

We watched the man leave with his guards flanking either side. The crowd parted like a sea to avoid him and his men. Whether it was fear or admiration keeping them away, I couldn't tell.

"What now?" The bearded slaver asked.

Master Carter spat. He whirled on us, trying to come to some sort of conclusion within his mind. His eyes focused on me and he mastered himself. Carter rubbed his head.

"Get them cleaned up, packed up, and shipped out. I will not cross Yalor. We'll make a good enough profit this season. It will be better next year."

"But, Master Carter, I—"

"Did you not just hear me? I will not make enemies with Yalor. You've no idea who that man is." Master Carter shivered underneath his furs.

## The City of the Golden Age

Master Carter gave his orders and set off, clearly suppressing any further thoughts. He was resigned to his misfortune and would not tempt fate further. His son and men were none too quiet about the injustice of it all, but before long, they too, became resigned. Master Carter's son stormed off after raising his voice to uncomfortable levels. Master Carter did his best to pacify the boy but failed to do so. The bucket clambered to the ground, and our wealthy audience watched him leave, much the same way they had watched Lord Conarance, albeit with less awe and more ire.

An essence wielder came before we left the market and placed a seal emyon on my back. After it was filled, the seal washed me over with a cooling energy. The relief was instantaneous. It was as though I were home back in the glacier. The pain from the wound on my back was dulled in moments. It almost put me to tears, the stark difference. She must have put a bit of healing into that small emyon seal. After I saw her eyes, I was sure of it. An act of kindness she wasn't paid to do but did anyway. I wanted to thank her. But she was gone before I could get the words out.

They moved us out of the market and we were bathed and changed into something more appealing, almost like we were packaged in white paper for a holiday gift. The slavers led us to the main road and put us into carts to be shipped off.

Apparently, there had been a slight change of plan while I was busy studying the terrain. Master Carter wanted us out of his hands as soon as possible and to be far away from anything Yalorian. Lord Conarance was going to leave with us in a convoy rather than awaiting the shipment. I could just make out his coach at the head of the line. The guards in white plate mail were numerous, but I wasn't sure there were enough of them to guard the whole slave convoy and whatever else they had been in this city to pick up.

Disinterested in further evaluation, I went back to my study.

"What are you up to, hatchling?" Leegius snapped me back to the real world some time down the road.

"The grass."

"The grass? Fool boy, ain't nothing interesting with grass."

Neither Leegius nor myself responded to the man. He was obviously in a poor mood for his chains.

"What do you see there?" Leegius now looked at me with a new set of eyes as though he was starting to understand something in a new light.

"Change."

"Change? Like with the seasons?" The other man, bored enough to join in our conversation, wanted to know. I wasn't sure if he was preparing to insult me further.

"What is your name, friend?" The longer I got to know Leegius, the more I understood how he was just like that. Everyone was a friend. None were strangers if he could help it.

"They call me Ffffryer." He extended his name for some odd reason. "Been told I can cook decent enough."

"Fryer? A pleasure to meet you. This boy here is something unique—"

"I know that. He's a damn blue lizard dragon thing. I can see it plain."

"There's more to it than that, isn't there, Alerez? Was Fryer right? Are you watching the grass for its change with the seasons?" For a moment, I couldn't tell if he was making fun of the man. I learned later on, that this was improbable. Leegius never insulted anyone. He spoke the truth, but he didn't verbally attack others.

I shook my head. "If you watch closely enough, you can tell where we are based on the grasses."

"Like in the ffffiefff?"

"Not necessarily. Grasses don't abide by fief or provinces demarcations. Grass is one of those plants that can be found anywhere you go, even if scarcely. They are diverse and extremely adaptive. Since they must adapt to the climate in which they find themselves, they possess different characteristics. With these changes, I should be able to tell where we are going and how to get back."

"Oh," Fryer chuckled to himself. "Now I get it. You still think we can get away."

I said nothing and kept to my grass watching. Our convoy started to move.

"See, we ain't going nowhere, 'cept where they say."

The journey took days; I lost count of how many. All the time, I watched the grasses. I realized after some time, though, that Fryer was right. It didn't matter if I knew how to get back home or not if I couldn't get away. After a while, I stopped reading the grasses, accepting how futile it really was. Leegius became solemn as we went on, as though he knew what awaited him on the other side of this trail. I let him be. Though I had wished he was available to distract me from my own anxiety.

The white armored guards were strictly professional, and at times I believed them to be mute. They guided us off the wagons without having to say much at each stop. They were practiced in their system. This was not the first time these men had delivered slaves. Even the cook that served us water and gruel seemed of a higher class. He wore a fine tunic and not a splash reached his apron.

The meals on the road were small but sustaining. It became clear early on that bathroom breaks would not be taken. Those were reserved for when we made camp in the evenings and under very watchful eyes. The trip was especially long due to those stops. Each seemed planned, but with all those wagons, slaves, and cargo, it took time to settle in.

Each wagon of slaves was dismounted and corralled to a strong stake away from the main camp. No fire was lit for us, much to the irritation of the others, but I was happy for it. The cool night air was welcoming. It was amazing to me that the guards trusted themselves enough to sometimes guard us in complete darkness on cloudy or half-moon nights. The gemmed bracelets we had worn with Master Carter had been left behind. Still, no one made to escape when we made camp.

The restraints for my horns and tail had also been removed. I didn't even mind they had left the weight on my wings. It was a welcome relief. I sat in the darkness and ignored the complaints of my peers as they held themselves against the winds and frost. Elder Sister, the smaller of the two moons, watched me closely those nights, it seemed.

The peace was short-lived, however. One night in the dark, we could hear shouting and further altercations. I couldn't make out what the matter was at the time, but the others agreed that a slave or two had been trying to escape or had a disagreement with the guards. Mounds were discovered on the side of the road as we loaded up for the next leg of travel the following morning.

We passed by many cities and towns. Each flew the flag of the empire, Avalon, superseding their own; a crown fit for a king and a crown of thorns fixed to the handle of a sword which was skewered into the ground. It wasn't until we reached the largest city that we saw a different flag, standing alone: a sun promising a new day. Our final stop. The convoy circled around a large processing station on the opposite side of the main road and we started unloading one wagon at a time.

There was a disconcertingly low level of security here. People walked around unshackled in the streets between the buildings. More than a few appeared to be slaves. Their clothing lacked anything beyond utility. The few guards did not seem too keen on preventing escape. They were there to direct rather than control. There wasn't even a wall around the outpost.

My gut sank when they approached our wagon and told us to stand. It was only a small team. One man to record each of us, one guard, and a pale woman in robes. She alone was unnerving, but not as unnerving as the precession that followed the small group, Lord Conarance in the middle. He strode through the mud perfectly fine with what flecked up and added itself to his boots and trousers, all smiles. The men and women flanked either side of him and came to rest in a stiff posture, hands clasped behind their backs, dressed in finery. It looked like the arrival of a nobleman, staged and extravagant, but it drew our eyes still. Was this for us or for him? Were *we* supposably the nobility in this scenario?

Lord Conarance flourished his arms in presentation and opened his mouth to speak. At that moment, the first of the slaves from our wagon was released from his shackles. Fryer rubbed his wrists for only a moment before he launched himself forward. He shoved the guard back and knocked the record keeper down into the mud.

Fryer had gone a hundred paces before anyone reacted. His speed was astounding. The other slaves held their breath for him, but before too long, we let it go. Something was off. Fryer felt it too. Two hundred paces out, he slowed. Fryer glanced back quizzically as he was not being pursued. No one sought to reclaim him. He felt it too: he had failed the escape before he tried. He jolted forward, quickening his pace. He was committed, if nothing else.

Conarance's smile was always there, always. But it widened then. It was as though he had an extra hinge somewhere in those cheeks. I started to understand that famous expression of his. It was his signature 'I win' grin.

The woman in the robes made a small gesture toward the ground and followed the path Fryer took with her hand. A root the size of a small tree shot out of the ground and grabbed the man by the leg. He would have slammed into the ground at a full sprint, but another root caught him by the arm and pulled him into the air. I could make out what happened close to the ground near Fryer from the top of the wagon, but Fryer was brought high enough for all to see. This was a presentation. The slaves already in the outpost swarmed to the edge to see what was going on. Two more roots shot up and grabbed Fryer by his limbs.

There was a collective sigh, even from some of the guards. A part of all of us wanted him to escape. The roots created large trenches in the earth as they carried their prize closer in.

With Fryer dangling awkwardly above us, Lord Conarance turned and nodded his head to the pale woman. She made another small gesture with her fingers underneath her long sleeves. The lord turned to us with his arms thrown wide and shouted to be heard over the screams that followed.

"Welcome to orientation!"

We watched Fryer as he was pulled apart. If not enough came away with the individual root, they would quickly drop the chunk of meat, catch him again, and pull more of his flesh away. His screams left his face with a tortured expression as his life departed.

The roots did not relent as they dismembered the last of him and disappeared back into the ground.

*Orientation?* Like this was some sick fecking club and we patrons vying for entry. I knew it. I wasn't sure at the time why, but I knew Conarance was a sick bastard. I wondered then what Overlord of Disiea I had pissed off enough to be dragged, fingernails splintering, into their realm.

I could feel my heart throb. There was no other sound. They released me from my shackles as they did the others, all of them. I couldn't feel the relief of all that weight taken from me for another had taken its place. Conarance watched each of our faces as we passed between his precession, but when he made to turn from mine, his eyes lingered on my own. There was a special purpose he had in mind for me. I broke my eyes away and shuttered.

The other slaves and I were lined up in ranks in the center of the outpost. I kept close to Leegius. He didn't seem to mind. After all the slaves were in position, Conarance and the others that followed him stationed themselves in front of our group. A draft horse was beckoned forward, drawing a large wagon. The finely dressed people pulled from it a great many leather sacks. Each sack was documented by the record keeper and directed to individual slaves.

At length, Conarance presented each sack himself. Conarance wasn't a man given to whispers, but I could hear nothing of what passed between him and each person. A rushing sound was all that my ears could make out, as though my blood pressure were a torrent. It increased in intensity, threatening to bust whatever damns held the blood back as Conarance greeted each slave to their new lives. Finally, Leegius was the last slave to be greeted prior to my individualized greeting. The way Conarance shook Leegius's hand so confidently, had me lacking any such feeling. I wished one of my heart chambers would burst and remove me from the situation.

I could hear the world again when the man walked up to me.

"Ah, my prize-find, the Alerez with no name. I'm certainly glad you are a glacier variant. I don't believe we could have accommodated one of your aquatic cousins." He snapped his fingers and leaned in close. "There's no need to fear, hatchling.

You'll find a good home here. Yalor is truly a place of opportunity. Ah, you are the only one with a green mark this time around. I have high hopes for you." Conarance placed the leather sack before me, a green mark painted across its face, and set off to the next person in line.

When Conarance finished his rounds, he centered himself in front of our mass formation again. "My apologies for the time I've had you all standing out here, but I had to make sure I met every one of you individually. I am chief of operations here, Lord Conarance Vaux. *Here* is Mistress Hydel's estate, Yalor. My mistress has many philanthropies she wishes to accomplish in her lifetime, and Yalor is the *how* she will achieve these ambitions. It is my duty to oversee them to fruition. As *overseer*, it is one of my many, many pleasures to find those I believe can be a grand addition to the citizenry. You have all been judged as such, the finest Orecul has to offer. Please open your packs." He continued as we did what we were told. "These are your welcome gifts. In Yalor, there are no whips, no devices to instill fear. There are no men to watch your every move."

The first item in the bag was strategically placed so as not to be missed. The epaulet was different in each bag. Mine was of a polished leather and a dark green cloth. Set in its front face was a cut green gem. I glanced up. The men and women standing so formally next to Conarance had clear gems on their left shoulders. I had misjudged them.

"However," Conarance continued, "You are to start wearing these immediately. I cannot ask for Estry's assistance every time one of you runs off." He chuckled to himself, alone with his gruesome joke.

The formal slaves came around and helped each of us into our new shoulder equipment. They made sure these were fitted and secured properly. When they fitted mine, it seemed to come to life as soon as they were done. Instantly, a powerful cooling effect washed over my body. It was much stronger than the seal emyon the essence wielder had placed on my skin. I felt invigorated, but I kept my head down.

"With the added purpose of protecting my mistress's interests, these shoulder pieces signify your position and rank. As you earn favor, these will be replaced with new pieces. As you can see—" Conarance flourished and a number of slaves stepped up past the ones in finery. I hadn't noticed them lining up. The finely dressed slaves departed. Those who replaced them each had a different colored gem on their left shoulder. Their shoulders were also adorned in varying ways. "—we have quite the elegant color-coded division of labor for our family. I expect each of you to respect your superiors and follow their lead, for they have earned Mistress Hydel's grace. The color of your gem signifies which of these divisions you belong to. Jarce here will call out your color and division, and your ranking official will take you from here because, quite frankly, I've grown tired of my own voice. Welcome to Yalor. I will see each of you very soon to check on how you are acclimating to your new lives. I wish you well." Conarance stepped back and set off to his coach. A man with a round hat who seemed to come out of nowhere, followed him away.

The man Conarance had indicated stepped up with his scroll, the mud on his back and rear still fresh from when Fryer made his escape attempt. He took a deep breath:

"Lilac: Water Purification and Sanitation Division. Your Chief of Station is Anglus." Three slaves with purple gems stepped forward nervously, not entirely sure what to do. Jarce waited patiently, but nobody moved. Finally, Anglus moved into our crowd, agitated, and pushed them out. One slave doubled back to retrieve his sack and earned a slap on the back of the head. The team moved to a coach much less fine than Conarance's and the coach set off to the city.

Jarce cleared his throat and continued: "Citrine: Theater. Head Performer Dulepia." The slaves that stepped forward were not at all what I would imagine human actors to look like. One had so many boils, I thought him a different race than Man.

"Sapphire: Realm Enforcer. Commander Grenlic." The strange creature to whom the name belonged moved forward and I half expected the earth to break with his steps. He was built as though a mountain were attached to his flesh, craigs and all. It was astonishing the white plate armor could fit him so well, albeit they had been forced to redesign the whole suit. He walked back to the city, following alongside the coach that carried his new men.

"Crimson: Court of the Age. Coliseum. Master at Arms: Beast Flesh Krolec." My heart sank further still. Leegius pulled his pack from the earth, gave me one last glance, and set off.

"Emerald: Alchemy Division. Lead Researcher Estry."

Wait, green. Jarce indicated the pale woman. A yellow sense of abandonment crept over and held my hand as I watched Leegius leave. If you'll pardon the further use of color. I hesitated, fighting against a primal preservation of self, but I eventually moved forward. Jarce continued to make his announcements and I followed the crone wrapped in black.

I trailed behind her, half expecting a root to lash out at me at the slightest displeasure I might cause her. After I noticed my feet scuffing the ground was the only sound accompanying us, I focused on how I placed each step to quiet them down. At the coach, she stood and waited expectantly. It was a long, awkward moment before I realized she was waiting for me to open the coach's door for her. I did so, again awkwardly, holding on to my sack of gear. I pried the door open with one finger as I needed the rest to hold on to the sack. I could practically feel her thoughts as she scowled at my efforts and went inside. I followed her in and fought with the equally palpable feelings of not wanting to sit next to her and not wanting to make it easy for her to look at me. In the end, I sat across from her. I couldn't seem to let go of that damn bag.

We were well on our way before she spoke. All the while, she examined me. "Simple, are you?" She asked. "Pity."

"Sorry?"

"The correct answer is: 'Yes, Lady Estry.'"

I didn't think I was safe from the roots in the carriage. "Um, yes, Lady Estry."

She continued to stare at me as though I were an offensive smear of shite that had found its way onto her favorite carpet.

"What is your name, simpleton?"

"I do not have a name...Lady Estry."

Her eyebrow shot up. "No name? Do your people not address each other like the rest of the civilized world?"

"No, I—"

"It matters not. I care not for a lesson of the inferior races. But I cannot have one of my members walking around nameless like some cur brought in from the streets. I've never heard of a glacier razor possessing any alchemic talent, either." She scanned me thoughtfully as though a flower forming from my ear would be proof. "Harvester? No, doesn't feel right on the tongue. Bringer sounds better to me."

"Bringer?" I asked. It hardly sounded much better.

"Yes...I will assign you as a collector. There are plenty of talented alchemists who require ingredients for their research. Other tasks will be assigned to you, but this will be your primary function." Estry more spoke to herself than me. When it appeared she was satisfied with her own responses, she turned to watch the road as we moved.

As we approached, Yalor loomed. We passed through a great gated wall, stopping only for Estry to present a piece of paper to one of the guards. He leaned in and peered at me through his visor and waved us in. The architecture was difficult to place. I was no student of the craft, but I could make out details that were foreign to the region. I couldn't identify if the designs were entirely human.

Perfectly lain flagstones lined the roads so close together that weeds had no hope of finding purchase. The routes were established for flawless efficiency. Stone and timber made up the accents of the buildings, dependent on the purpose of the structure, but all had a metallic gold band just below the roofs. Two structures were pronounced above the others. A keep on the far side of the city and a clock tower nearer to the route Estry and I took.

On the sidewalks, whether the individual was moving with a purpose or speaking with another, I couldn't make out one person who didn't have the shoulder piece as I did.

The Alchemy District was smaller than the others. An underappreciated art, if there ever was one. It had taken us an hour at least to make our way through the Artisan District alone. But to me, it was still incredible. My mother and I were the only alchemists back in the glacier. There were enough alchemists here to fill my entire village and then some. I wondered what I could learn here in one disconcerting thought. I had started to accept my fate and I didn't like that. I would find out later how exhausting it was to remain obstinate about your circumstances; how hard it was to hold on to hope that someone would come and rescue you.

Our coach came to a stop in front of one of the larger structures in the Division.

"Here is where you will live. Report to Professor Resin. He will show you to your quarters," Estry said. There was no room to ask questions. It was a clear dismissal. As soon as I was out of the carriage, the door was closed, and I was left there in the street.

The sign on the front of the cottage labeled it the Novice Apothecary. Apparently, the conventional naming in Yalor would be unimaginative.

As I approached the entrance, I narrowly avoided some richly dressed slaves exiting. I had to work to keep my sack in hand. I pried the door open much the same way I did for the coach, sparing only a few fingers so as not to lose the one thing I owned.

"Welcome," a younger human male greeted me from behind the counter. "Oh. A recruit, not a customer." He examined me from above two pieces of glass fixed in a wire frame on the bridge of his nose. "An Alerez? Odd day I'm having. Interesting, if nothing else. First, had to put out a fire in the back. Novices aren't good for making much, but fires they are quite good at. And now a lizard who can talk comes through my door." He hesitated. "You *can* talk, right?" I nodded. "A fine display of the skill, I must say. Come around the counter then."

I did as he asked. I appreciated how less threatening he was compared to Estry. His smile was genuine.

"Place your bag just there. Good. Now, I'm Ulinor, a student too. I run this shop when the professor is away and welcome in the new recruits. This shop will be your home for a long while. You will help manage the shop as well as participate in class while you're not about on your duties. You do not make a lot of marks yet, but a number of them will be given to the shop for equipment rental, tuition, and room and board. Meals are provided at the mess hall in the district..."

"Marks?" I asked.

"You haven't gone through your pack yet? No, I supposed when being escorted by Estry, one would not have the mind to do so. Well, let's open it up then. Go on. You can use the shop counter."

I started to unload the gear and lay the pieces out. Inside, there were two outfits, none too glamorous, a manual and map, and a smaller leather pouch. Inside the pouch were a number of copper coins with the number one stamped on one side and a rising sun on the other.

"There should be a number of those in there to get you started since one typically arrives here with nothing. You'll see in the *Welcome Guide* that you receive ten marks per month. Five of those will go to the Division. Those uniforms are all you're allowed to wear as soon as I show you where you'll be staying. That's just upstairs. In your room, you may wear anything you purchase for sleep attire. I promise you'll want to purchase more uniforms too. It's messy work here. Your own mistakes will ruin plenty of them."

I barely heard him as he spoke. I was in awe of the apothecary around me. I had never been in a shop before, let alone a shop of my profession. With little iron in Korigara, my mother and I didn't have access to the up-to-date equipment models in this room, and glass was also a rarity in the glacier. I later learned the pieces in this shop weren't by any means the best on the market, but they were a sight better engineered than my own at home. At the time, they were the best I had ever known.

"Careful with that. We have a strict, you break it, you replace it model here."

"What's the cost of this?" I held the flask closer for inspection. The glass was purer than I've ever seen.

"That there is a round bottom. In the market, they are worth about nine marks. It sounds cheap, but it is above what you could afford to replace at the moment." I returned the item to where I found it. "I see you are curious to learn. That's good. What's more, I already don't have to pick up after you, I see. Keep that up, especially. Now, what that guide doesn't tell you...you better write this all down. I know you don't have any paper, check your bag. Er, you do know your letters, don't you? Good. Stick with Oreculian. Professor Resin will not have you cursing my or anyone else's name in whatever language your people typically curse in. No, we journal our discontent in common here."

That made me smile and Ulinor returned the notion. "Class is every day starting at mid-day and in the afternoon after supper. It will be held in the backroom there. The end of the week is devoted to honing the skills you acquire in the class in the form of research projects. No cheating now. The instructors know what the results should be and your proficiency level. During the day, you will be given chores to help keep this shop open. The products you and the students create are sold here at a discount as they are imperfect, but the funding keeps the doors open and allows Professor Resin to teach you lot. Only the top students assist the Professor in the management of the shop, helping customers and the sort. That's me. You will work here until your rank and graduation lead you to the other parts of the Division. You getting all this? You write slow. You don't need to record every word, just the bits to help you remember. Oh, how rude of me. I introduced myself; I never gave you the opportunity."

My writing hand stopped short. "Well, uh, Estry called me...B...Bringer." The whole statement felt sour in my mouth.

"Bringer? Damn luck to have her name you." He shook his head. "I see why she didn't accompany you in. Your name is instruction enough for her intent for you. You'll be needing papers then. I'll have them drawn up."

"Papers?"

"My lad, do you think all these ingredients grow here in the city? A number of the alchemic components we use are found outside the walls. You'll need something to say you have permission to leave the city. We'll go over that more in due time. I suppose I'll need to give you an escort for a time so you don't get lost. For now, go change out of those drab garbs. You'll not be able to get under the shoulder piece you have there, so cut away that part of your...whatever it is you're wearing. Go upstairs. You'll be in room four. Chop chop. It is almost supper time."

I did as I was told and went up the stairs. I felt for a long time that I was betraying myself. I found that, despite my circumstances, I was excited. I was about to become a true alchemist. My mother taught me a great deal in the ice burrows, but this was going to be a whole new side of the craft.

The room contained little else other than four beds and a window. It was apparent the trunks at the end of each bed were for personal items, though there was no latch. It would be impossible to lock it. After the second trunk turned out to be owned, I found the third was empty. I ripped the seam of my clothes with my tail blade and changed into my uniform. An undershirt, a jerkin, and trousers complete with a hole to slip my tail into. The boots wouldn't fit over my feet, so I left those in my trunk along with my other uniform and what was left of the fabric of my old life. Ulinor helped me lace up the backing of my jerkin, which had been modified to admit my wings.

The meal was a gruel of sorts but a damn sight better than what the slavers had provided me. I slurped it alone, as far away from the others in the hall as possible, trying to ignore the stairs and the void in conversation I seemed to produce. I wasn't sure how the others received such lavish meals compared to my own. Though slightly envious, I didn't let a complaint creep into my mind. I was grateful just to have something on my stomach. Others turned to watch me and turned back to remark on my presence to their colleagues. These were all alchemists. I tried not to make my first impression a negative one, but given who I was, I realized I wouldn't have much control over that. I quietly finished my meal and left without much else.

Back at the apothecary, I made my way to the classroom in the back and waited. I wasn't sure what I should be doing. After realizing I would probably need my journal and writing utensils, I ran back up to my room and retrieved them. When I got back to the classroom, I placed them down but did not return to my waiting. The equipment had been calling me and I was obliged to answer.

Instead of the pewter I used at home, the mortar and pestles were a fine stone. The glass equipment was all banded with copper to keep them from shattering under the heat we would require of them. In Korigara, we were required to use other means. The mineral deposits of a glacier are very different from the rest of the world. Instead of leather pouches, the final alchemic products were contained in small glass vials. I examined two of these vials. One was a clear glass, and the other was colored. I hadn't known glass could be colored. I wondered if this vial kept with Yalor's color coding system they seemed to favor.

When the other students started to make their way into the room, I snapped around as though guilty of something. They hesitated at the doorway.

"So, it is true," one laughed. "We got a pet lizard!"

"Enough, Yuti. He isn't the oddest thing that we've seen in this city." Ulinor squeezed by, between the large boy and the door frame, arms full of scrolls and papers.

"He? Are you certain?" The large boy called Yuti eyed me. The prepubescent mustache on his lip would put other men to shame. Two long muttonchops decidedly stopped short of a decent beard. Seeming to come to some sort of conclusion, he offered me his hand.

I looked at the hand, puzzled. "Bringer," I said.

"Okay, Bringer. We shake hands or lock arms here in the empire. Depending on where you're from, you see. Yes, like that. I'm Yuti."

"'The furry one' also works," Ulinor shouted back from behind the teacher's desk.

"'Teacher's pet' works for that one," Yuti pushed his chin out to Ulinor. He stepped aside to admit others.

Ulinor paused in his attempt to organize the desk and pointed to each student as they came in. "This is Bik, Holin, and Fredrick. Others will make their way in, but for now, everyone, this is Bringer. He's here to learn just as the rest of us. Bringer, I believe that seat over there is free. You can have that workstation."

Ulinor retrieved a piece of paper. He recorded my name on there and visually inspected it to see who was missing. At the station Ulinor pointed out, I started to unpack my things from the ugly satchel with the green mark. The others had finer and more robust bags. I should consider upgrading when I could afford it.

Yuti flipped one of the notebooks on my desk open and flipped through the first few pages.

"Well, Bringer, your handwriting is shite. Not your own language, I suppose." Yuti handed the notebook back to me. "Don't let Ulinor fool you. He's friendly enough outside of class hours but very competitive any other time and the highest-scoring bastard we have here."

"You are just mad because this is your third year round," Holin shot back. She smiled at me. "Yuti is not cut out for alchemy like the rest of us."

"I believed you and I received the same score just last week," Yuti lazily snapped back with an exhale. He settled into his workstation and fingered through a book. "Now, if you don't mind, I need to ensure I outmatch you in the next."

Holin blushed at that and turned her attention back to setting up her station.

The rest of the students made their way into the classroom shortly thereafter. It wasn't long before they all abruptly stood up. I thought my eyes were playing tricks on me when a dark figure came into the classroom and disappeared, quick as that, behind the other's workstations. Almost as soon as I was sure my mind had been making things up, a rat jumped up onto the desk at the head of the classroom. The creature was dressed in a tunic and slacks, though. He pulled a pocket watch from his vest and checked it before returning it to the same pocket; the chain glittered as it dangled.

"Bringer," Yuti hissed. In a muffled speech, he gestured to me, saying, "Stand your arse up."

I did.

"Everyone is accounted for, Professor Resin. We have a new student over there. Bringer."

Professor Resin peered at me over the list through a set of spectacles. The page hid half of his body. "Bringer, huh?" His whiskers twitched. "Thank you. Take your seats. Seeing as though we have a new student, I believe it will be prudent to go over the basics."

A collective groan followed.

"Bringer, you were sent here to be an alchemist. Tell me, what do you know of alchemy."

"Little to nothing...Professor?" I felt then I had disgraced myself.

"Typical. I relish the day I have a promising pupil enter my classroom rather than departing it. Bik, share your tome with Bringer. Open your *Basics of Alchemy* chapter one."

The nearest boy looked at me hesitantly before scooting closer to share his book.

The first basic lesson was, well, basic. We covered the equipment, some basic techniques for preparing the ingredients, and some easy-to-learn ingredients and where to find them. It covered nothing I hadn't heard before but did give me insight into how different the empire approached the craft than my mother did. For them, it was closer to science than her art. A sentiment she instilled in me. One observation did pique my interest:

I was asked to read aloud, "Alchemy is the process of drawing out magical traits from the mundane. Alchemists, through research and technique, bring out the emyonic attributes of ingredients and apply them to their purposes. Unlike emyon, which uses the wielder's soul essence to produce, alchemists manipulate the essence of worldly objects to alter reality."

"Thank you, Bringer. Bik, why don't you read next."

"Professor." I didn't take my seat.

Professor Resin removed the set of spectacles from his eyes. They were only slightly different from Ulinor's and had arms that hooked around rodent ears.

"Yes, Bringer?"

"I don't understand what I read."

He sighed. "It is saying we are different from the essence wielders. Our limitations are creativity and the available alchemic components. A wielder will run out of essence while performing emyon. We, as alchemists, need only to ensure we have the proper ingredients. Some are obviously rarer and harder to use, but as long as we have them and know how to use them, we can make wonderful things happen. Our souls do not play a part in it."

"Th...Thank you." I sat down then and heard nothing of the other students' readings. There was nothing left to listen to. They were far behind my capabilities. The only thing I could think was, *how could they not know?*

## One Taste

The class was instructed to create what they assumed would be my first elixir. The product was basic, but I spent an extended period of time prepping my ingredients and station. I used this to my advantage because I was trying to decide who I would be. It looked like I would be in Yalor for a long time and I wasn't sure if I wanted to be *seen* yet. If I could keep my talents to myself, covertly, maybe I could force this new world I've been thrown into, to be what I wished it to be. It could also save my life from jealous colleagues. What was the murder rate in the cities?

I placed my hands on the glass condenser and itched to get started. I could make something special in that moment. According to the guide, if I were to be promoted far enough, I would be moved into another part of the Alchemy Division. There were more advanced schools, specialty positions, Golden Age projects, the opportunities were endless. But I wondered what that would look like. When I thought of my skill putting me at odds with Estry, I realized this would more than likely cause me to be around Conarance more often than I'd like.

The itch subsided then. I carefully watched the others as they worked and gauged what I should do. I created a product below the average of the class. I was afraid it was still too much to keep me unnoticed.

"Let's see it, Bringer. Hmm, though I appreciate the showmanship, this vial you put it in is far more expressive of the expense than this elixir would go for. We save these for the more costly products. Be sure you change it out for another. There are still scraps of your ingredients within the liquid. That's fine, but see if you can filter some of that out." Professor Resin pulled the cork out and sampled it. "Your potency leaves something to be desired.

It will cure only the mildest of stomach aches. Good first attempt, though. I must say I'm impressed."

*Damn.*

"Be sure you fix those few things and Ulinor will show you where to put it in the shop. Should go for about seven marks." The professor returned the bottle to me and moved on to the next student."

After the class was over, Professor Resin checked on the assignments for the following day. He assigned me a simple research project, which I was to have complete within the week, shop clean up and collection...or *bringing*. I scorned Estry in my mind.

"Your credentials to leave the city gate should be ready by the morning. I'll have it delivered to the shop. Yuti will be your guide for a time. He, at the least, knows what you're looking for." The class had a shallow chuckle. Yuti reddened but kept his tongue. "Ensure you're back in time to clean up for the afternoon shift with the shop. Oh, also, Yuti, make sure he goes to the market some time to get all that he needs." Professor Resin made to hop off his desk and stopped. "And Yuti, be sure you both stay away from Blackwood."

"Yes, Professor," Yuti looked grim at that.

"Professor," Ulinor raised his hand.

"Yes? Be quick about it. I have strawberries to harvest."

"Not that I'm keen on another field trip, but has there been any progress on the Blackwood project?"

Professor Resin shook his head. "I'm afraid not. It's spreading too. That's the biggest issue. Pay it no mind, students. The council is on it, among other things. Focus on your research for now."

The rest of the evening was ours. Some saw to their research while others disappeared from the shop as soon as they were able. I just wanted to sleep. I had been yawning through the end of the class as the newness of everything began to wear off. When I opened the door to my shared room, I paused. I wasn't sure I was going to like the sleeping arrangements in Yalor. 'Too comfortable' was the first thought when I looked down at my bed. Father always warned comfort was a danger. When I lay down, I ceased my complaints. I was out to the world in a matter of moments. I never stirred as the others came in.

I woke early. A habit instilled by my father, though the comfort of the bed caused me to sleep past what he would have accepted. I didn't need to change, so I tied the marks pouch to my belt and set out. Yuti, Bik, and another boy I didn't know the name of stirred only a little as I made my way out of the room.

The moon was still high and bright through the windows when I opened the shop shutters. The streets were hardly beginning to stir. There was only one person who came to the shop that morning.

"Oh, someone is awake?" A boy baring a brown gem on his shoulder startled when he came into the shop. "I have a few things for your master this morning. I'll just place them where I normally do."

I helped him unload the boxes from his cart outside into the corner of the shop behind the counter. He thanked me for my assistance and set off about his rounds. The parcel promised to me the evening before lay on top of the boxes. I only happened to notice it for that dreadful name written over its front. I opened and read it as I made my way to the eating facility.

The list of ingredients I was to obtain was...juvenile, to say the least. Clover, dandelion; most people would see these walking across the field. I decided maybe I could use this to my advantage. If I spent the extra time I had outside the city, I could start some research projects of my own. The only problem was my chaperone. I pocketed the list along with the credentials that accompanied them, which would need to be renewed each week.

Irritated at the dining facility being closed, I found a still-burning street lamp and examined my notes on my research topic while I waited. It, too, was nothing special. I was given a week, but it could take me twenty minutes. I was beginning to think I should have forced my way up the ranks after all. My time would be better spent on real projects. Things that actually interested me.

"What's this then?" A blue gem seemed to manifest himself from the shadows. I hadn't been paying enough attention to my surroundings. He was unsure on his feet and smelled of strong spirits.

"Good morning."

"Morning?" He shot a look into the sky quizzically, looking for the sun. Rubbing his mustache and chin, he said, "It is not morning. And since when can a thing like you talk? You don't pass the sniff test, boy. You're dressed like a person but could be a pet, for all I can tell."

"I...uh, I'm an Alerez, sir. We are people just the same as you."

"You don't look like any people I know! Well," he pulled a set of shackles from off his belt. "I'm gonna take you in, I suppose. You don't make sense, and I need someone to help me figure this out."

I jumped back when he reached for me.

"I'm a student here, sir. I just got here yesterday."

"Now, don't make me have to be this guy, boy." He drew his sword.

It hadn't occurred to me until then, that these blue gems were quite possibly the only armed slaves in the city. I made a run for it. I didn't like being defenseless.

"Hey!" He shouted and somehow his feet were more stable underneath him than they had been.

I shot down the slope over a creek and back up the adjacent bank. On my way up, he grabbed me by the leg and we both fell, sliding back down to the creek. I smashed my heel into his face and scrambled up the bank, now free. I didn't know the area enough, so I ran wherever I thought could conceal me. It was no use. Though drunk, the guard was still an athlete. He was just behind me the whole time. In between some buildings, I ducked as his blade cut the air. It bit into a support beam and he stumbled out of the alley over some crates.

I didn't run from there. I knew this was going to get worse the longer it went, but I wasn't going to surrender. I was sure he had forgotten he intended to bring me in at this point. That option was gone. I lowered my stance and waited for him to get up from the ground. Honor, my father always told me to be honorable in a fight even if the opponent was dishonorable in his actions.

He swung at me with his sword. I deflected it with my tail blades down to the ground, he followed the motion more than a sober fighter may have. I sliced upward. The bones in his face gave. When he fell, I had to catch myself from going down with him. I wrenched my tail from the bridge of his nose and quickly checked all directions for other enemies. Another lesson from my father. When I was certain I was safe, I checked all directions again. This time for the getaway. I had to know where I stood. Would a witness report me and therefore make escape impossible? No. There was no one there. I was lucky I killed him as I did. The boxes he stumbled over would be the loudest thing to have happened.

I didn't wait around any longer. I was sure no one had witnessed the altercation and I wasn't keen on being found next to the body. I disappeared from the scene following the route we had taken so as to not get lost. I found his shackles on the bank of the creek and buried them deep in the muck. As I knelt down at the creek and washed the blood and mud from my tail, a smile cracked across my face.

*That felt good*, I thought.

<hr />

It wasn't until the sun started to come up that I began to panic. I checked myself for any blood splatter, mud, or anything that could give me away. In the rush, I had forgotten to ensure I couldn't be tied to the killing. The mud on my back fit the streaks we created on the bank of the creek.

There would be no breaking fast this morning. I washed my feet off in the creek. It was no small feat to avoid those who were now in the streets to begin their work for the day. Back at the apothecary, it was too risky to go in through the front door. Instead, I climbed up the back side of the shop. It took too long to remember which room I had slept in. People would start opening their shutters any moment and I'd be out in the open. Luckily, it was exactly that which saved me.

One student in my class opened his window shutters just in time for me to make out Yuti's voice. I slid in as the boys left the room. I wasted no time changing into the spare uniform. I was tying the clean trousers to my waist when the door swung open.

"I got to see if I can fix the sole. I'll be down in a moment." Yuti closed the door behind him and stopped. "Bringer? I thought you were already out for the morning." He looked around the room for where I may have been hiding. His eye lingered on the window I had stupidly left open. I had thought to go back out the way I came.

I couldn't think what to say. There was nothing I *could* say. I gave him a cold shoulder instead. It was the best option. If I gave him enough time, perhaps he would convince himself of the best explanation.

"Can you..." There it was. "Can you change colors?"

"What?" I had to smirk at that.

"You know, like some lizards. I've been told they can change the color of their skin." He smiled knowingly and let it be.

I finished dressing and watched him work on a boot. The bottom portion had flopped away from the frame of the thing. The style of boot was sturdier than the ones humans wore in Korigara. I marveled at what the hell this boy had put the boots through to wear them so thoroughly. He ended up tying a strip of fabric around the boot to keep the bottom in place.

We headed down together then. The other students were going about their various businesses in the shop. Bik and Ulinor were prepping the shop for its opening hour.

"Bringer, don't forget your lists." Ulinor rubbed the sleep from his eyes.

"I already have them." I pulled the documents in question out of my pocket.

He shook his head and grabbed a stack off the counter. "These too. You're supposed to get *all* the ingredients the class requests."

I grabbed the papers with a groan.

Yuti and I made our way to the coach services. The guards had cordoned off a section of a small town square and we were forced to go around. I watched them examine the body I had left behind as we passed. They were questioning the local population too. I was struck to see there were elderly people here. The slaves that were brought in made lives here almost like any other civilization. The only difference being, they were not free. As the elderly lady spoke to the guards, I wondered if her grandchildren were there. Were you born into slavery if you were the child of a slave?

"What's all that about?" Yuti asked.

"You know this place better than I do."

"Looks like someone got taken out. That's not something you see every day in Yalor."

The coach took us through the same route out that Estry and I took to get in. I took this chance to examine the city now that an old crone wasn't staring daggers through me this time around. The looming clock tower rang deep and long as the city seemed to burst to life. You would never have guessed each person was a slave if you hadn't been told. Now, knowing about the shoulder pieces, there was no way to avoid noticing.

Otherwise, life seemed to be normal here. Shops sold their goods, homes opened their shutters to let in the sunlight, and children played in the streets before they were chased off by the guards. The buildings were tall and seemed to possess the architecture of many cultures. Stone and timber were the primary materials. The roofs appeared to be made of a ceramic material of sorts, lain flat and tiled. And of course, each building had the golden band just a few feet below the roof. They could've been solid gold, for all I could tell. The keep and clock tower, as well as the other taller structures, were stone. None of the stones were natural on any of the buildings. Rather, they were cut and fitted and didn't look to be from any nearby location. The expense put into this city was mind-boggling.

At the gate, another guard opened the coach door and poked his head in. "What's your business?" He asked curtly.

"Harvesters, sir," Yuti took the lead. "Sent by Professor Resin for ingredient collection. We will be returning with controlled items on our way back."

"Papers." The guard held out his hand and we provided the documents. He returned our papers and waved the coach to depart before closing our door. I watched the inbound traffic through the window as we made our way by.

"Are there settlements outside of the city?" I asked Yuti.

"A few. Some are said to be used for retired slaves, but I haven't seen any without these shoulder things. Thems that don't have one are not from here. Those are usually dignitaries or something."

The coach dropped us off at the road just before the outpost where orientation had been held. I timidly checked to see if the blood pools were over there where Fryer, the runaway, had been seized. I couldn't make anything out from where we stood and I wasn't keen on investigating further.

"Where to then?" I asked.

Yuti led me out and I started to realize how large Yalor's territory really was. My feet began complaining after a while. When we got to where some of the ingredients grew, I surprised him by gathering what was on our list without needing him to point them out. A misstep on my part, but I let it slide, hoping he would do the same.

He didn't. We rested on a steep hill for food and he handed me some bread since I had not packed anything. "You're a liar, huh?" he asked when I reached for the loaf.

I took the bread without answering and ate.

"I saw you eyeing the class. You could've done better. Why didn't you?"

"You never wanted to be an alchemist, did you?" I asked in response.

"Fine then. A truth for a truth. I'm willing to make that deal. Are you?"

I nodded slightly.

"I have no idea why I'm in that class. Side from the person that assigned me being a fool. I'm not cut out for it, and it bores me to tears."

"Thought I heard you sniffling last night."

He laughed. "You're not out of the deal. Spill it."

I got up and leaned into the wind. "You're right. I am a liar. I don't know if it's just in my nature or why I really chose to hide my talents. Maybe I just knew it wouldn't do to come in and immediately show up the whole Division. Maybe I just instinctively deceive and manipulate. I really can't say."

"A man should know himself, Bringer."

"I suppose, but we are boys. I missed my chance to become a man."

"Nonsense. We are young men. You're a bit smaller than the rest of us, but men to be. These days are how we decide what and who we will be."

"And what will you be?"

He pointed at a large complex close to the mountains. "That," he said.

"What's that?" I asked as he joined me on the hill. The fabric strap on his boot had come loose and an audible flop accompanied his steps.

"The only place in Yalor worthy of a warrior. The Coliseum. The Blood Gems of Yalor."

A realization crossed over me. I looked up at the sun. "Maybe we can go by there next time. Time permitting, of course. Be sure you explain to them how hopeless I am out here and how lost I would get. They are sure to let you continue accompanying me."

His face lit up, and he jerked his head back to the Coliseum. "You, my reptilian friend, have a deal."

## The Coliseum

The next day, Yuti once again struggled with his boots. I noticed the sores on his feet before his socks came on. I admired that he didn't complain about the wounds.

"Here," I said.

He looked down at my feet and then at the boots in my outstretched hand.

"I think they gave me a bigger pair, assuming my feet could fit if only they were big enough," I said and tossed them his way.

"You sure? I'll pay you back, I swear."

"For what? They cost me nothing. Just put the damn things on already. We got to get moving."

Once outside of the city, Yuti and I collected what we needed. We had to split up. My collection satchel was bulkier than last time.

"Got it all?" I asked him when I came up the hill we decided to meet on. It looked like he had been there for some time waiting for me. I was sure he rushed around to finish as soon as he could.

"Yep. We're free for the rest of the morning."

We hid our satchels near a bush. They would not be messed with. Yuti assured me no one ever came out this way.

I hesitated at the crest of the hill as a gust of wind threatened to fill my wings. They twitched then. A calling of my ancestors. I should be learning to fly. I thought about gliding the entire way to the Coliseum. I would never have made it of course, but it was a nice thought.

"What are you doing, Bringer? Like you said, we gotta get going if we are gonna make it."

I let him lead me away from the siren call.

We approached the Coliseum from the front entrance. The only soul to greet us was a bored-looking guard who jerked his head up from the hand it was resting on when he noticed us.

"What you doing here?" The guard yelled as if we could answer properly at a distance. It was only a half-challenge, so I closed the gap steadily. "What er you doing here?" He demanded again, irritated this time.

"We are seeking ingredients, my good sir." I pointed at the emerald on my shoulder as though it explained everything. I impressed myself with how I was handling my new life in rare instances such as this. Here, I gave myself a persona as though I've been at this business for years. It was always easier to pretend when one wore a mask over one's true intent. Mine happened to be constructed of little more than a smile and an air of joviality.

"Ingredients?" The blue gem looked confused. "There's plenty out that way." He pointed us off. "Now get on, youngling."

Ah, 'youngling' not 'razor' or their variant of, I could work with that.

"But, sir, this is a special request. It's a mushroom. Aris Cap." I presented my list, omitting the drawing that had been provided to me. Aris Cap wasn't on it, of course, but he and I both knew he couldn't make up or down of the damn thing.

Yuti shot a look at me when I handed it over and I kept my face forward, but the smile was for him. To his credit, the blue gem guardsmen made a convincing effort to show he understood the markings on the list, albeit upside down for a time.

"Fine," he said and Yuti relaxed. "I've seen a few shrooms down below, probably what you're looking for. Follow me then."

I nodded appreciatively and followed him to the portcullis. It is odd that so many of men's contraptions were made from various iron alloys. Essence wielded to flame could easily break the siege at any fort with the right man. It could be I was giving too much credit to the strength of essence wielders as a whole, but it got me thinking. The Alerez's affinity for ice emyon made siege with fire almost impossible. But there was no siege. The humans were just there all of a sudden like. They flooded in without anyone noticing. How in the hell did they get in? Korigara was heavily defended by the sure nature of it. Blizzards above and a large chasm below.

It had to be a very specific operation somehow. I couldn't have been the only prize they won. No, I was a byproduct of the invasion. That raises another question then: What *were* they after? Are they still there? I suppose they could have been soldiers, but I wasn't certain. If they were soldiers, then was that part of a campaign to occupy my home? Our glacier had washed up on shore centuries ago. Did we pose a perceived threat to the empire by not becoming part of it? No, that can't be exactly right either. Humans didn't want the other races involved, but their land, on the other hand. What could we have possibly possessed that would merit an invasion?

"Bringer," Yuti brought me back out of my mind.

The portcullis had been raised and the guard was waiting but losing patience.

"In ya go," the blue gem said. "I have to stay here. No time for sitting the baby, as they say. Any limb loss ain't my prerogative, so keep your nose to yer job and the big guys'll leave you be. Prob'ly. They like trophies, so maybe cover those 'orns of yers."

"Thank you..."

"Agris," he supplied. "Corp'el if you please."

"Um, thank you, Corporal Agris." Damn lucky that. His name was dangerously close to Aris. He didn't even know the letters that made up his own name.

Inside, the structure was wide open. Gates were scattered across its inner walls and led to the field. The field itself was huge. You could almost place a small mountain within it. Up above were seating for thousands, along with two areas that appeared to be for distinguished guests.

"Alright," I said. "I thought coming it would help shed some light on what this place is, but I was wrong."

"They don't have something like this where you're from?" I shrugged at Yuti. "Ah, well, Yalor having it confuses me too, I suppose. The Coliseum hasn't had an event so long as I've been here. What they are typically used for is sport. That's why they send all the big fellows here, the real warriors of their own rights. Sometimes, they're legends of their homeland. They come here to train and fight."

"Wait, blood sport is conducted here?"

"It's supposed to anyway. Like I said, they haven't used it."

"But they are still sending slaves here."

"To train, I guess. That's why I wanted to come. I want to train. I want to be a warrior."

Humans did seem to enjoy the bloodier side of things and a bit more than I thought natural. It would only stand to reason they'd discover a sport to it. When peace becomes too dull and suffering is a distant memory, humans delight in other's suffering. I could see old blood in the soil when we approached the edge of the field. The men they employed here must certainly be bloodthirsty, or at least enough so to stay alive. But Leegius, he wasn't bloodthirsty...was he?

"We shouldn't be here, Yuti," I said. He didn't respond. He was fixated at something behind us, so I turned, knowing it was too late.

"Green? And an Alerez?" It wasn't *just* Leegius. It seemed to be every damn brute Yalor had to offer. Their line grew larger as they exited the structure of the Coliseum onto its field. Each of them was armed; wooden weapons, yes, but a toothpick would have looked dangerous in these men's hands. I know this because one was picking his teeth with a sliver of wood.

"What the hells are you doing here, boy?" Leegius had pushed through, obviously not the alpha of the group.

*Shit.*

"Hello again, Leegius." I tried on a smile. It didn't fit well. I tried to reshape it. "I was sent to gather a few things."

"What are you doing here, greenling."

If wetting yourself could itself be constructed strictly into an emotion, then every fiber of my being would've been drenched in the acrid stuff when this one spoke. He looked like a man who could take Leegius's arm off and beat everyone here to death with it. To put that into perspective, in case you haven't fully grasped that image yet, Leegius is a fecking minotaur. It wasn't just the size, but a protruding layer of scars that were etched purposely all around his skin in a tribal style, making him look more like a beast than humans ever could have been in my dreams. They formed a new shape in his body, and the raised skin was tattooed in dark inks. This man chose to look like a monster. If I hadn't known any better, I would've guessed he had been spat from Disiea itself. His red eyes burrowed into me, oozing malice. Yes, this man was exactly as I described, every bit of it. A demon without being one. I believe I feel it necessary to reiterate so because today, here writing it down...It still sounds like exaggerated nonsense.

Yuti didn't look like he could get a word out. I couldn't blame him; his size was no better for the situation than my own. Though Yuti was much larger than me, he was still a child to these men.

"We...were sent to gather mushrooms from accumulations of old blood." I prayed Leegius would help me if things went awry. Regrettably, I admitted to myself that I was hoping he'd be willing to die for me whilst I ran away.

I made to take a step back. Doing my best to avoid the action looking like a flee or a challenge. Either way, it could go bad. They smiled, taking it as a flee. I felt trapped like a fox in the hunt, but even a fox has a chance to rip out a few throats before he's brutally murdered by the hunter's rabid dogs. The thought must have painted a snarl on me and the tattooed man was fully amused.

"Look at this," another giant laughed. "Must've come to join our ranks, Krolec."

This was going exactly the way I was afraid of. Leegius didn't look ready to step in. What the hell was I expecting? Sure, we were shipped here together. That makes us best friends now, does it? Why the feck was I here again? Something about recruiting?

The tattooed man, Krolec, slapped an arm to the painfully amused giant. "Well then, I guess we'd better induct them proper, aye, Browler."

I wasn't sure what a browl was, but I didn't want to find out.

"Alright, fine, but I get the horns."

Note to self: when a person who works around men such as these all day warns you about said men, take the damn advice to heart.

"I'll fight." Yuti was shaking. I was afraid he would collapse. The men laughed heartily and that seemed to either offer him some courage or piss him off.

I placed a hand on his chest to hold him steady.

"Bring—"

"Yuti, I know you fancy yourself a warrior, and I'll teach you." I hissed under my breath to him. "But I can't do that if you're dead. I need to get us out of here. Be ready to flee."

I could tell he wanted to protest. He looked at my smallness, but he nodded and stepped back. I could tell what confused him the most was that *I* could teach him. I wasn't sure that was true either, truth be told. I just needed him out of the way.

Browler, with his extra bit of gut and massive wooden sword, waltzed over without a single care as if this were a simple chore.

"Coward!" The word shot from me like the tension was pulled back in a bow rather than my bones. I fought the shakes in my limbs and shot a look at Leegius. It had been directed at him and the shame was written on his face. He was going to let me die.

"What?" Browler looked flustered, clearly thinking the outburst had been intended for him.

An on-my-toes plan stumbled in. When the rules are against you, change the game.

"I'm a third your size, you bastard, and you are going to bludgeon a defenseless boy to prove what? Your strength? Your battle prowess? Or so you can use my flesh to pretty up that devastatingly ugly face of yours?" I shouted, hoping my voice didn't sound as high as a child's should be.

"Wha...you've got those horns and that bladed tail. You've got plenty of—"

"Are you serious? Everyone knows an Alerez has no natural weapons. These are for show, you big dummy." Leegius was studying me. I probably should have pulled back on the insults. "These are to attract a mate, nothing more."

Browler quested for the truth of my statement toward the group of giants. Someone tossed a wooden sword and it clattered between us.

"There ya go." Laughs from the crowd.

"There. Now shut it, ya little shit. I've got food waiting on me and you are pissing away training time." Browler started forward again.

"Training?"

"Yea—"

"Training! Are you telling me there's no real steel here? You *are* going to kill me, aren't you? A sapling versus a mountain and you won't even give the sapling a thorn?" I shook my head. "You guys are pathetic. Hell, even your leader over there tries to hide the scared child within. That full body mask of his and all—which, in fact, looks like a child's fantasy nightmare." I will not claim to be skillful at getting under an individual's skin, but the red growing in the tan of Krolec's hide was impressive. I believed my stumbled-in tactic had some standing after all. "A spear or halberd, if you please." I spoke directly to Krolec this time. He did not appreciate it.

Leegius shoved back through and brought the spear quick enough. He jogged up and we locked eyes for a moment. I was trying to hide my fear with a smirk and he was looking at a dead man. Another man brought a massive sword to Browler. This sword would've taken any normal man both hands to operate. Browler one-handed it easily.

"Are you a brave man or just an idiot? Because I'm seeing a pattern of you trying to enrage bigger men than yourself, but I'm failing to see a root purpose." Leegius dropped the weight from his grip and it very nearly brought me with it. Laughter broke out behind him.

"I truly believe I have a death wish," I responded, finally winning over gravity. "Besides, if I've learned anything these last few days, I'm on my own now. The world is my enemy."

"That's a dark way to live, Alerez." Leegius sounded saddened by what I said more than the fact I was about to die. Maybe internally, he was part of the Breathing Church, more concerned over my immortal soul than my physical well-being.

"Oh, you mean for these last few moments?" I met his solemn gaze and cocked my head, instructing him to move out of the way.

"You shouldna done that, little lizard." Browler grinned. "Krolec isn't the most forgiving. He wants me to put the hurt on y—"

I handled my spear with one arm wrapped around the haft and stepped back from Leegius, ignoring the hot air pluming from Browler. I moved like fluid, doing a little blade dance. The spear and my body moved like two serpents in coitus. A lot of faces went rigid. My ballet of blades ended in a sort of bow, coiling my intensity.

I threw my wings out and they sucked in a full lung-cracking breath. The breath released in a gust of sand and heat, launching me forward. My horns were finally given to Browler as he wished but delivered in my own method, directly to his nose, horns piercing both cheeks and crushing eye sockets. Another breath to my wings and I launched over him, levering off his face as he fell in spit and blood and teeth. I flew over the head of an idle Krolec, who seemed more awed than the rest who moved to oppose me. Blood flew like an avalanche when I opened up the first wave of giants with a wide arch from my spear. The end of the arch found a wooden shield and I almost lost my grip. Massive hands moved to restrain me, not one of them tattooed, I noticed. Krolec being the leader, I suppose he also had to be the smarter one. The blades of my tail freed from their tear-drop-shaped fin into a fan of many severing ends and, in turn, freed a few fingers from ugly knuckles.

I couldn't gain much air into my wings with everyone surrounding me, but I made do and launched myself in the direction of the screaming, bleeding giants. I could only get part way up and had to crawl over them. I lost my spear in one thus far unwounded giant to lose the extra weight and pole vaulted over the last few men outside the circle with one final gust of wind. I landed in an uncontrolled way to keep my limbs from reaching crushing hands, taking the full impact from the earth. All necessary. If they had grabbed any part of me, my story would've ended in the worst, bloodiest possible way. I quickly found my feet, ignoring my hurts, and sprinted.

"Run, you idiot," I screamed at Yuti, who was overly mesmerized at that moment. He snapped out of it and followed. He helped push me along as his legs brought him along much faster than my own.

"Hey!" I shouted as we ran at a full sprint to the portcullis. The shout caught the attention of Agris, who was looking half asleep. "Close it...or...they'll escape." I was winded and had to speak between gasps.

Agris shook his head, irritated and went back to his prior task of lighting a tobacco leaf in his mouth. Then the tremors reached him. He peered to see what was happening and saw the warriors moving like a rock slide toward us. The leaf dropped from his gaping mouth and he moved out of sight.

The power rushing down with the portcullis made me cringe and I experienced a quick prayer as I dove feet first. I slid surprisingly far and a rush of iron slammed by my head, dazing me. But I had made it to the other side. I didn't hesitate when I came to a stop, though. I shoved Yuti and myself the rest of the way before another rush slammed into the iron frame, arms seeking purchase. With a quick scoot on my ass, I narrowly escaped the final inches bringing my tail the remaining distance.

My adrenaline rush faltered and then exhaustion hit, I felt weak. I collapsed despite the colorful curses precipitating from the bulls in the pin two feet away. I thanked whatever deity got me through. The giants would have helped me through by way of pushing meat through a mesh screen.

"What the hells," Agris said, looking exhausted too despite only having to pull a leaver. "You shouldn't have done that, razor."

"Me?" I rolled to my side to face him. "You are the one who kept them from me. I completely appreciate it, but you're the one who has to work with the bastards." Agris flushed.

Color washed from his face and the stillness behind the portcullis drew me. The giants were retreating? I know I pissed them off more than that. When I looked back, Agris was stiff and attentive to someone behind me. My body wasn't cooperating and I figured it was too late for me anyway, so I flopped fully onto my back. My limp hand slapped down on a very expensive shoe. There, standing over me, was Conarance. Smiling.

Conarance had us before the professor before any excuses could reach our lips. What was scary, was Conarance didn't seem angry about the whole exchange. That smile never left him.

"I found these two at the Coliseum today, Professor Resin. They held their own quite well, it must be said. But we all know that they should've been about other duties, yes?" Conarance paced about the shop, examining the stock as he spoke. I couldn't tell if he knew enough to determine their quality. He placed one bottle back and tried to rid the dust from his fingertips. The man with the round hat that seemed to accompany him most places provided a handkerchief. The tattoos on his arm peaked from behind his sleeve as he did so. He snapped back to his easy but ready stance with fluid motion. A killer then.

"My deepest apologies, Lord Conarance. This was not the task assigned to them. I will be sure to administer severe punishments." Professor Resin looked more afraid than angry. His eyes never left the ground. We tried to follow suit and kept our heads low. Yuti was beginning to tear up, but he fought it hard.

"I should hope so. On another note, may I make a suggestion?"

"Please, your grace." Resin bowed his head further still.

Conarance ran a hand through his black hair. "The Golden Age is coming and we need to get the Alchemy Division involved with the Coliseum. Ensure the message reaches Estry. I would not be opposed to these two accompanying the team as they have shown they can handle themselves with those brutes."

"Of course, your grace."

"As for the punishment, I will leave that to your capable hands. I'm in no mood to administer the punishment myself and it wasn't Theater worthy."

Yuti went pale then. He lost his fight against the tears.

Conarance walked out of the shop then, and the man followed him, returning the round hat to his head. When the door closed shut behind them, Yuti relented to the tremors he had been holding back. I stood there stupidly, not knowing what to do. Professor Resin stood there and rubbed the bridge of his nose for a time.

Yuti and I settled in for a long, labor-intensive evening then. We rearranged the shop, stacking boxes, and cleaning all the inventory on the shelves. The class went on without us that evening and the others could be seen eyeing us from the doorway. Yuti didn't speak to me the whole time. That night, when we stripped off our uniforms, he still said nothing. We lay in bed staring at the ceiling. He and I both knew we were not going to pass out quickly after the day we had.

"Teach me," he finally broke the silence almost an hour after the others had fallen asleep.

"What?"

"I don't want to be weak anymore. Teach me how to fight."

True Alchemy

Professor Resin wouldn't let us out of his sight for a long time. During our punishment sessions, he would stand nearby with his arms crossed, almost like he was studying us rather than ensuring we got the job done. We were not allowed to clean ourselves of the sweat and dust before each class as we were working hard right up until the start of it. His punishment didn't stop there. He called on us extra during the class and judged our projects harshly and loud enough for the others to hear. There was a moment toward the end of the punishment routine where Resin examined my work and hesitated. I prepared myself for the tongue-lashing I was about to receive, but it never came. He handed me the bottle back after sampling it and left the class. He did not return that day. The class was understandably thoroughly confused as he had not made the full rounds. It came to Ulinor to dismiss us for the evening after he took up the mantle and checked the other's work.

The next class came after the end of the week was over, and our research projects were due. We all stood at our stations, projects in hand, ready to approach him for presentation.

"I see everyone is ready. Your projects look good. Today, we are going to do things a little differently. Yuti, come pass these out. What Yuti is handing to you is a test. I expect you to do your best on the exam as it is quite important."

My heart fluttered heavily in my chest as I read the paper's header. Resin stared back at me knowingly with a smirk. It was the test for promotion. After reading the first few questions, I could tell this wasn't just to graduate the class; this was something far more.

"Yes, Ulinor?"

Ulinor dropped his hand and stood to speak. "Sir, this is very complicated. We haven't covered most of what is on here."

Professor Resin watched him. "Was there a question in there?"

"Well, um, sir, we can't do this. The newer students can most definitely not do this. Why are we taking this test?"

"Take it as a gauging tool, Ulinor. I feel as though some of my students, well, it's time they moved up. This apothecary is not meant to house each of you forever. Alchemy is a very complex science and there is only so much you can learn behind those counters. It is time some of you moved on, yourself included. Take the exam. There are no negative repercussions for failing. Indeed, I expect most of you to do so. But even failing this will allow me to recommend you accordingly."

I flushed as I picked up my quill. I had no idea how best to approach this. I couldn't think of a better reason than just wanting to go unseen when I tried to come up with an excuse as to why I should fail on purpose. Looking back, I think that I was comfortable there. It was easier in that position to pretend that I hadn't become a slave and I could have a simple life working at that small apothecary. This would not have been enough for me, I knew. I wanted to continue my exploration into the art of alchemy and I could not do so with my current circumstances. I was expected to be at a level of skill that required a large amount of supervision. But if they were to know, if I were to be seen for the skill I possess, what happens then? Would I ever have another day to myself? Would they turn me into a weapon? I still had no idea what Yalor really was. Sure, a city fully operated by slaves, but the slaves produced something for their owners, right? What was Yalor selling and to whom? I didn't want to find out.

I failed the test as convincingly as I could. The effort in doing so was greater than it would have been to get full marks. It pained me greatly to even attempt ignorance in the subject. When I brought the pages to Professor Resin, he hopped down from his chair and met me in front of his desk. He looked at my face, rather than the paper when I handed it to him. Then he took the papers and threw them in the bin. I stood there, wide-eyed, staring at the test, but I didn't protest.

Professor Resin curled a stern finger at me, indicating that I should follow him. He checked to see which students remained and announced, "When you've completed your exam, place it on my desk and go enjoy your evening." The few students nodded. Bik scowled and returned to his paper.

Professor Resin said nothing until the front door of the shop was closed behind us. "Why are you holding back, Alerez?" I followed in his wake but said nothing. "I suppose someone's reasons are his own. It doesn't matter. You show no reverence for the craft and I am beginning to resent this in you."

Professor Resin led me to a trap door not far from the apothecary, only a few blocks away. At first, it seemed odd to find such a thing in the center of a garden, and then I understood. This was his small cut of land and he grew ingredients on the surface. It had never occurred to me how, whatever he was, would normally live. As I closed the hatch behind us, I noticed an odd fruit. Blue strawberries?

Professor Resin lit some candles and his fireplace before we moved on. His home underneath the ground was simple but cozy and pleasantly cool. Passed his soft armchairs and bookshelves, he led me further still underground. Down a narrow tunnel he continued to light candles and sconces as we went slowly, revealing the place. A large room opened up before me, his personal alchemy workshop. I admired it from the entrance before finding my way in. It resembled mine and my mother's little cove of alchemy in the glacier. The only difference really was the cultural style and the fact that we dug ours out of the ice rather than earth.

"Sit down." Resin demanded and I did so. The furniture in his home was a more comfortable size for both of us. He leaned on his counter rather than having to hop onto it. A bowl of those same blue strawberries sat at his elbow. "Bringer, I'm not going to ask you to explain yourself to me. But listen to me: You must move on. Whatever is holding you back, you need to work around this very moment. Tell me, do you know what is done with the dross in Yalor?"

"Dross?" I asked. This didn't feel like an alchemy question.

"Yes, dross. Wasted investments. Slaves that didn't live up to expectations. Dross." I shook my head. "They're thrown away, Bringer. Sold to traditional slave work. Or worse when they're...well, let us pray you never find out. You don't get a second chance. You, like myself, may be small, but we cannot go unnoticed in this city. When people see a large rat checking his pocket watch, that's worthy of conversation. Same goes for you. People don't expect to see a pocket-sized dragon, let alone a pocket-sized dragon working at an apothecary. Wasn't it Conarance that discovered you? I thought so. You, my boy, are not going under anyone's notice. Conarance is not a patient man."

"Professor, fine, I'm a liar. But so is this place. What am I supposed to do! I didn't get a proper name, I've been stripped of my family, I'm not allowed to fly."

"What does flying have to do with anything?"

"In the margins of the guide I was issued, there's a handwritten entry, scribbled in for my convenience, stating Alerez are forbidden from flight. My people have a saying that those who cannot reach the sky in life, cannot reach Nybe in the afterlife. Not only that, but taking flight is a rite of passage into adulthood. They took my name, my right as an Alerez, and my afterlife."

"You don't believe that about Nybe."

"Well, no, but the rest is true."

He sighed. "Bringer, try to understand something, and the quicker you do, I promise you will feel better one day: each and every one of us has lost something being here. This isn't a bunch of people sold to commute their prison time. Well, maybe some of those at the Coliseum. We are skilled workers, people who were going somewhere in life only to have it taken completely away. I lost a wife and a few children. They pulled me from the sewers one day and I never saw them again. This was almost thirty years ago now, Bringer. I said you'll feel better. That wasn't right. The truth is it never stops hurting, but you do learn to live with it. The best we can do is make the best out of it. Nothing else. This thing on your shoulder, on mine; it condemns us. We can only work with what we have left. Bringer, please. Show me how much you really know of alchemy. I promise I will recommend you for the best possible positions I can."

"How?" I asked, resigned.

Resin looked around as though lost in his own shop. "You've been sort of convincing in your deceit. I'm sure you are something special as an alchemist, but I'm afraid I have no clue which direction to send you." He clapped his paws. "You'll pick. Forget the tests. Just show me what you can do. Use my equipment here. Make something spectacular."

I walked around his workspace and ran my fingers over the surface of a fine calcinator. I opened its face hatch idly, just to buy some time to think. I let my mind open up to the possibilities. I melted away to those late nights in my mother's tutelage. The burning away of the chaff until the true essence of an ingredient is all that is left. The boiling and refining. The drops of purity falling into the bowl, ready to be harvested. I worked with all my will and soul to create products only imagined up till the point we brought them into reality. Wiping sweat from my brow in the low light, I relished at the thought of putting the creation to use.

I was back holding the calcinator hatch door. "I'll do it. But I need you to keep a secret. Can you do this?"

Resin wiggled his whiskers. "What sort of secret?"

"I promise, you'll know when you see it. Give me one month. I'll make something you'll never forget. I'll create what only the gods can."

Yuti and I were forced to go on our trips with either Ulinor or another each time, a continuation of our punishment. I couldn't relinquish my duties in bringing the other students their ingredients, but the workload did ease up as the others were moved to other sections of the Division. Ulinor had been promoted too, but after he noticed the extra ingredients I had been collecting, he chose to continue joining us to see what was happening. I gave him no indication, but when I collected those rarer items that he recognized from the textbooks, his curiosity was piqued.

I made time to teach Yuti how to fight as promised. The boy had been right; he was made for it. I tried to show him ways alchemy could make him a better fighter. He was apprehensive until I showed him how to wield a flaming sword. We had only sticks, of course; no slave other than the blue gems could possess such a thing, but my point had been made.

I was removed from class and allowed to spend my days under Professor Resin's roof. When I gave him the list of the items I needed, he told me I would need to pay him back, but he agreed to fund my project. I promptly agreed. Some of the ingredients on the list were pretty rare and he would be the only one that could order them for me without raising suspicion. While I waited for them to arrive, I worked the other ingredients into what I needed.

Some required to be cooked down in the calcinator. When it came to cooking down limestone, I was afraid I would owe Professor Resin a new calcinator for the abuse I had to put his through to extract what I needed. Luckily, the stones met their new form before I burned a hole into his wall. Other ingredients required more care because they were volatile. Some condensed, some extracted. I worked diligently and each came to fruition in a timely matter. The time eventually came, and I was forced to show Professor Resin what my secret was. Though everything in my body told me to keep it to myself, my desire to be seen for who I was implored me forward.

"What is up with those berries of yours?" I asked.

"You're stalling?" Professor Resin fixed his glasses at me.

"I am," I said dryly.

He said nothing for a long time, just watched me, thinking something over.

"Bringer, do you know why I sell blue strawberries?" I shook my head. "It is because I have hope."

"Hope?" It wasn't where I had expected the conversation to go.

"Mmm hmm. It is no small task to do so, but we are allowed to buy our freedom from Yalor. Most do this with retirement. Me? I want to buy my way out. I take these berries, every chance I get, to the market. They sell for exorbitant price." He shook his head. "It is asinine how much someone would pay for these berries. The mistress wishes for me to find a way to sell them worldwide one day. Maybe it will happen. I can't say. But these nobles we have visiting will even give me gold for these berries. I trade the gold in for marks, and, once I have enough, the marks for my freedom. The chances of me achieving this are lower than a Fezdt's dwelling, like this one." He gestured to his home. "But, I do it every week, sometimes twice a week, because I have hope. Hope that one day, I will see that blasted clock tower for the last time."

He walked over and rummaged through his cabinets. "They really do sell quite well. People say they taste sweeter than regular strawberries." Professor Resin placed a bottle on the counter. The label only said the word *dye* on it. "Funny what people are willing to believe when you just change the color of something." He had to readjust his glasses when his smile shifted them on his face. "Now, there, a secret for a secret." Resin motioned for me to proceed.

I swallowed. "What I'm about to show you is going to change how you view alchemy. The others cannot know. I'm not sure when this should come out. With this technique...the implications are high."

"Fine, fine. I swear I will keep this to myself, Bringer. Show me already. I know I agreed to a full month and your ingredient preparation is superb, but I'm beginning to think you've tricked me. Show me already and let it be out." Resin was clearly losing patience with me. I was starting to think I had overstayed my welcome, but I pushed through it.

I nodded and turned to my ingredients. Three parts of the whole product lay before me. Kilician Powder, sigil oil, and a small heart I gathered from a toad. The former two were highly difficult ingredients to produce and expensive. Part of my hesitation was knowing if I screwed this up, I doubted Professor Resin would finance me further. I took a breath and tried to trust myself...as far as anyone could trust me.

I added the Kilician Powder to the bowl of sigil oil and stirred slowly. The oil and the powder combined well and became a soupy white. I let the chemical reaction take place before I continued.

"Don't breathe in fumes," I warned.

The mixture became hot and started to boil over violently for a time until what was left was a brown kind of paste. With the spoon, I added the heart to the paste. Professor Resin watched closely over my shoulder.

"Why the heart? From a toad even."

"The specific heart has nothing to do with it. The trait I am seeking within this heart is the spark of life."

"Life? That has nothing to do with alchemy, my boy. A toad heart has many uses. The traits are water or adaptability-based, but life isn't a trait."

"Shh," I hissed. I couldn't let him break my focus for the next stage.

I ladled the paste over the heart, one small spoonful at a time. Secretly, I had carved a sigil into Resin's spoon. Now, I pushed my essence into the sigil. The spoon began to glow and Resin's eyebrows shot up. I continued to ladle spoonfuls of the paste onto the heart, only now, the paste took on a dim brown glow. The heart reacted underneath. It started to change slowly, too slowly. I pushed my essence further than I thought I was capable of. I held on as long as I could, ignoring the dark spaces forming on the sides of my vision. Finished, I collapsed, dropping the spoon and splattering some of the now paste onto Resin's table. I was able to catch myself before knocking myself out on the corner of the table.

Resin was so excited, he paid me no mind and went to retrieve the heart with a pair of tongs. He returned to my side, holding it, confused.

"What did you just do, Bringer? In all my years, I've never seen such a thing."

I ignored him as I regained my feet. I had to check on my work. When I saw it, I couldn't help but give a triumphant smile. There clamped in the tongs was a root.

"Plant that if you please, Professor Resin, in that fine garden of yours. A few weeks from now, we'll harvest it and its offspring."

"But...what...what was all that?"

"That was the secret I promised you, which I'll remind you of your swear to keep it. I used essence."

"You mean like a wielder?"

I shook my head, still finding reasons to catch my breath. "No, far from it. In order to wield, one's soul must have an elemental affinity. I do not. Nor can one do what I just did if they have an affiliation. You'd freeze or burn the damn product. To do this, you must be malleable rather than fixed. This lets you tap the *soul* of nature itself and re-write it. That, in your hand, has no name because it does not exist. Call it an abomination, if you will, but not lacking nature's permission."

Professor Resin opened his mouth to ask more questions, but I held a hand up.

"In due time, Professor. Plant it. You will be the first to see."

He scratched his chin. "Plant, eh? Takes time to grow. You said one month, my boy." He smiled mischievously, anxious to see what was next.

"A few weeks more. I can only demand so much of nature. Lady Ecyila cannot be usurped by a mortal."

"Bringer, I...I don't know what to say." He held the root in his hand as though I had gifted him gold from lead. Theories have been made, but so far, there is no record of anyone doing this. "Where did you learn this, my boy?"

I shrugged. That was one secret I couldn't reveal to him. When I thought about it, I noted to myself how I should return to the craigs I had called home one day. Even if it turned out no one lived there anymore, I needed to return to Korigara to retrieve the *Soul Apothecary*.

"My mother," I said instead. I knew he wouldn't have let me off the hook with a shoulder shrug. Accusing my mother removed a further investigation into the matter and ceased all other questions simultaneously. It was rude to ask the slaves about their past lives unless they themselves offered up the information.

"She was a genius, Bringer...you are a genius. You have created something unimaginable. Conarance will be most pleased to hear how skilled you truly are."

It is said that Alerez have ice in their blood, but at that moment, I had never known anything more chilling.

## The Blackwood

Professor Resin thought the root had to be the final product I had promised. I let him think this and even let him name the new item: stopped-heart root was his choice. A name I wasn't opposed to, but it took some time for me to warm up to it. I'm embarrassed to say it hadn't occurred to me to name the items nature and I had brought into existence. This may be attributed to my younger self's arrogance or selfishness. I wasn't concerned about improving the world. Each time I made one of these abominations unto Ecyila, it was for me and my use alone. The possibilities and advancements they could bring to the world as a whole were never my concern, not until I was far too old to enjoy changing the world for the better.

If I had to rate my regrets at the end of my life, this would be among the highest. If one were to read my story and examine my actions, their opinion may be different, but I was never all monster. I had dreams once. I had innocence. I was a normal Alerez, ready to take on the world and be something. I was going to leave my mark just as all the young wished to do. They took all that away. The day I was assigned to Blackwood solidified what I was to become. When I look back, that is the day I truly changed for the worse. That was the day I could never go back to who I was supposed to be. Whatever my name was to be once, it didn't matter. On that day, Blight-Bringer was born.

Our promotion ceremony was a small affair held in the back of the apothecary. No distinguished guests were invited, and the rest of the Division made it along just fine, not knowing who had been added to their ranks.

Professor Resin added a thin piece of metal to the uppermost tier of my epaulet closest to my neck, and that was that. The ceremony was complete with a handshake and it was time to be off. Only the destination wasn't our new quarters across the way or being added to a prestigious research team. We were on our way to the Blackwood.

I could only tell by the reactions of the others that this was better described as a demotion rather than anything favorable. We walked alone in the direction indicated once the carriage dropped us outside of the city walls. My feet almost took me in the opposite direction when I got out. Yuti had to correct me. He and I had been going north and west each time we left the city; now we were to go east. I thought it was ridiculous to suggest I had missed an entire forest nearby, but there it was, looming over the horizon jealously. Even from a distance, I could tell whatever ailed the trees groped out to claim more. My opinionlessness about our new position quickly fell in line with the opinion of my companions.

"Tell me," I tried to keep the shake out of my voice as we approached. I was their leader now; I couldn't appear without confidence. "What is the story here?"

"There's something not right here." Yuti was the first to speak up. I didn't shame him for the uselessness of his statement.

"For a few months now, these woods have been corrupted with something we can't define. No one has been able to stop it either," Ulinor said. "It started with a hunting trip. A large cocoon sort of thing was discovered. The Alchemy Division was sent to figure out what it was. After a while, whatever it had been started to spread, radiating from the cocoon, and it hasn't stopped yet."

I didn't want to sleep within the boundaries this disease had claimed as its own, so we sent up camp just outside the woods. We positioned our tents in a half circle around a campfire as though its light would keep the encroaching darkness from the woods at bay. Bik pulled up a carriage loaded with alchemy supplies, and we set up a few tables with the equipment. It was apparent by the supplies and setup, we weren't to leave until we solved this problem for Yalor.

The first night, none were able to sleep much, for a low moan reached out of the darkness to claw at our backs. Some tried to keep the fire as bright as possible. I wanted to help them, but something drew me closer to the edge of the darkness. I wasn't foolish enough to leave the light. Within the wood, we could make out the sound of a large set of claws groping around, scarring the land. A moment passed where there was silence and each of us paused to peer into the dark. Suddenly, the moan returned angry and it sounded like a large tree was slapped down out of its root system and snapped with a loud crack. I promptly helped keep the fire alive.

The next morning, we moved the camp further away before we got to work. Even then, we stared from the edge. There was a point just past the tree line where every part of you said it was a bad idea to proceed further. Ulinor took the first step past this, I am embarrassed to say, as I had been appointed the leader of the operation. Given normal conditions, I am certain I would've performed just fine. But this wasn't a normal thing. I remember wondering why the church wasn't assigned to the Blackwood rather than the alchemist. This was my last internal complaint before I followed Ulinor in.

With each step further into the woods, it became undeniable that this place was a crack in the world. Every instinct raked across my back, begging that I would turn back in self-preservation. The air tasted stale and it was heavy in the lungs. Trees hung their heads and watched us pass, defeated in their misery. Bits of a husk-like substance grew in patches amongst them. Nothing grew on the forest floor. Only the corpses of the past held on there as underbrush tends to do long after its departure. As we approached the location of where this cataclysm began, we had to step carefully over longer, root-like bits of the husk material. Yuti pointed out the cocoon in the center of the husks. From it, the husks crawled across the forest floor to reach out into the world, slow but ravenous. The stuff webbed out like mycelium, suffocating trees and sunlight alike. We stopped short of the epicenter, unable or unwilling to proceed, too concerned with making contact with this unknown material. Whatever the soul was within us, all warned that we may be lost if we got closer. I wasn't sure what was meant by lost, but I didn't want to find out.

"Where are the animals?" Bik wanted to know. I did too, then.

We listened for them. If there were songbirds nearby, their songs died elsewhere. Though the sunlight was present, there was a need to squint to try to see regardless. It was as though the light it provided was less vital, complacent in its duties.

"There." Yuti pointed as one would trying to get the group to notice a ghost. He was on a roll with that finger of his.

His deminer wasn't unfounded. The silhouette of a deer, unmoving and blending in with a tree, stared back at us. The wrongness of this set me on edge. It could've been a predator for the way it watched us. Subsequently, the shadowy outlines of other animals began to reveal themselves to us. The animals could have formed from the trees themselves for the suddenness of their appearance.

"Why are they watching us like that?" Yuti asked.

"Does it matter?" Ulinor shoved past our stricken forms and started closer to the cocoon but hesitated.

The next sound was enough for all of us to forget the horror before us in light of the horror behind us.

"Ah." Not the call of some deeply disturbed soul or monster of unspeakable horror, just a single word. We each turned slowly to see Conarance standing nearby. The basic physics of sound didn't work right in these woods. Footsteps were muted, and voices didn't carry as far. The predator had approached unannounced.

"My Lord Conarance," the words tasted foul in my mouth, but I bowed to the bastard anyway.

He smiled, pleased I had learned some decorum. Professor Resin followed closely in his wake but not close enough to be between Conarance and the man with the round hat. I hadn't gotten a decent look at the man until now. If you paid attention to only his garment, you would think him a manservant or high paid retainer. His eyes told a different story and they were fixed on me. He wasn't a large man, but he held violence in those eyes. I wondered at the number of men he's strangled in their beds.

"So, this is what is all the way in here, eh?" Conarance examined the black-purple mass from a safe distance with his arms clasped behind him. He only reached to run his fingers through his hair and nothing else, as though he was sickened to risk touching anything nearby. I couldn't disagree with him.

"Yes, my lord. We had only just discovered it ourselves."

"Just? How "just"?" He glanced at Resin.

"Lord Conarance, these boys have only just been promoted and assigned to these positions. They haven't been authorized or tested for capabilities until now."

"Did they not arrive yesterday?"

"Th...They did, but—"

He turned his attention to me then.

"Then why is it today that we approach this...thing and not the day when you arrived?"

"I..." I wasn't sure how to explain the monster we all heard. It sounded like a child's night terror when you thought about it. There was no damage to the woods to provide as evidence.

Conarance combed his fingers through his hair again, this time with care. He sighed in such a way that you would swear he was on the brink of ordering an execution.

"Fine then," he said instead. "Alerez and the rest, further orientation appears to be needed. This is Lord Eneric's leisure grounds. Lord Eneric is set to be Mistress Hydel's general when we claim this land as a fief of the empire. These woods are Mistress Hydel's gift to Lord Eneric so that he can be at peak performance. He enjoys hunting, you see. The condition of these hunting grounds is unacceptable. The caretakers have lost control over the situation, so it fell onto you, alchemist."

Conarance noticeably grew less tense. "That means you, Alerez. When I found you, this is what I had intended for you. Resin here has told me all about your talents. It pleases me to know I was not mistaken. This situation has gone on long enough and my mistress is losing patience, which means I...am losing patience. Fix this."

He took a look around and the side of his lip arched. I imagined this was his first time so deep into the wood since its corruption began.

"Whatever *this* is." Conarance produced a handkerchief and covered his mouth and made to leave.

I gave myself a moment to sigh out the biggest breath of air I think I've ever held.

"Oh, and Bringer..."

I stiffened again.

"Do hurry."

We followed Resin's example, bowing as the two departed. None of us relaxed until our professor's shoulders came down. Even then, he kept to whispers for a time. He checked his pocket watch out of habit more than any sort of deadline. Conarance had made it clear, the deadline had passed. The rest was borrowed.

Cocoons always have something within, a mutant of its former self, a more perfect form. Adject monsters in comparison. I watched the cocoon for a long time after Conarance left. The howling and violence we could hear in the woods the night prior came to mind. I wondered if I was more afraid of the monster within or the monster without.

⁂

I set everyone to task. I sent Ulinor off to the libraries for references on Celn creatures, demons, and the like. Nothing in my mind convinced me this was normal or mundane. This cocoon wasn't natural, but I needed to keep my options open with the manual of creatures. I haven't been far enough from Korigara for long enough to decide I knew everything about the outside world. My glacial home had monsters of its own, but nothing that felt the way this cocoon felt. Next, I set others to build scaffolding around the cocoon and above the husk. I needed to see what would happen when someone made contact with the stuff, but was unwilling to do so with my team or myself. Finally, myself, Resin and a few others erected our workstation, which consisted of three large tables and all the wonderful bits of equipment I never got to use until I came to Yalor.

It was only after I placed the last beaker down that I took a moment to decide how I was going to approach this. Not 'this' as in the task, but the mentality I wished to use. If I were to take after my mother, I would try to earn the respect of this bit of nature until it basically requested I take from it for my work. She was that kind of woman. She approached alchemy with love, care, and admiration to coerce nature into relinquishing bits of itself in the name of our work. But her methods were never good enough for her impatient son. I could see the true potential within and was unwilling to wait to see the end result. There was also the Yalorian approach...at least as far as I've seen since joining the Division.

Professor Resin and the others seemed to see our craft as pure science. Sure, Resin cultivated some of his own ingredients, but he was methodical and expectant. There was, however, another approach this city and myself had not seen or fully explored...mine.

Lady Ecyila may have set this world in motion, but we were its masters. If a Golden Dawn could be brought forth, we alchemist were the only ones capable of doing so. Alchemy wasn't a negotiation with nature. One may care for it but it cares not for us. Alchemy is not a science. Scientists spend too much time musing over scroll work and text books. Only so much learning may be had in the lab. Alchemy is a demand, plain and simple. One may play coy, but in the end, your will must outweigh that of your opponent.

I flipped a knife from my hip and sliced off a hunk of the husk. After retrieving the bit of material with a handkerchief, I smiled, eager to get to work. Eager to understand whatever was happening here, and take it for my own.

"Hmmm." Yuti mused. "Is there a way we can study it without tearing it off?"

"We can only do so much from an alchemic perspective if the stuff is still attached," Ulinor spoke for me since I was preoccupied with rubbing the sides of my head.

Yuti drew his wooden sword and hacked a piece of the husk away. He let it fall to the ground and stood face-to-face with it. The material dissolved soon after.

"Aye," Yuti said. "I see the problem."

I rubbed my head all the harder. The equipment on the tables mocked me. We hadn't been able to retrieve anything for research purposes. My enthusiasm from before had been replaced by a healthy dose of anxiety. Conarance's time frame was growing ever thinner. I wondered how long we may have before his next visit. The sun had already set twice since our arrival. I wasn't sure how many there were left.

"I got it!" Yuti slammed a fist down on his palm. "We hack it away just like that. Problem solved. If it cannot survive without being connected directly to this spindle of silk then we keep lopping until there's nothing left."

Ulinor pointed. "Yuti, you see there?"

"Yeah, why?"

"Is that husk attached to the cocoon there?"

"No. I suppose not. It's just in that tree all alone like."

"So no, that won't work. Plus, there's no chance for us to understand this thing if we just destroy it like that."

"Understand? I thought the point of this trip was to be rid of it. Why the hell are we looking to preserve a single inch of the stuff?"

"Because they don't own everything!" I snapped. Despite sound having a difficult time in those woods, my voice carried well.

"Bringer, I don't like being here." Yuti's shoulders slumped. "Shouldn't we be finding a way to go home?"

"Home? Since when do we have a home? I'll be a dead man walking amongst the living before I'd call THAT home." In case I hadn't been clear, I threw a glass beaker in the direction of Yalor. "How could you use that fecking word, Yuti? Are you enjoying this little situation we find ourselves in?"

"No. But that's why I want to go...back. Brighter minds than ours couldn't figure this out. How the hell are children like us supposed to? We aren't great alchemists."

"*You* are not great alchemists. I have to figure this out before we can leave. If I don't, then this is never going to stop. Take a look around, Yuti. That thing there isn't part of our world. Tell me you haven't felt a little off since we've arrived."

"Now that you mention it—"

"I wasn't sure either. That I will forgive you. Ulinor, bring me that book over there."

Ulinor did as I asked. The tome was heavy but nothing compared to the *Soul Apothecary*.

"This is a book by a man called Khtri Farish. And you see, this man traveled from coast to coast learning and documenting all the things others couldn't be bothered to." I took the book and slammed it down. Everything upon the table rattled its disagreement. "There is not one sentence about this thing before us in the entire book or any other volume in the series." I left out how quickly I had to reference the material. "Which tells us what?"

Yuti thought, hard. "We've made a discovery."

"This isn't something from Celn," Ulinor said with stress building in his voice. He stumbled when he looked up.

I focused my attention on him now. Yuti was going to make my brain bleed.

"Which means?" I encouraged him forward in his thought pattern.

"Which means, this cocoon would have to be from the other realms."

I let my arms down, the anticipation satisfied.

Resin went pale, which was impressive for someone covered in fur.

"You can't mean that," he said.

"So now the question is: Who the hell does this cocoon belong to?"

"Should be a moth of sorts, right? A big one."

"I don't care about the being inside nearly as much as the being that transposed it here."

Yuti fixed a surprised "oh" with his mouth and his arms dropped from being crossed at his chest.

Professor Resin stepped forward. I let him have the attention of the others. Questions I had no way of possibly knowing the answers to were about to come up. I had hoped he would know those answers. As much as I knew about alchemy, I knew nothing about the world. I needed someone with experience to guide me further. I needed to sample the world like Khtri Farish. Until then, these boys' lack of experience and one large rat were all I had to go off of.

Resin squatted down and stared at the husk for some time. Then he walked up the scaffolding to the side of the cocoon and did the same. He reached to touch the cocoon and a number of us moved as though we would've been fast enough to stop him. I was relieved when he pulled away. His hand snapped out anyway and grabbed a handful of the husk.

I stiffened and held my breath. Nothing happened and all of us let out a sigh of relief. Each, in turn, smiled at each other, feeling foolish for our worries. But then the husk in Professor Resin's hand collapsed as it always did when removed from the greater structure.

I believe we all had the same thought at once. It was one thing to hold the husk in your hand; it was another to breathe it in. Resin must have had the same thought, but he sucked in a breath as though his head were about to be submerged in water instead of ceasing the breath entirely.

Resin's head cocked back as though he were in instant agony. His gaze shot up into the sky but he was not seeing what was in front of him any longer.

"Get something over your mouth and nose now, hold your breath, and help me!" I shouted, suddenly desperate, to the others.

We all worked to steal fabric from our shirts, towels, or any other cloth lying about and fasten it to our faces. Resin fell into the husk over the edge of the scaffolding as we did so.

"O—Oshhhh." He convulsed as words tried to work their way out of his mouth. "No...n—iz." The rest he spoke were a series of squeaks only a desperate mouse had the capacity to make. Some could have been in his native language. I had no way of knowing.

My hands fumbled on the string for my cloth mask. An Alerez beak was too odd to make a proper one. Frustrated, I dropped the fabric and rushed in to pull Resin out of the husk, hoping the others were not far behind. I would not be strong enough to pull him out myself.

I ran up the wooden frames and grabbed at the rat's clothes, tail, or fur, whatever I could gain purchase on. I started to grow weaker with my held breath before I had arrived. As I was beginning to fear I could not save him, Yuti grabbed Resin by the tail and yanked him out. I heard something break within but ignored it. Ulinor joined in and we dragged him, far. The clouds of husk his body produced in its thrashing covered too much ground to risk staying near the research site.

After we stopped, I spat out a large chunk of ice molded to the inside of my mouth and collapsed.

"Get...the others away...from there. Go!" I struggled to catch my breath between words. I resorted to sucking in deep rasps of air. The vision in my eyes slowly returned.

Ulinor regarded my ice sculpture for only a moment and then obeyed.

I held the trembling rat. I wasn't entirely sure what to do, so I held him tight to prevent him from inflicting injuries on himself or me as he thrashed. I had nothing to prepare for him. I cursed. My mother knew of other ways I could have helped him, but when we had gone over those lessons, I had been too fixated that they felt more like herbology then alchemy.

I was glad when he started to speak; it meant not only that he was still with us but that I would not be required to fish his tongue out of his throat to ensure he remained so. Old as he was, those rodent teeth were well taken care of.

"Sh..sh..she is here. She is...now." More squeaks of his language. I couldn't tell you what a single word may have been. "Oshoku." His only clear word and it meant nothing to me. He may as well have been squeaking again.

Resin passed out in my arms after a series of squeaks and other nonsense. I made sure he was breathing before I set him down.

"Yuti," I said. "What is an oshoku?"

He was stiff but started moving to the cloud of husk Ulinor was busy evacuating. "I better help him. He looks like he could use a hand.

I looked down at Resin, anxious at Yuti's response but too nervous to pursue further for the time being. I set off to find him a proper place to rest.

⁓⁓⁓⁓⁓⁓⁓

Yuti and Ulinor had been quick enough. Only one other person breathed in the husk dust. She too, fell unconscious after muttering a series of nonsense. At least, this was according to those who found her. We placed the girl and Resin in a small tent back at camp by themselves. By the time we got the girl and Resin back to camp, the sun was too far gone for us to continue for the day. I couldn't help looking over my shoulder. Since sound had apparently forgotten how it was supposed to work in this area, I was afraid Conarance would sneak up on me again. Things were looking too bad for me to have anything good to tell the chief of operations if he were to show.

*"Ah yes, Lord Conarance, please come in my tent. We will discuss things. Oh, the project? Yes, well, it turns out that the*

*whole forest is now in the possession of some great deity. If we offer it a child sacrifice, mmmmaybe Eneric can have his hunting grounds back. Only issue is that it would have to be HIS child. Is Hydel showing yet?"*

The distraction I had given myself worked for a time. I felt so helpless as each of the scenarios I played through in my head was as useless as the next. I call it a distraction, but it was more torture playing through how the next meeting with Conarance would go. The fire was low before I brought myself back.

Yuti threw a log onto the fire and sat across from me. I didn't give him long before asking my questions.

"What is an oshoku? Why do I recognize that word?"

"Do they not have Titanism where you're from?"

"I'm not sure what you're asking."

"You know. Religion. *The* religion." Yuti produced a necklace I couldn't recognize. When he noticed the blank expression on my face, he continued. "It's called Titanism as an umbrella term. They aren't actually grouped together."

"One was born. One was grown. One was hatched. One was made. One simply was." Ulinor took a seat with us at the fire.

"What? Listen, I don't need a lecture. Of course we had religion in Korigara. So, what is a titan?"

"He must've had a religion of gods," Ulinor said to Yuti, who nodded his agreement.

"Titans are precursors of the gods," Yuti said.

"I would've guessed this cocoon and aberration to be a lesser demon or up to an Overlord. But Professor Resin's outburst like that..." Ulinor's knee kept hopping as he sat there at the fire. "Oshoku the Abomination, the one born. Of all the places for a titan to be, this is where she shows up?"

I wanted to ask what the big deal was, but talk of things that would give the gods pause, gave it to me also.

"Ulinor, you're smart—"

"Thank you."

"No, you idiot."

He smiled at me and I understood. I couldn't help but smile back.

"I need you to get close to the animals. Maybe if we understand what is happening to them, we can find a way to save Resin. See if you can't catch one. I am not confident in it, but I will send for a priest. They could know something I do not. I've never concerned myself with the afterlife, but now it appears to have concerns with us."

Almost on cue, those same monstrous moans and gnashing ripped through the woods. We all stood prepared to run. Whatever it was could come out of the woods for revenge for messing up the husks. It never came, though. The night grew old and the fire struggled to stay alive. We only struggled to stay awake.

The creature seemed angry this evening. It sounded like the beast was ripping up all of our scaffolding and workstations, tossing them clear across the way. Glass shattered, and more trees groaned under pressure.

The next morning, however, nothing had changed. The pestle hadn't even fallen out of my mortar, and I was famously irritated by the poor weight distribution of the thing. I touched it as I walked by. It promptly fell out. I kept walking by, lest I react irrationally. Poor design as it was, it was the best one I had.

The scaffolding remained steady as well. Hardly any wear on the planks yet. Not a nail out of place.

Satisfied we had all shared in a rather terrifying fear dream, we each did as we planned the night before. Ulinor set out to find the animals. It had been at least a day since we saw one, but they appeared to be curious at the least. Maybe Ulinor's awkward footing would attract spectators.

I stared at the cocoon as a fool regarded a cliff's edge. Yuti stayed nearby, a piece of cloth on his face, to muscle me away if this went awry. It never ceases to amaze me just how small a wrong move will end even the most heroic of stories. I was no hero, but I recall having the odd thought that if I died here alongside Resin, I would not be remembered. Who would there be to do so?

Were any of the hatchlings from my cluster still alive? Was discussion of my disappearance abandoned after their naming day? And then it occurred to me, how can you be remembered if you have no name.

Bringer was nothing. Just an odd thought from a haggard old woman with a lasting consequence. I was only a "bringer" for a short time. How could that be the word to define me. In my world, that could be a name for a simpleton. But not someone like me.

I reached out and pulled a large handful of the husk away from the cocoon. I rushed to Yuti and shoved the husk into a leather bag he carried where it could safely fall apart. We sealed the bag and ran diving behind a boulder as though the thing were set to explode. After it didn't, we realized that may have been a little much, but neither of us were keen on joining Resin's bedside. He had begun to fever this morning.

I started back to the leather bag, but an arm caught me.

"No," Yuti said. "I'll go. If anything happens to any of us, you're the best chance we have to come back."

The first thought that came to my mind when he offered frightened me. Well, there were two in rapid succession. The first was how someone else would die rather than myself. The next was how well it suited me to send someone to die in my stead. A whole lot of conflict occurred in my mind then.

Despite myself, I nodded my agreement. Yuti fixed the cloth over his face and peeked into the bag. When the smallest of husk mist crawled out and dissipated, he paused for the worse, but when nothing happened, he waved the all-clear.

The husk powder wasn't what I expected. Instead of a lose flaky material, it was—

"Sand?"

"Why?" Yuti seemed to raise the best questions despite his lack of alchemic skill.

I had no answer, but my curiosity was piqued. I wanted to reach my hand in just as Resin had, but I stopped short of the twitch in that destructive direction. I poured the sand into the nearest glass container. I noticed there was no powder this time, as though what was vital had already been lost. The crystals were a pale black-purple, just the same as the cocoon, but now it was impossible to tell that it had been part of the structure to begin with. How did sand become cocoon husk?

I searched around somewhere, anywhere, for direction. I could tell this cocoon was going to be the death of me. The mystery was unraveling all too slowly to succeed before the man with the doubled-hinged smile returned. To do alchemy properly, I needed time. I needed to study this material and slowly discover its properties, but—

"Yuti, do you trust me?"

He was taken aback. "Sure? It's the thing you are about to do that I do not trust."

I handed him the vial of sand and rummaged through my pack behind the workstation.

"Don't tell Ulinor about this, okay?"

Yuti handed the vial back to me, eager to see.

I pushed him back from over my shoulder. "Stand over there. You'll be able to see plenty."

I poured the purple-hued sand onto a piece of paper.

"I wanted to keep this from the rest of you, but if I don't do something, Professor Resin is going to die. We don't have the luxury for experimentation." I picked a few grains from the paper between two fingers. "It is time for Oreculian alchemy to evolve." The grains lit a dull white-yellow and I tossed them, angled to keep any remaining unseen powder away from my face.

Upon contact with the air, a complex, volatile reaction occurred. The grains of sand disintegrated, releasing their essence. The fire-like crystals stabilized into a green hue and burned softly on the tabletop, digesting and repurposing its own material, each iteration slightly weaker than the last.

Four sigils floated within the flame. This is when I approached, Yuti in tow. This is also when I began to despair. The color of the crystals told me nothing of interest. Perhaps the green coloration could've led me to other conclusions if I had been in the right mindset.

"Funny shapes?" Yuti looked closer than I would have advised him. "What do they stand for?"

"I haven't the foggiest of ideas."

"What do you mean? What was with all that build-up just now if it meant nothing?"

I stared as the crystals sustaining the fire collapsed and began to fail to repurpose themselves. A hope flickered and died. Resin was going to die now, and there was nothing to be done about it.

"Brin—"

"It meant there is nothing," I snapped. "The runes...none of them made sense." I set off toward my tent, defeated and ready to curl up in my self-loathing.

"You can't give up, Bringer," Yuti said with a tone of uncertainty. "Conarance isn't going to keep going easy on us. You haven't seen it, but he has a nasty side about him."

"There is not always something tangible to fight against, Yuti. I don't understand why we are the ones here in the first place. Why is Estry not the one running this show?"

"Estry isn't an alchemist, not really anyway. Besides, she's needed elsewhere preparing for Yalor's dawn of gold."

That perked my ear but not enough to distract me from my gloom of a near future. I returned to my tent and left Yuti to figure it out on his own.

"Bringer!" Yuti whipped open my tent flap abruptly. It could have been minutes or hours since I last saw him. I snapped up off the bed roll, alarmed and upon seeing his face, I asked nothing. I shoved out past him. I feared Conarance had come this morning and I had yet another day unaccounted for. There had been no progress and not so much as a good night's dream to report to him.

"This way, toward the cocoon, hurry."

Once again, I did so without questioning and ran close behind, relieved no smiling monsters had been waiting.

He brought me to the cocoon as promised. At dawn, it was typical to find the other alchemist following my overarching orders about the cocoon. Mostly, it was for them to figure out what the cocoon was. When I approached this time, it was the first I felt I was going to have to get mean in my leadership role. I found I was both angry with them for being slackers and with Yuti for wasting my time. They were all just standing around useless like. But no amount of foreman whip-slinging was going to get us any closer to the answers we so desperately needed.

I followed their eyes up the massive tree overlooking our research site and the cocoon. There, impaled into the trunk high above us, was Ulinor.

"He's been up there at least the last few hours. We've been working down here. Nobody has climbed the tree. The antler in his chest would've made him look like a branch with moss or that husk stuff in the early light."

"Why has no one gotten him down?"

"We—"

"Get him down!" I snapped.

It took throwing together a ladder out of the scaffolding and a great deal more time than I was comfortable with, but we managed to get Ulinor's body down. We had to pry him away from the tree itself with an axe head as a lever. The antler had been impelled deeper than expected. Yuti, myself, and two others carried his body over to our workstation. I broke a lot of expensive glass when I shoved a space clean for him.

"Leave us. Yuti, you stay. Tell the others to pack up camp. It is not safe here any longer."

The other alchemists slinked away and they hurried to fulfill my order. No one wanted to be in the Blackwood in the first place. A dead leader seemed like a pretty good excuse to abandon the mission.

"Can we do that?" Yuti asked.

"Go with them if you would like. I won't stop you. I'm calling everyone off the research sight." I held my face in my hands. "We were so clueless coming out here. I should've closed shop when Resin was struck ill. I should've convinced Conarance to give us more time to understand what was going on here."

"What could've done something like this?"

I had kept myself at an emotional distance until then. Now, I gingerly examined the catastrophe before me.

Ulinor's face was frozen in more surprise than anything else, as though he barely had time to register what had happened to him. The antler had been stabbed straight through his heart. The end that would normally be fastened to the head of the deer was the part protruding out of his back. The rest of the antler was grotesque with husk and rot but without gore.

"It was a message. One without malice but clear."

"What message?" Yuti's emotions seemed to be catching up with him as well. His eyes glittered as he shut Ulinor's eyes. A gesture Alerez didn't share with humans, but one I have never forgotten since then.

"To leave. Or join him."

Oshoku

We knew Conarance would be coming for us, but there was no measure of time that would've made his visit any amount of pleasant. Luckily, Yuti and I were outside the Blackwood, away from the husk, and could hear every step he took in his approach. We counted them in heartbeats though, as the blood pulsed in our ears. We kept our heads down in anticipation of what was to come.

Conarance came to a stop just inside our small camp and took in the scene, resting on his cane. The man with the round hat watched passively behind him. The wisps of smoke from last night's fire reached for us spitefully as though to cause more discomfort in the situation. I fought to keep my eyes from watering.

I remember glancing at Yuti and wondering why he was shaking so. I admit, Conarance had me feeling ways too, but the terror written on his face...it never occurred to me that I was missing something.

"Where are the others?"

A long silence grew between us. The trees barely rustled in the breeze.

"I sent them away."

No sooner than the words leaving my mouth, I found myself staring at rocks with my vision in sparks. No one had moved. What the hell happened?

"You, young man, where is your professor?" I heard Conarance, but he sounded far off.

My field of view centered loosely on Conarance speaking with Yuti. I couldn't tell you where the man in the round hat had gone, but I hung in someone's arms like a loose puppet, vision splitting like my head.

Yuti was in full tears and snot when he pointed to the tent Resin resided in, his shaking uncontrollable now.

"Get him," Conarance demanded.

Yuti went on as he was ordered and Conarance held me in his regard for a long moment. Suddenly, all the pain I was experiencing stopped and my vision recentered. I fell to my knees and retched. After a while, I realized his glossy boot was in front of me and I arched my head to see him.

"I can tell you're wondering what happened, aren't you?" He asked.

He was right, but I couldn't vocalize it. Further, it seemed to correspond with Conarance's disposition and I knew I wouldn't be able to ask politely.

Yuti came out of the tent, supporting a barely conscious Resin on his shoulder.

"Here he is, Lord Conarance, just like you asked."

Conarance combed his fingers through his hair. "So, he is. Pray tell, what the hell is wrong with him?"

Yuti shot me a glance and collapsed. His body fell into an epileptic fit and Resin guarded himself from Yuti's flailing limbs.

"Did he ask you a question, or did I?"

Yuti was quick to find his feet when his fit ceased. He bowed so close to the ground I could swear he had his face in the mud. I had never seen the other humans bow like that.

"I'm sorry, Lord Conarance. Of course, it was you. I showed you dishonor. Please forgive me. Professor Resin is ill. He inhaled part of the husk from the cocoon within the woods. We don't know what it did to him, but he hasn't been himself ever since."

"I'm just fine, Lord Conarance." Professor Resin pulled himself from the ground using a fallen branch. He used it for support once he was standing, proving the lie. "I've just been feeling a bit weak of late. Please, leave the boys alone. This was my project, remember?"

"And where are we in that regard?"

"We are making steady progress. This is a very complex issue. One to such a degree that we are unable to confidently portray to you, my lord, accurately. What you should know though, Lord Conarance, is that this issue is beyond what we'd be able to achieve results from within the decade. For—"

"Decade!" Conarance ran his fingers through his hair, mastering himself.

"Your pardon?" Resin's strength was failing him and his bravado was close in tow.

"This should have been dealt with months ago, Resin. Our mistress grows..." Conarance combed his hair again and smiled that smile of his. "Let's take a walk, shall we?"

A deer, black as malice, came through the brush to witness our foolish return. It was the same tar-colored being that watched our final departure the day Ulinor was found. His body was frail and pitted, with rotted eyes that watched us still. Broken sections of chitinous material, like hardened cocoon husk, coated and deformed the rest of his body. I was no hunter, but I knew antlers were a thing of pride for deer and hunters alike. This dear had one broken off. After he settled down and lost some interest in what we were doing, he kept his eyes on me individually as though interested in my next move.

At the cocoon, Conarance did not show any of the apprehension that myself and the others did in our awe of the thing. Was he too stupid to be afraid, or was there nothing but the displeasure of Hydel that gave him pause?

"This is a thing of Oshoku, Lord Conarance," Professor Resin continued his discussion, doing his best to catch up with the rest of us. "*We* cannot do anything about it. Not without a lot of time. If you wish for hastier results, why not call on the Ceths or Father Freitney. A titan is not in the purview of an alchemist."

"Enough." Conarance kept his voice pleasant, but there was nothing of the word within. "I will not start the project over. It has become apparent to me that the Alchemy Division does not seem to take their duties seriously enough." He walked up the scaffolding to the cocoon, dodging the gaps removed to make the ladder when we retrieved Ulinor and leaned forward to examine the husk of it closely. His hands remained clasped behind his back though. Not a fool, then.

"Lord Conarance—"

"I said...enough." His voice shook with the restraint. "Cut it open."

We all stared at each other for a long moment. To his credit, even the man in the round hat looked taken aback.

Suddenly, the idea of losing this specimen for my personal research became unbearably real.

"Lord Conarance, there's simply too much we can learn from this being growing within. If we can contain it, then—"

Again, I hit the floor without any provocation. This time, I retched and continued to convulse far longer than my stomach had the capacity to contribute. Just as I was starting to fear my organs would come up next, it all stopped abruptly.

I tried to blink the tears away and catch my breath. "Wha...what the fuck is that?" I shouted at the earth.

"Bringer," Resin's hand rested on my horn with pressure. It was enough to get the message: *stay down*. "I'll go. Someone get me a knife."

Yuti offered his belt knife to our professor and the field mouse staggered his way to the cocoon. From the ground, I got my first good look at him since he fell ill. I wasn't sure if he even had the use of his left leg anymore. It looked as though it had been atrophying. Resin hadn't been bedridden long enough for that to have happened. I wondered what else was wrong with his body. That's when I remembered the deer that had watched us approach.

"Stop." I found my feet and rushed over to Professor Resin, but the man in the round hat was quicker than anyone dressed in fine clothing had the right to be. He shoved me to the ground, locked my arm behind my back, and slammed his knee into my back. I let out a sharp cry when the air was forced from my lungs.

Professor Resin didn't look at me. He kept up his slow hobble up the ramp and down the wooden frame until he was next to the cocoon itself.

"Yuti," I pleaded. "You said you wanted to be a warrior, right? You said you wanted to learn how to fight. Then why aren't you! Stop him!"

Yuti watched on, defeated before the battle had begun. After a moment, he slinked away. Where to, I couldn't say.

There was nothing else for it. Resin cut into the cocoon and another gust of the powder burst and spread over him. He covered his mouth but couldn't hold it in long enough and resorted to coughing harshly. He kept cutting through. The husk proved to be a great deal denser than the rest spreading across the woods. Given his weakened state, Resin relied more on his body weight to make the cut than any amount of strength. Once the gash in the cocoon was large enough to fit a human child in, Resin fell to the ground, wheezing to avoid the cloud of decay he had unleashed.

Among the cloud, something flew out of the cocoon. It had only been large enough to fit the palm of your hand, a moth, maybe. No one else seemed to notice it, though it presented the only thing with substantial mass coming from the cocoon.

Conarance gestured and the man with the round hat let me up from the ground. I used the chance to rush over and pull Resin from the area. Given my size, pulling the large rat proved to be difficult once again. I allowed myself to breathe once I had brought Resin a confident distance from the cloud. Trying to settle my breath, I dragged him further still. I couldn't think what else to do. When I saw his sunken face, I panicked. If there had been anything I could do for him with all my alchemic knowledge, it fled me. I began to cry. If it had been for Resin or myself, I couldn't tell you.

I thought of what Resin had been trying to teach me about hope. As Conarance approached, I couldn't make anything of it. I respected Professor Resin greatly, but hope and I hadn't been able to find common ground.

"Let's see what's inside then, shall we?"

"Cona...Lord Conarance, this is not alchemy anymore. I can do nothing with what you ask." I really did not want to go back up to the cocoon. "Please call in others."

For once, Conarance did not let the man with the round hat do his hands-on work. The abruptness of it was more frightful than any of the brutes at the Coliseum could manage. His face twisted from his emotionless glair to murderous intent. He lifted me up, first by the horns until I was standing and then by the throat. He shoved me against a tree, knocking husk bits everywhere. The powder release stayed low, but I wasn't sure he was in a state of mind to care one way or the other. He dragged me up the side of the tree until I was face to face with him.

"I've seen what you can do, Alerez. I did not purchase you for your expertise in biology. I purchased you for Yalor's Alchemy

Division because you can do something all the others could not. You have a gift!" He let me fall and continued while I gasped for breath. "Never mind how angry I am that you neglected to teach the other alchemists this talent of yours to improve our overall design. We can cover your selfishness in that regard at a later time. Your ability to do alchemy as though it were emyon has more potential than I can imagine, but what I do know is you and yours have not been taking this cleaning up of the hunting ground seriously. Why?"

I wasn't sure what to say. I had no idea how the other alchemist had handled the job before we were sent out. There were whispers that the intent was to get fresh new eyes on the issue. The more experienced alchemists had been unable to figure out what to do either. I wondered if they had come to the conclusion we had concerning the nature of the cocoon. I wondered if they had been killed like Ulinor.

"I think there is only one way to convince you to do your duties, young razor. The stakes simply are not high enough."

He grabbed me by the horn then and started toward the cocoon. I didn't know what he had intended, but I knew I did not want to find out. I fought back as hard as I could until I wrenched myself free. Then I stood back in a fighting position and wished I had a spear or good solid staff, at the least.

Conarance held up a hand, stopping the man with the round hat from coming closer to me. Whatever the man held behind his wrist, he magicked away again. Conarance ran his fingers through his hair, placing the errant strands back where they belonged and walked over to his cane. Cane in hand, he faced me, and my body went numb. The tingling was so harsh that I thought I was being stabbed by a thousand needles for the first few moments. I fought to retain my control, but each muscle in turn, failed me.

Conarance strode up and dragged me by the horn then. I dangled there, helpless, heart racing at my fate to come. I remember wondering where my soul would go now that the other realms were broken. With Ald'Kair's throne abandoned, the afterlife has become too uncertain for all of Orecul, Alerez's included. I was not only afraid of what would happen to my flesh but the rest of me as well.

We stopped, but not for long. My body's numbing had taken full effect. I could not turn to see what had halted our progress. A quick jerk and Resin sprawled hard to the side. Conarance dragged me by. Resin did not move.

At the cocoon, Conarance picked me up again. Over his shoulder, I could see the man with the round hat pulling a metal wire tight across Yuti's throat. A sword lay in the dirt before them. I wished I had a better thought the last time I saw his purpling face, but the only thing I could manage was: *where did he get that sword?*

"You will fix this, Bringer. Because if you don't, it will devour you. I didn't tell you what happened to the other alchemists that worked the hunting grounds, did I? They became infected with this stuff. And we burned them alive, Bringer. That's the only way to deal with such diseases."

He forced my head to look at the opening in the cocoon. It was hollow. I wanted to check over my shoulder for what had been within. I didn't believe it had been empty this whole time. Instead, Conarance shoved me in.

Far too late, my body started to come back to life and I scrambled toward the opening, desperate. I didn't want to be a part of whatever Conarance was about. He poked me back down with his cane like a rich man fending off a starving beggar. Though it was a weak and pathetic attempt, he retaliated with pain. How dare this wretch sully his fine clothing. I started to fight back the way an animal in a trap would. Careless of the pain or blood loss. Nothing else mattered but removing the greater part of the body from the metal jaws. The wrongness I had felt since placing a foot in the Blackwood was all the worse in the cocoon. I felt a set of claws, twice the length of my entire body, close in on me. Slow but ever tighter.

The feeling in my body came back further still and I split my tail fin into boney spikes. I thrust it at Conarance, intent on cutting that smile he fashioned himself so often into a permanent feature. He raised the cane with both hands and smashed it across the roof of my beak. I couldn't tell you if anything had broken, but stars flashed violently in my eyes.

When I was able to regain myself just enough, I watched Conarance pulling at the husk on either side of the gap closer together.

"Conarance!"

Still today, I am not sure what it was that I saw there in him or what came across his mind, but with that plea, Conarance paused. The silence that followed was the stillness after the cocking of a flintlock barrel resting on your head. Then he pulled shut the gap and left me in the dark. Those unseen claws pulled me down.

Down the darkest paths, one can see the dullest of truths. Truths so obvious, but one can never hope to notice it in the business of the world. You have to be swallowed up by the deepest of mires for them to be revealed to you.

Hope. That was what Resin told me I lacked. I had scoffed at that. He was right, but not for the reason he intended. Hope leaves you wanting and waiting as the world decides for you. In hope, you are only a victim. Vulnerable and weak. People use hope to try to smooth the edges of a life gone wrong. It never mattered how much you applied; it would cut you just the same. Hope is that thing you say you have when there's nothing else left and you slowly fade into obscurity.

*Hope is poison. A rot. A disease.*

Face down in the sands of Wohe, I couldn't help but swallow it whole.

She was there, when I lifted my head. Black blood oozed from empty eye sockets, as empty as the sandy plains. Though there was no flesh on her face to speak of, a distinctive snarl worked its way across her maw. It is said she wears different skulls in place of her own. Today she wore a deer's skull, antlers high and wide. Putrid furs clung to her back but then shredded toward her stomach as though something had ripped her entrails out through her womb.

I pulled myself to my knees and hung my head in submission. What else was I to do? Oshoku was a titan. No amount of want was going to free me from her presence. Least I could do was try not to piss her off. She prowled around me, investigating this trespasser to determine his fate. Crawling on all fours, each step she took dragged her ripped skin across the purple sands, leaving an ugly rotted blood color that absorbed too slowly into the terrain. Low growls made my bone itch as she hummed to herself.

I stole a glance around, careful to not lift my head. Nothing could be seen. The only detail I could make out was a thick purple haze that seemed to eat sight rather than deny it.

She crawled off then, but not too far. Oshoku reached her hand into the seas of sand and examined it. When she shot a look over her shoulder at me, I dropped my head again. It was then I realized how dizzy I was becoming. At the time, I didn't know if it was Wohe I found myself in, but I was almost certain the place was sapping my strength. I caught myself from toppling over.

The titan shuffled over and drew in the sand before me. It took her time with those oversized talons, but she managed. It was the runes that appeared when I scryed the sand. My breathing became labored as I looked up at her. I quickly looked away when my eyes reached those sockets on her wendigo face.

She roared then and slammed her fist. I call it a roar, but it was something I couldn't define. It was a mix of dying rabbit and screaming elk. I couldn't help jumping back, but I found my position just the same. Only this time, I was poised to run. All instinct, but there was no getting away from a titan once they'd taken interest. I had to push it down.

She stared at me for an extended period of time. Each moment, my bodily tremors increased in voracity. Oshoku plunged her long fingers deep into the sands of Wohe. A black, almost shadow, oozed from her fingers and started to crawl across the ground toward me. When it was close enough, tiny spires began to form in the ooze aimed my way. I went on watching, curious and frozen. The spires lanced through me all at once. I jerked back, but they held me in place. I gasped. The pain was deep and unrelenting. Experiencing that sort of thing, you can't scream. You can only bear it. Whatever she was doing to me, I could feel in my marrow. The spires had driven into the very core of my bones.

The spires ripped out of me. Only then could I find my voice. I screamed. It tore my voice up. It was all the hurt coming out in one long, harsh exhalation. I ran out of air. Oshoku's talon moved across my chin, almost motherly, and the world went dark.

I felt around, hoping I was not in some sort of prison now. The wiry material felt like a spider had created its den out of tree shavings. The husk. I ripped, tore, and shredded the cocoon's inner envelope, not caring where Conarance had sealed me away and making my own escape route. The outer layer of the cocoon gave way, pitching me forward into the mud.

It was dark out. No way to tell how long I've been in that cocoon. Or was I in Wohe? Already, the thought of that land was slipping from me like a dream. I remembered enough though, all pain and despair. The land of the afterlife, a dismal creation by the titans for our sake. It didn't make a lot of sense, but I decided these thoughts were best left to the clergy.

And then I remembered. Resisting the resistance to look, I turned my head. Yuti lay there. No movement. In fact, it looked like there hadn't been movement for quite some time. I fought with the part of me that broke at the sight of him and the colder part that wanted to check how long he had been dead, only to determine how long I had been gone. I was sure Wohe's time ran differently from our own. It had been three days minimum, by the way.

No flies had lain claim with their eggs, but the husk had other ideas. It had crawled across him but left his face revealed as though out of respect. Enough of his body poked out for me to do my analysis.

If he never got that fire in him, a fire I ignited, he wouldn't have been killed. I wondered if he died a warrior after all. The sword he had dropped was no wear to be seen. Despite not having a shovel, I look back at that moment and wish I had had the grace to at least bury him. Nothing else, just given him a decent send-off into the afterlife.

Resin wasn't far away. His body was in worse condition than Yuti's. *Withered* was the only word I could come up with at the time. A sad piece forgotten by the kiss of life. I collapsed next to him and finally allowed myself to weep. The cold calculation relented then. I even went so far as to hold his hands. It was then I jumped back. His fingers had moved.

I rushed back to his side. Two fingers to his throat could detect the smallest of pulses. It was later I learned the trick. This disease, this blight, was tricky; it was a liar through and through. Of course, I didn't know. So, I dragged Resin toward our camp. That is, until the animals showed up.

At first, they were but shadows, vague enough to be mistaken for shades of consciousness. But they stepped forward as though to challenge my presence. Less easily ignored than conscious. The deer with the missing antler stepped forward first. I remembered what happened to Ulinor and decided I was willing to die protecting Resin. The fight never came. The deer bowed.

Of all the things I would have expected, a bow from a deer was not on the list. All the other animals there produced actions to similar effect. I let Resin down easy in a sort of awe.

The creatures looked a lot like what Resin's body was beginning to. Each was as though nutrition decided their body wasn't worth the effort. Their skins, feathers, and furs were all taking on a blackness noticeable even in the pale moon light. Bits of the husk found their way into their flesh and took on chitinous likenesses.

I stood there stupid for a long time, but none of the creatures made a move to change their behavior. That is, until the deer pulled his head up and lay on the ground. We watched each other then.

"What do you want? I don't understand."

Obviously, the deer had no answer to give me. He watched me.

"It is not about what you want, is it?"

Something told me these creatures needed something more vital than life from me, a release from it. I wasn't entirely sure if it was my need or theirs that I decided to serve. Who could say? But I spent the better part of the next hour slaughtering the creatures. Not a single soul, I'm assuming, moved. My tail blade grew heavier and heavier with each pass through flesh. I went on slaughtering for so long, the original purpose for my actions became lost and I slaughtered out of habit more than anything else.

Panting, I resorted to throwing rocks at birds, hoping I threw with enough velocity to take them from this world sufficiently. I saved the single-antlered deer for last. I want to say I left him alive to serve as a witness to my killing of all of his friends, but the look in his eyes when I approached made it clear, he had no interest in that. All tears and mud coated my face when I locked my horns into his antler and antler stump. With a jerk of my head, I forced him to angle his neck, my forehead resting against his own. My tail blades cut cleanly through to the deer's neck meat to his esophagus. It was startling to see nothing change on the deer's face. I struck again rapidly until his head fell away.

I stumbled away from the deer's head and lay in the graveyard I had created. I screamed for a time in between the moments of emotionlessness. When I was ready, I pulled myself from the ground and made my way back to Professor Resin. I just wanted to leave this place, but the last gatekeeper lay on Resin's chest.

A large snake warned me away a few feet from Resin. I stopped as the warning requested, but I made no attempt to prepare for the strike. I assumed the creature wanted the same thing all the other creatures requested, but when I made to take its head, the damn thing dropped down and slithered toward me.

I stumbled back and crawled backward. The snake, black as rot, crawled up my legs and coiled about me. Face to face, I gave up avoiding the thing, but didn't shy away. It hissed a long, drawn-out fang-filled hiss and we sat there. It was either going to kill me or it wasn't. There was no in between.

"Do you not wish to be free of this fate as the rest of them?"

The snake lifted its head and, a moment later, smiled. I have claimed before to know little about biology, though this scenario, I was certain, was impossible. I quickly ran through my mind to see if there were sentient snakes in Orecul as well as rodents. There was nothing. I took a swing with my tail blades. They connected. The snake vaporized, and a moth crawled along my tail where I had made the connection. Suddenly, I was fed up with the fantastical. I grabbed the moth, threw it and lost track of it immediately.

With a huff, I gathered what was left of my energy and left the Blackwood behind. Sweating and parched beyond measure, I set Resin down to rest in my bed roll. Collapsing next to him, I checked my pauldron. The cooling emyon still ran strong, but the effort I expended that night had paled its effects. That's when I noticed the snake in the tent's shadow.

His appearance was almost demonic this time. I jumped reflexively. A set of great fans of flesh flared to either side of his head. Its face was only reminiscent of what a snake was supposed to be. Instead, he took on the likeness of death himself. Flesh drawn back; all lines wrong in a sort of primal sense. The skull of the deer I killed in the woods rested beneath the snake's coiled body. The deer's eyes had already sunk back and the skin appeared to adhere to the bone even less than before.

When the snake slithered into the moonlight, its features smoothed out and became more natural, with crisp black scales and crests of gold. It watched rather than accosted me. Suddenly, an insane part of me took over.

I stood up from the ground and held my arm out to the thing. It lunged forward with the offer, crawled up my arm in a serpentine, and rested on my shoulder. A flickering tongue across the side of my head told me he was secure.

Looking down at the deer's head, I wondered about the nature of this disease. Resin was a familiar sight next to it. How did it spread? What did it do to the body? I realized I too, must be infected. I thrashed about the cocoon before. There was no way I hadn't inhaled the husk powder too. A foggy memory of me coughing while I ripped away at the husk crossed my mind.

The world started to catch up to me then. My body remembered the efforts of the night in heavy exhaustion. My mind let me cross paths I had been holding back. I collapsed to my knees near the fire pit Ulinor, Yuti, and myself met every night since we had come to the Blackwood. I remembered that last look in Conarance's eyes when he shut me in the cocoon. I remembered where I had found myself.

Was that really Oshoku and Wohe? How could that be possible? Was the cocoon a harbinger of some great fiend Oshoku was planning on releasing on the world? No, that couldn't be right. It was empty until I fell—was shoved—in.

When you leave the Blackwood, that odd feeling of wrongness falls from you like passing through a curtain. I realized then, the curtain hung on me this time. I may as well have still been standing next to the cocoon. It was the final bit of feeling that set off a panic within.

Frantically, I tried to start a fire. Yuti had been the only one who could with a flint before. Frustrated, I tossed the rock into the shadows, hardly acknowledging the missing snake. I produced a vial from a pouch on my hip, grateful it hadn't fallen out before. I poured out a small amount into the fire pit. The bits grew ember-like on their way through the air and ignited the entire campfire in a whoosh.

With the light, I checked myself over, my panic growing. My blue-hued scales were nowhere in sight. Instead, it was as though I had been dipped in lies. I sat there unmoving for some time. The flame was flickering away by the time I came back from the nothing form of thought I was cycling through. All the while, a moth regarded me.

I snapped back to the world when my belly began to ache. Though it pained my body, I couldn't find it in me to care. Though, I couldn't stay there and wait for Conarance and his muscle to return.

The moth crawled about the vial in my loose fist. Somehow, I knew then the moth was the snake itself.

"You...you were the thing in the cocoon."

No response, of course.

"Well, unless you've had it with this life, I suggest you carry on somewhere else. I can't offer much more than a release today."

I crawled up from the ground, vial in hand. I retrieved Resin and dragged him further from the wood.

"You know, moth...snake, whatever you are, I couldn't figure out what my scrying revealed when I tried to see what this whole thing was about," I gestured to the wood, uncertain if the moth was even around given the lack of light. "But there was one, just one, sigil I knew by heart, weakness to fire. Resin, thank you for helping me produce this with the heart-stop root. With it, I am going to do one last act of kindness. I don't know that I've done many in my life. I don't believe if I were to survive until morning, that I would do many more. But this is one thing I can do for this world. I couldn't care less about Yalor or its working, but these woods are a blight that will not stop. I am the only one who can." I regarded his unconscious body. "Fine, I am the only one who knows how to, then."

I longed for Resin to wake up, though I cannot say it was for a good reason. I just wanted him to acknowledge this good that I would do. Just an approving nod would be enough. I thought of father and my constant stream of disappointing sighs I've saved up. There was nothing for it. I held the vial in my hand and used the raw essence I created within it and I set the Blackwood a blaze.

## Clock Tower

In total darkness, I dragged my feet back to Yalor with Resin on my back, with only the city lights guiding me in the proper direction. There were still many hours before dawn and I wasn't keen on being around when others arrived to my rather large beacon. I abandoned the main road, assuming Yalor possessed a fire-fighting division somewhere in its walls. Though I was on my way to the final step of my life, getting crushed by a creature and cart was not on my list of desired experiences. I found myself instead slipping through fields and then buildings to avoid the guards. The flames reaching out to the heavens from the Blackwood was enough to distract the guards at the gate. I slipped in behind them from the opposite direction.

Somehow, I arrived at my destination, fully winded. When you think of carrying a mouse, you don't expect it to weigh more than you. I took each flight of stairs as their own challenge, pausing periodically along the way. At the top of the clock tower, I sat Resin on one of the belfry's pillars. I hadn't known where else to go. I didn't feel the apothecary was safe any longer. They'd think to find me there. The clock tower was the only other structure I knew of. It would have to do.

I stood on the ledge, daring myself to step forward, still uncertain if I was going to fly away from this place or plummet. Of course, there was no escaping Yalor, even for someone who could fly. I've tried, as all the slaves here inevitably do, to remove the little shoulder piece issued to me when I arrived. There was nothing you could do to get the thing off. I wasn't sure Mistress Hydel could remove them if she wanted to once they were sinched down. It didn't matter how far my underused wings could take me. Anyone I encountered would know exactly who owned me. Or if Conarance's phrasing held, where my "citizenship" was held. I couldn't get back home before I was captured. All this assuming the heat didn't kill me first. The cooling emyon had to be recharged periodically.

Even from the clock tower, I could feel the heat from the fires. The Blackwood would be no more before the sun could rise. The sigil, which depicted the weakness to blaze had been a strong one, more than most plant life shows when scried. I underestimated it still. The fire spread and burned as though the entire wood had been made of oil. A blazed wielder could level all of Yalor with that kind of power. I wondered how many lives Yalor would expend fighting the flames.

"There's something about a good fire, yes?"

My emotional energy levels being as void as they were at the time, I lacked the capacity for surprise. I assumed someone had misplaced their beloved boulder up here when I walked about. Now that boulder spoke to me, drinking tea, of all things.

"Book illustrations do your kind no justice," I said at length.

The Olenous smirked at that. These large creatures were rare, so far as I could tell. One of the few that belonged to the empire alongside humans along with the Lignum and something called Triurgoath. Olenous were depicted as parodies of rocks, armadillos, or pangolins in the books. I could see why humans make such an association for the creatures, but it seemed a way to keep the masses viewing them as lesser beings. The depiction of Alerez, or glacier-razors, were none too better. Not much more than kobolds, really. I reminded myself not to use the word of designation humans issued such creatures. Seemed odd that Yalor still had what would be considered derogatory in their books for another race of the empire.

"I am afraid their material is a bit dated." The Olenous's voice was gravelly. I could feel the vibrations in my chest with the pronunciations of certain words. "Yalor's vast pockets and still they cling to the older texts. Is that so in your profession as well?"

"Alchemy is all old. You could say they use the newer texts."

"Isn't that your project kindling the night out there?"

I nodded.

We said nothing for a long time then. He played with a coin between his fingers one last time. Each turn clinked against his armored fingers, then returned it to a pocket as though he shouldn't have had it out. He watched me watching him as he did it but still said nothing. Out of politeness, I returned my attention to the flames growing ever larger. I estimated this would be the zenith of the cataclysm. The fire would burn out now instead of growing any larger. It had reached its limit.

"It's faster than any flame I've known."

He left it there, as one would expect the other to fill in the rest of the conversation. I only nodded.

"Come." He gestured opposite of himself. I hesitated. "It has been a rough night, has it not? Come."

I sat near him instead of opposite. I didn't want my back to the flames. I had to watch it all go down. In part to ensure everything burned up, otherwise my efforts were wasted. But in truth, I was counting the time I had left with each felled tree.

The Olenous poured me a cup of tea with deliberate movements. His hand held the top of the teapot steady as he poured. After pouring, he returned the pot to its resting position while moving his opposite hand's fingers across the surface of the pot in a seemingly pointless but reverent gesture.

"I've seen those motions before." It had me in mind of the tea shops here in Yalor. I've never participated myself, but I've seen the Wahyn humans do something similar while serving tea to their patrons. Yuti flashed in my mind. I looked away from the Olenous to contain myself.

"Our mortal coil may not be free, but it is impossible to cage a mind. There is always something to learn from others." He offered me the tea cup with the same deliberate movements, just as awkward and misplaced as before, given his massive form. "I am a terrible host. It has gone cold."

I accepted it graciously. It tasted of dandelions and lavender.

"I'm Bringer now. Or so they say."

"Grenlic. Now, eh? Estry tells lies when she says she has no sense of humor."

The moth inadvertently tickled my cheek and I slapped at it. The thing fluttered and landed on the opposite shoulder.

"You should name it instead, this thing. Since you share your secrets with it."

I must have been mumbling when I stood on the ledge. "How do you know I wasn't praying?"

"I've seen many a holy man. It is rare that I meet someone so far from the gods as yourself."

I couldn't help but tear up when I looked Grenlic in the eye then.

"You're right. It has been rough, but not just this evening." I fought against the cracking within that came on suddenly. "You know, I am not sure if I should mourn. They killed another hatchling when I was taken. It's a difficult thing to mourn something without a name to give it. There hasn't been a chance to consider it since you walked us into the city. I don't know who else they hurt. I don't know if anyone else was killed or sold like myself. Is my mother even alive? Father wasn't there. How could he protect her when he is always gone?"

Grenlic's tea cup sat idly in his palm.

"I'm sorry." I whipped a tear from my cheek. "I'm just frustrated at the name I've been given." I laughed and got my composure back.

The fire in Blackwood was failing. The heat no longer caressed our skin from this far away. Men silhouetted against its light as they fought back the flames. Their emyon caused bursts of light as they threw water at the mass of the fire. It wouldn't do them any good. The flames were dying for lack of food. The volatility of the Wohe disease was too nourishing to them. You could only let that type of fire die out. I supposed they would have to make a show of it either way. Conarance or someone else of high prestige would be out there demanding they do something.

"You said 'now'."

"Yes."

"What did your people call you?"

I sucked at the bitterness there, forgiving the fact Grenlic suggested I name the moth when I myself wasn't given such a luxury.

"I see," he said. "Close your eyes, hatchling."

I did, allowing myself to forget for a moment I was watching the last moment of my life burn away.

"Your mother, on your name day, do you see her?"

I did then. I could smell the soil down in the ice caves. She was tending to her flowers as she always did when her time wasn't already spoken for with my lessons. The light brought in from the mirrors through holes in the ceiling angled just right to illuminate her already bright smile. Funny, her smile only seemed that bright when she looked my way.

"It is your name day, yes? When she sees you, what name does she use, hatchling?"

She embraced me, proud, loving in only a way a mother could be. Proud for no other reason than I was her son. Her lips moved, speaking my name. I couldn't hear it, but I could make out the shape of it.

I opened my eyes then and cleared away the tears. The fire out in the distance was nowhere to be found. Only the memory of embers.

"Alcillis." I could make out little of Grenlic's face in the dull moonlight. He waited. "The moth, not mine."

"A fine name."

I drank a bit more tea and stood up from the ground. The Blackwood was no more and with it so my direction. But I had a name. I did not know it, but I had a name...somewhere.

"Where will you go?"

The city guard would come for me soon, but I had no inclination that Grenlic asked for professional reasons. He wanted to make sure I would be okay.

"I will not hide," I said. "Will you ensure his safety?" Resin's breathing was still weak and growing weaker so far as I could tell. I wasn't sure what I could do with him. I thought about throwing him over the edge to save him from being accosted further. To my relief, Grenlic nodded.

***

Within a few hours, I discovered the true limits of the pauldrons each slave wore. Once Conarance had me in his possession, he spent a long time demonstrating it. His cane had something to do with it. Something he did to the lion's head on the handle allowed him to cause severe pain to whatever citizen he wished. After too long with us alone in the throne room of the Yalor palace, Conarance grew tired of the pauldron's abilities and he tossed the cane aside to conduct the more traditional corporal punishment. I wish I could say I stood unmoved by his means of torture, but there is only so much a child can withstand. The only thing that lessened the impact of his backhands and fists was the quite possible concussions he delivered. Instead of him being so creative in his spouting of obscenities and methods of inflicting pain upon my body, he should have ended me there. It could have saved the world a lot of trouble.

"First thing you do. The first thing!" He hit me again. "And you burn it down." Again, he struck. This time a rather large ring sliced my cheek. He grabbed my face, forcing me to look at him. "What the feck possessed you to think that was what I wanted?" He guided my face into a rising knee.

A door opened in the back of the throne room and he tossed my head aside. He fixed his hair frantically with that combing motion of his and stood next to me as though he had been there the whole time. He checked his bloody knuckles, tried to clean his hands with a handkerchief, gave up on his efforts, and clasped both hands behind his back. Seeing this, it occurred to me how much trouble he had to be in for bringing me to the city in the first place.

Too many stern faces joined us in the throne room in this all too early morning hour, Lady Estry among them. Not only had this situation woken the mistress, but apparently, everyone of importance in Yalor. Each stern face took their place on either side of the throne in order from most grumpy to most annoyed. I could hardly tell Mistress Hydel had been rudely awoken from her slumber. Hydel was a beautiful woman, it had to be said. The flowing white of her garb and gold accents complimented her dark copper skin. Her braided hair showed not a bit of bedhead like she was a goddess lacking the need for sleep. The way she approached the throne, for a moment, I thought she could be. If nothing else, my fate was completely in her hands at the moment. For all intents and purposes, she was my god.

"One stands when in the presence of the Lady Hydel, citizen," the large Tréges Denkian in leathers snapped, the fur laying over one shoulder reminiscent of a cape. He looked like the sort of man who would use my kind's bones as a comb, or maybe a toothpick.

A defiance came over me. I supposed that Conarance had beaten any whining out of me, or I was simply past my limit of caring. If they were going to kill me, maybe I could go with a smile, knowing I could cause a little bit of hell on the way out.

I looked around, drunk in my pain. First to the large man who grew infinite shades of red as he waited for my response, then down the line of bleak faces. Finally, to Conarance, who looked ready to murder. All were standing. Halfway through my 'who, me?' gesture, Conarance's fist bared down on me. With a twitch of my neck, my horns interceded and a wonderful crunch of breaking bone filled the room sharply. It brought me part way back to normalcy. Not the kind a hatchling of Korigara may exhibit, but a new sort of desire for blasphemy I brought back from the clock tower. Defiant for the sake of it. Resentment, bitterness, calamity.

The youngest human in the throne room, barely a man really, attended the screaming slaver.

"Pardon my lack of courtly etiquette, M'Lady, but I find it rather difficult to stand given the excellent care provided by Lord Conarance."

Mistress Hydel's face barely twitched. A woman of self-mastery. The others stiffened, fighting their individual reactions and regarded the mistress, anxious as it seemed she was going to tolerate this behavior of mine.

"Bringer, is it? Of the Alchemy Division. Estry tells me that you are the newest addition." Hydel had an abnormally normal voice, beautiful even, elegant. I expected one who would own so many slaves as to fill an entire city to be monstrous, something even beyond the Tréges by her side. Something closer akin to that monster Krolec.

Her pleasantness put me off. "Yes, M'lady." Even the contempt for my name was numb.

She watched her nails; each was gilded and golden with a different design and complimented the accents on her face, in her eyeliner, and in her hair.

"She also tells me you have yet to show any value to the Alchemy Division or to Yalor for that matter."

I met Estry's eyes. She made no apologetic gesture and her eyes were stern.

Has she?

"Bringer—" Ah, there was the contempt. "—I must say I am quite displeased with your performance. It has brought into question your worth in being a citizen of Yalor. And much to my own chagrin, it has brought into question Conarance's judgment. You see, the Yalorian Forest, what you and others have begun calling Blackwood, was a labor of love and a gift to my lord Eneric..." She gestured toward the large Tréges by her side. "...for his services as my top advisor and soon-to-be general. As you can see, he is quite upset at this whole ordeal." She lowered her gaze. "*That* is what displeases me the most. A razor is always a costly investment, but the cost and man hours it took to grow that forest in these rocky lands was of greater cost than a thousand of your kind.

So, there we have it. More than enough on the cons side of the page of your fate. I will figure out what to do with you later, though the Theater has been most monotonous this season. Take him away."

She gestured and two high-ranking blue gems flanking either side of the large entrance approached. It was only after they slipped their white armored arms under my shoulders and started to pull me away, that I found my tongue.

"Was your life worth my investment?"

My shackles clattered as the guards came to an abrupt stop with Hydel's hand raised. I wasn't sure how they could see her gesture while facing the other direction.

"Was that a threat, ice-lizard?" Eneric asked quietly, ever redder in the face. "Mistress, please allow me to show this pair of boots—"

"Excuse me?" The displeasure of our interaction finally reached her face.

I gained my feet and shrugged off my escort, easy enough. No one here considered me a threat. They maybe should have. Though, I stopped far enough from Hydel's throne. No need to give any hidden archers the excuse.

"Was all this worth your life, M'lady?" I spoke clearly, but the whole congregation lost their silence then.

Eneric demanded I be put to death there and then. Estry tried to apologize for letting such a creature as myself cause so much chaos. Conarance spat his own line of obscenities to my back.

"Enough." Hydel barely whispered the word, but it cut through the others and they became silent. "Explain yourself. But I warn you, if you fail to do so to my satisfaction, we now have in our employment a priest from Houlian Thicket. I will introduce you without looking back."

I wasn't sure what she meant, but when the priest in Hydel's precession paled, I decided I would not like to.

I nodded. "The forest would never have been yours again, Lady. That was no disease of Celn but rather a blight from the bowels of Wohe itself."

"He's mad! Take him away before I stuff him for bow practice."

Mistress Hydel stood up with such deliberate and authoritative movements that I hadn't realized she was moving until she was halfway to Eneric. Her hand placed on his chest and he calmed instantly. She brushed past him and he followed to the back of the throne room and in semi-privacy, she held his face to hers. She spoke sternly but with such care in her eyes. Nothing was above a whisper, but I could hear her apologize about her gift being ruined. When he was sufficiently calm, they returned to us, Hydel returning to her throne.

"Father Freitney?" she asked the priest.

"Little is known about Wohe, M'lady. We do not have a connection to such a place the same way we do Nybe of Disiea. Some scholars anticipate it as a concept more than a realm. Dreams and horror stories told over the hearth or to children as they lay to rest to keep them on their best behavior. Others take it seriously...The Abomination's throne. A prison for all lost souls. When loved ones' souls are found to not have reached Nybe, it is often told they are lost in the sands of Wohe. Ghosts trapped between lives. How do you know what you have told us, my son?"

I glanced over my shoulder toward Conarance, wondering if he would interject at any point, an objection to the contrary. But I knew he felt it too. It wasn't something you could ignore.

I tried to decide what the best approach would be. Who could say that they have knelt in the plains of Wohe? Would they believe me?

"When my team came to the wood, we heard horrible things beyond the tree line when night fell. One of us, Ulinor, lost his life when venturing after sunset." I regarded Estry. She had the grace to show some remorse, and that surprised me. "Eventually, Oshoku approached me. It is my belief our constant presence interfered with her work. She wanted to know what it was we were doing there, and, in turn, for us to leave."

Father Freitney took a small step forward. "What did she want? Did she say anything?"

I shook my head. "We did not exchange words."

"I...I've heard these sounds coming from the woods," Eneric said. He didn't look pleased in agreeing with me, but as I've said, it wasn't something you could ignore. "When the cocoon first appeared, it always felt like something was watching me and the hunting party." He shook his head. "I am not saying it was The Abomination..."

"That's it, isn't it? Tari, please." The priest beckoned a boy who had attended Conarance before forward. In his hands was the oldest tome of The Breath's faith I've ever heard of. It wasn't too surprising though; the church guards its resources jealously. Only a few have confirmed the existence of faiths.

The boy held the book in both palms, straining against its weight as the priest flipped rapidly through its pages until he found the verse or instruction in question.

After the father read for a short time, his head jerked up. "M'lady, I am sure of it. The Abomination has corrupted this boy."

A shutter ran through me. "N...No—"

"Look at his flesh. Estry, he came to Yalor in his natural blue, correct? His eyes, they are the only natural color left to the boy. We must burn him. Cleanse the body and the soul."

"I saved everyone!" I shouted over the growing tide of comments. All on the verge of agreeance with the priest. "You also, father. The Breath's throne is empty. He didn't do this. I did!"

He looked pained at that. "Maybe so, but his works and miracles are still at work, my child. This is the only way to ensure your soul reaches Nybe to await his return."

"Nybe was the furthest thing from your land just last night. Wohe was closer than any time in history. I sent Oshoku and her fiends back. Do you not understand this?" The guards took it upon themselves to restrain me.

"I do, dear child, I do." The priest closed the tome with a thud. The book holder staggered.

"Burn the boy. Be rid of him!" Conarance still held his crippled hand, the loose hairs on his head going unattended. His comment raised the room in a fuss.

Eventually, Hydel silenced the room again. I had the distinct feeling that though everyone spoke over each other, she had recorded in her mind each point of view in turn.

"What do you have to say, Bringer? It would appear the Breathing Church has the right course," she said.

Frantically, I watched my future unfold before me. All their minds had been made up. I said the only thing I could. "I can cure myself."

"None sense!" Eneric pointed a stark finger in my direction. "A child taking on the works of the titans? The gods can do nothing against them, so how could you?"

"Because I have read the *Soul Apothecary*! I alone am the only true alchemist in your blasted city. Estry here is barely a verdure wielder. Her knowledge of nature pales to mine." I shot around to Conarance as much as the guards' grasp would allow. "Resin knew that. That is why he recommended me to the Blackwood project."

"M'lady, no one can change the course of a titan's will. The *Soul Apothecary* is much like Wohe, shrouded in myth, believed to be a figment of tales," the priest said.

"What is this...thing you have read?" Hydel asked.

Thank the gods she was a curious woman. "A thing which tells of the truth of alchemy. From it, I've learned what we can really do. Or, in this case, what I alone can do. Did it occur to anyone here as to why an entire forest could burn down in half a night? Such a process would take days, at the least. If you'll allow me to show you, M'lady?" I shook my shackles.

She nodded and the guards released and unchained me. I took a moment to stretch my wings, hoping to look a bit more intimidating and buying some time to think. I was working one step at a time. Each began before I had time to plan and steer the conversation. I wanted that control back. I had to do something unexpected. Something so convincing that I wouldn't be questioned.

"A knife if you please." The guard checked for Hydel's approval and handed me the knife from his belt. I hesitated with the blade on my palm. Then I sliced. With a wave, I scryed my own blood. The particles evaporated in a pale gray and reassembled into a number of sigils. Though Estry was the only one not to make a gasp of surprise, she was the most affected. Her eyes showed the first bit of emotion beyond contempt for me for the first time.

"Each of these represents a different aspect of my blood." I shuttered at what the sigils revealed but pushed on. "This is how I found out how to solve your problem. It's called scrying. I scryed a bit of the husk found spreading through the wood. It revealed how volatile the entire area had become. You're right, Father. No one can stand up to the titans. But what about the titan's own creations? The laws of Ecyila still hold. Fire, the most primal of all the elements, a tool of the titans and gods in turn, was enough to send Wohe back from the world. I pushed back an entire realm with one move. With just this skill you see before you." The sigils in the air fell away, forgotten. I begged Estry didn't recognize any of them. "To burn someone is to send their soul straight to Disiea, Father. What the scry has revealed to me is that this disease is in my very soul. M'lady, if you do this, you will send me as a weapon directly to the enemy. Disiea is no longer a place of purification. Nis no longer reigns. Isn't that right, priest?" I spoke the last bit with contempt. "Killing me outright leaves the disease to fester in our world. Let me fight this. If I can kill the infection, this blight, everyone wins. If not, we all lose."

Hydel sat back and regarded Estry, who offered nothing in return.

"This *Soul Apothecary*, you learned to scry from it?"

"I did." I bowed.

"What else, have you learned from this tome? Scrying seems to be of little use in taking on a titan. What sort of things does the book teach you?"

"Hmm," I said, feeling a little cocky. I was winning her over. Perhaps I was giving too much away, but I was also selling myself, making myself indispensable to her. I made my way up the dais to her throne. She was so intrigued she stopped the guards from restraining me again. "Did you know that you humans have an unraveling point?" I shot a finger out and touched her in the appropriate location toward the lower half of her stomach "Here. Yes, the mark of your birth." I pulled up my filthy tunic revealing my filthy but smooth stomach. I wondered if I wasn't repulsive to her. "Notice, I do not have one. One could say that my kind is not of birth. This 'belly button' is not a mere testament to your birth. No, in my world, it is the point that remains when the gods pull a person together. With the right methods, an alchemist can collapse one of birth into the components that constitute their being. You see, we are all made up of ingredients. Each of us. I can extract them. Including your soul, in the form of salts. Incidentally, this is where we get the phrase of someone being 'worth their salt' comes from. The *Soul Apothecary* gives knowledge on all this. Alchemy of the soul." I jammed a finger into my temple. "It's all up here. Only here. This is why I can cure myself. I know how to do the work of the gods. I can extract and repurpose essence and the soul itself. I can remove this blight from my own soul and light it up like I did the woods. I. Can. Do. This."

When my attention returned to the throne room, Conarance and the young man attending him returned to us. I wasn't sure when they had left, but Conarance had come back pale. His bloody hand was bandaged, a look of concern restraining that smile of his. I thought of the cuts and other damage he contributed to my face and checked with two fingers. Blood came away bright and vicious.

Mistress Hydel thought for a long time, her fingers interlaced before her. The throne was too large to accommodate her position. She was forced to lean on her knees, a decidedly un-lady-like position.

"Salts?" She asked. She shook with intrigue and no lack of terror.

It was then I realized I actually liked her to a degree. "Yes, m'lady, salts."

"You can't possibly be—"

"How long?" She cut Eneric off. "How long would you need?"

"Until the comet crosses the sky," I said. Ecyila's Comet would pass months from now, marking the end of the year. It would be ample time to cure myself and, if nothing else, orchestrate my escape.

"Two weeks. I will afford you two weeks, Bringer. At such time, Father Feirtney will test you. Such time as you fail his examination, he will have the authority to decide what to do with you then. You will be confined during your time to ensure the disease doesn't spread. One of my house attendants will assist you." She stood up and all in the throne room snapped to attention. "Court is dismissed."

Hydel strowed away, the cloth trailing her body with the same grace she exuded. A house slave followed in her wake. The girl stole a glance my way before leaving with her mistress.

Each face left behind watched me with murder, but I barely saw them. Instead, I considered the two weeks. That's barely enough to compile a list of ingredients. Suddenly, my job as a bringer seemed far more important than I had given it credit for. How would anyone know what I needed better than myself?

"Oh, and Bringer." My head snapped up to see Hydel standing at the door at the back of the throne room. She regarded Conarance still holding his broken hand. "If you use your natural glacier-razor gifts to cause harm to any other citizens or nobles again, I will have them cut from you with hot iron."

# 10

## The 'Cure'

It took some convincing, but they let me use Resin's home for my two-week confinement. The selling point being: it would be easy for others to keep their distance from me. The only access point was the hatch in the middle of the garden. I would be allowed minimal time on the surface, but two blue gem guards would remain nearby to cut me down if I were to take a single step outside of Resin's property line. Their white honor guard armor told me there would be no negotiation with them. No amount of convincing could get me to have them look the other way, let alone set me free.

"Here we are, Bringer." Grenlic had become impatient waiting for me to cross the property line into Resin's garden.

"Yes," I said blankly. The moth crawled along a purple nightshade flower near the hatch.

After a moment, Grenlic sighed and placed a hand on my shoulder. "Look, little Alerez, you can let the pressure end you now if you like. Or you can fight this. Two weeks isn't long in such times; this is true. But if you let it weigh you down, you are defeated already."

Oddly, my first thought was whether or not he needed that plate male, given his body's natural armor underneath. Grenlic was especially large with that extra layer. I was surprised at the delicateness of his touch then. It would be nothing for such a man to crush me with a slight gesture.

"We'll have tea again soon, Grenlic."

It was the wrong thing to say. He dropped his gauntleted hand and shot a look at the other guards.

I felt like I broke something precious to another. Stepping forward, I crossed the property line, thus beginning my confinement. I didn't look back as I made my way down the hatch into Resin's home.

The place felt wrong without Resin scurrying about as he did. I wondered where Grenlic had deposited him. Did he survive the night? It brought me to mind his ailment. He had collapsed and more or less had not recovered in any way. I was out and about with only the color of my flesh indicating any sort of change. There was no way to be certain we had the same disease, I concluded.

Wondering if I should request my old mentor's body for examination and feeling guilty for such a thought, I went about lighting the candles and lanterns. Thankful Resin was a man who enjoyed a clean work area and home; I took account of all I had to work with. It occurred to me I would be able to do little true alchemy with the equipment. What I would need to do so would need to be designed and manufactured.

Alcillis made its way down the latter soon thereafter, sliding between the rungs and then disappearing underneath a cupboard.

"Stay out of things. Show some respect while you are here...and don't eat any mice."

"Hello? Is someone down there with you?"

Stiffly, I peered through the hatch entrance stern with myself for not closing it on my way in. The small girl who had attended Hydel in the throne room stared down in such a way I wondered if she could see me. Her blond, almost white, hair shone in the sunlight. It was held so closely to her head in braids that hardly a strand wavered in the breeze. It was hard to make out the gem that marked her a slave, given how white her dress was. Hydel wouldn't allow the typical garb of her citizens for her attendants. The first thought that came to mind was 'spy.' This must be the help the mistress alluded to before.

"Yes. If you count the mushrooms. They could be Ligshrum for the number of them."

"I doubt a Lignum would entrust its parents to you. I heard they were trouble even for the Lignum anyway. It's rude to leave the guest waiting at your door, you know?"

"Do rats share the same customs? Since you lot keep them in the sewers and all? I figured humans would just toss toilet paper correspondence instead."

That stung her a bit. The girl stepped back out of view. There were not enough steps to take her further than a few plots of the garden. With the distinct feeling that I was being unfair, I climbed the ladder.

She bowed, both hands in front of her, holding a covered basket. "I am Mistress Hydel's personal house...em a palace citizen, Kyda. I have been assigned to retrieve anything you request during your stay in this..." She checked over my shoulder. Her demeanor was forced enough to have me guessing how long she had been in the mistress's service. "Home? Given you provide the marks for me to obtain the requested provisions."

"A pleasure. I noticed you omitted the part about providing the aristocracies with any updates along the way. Bringer, or so they call me."

To her credit, she said nothing about the reports. No excuse or ask for pardon. "I understand you are an alchemist?"

She brushed past two of my provocations at this point. I wasn't sure what to do with that. This more aggressive Bringer would need to learn how to navigate these waters more akin to my father.

"I am."

"Very interesting."

We stood there, awkward as anything. She was my height. My eyes fell, and I caught myself. I've been told human females don't approve of males looking down. At what, I wasn't sure.

"What's with the basket?" I asked.

"Oh." She pulled the cloth from the basket. "I thought you could be hungry from the day...and night you had. I heard you enjoyed—"

"Apples!" It shot from me, half-whispered and the other half bubbling in saliva.

She smirked and tossed me one of the glorious jewels. As soon as it landed in my hand, its lifespan dropped. The act may have seemed a bit feral, looking back.

"Maybe a little gentler with this one? I'm not sure I can save an Alerez from choking. Oh, and it's customary to leave the core remaining."

I took the fruit calmer this time and more than a little embarrassed.

"How did you know I like these?" My stomach no longer aching, I returned to my skepticism. "All the people I know are dead." That last part was supposed to be a joke, but it left us both feeling rotten.

"I may have checked your mark use history. No one knew much about you. Lady Estry only scowled at me. Apples were the only thing you consistently purchased."

"They keep track of those?" I took a bite of the next apple. "How is Soe doing then?"

"The man in the market? His apples are coming in good. I told him these were for you and he gave me a discount." She took on a gruff demeanor and voice that didn't suit her. "'A good customer for a lizard,' he said. I think he may have thrown a few extra in here. So, I...made you a pie."

"Pie? What the hell is that?"

That shocked her. A sly smile crossed her face, the sun cresting a cloudy day. She produced a small box from the bottom of the basket, apples rolling off its surface. I approached intrigued and bit off another chunk of apple. The juices filled me with joy. I told myself that is why I was in good humor with Kyda.

"Can we?" She gestured over to an empty patch in Resin's garden. "I need to cut this."

I shrugged and led the way. The pastry in the box left me unenthused. That is, until she cut a slice off for me. Slivers of caramelized apple covered in a thick sauce ran from in between two layers of pastry. My heart sung and I must have lost the rest of my apple because I accepted the treat with both hands.

"Go ahead." Kyda smiled widely, handing over a fork.

I layered a too-large bit onto the utensil with the care you save for holding your firstborn child. The aroma filled me like a hug. I placed the mouthful on my tongue, the body of the host. The flavor covered every magnificent nerve ending it could find and it was...the worst creation to ever curse this world of ours.

"Are you okay?"

"Mmhmm." I choked back bile. "Yeah. Yep. Just fine. I'm going to get to work, I think. Only two weeks, you know. I'll finish this...marvelous...thing in my work area."

"Bringer, what's going on?"

"No, no. Stay here. Actually, come back tomorrow. Down there is only for me."

"But I'm authorized to come down there."

"Yep." I shut the hatch door behind me, narrowly holding back from locking it also.

Now that the initial pain of eating the pie had passed, I set it down on a nearby counter and took another look around. It was then I felt the weight of the loneliness. Yuti and the others may have been human, but they kept me company, if nothing else. It was too quiet down here without anyone complaining about Resin's assignments or announcing frustrations about a particular experiment.

I should have taught them what I knew. True alchemy could have saved them in enough ways. Elemental oil for Yuti's sword skills. I could see Ulinor taking to grenadoes or even inventing something new. The smallest glimpse into what could really be done through alchemy would've been plenty and they could have fought back. I shouldn't care that they had died, but I did. Humans were all the same, but they were my friends to a degree...I think.

I checked to see if Kyda was still in the garden but was greeted by the basket of apples instead. The pie was nowhere to be seen. I hoped she could find a use for it worthy of her gift. As I brought the basket down, I thought I should repay the marks she spent on my behalf.

The hatch closed again; this time, I locked it.

Going through each ingredient in Resin's cupboards, I compiled a list for Kyda to obtain. I didn't have Resin's income this time, so counting my marks was a careful process. I wasn't sure I could afford food after this endeavor. I thought it better to worry about my stomach after Freitney's holy fire had passed.

The list for Kyda, in truth, was weak at best. I had no idea where to begin. It wasn't custom for an alchemist of any caliber to experiment on their own soul. Too many mistakes could be made. I could become an idol if I wasn't careful. Though that elemental hell is usually the result of careless emyon use, I could easily commit myself to such a fate even though I've never used emyon. I could also end up killing myself and saving everyone else the trouble. I placed that idea in the back of my mind to perhaps recall for later. If nothing else, to beggar Eneric.

The least useful bottles of Resin's creations, I cast aside, and they clattered to the ground. I paused when I came across Resin's dying reagent. I scoffed, sneering at his musings on hope. After I set it on the table, I noticed the snake examining the rest of my pie slice. Its tongue shot out to tickle its contents. It regarded me with a questioning look, and I shrugged. Alcillis changed into the moth and licked at the pie.

"Settle in then," I told it. "Two weeks is going to be one long day."

I watched it, disgusted at its pallet. Of all my uncertainty, there was one thing of which I was most certain beyond any doubt: cooking apples is a most grievous sin.

"No, no, no!"

The compound fizzled and consumed itself like there was an internal fire; the second one today. Another failure. I was starting to believe I could hear Oshoku cackle as each one piled up in the corner. I threw this burnt mush to join the rest. Kyda had made the comment, with her eyes rather than her lips, it was starting to look like a landfill in Resin's home. I couldn't disagree, but with my days falling from me like a leper's sour flesh, I had little time to be concerned.

"When was the last time you slept?" She asked, replacing the mortar and pestle I had knocked over in my frustration. The sigils I chipped into the sides now dark burns on the otherwise perfect granite.

My mind felt like lead as I considered. "What...the day before I became infected? That sounds right...right?"

Even as I spoke, dreams fluttered beneath the surface of my eyelids. I fought them back as though my life depended on it, because it did. Over half the time limit was spent and I wasn't any closer to a cure than when I started. I had been able to keep the experiments to my essence rather than my soul. All failures had minimal detriments, but I was starting to think I should do more and accept the risks.

"You need to sleep, Bringer. Come at this with a fresh mind."

"You know I can't." The only thing I've been able to do was discover the infection was growing deeper. "Why are you still here?"

I had more or less attacked her during this visit. She had made it a habit to show up every day since she left the basket of apples for me. Each day it was a delivery of requested ingredients and a meal. Today, I accused her of trying to make me weak, of poisoning me and ruining my work. I hadn't asked her to show care for me. Why would a human care about an Alerez anyhow? All these and the like. The contents of the basket decorated the floor in smashed green, and various other bud-borne colors. I knew I had hurt her. We had become friends to a degree during her visits. And I returned her kindness with cruelty. I wish at the time I had cared enough to stop myself.

Each tap of the pestle into the mortar set the sigils on its side to light. I ached at the fact that these were the first steps to most alchemic processes. I was starting over again. The leaves gave way to powder easy enough, but then I used too much essence and the contents went to gel, ruined before the completion of the first step. My grip grew tighter on the granite and I hunched over in repressed rage.

"Bringer, stop." Kyda held my hand still on the pestle. It still shook despite the amount of effort she put into it.

I don't know if it was the complete near collapse from exhaustion I was experiencing or the impending fiery death awaiting me at the end of this lingering failure, but a heat banked in me.

"You need to stop," Kyda said softly, still shaken.

"I ...can't."

"What?"

Apparently, I had whispered.

"I can't," I roared flinging her back. "I can't stop. In seven days, I die, Kyda. Don't you get that? I'll be killed in the worst manner possible and I can't—I haven't made any progress. I can't win. I am going to die."

Kyda got up slowly. I expected her movement to be as though trying to not provoke a rabid dog. She surprised me by simply brushing off her skirts and a swift crack across my face. She may not be a big intimidating Tréges like Eneric, but her hand told me about her heritage. Stars and dark spots swarmed in my vision. The rage fell from me with the spittle. My vision had only just cleared when I realized I was on my way to the ground. Despite trying to save myself, I clattered to the ground with a handful of Resin's dirt wall accompanying me.

"Shut up, shut up, shut up!" I think Kyda found the anger she had smacked out of me. "Bringer, you are an idiot. I've read your research. You are a brilliant idiot. If you would step back, if you would just rest and calm down, I know you can find the answer."

After she stopped shaking, Kyda helped me up and moved me to the couch in Resin's sitting area. I was out before the blanket she unfolded lay on my skin.

From a distant place, I heard her say, "I don't care if The Abomination is behind this. You can beat this, Bringer."

Without windows, it was impossible to say how long I was out. I shooed Alcillis off of the ladder rung and checked what time it was. It was too dark to say. Kyda would have had to be gone by then. No apologies today. My workstation was a mess. Kyda would've normally put everything back for me. This time though, I would have to pick it up myself. Just as I made to retrieve the small calcinator from the floor, my mind brought with it a thought as though from someone else's genius. I jerked up from the ground to check the table. I didn't want to spend the next few hours searching for the damn thing under furniture or anywhere else it could have fallen. It was there, just like I had left it. I clung to the bottle and held it to my chest.

⸱⸱⸱ ❧ ⸱⸱⸱

The following is a bit I gathered from the conversations I had with Grenlic. He didn't speak much, but I had always wondered what brought he and I so close. As he made to find his way to the next life, even a man such as he wishes to stave off the inevitable with talk:

Men in heavy plate clattered indiscreetly along the cobblestone road. More men than necessary. Grenlic led the formation himself. He didn't know the Alerez boy well, but still, it gave him anxiety.

Not for fear of the rumors sprouting from the ashes of the forest. Grenlic didn't believe in ghosts like some. He just never liked carrying out his duties. When he had been a soldier, a Writ Executioner no less, the tasks were honorable, victorious to the heart...mostly. Now a slave and head of the city guard, a city of slaves, his jobs felt...dirty. Not once have the actions he had been sent to felt just. There was no fighting this one. Lord Eneric was in town and Grenlic discovered early on Eneric called the shots while he was in proximity of Mistress Hydel. Much easier to swoon her to his way of thinking that way. When was he leaving this time? Not soon enough for the Alerez. Grenlic's influence over the Lady is worthless for now.

This wouldn't be the first time Grenlic was sent to bring a child to justice. It never got easier. Worse, he knew the victim this time. Sure, it was a short introduction, but he liked the kid. There was something special about Bringer. Maybe his darkness reminded Grenlic of his own demons.

Grenlic halted the formation with a fist over his shoulder. "Anet, take squads four and five and set up a perimeter," he instructed his second. "No one gets in or out. The...Burned Forest is now quarantined."

"Aye." Anet made the necessary commands via hand and arm signals and the squads were off.

"The rest of you are with me. Squads two and three, flank the shack when it is in sight.

Grenlic thought, as he did every time, how he wished there to be an end. Some say things aren't so bad. They aren't wrong, but these are concepts held in the sight of the observer. We could all be living in Disiea and someone would still have the thought that things aren't so bad. Grenlic imagined how the hound loves its owner so based on the table scraps it receives. Near meatless bones and cropped gristle, but the hound still considers itself blessed.

The slaves, as a whole, did live pretty well. As long as you didn't stir up too much dirt, you could live a pretty productive life. Mistress Hydel has even set a few slaves free under Grenlic's watch. But these were elderly people, their lives more or less spent. Yalor did do grand things with those lives on one hand, all to benefit Orecul greatly in the near future. But they were all still slaves.

There was no choice or willingness to bring about those great works.

They could be judged in any way they choose at the moment. Cast aside and used for the Theater simply because someone grew bored of them. Grenlic gambled his day was coming for just that. He and Eneric clashed quite often and he almost always ended on the negative end of it. Eneric was keen on Theater entertainment. A show bloodier than the Coliseum.

Grenlic wanted an end. Not for his end exactly, but he wasn't exactly opposed to it either. He was tired. He was tired before he became a slave. He was fed up with the idea of doing his 'duty' being the only thing keeping him from the entertainment industry. He was sick of being used and sick of letting them do it. His own end would be nice, but the bigger picture showed that would never be enough. Yalor was just a minor example of how bad things were in Orecul. His years as a Writ for the empire traveling from shore to shore was all the proof he needed. A mass end would be more desirable. Looking back, he decided maybe there hadn't been as much honor as he would like to believe.

The formation now in position around the shack made up of dead trees, Grenlic spent a moment with the environment. He simply couldn't believe a boy did all this. Then again, he did meet the Bringer soon after he committed such an act. He had come to Grenlic broken in such a way that a boy should not be.

The forest was dust in the wind. Only the corpses of trees remained alongside piles of out-of-place bones describing vaguely what they used to be. Grenlic certainly didn't feel any ghosts.

"Bringer, we are here to collect you," he said, no emotion one way or the other, all professional-like.

Not even the chirping of birds replied.

He walked up and racked on the door. Surprisingly, it didn't cave in. "Bringer? I don't want to make this difficult, son."

Still no reply. Grenlic's anxiety spiked. He didn't want to do this in the first place, now he had to hunt the boy down like an animal? The beast races like Grenlic have had enough of that. It was almost too much. The final step to throw him over the edge in this damned life.

"Send runners to Anet and—" He cut himself short at the sound of the door latch.

The door didn't open until Grenlic reached for it. It was slow. Any uneasiness crept up his spine and he backed away. He grabbed the hilt of his sword in anticipation. His men followed suit. Ghosts seemed to be something he could believe in for a long moment.

All this melted away in him when I stepped out, yawning and rubbing my eye.

"What? What is it?" I finally caught on to the clatter of steel. My eye came to focus. "Oh, hi, Grenlic," I said with a gingered wave. A wave conducted with a hand in shades of blue.

"Br...Bringer?" Grenlic slammed his hilt down to its scabbard. "What took you so long to answer, fool boy?"

"Sorry." I yawned again. "I've been sleeping heavily the last few nights."

"Your skin. You are cured?"

I grinned. "Happened about five days ago. Isn't it great?" I put my hand back up and showcased it, and then I spread my wings to do the same. "It's all gone."

A few men spoke a breathy prayer into the broken crown pendants hanging around their necks. A holy ward for the boy who took on a fiend and came out...normal. Grenlic's hand twitched to do the same.

I looked around at them. "Did you really need the entire city guard for this?"

"You'll learn how Lord Eneric operates soon enough, hatchling. You weren't supposed to leave that hole, Bringer!"

"The deal was I was free as soon as I was cured, was it not?"

Grenlic made a gesture with his hand with a huff and the formation dissolved back into matching ranks.

"Okay," He stretched his back forward, old age complaining. "Let's get a move on, Bringer."

"Wait, I'm coming with you? Back to the apothecary?"

He looked back at me, concerned. "No. They didn't tell you? If it appeared you were cured, I was instructed to bring you to Father Feirtney."

"To the cathedral? Shouldn't I be getting back to work?" I stepped from my makeshift shelter, nerves and heart spiking. *What if they found something?*

Grenlic shook his head. "They need to test you, Bringer. They won't let you live until they are sure Oshoku's influences are dealt with."

Good mood snuffed out, I grabbed my new ramshackle bag obtained from a dumpster, made sure it was closed properly and followed.

I despaired more and more as the cathedral came looming closer. Throughout history, the Breathing Church has never been kind in manners involving, or merely perceived to be involving Disiea, let alone Wohe. It was always the claim of a holy war or purification of sorts. The result was always the same, mass numbers of people dying. When emyon was first discovered, many were burned or crucified for claims of witchery and the like. This was considered a situation with direct involvement with another realm other than Nybe. I should have lied and said some lesser entity had approached me. I doubt that would have saved my life before, but now my chances were looking quite scarce. It was unlikely the church would miss anything I may have missed.

The clock tower struck eight. Each bell was a quake as we waited for the morning commune to end in front of the great cathedral doors. Grenlic still hadn't persuaded himself to restrain me, but he stood close all the same. I think he could tell I was poised to run. The tremors of the tower bell rippled through him as well, though I assumed for different reasons. I watched as the massive piece of metal swung on hinges far up the church's high aesthetic walls. I wondered why Grenlic spent his nights up there. Did he wish to get closer to Nybe? Did he know I had come up there to fall from grace? Finally, the last bell tolled. Its echoes died slowly and the silence that followed was deafening.

We paid no mind to the exiting crowd we pushed through, and they paid us little mind in return, aside from a wide enough birth so Grenlic's bulk didn't bowl them over. After a few feet, I pushed passed Grenlic and the others. No sense in cowering behind the boulder. Those ahead parted before me like you would for a leper, interested but cautious of the infection. I hoped my bravado unnerved them. A spit in their faith's face, confident I had won. In truth, either I had succeeded, or I hadn't. There was no running away if not. May as well take my fate with a stride.

With us before the altar, we were soon alone with Father Feirtney, save the guards. His head was bowed in prayer, breathing as they do when concentrating solely on the soul's white essence, the essence your soul generates for religious endeavors. Grenlic set his guardsmen to the entrances and any possible improvised exits. No one would be permitted to enter until the priest was satisfied.

Grenlic and myself waited quietly behind the old man. I have never been truly affiliated with white essence, but the place was heavy with the stuff. It was hard to ignore. Monetary tithing wasn't the only offering presented in the Breathing Church. It was almost paramount to offering parts of your soul to The Breath. Granting a mass of meek energies for him to use as he saw fit. I had no use for a god or a titan, especially one that had abandoned his station without a successor. The Breathing Church knew this, but still, they prayed and offered themselves. They still held faith he would return. It was an infection I did not want. Presuming, implacable, and corrupt in its own holy way. A discomfort I simply could not take.

"You shut yourself off like one does a disease, Bringer." Father Feirtney speaking startled me. No one had so much as moved for a full ten minutes. "That's disappointing, son. Especially since He saw fit to cure you."

"I cured myself, priest," I spat.

"Ah, but it was He who gave you the talent to do so, my son." He proceeded from his altar, robes flowing, all a glow but not with candlelight.

"That was my mother's doing," I muttered, gritting my teeth, not anxious to contribute further to the debate, but I would not relinquish the proper credit. "And before we continue this back and forth, it was her mother before this and her grandfather before that who passed down the knowledge. Shall I continue down the lineage? Or would you like to know what I've acquired from my father's blood?"

Feirtney didn't push the subject. He smiled kindly and bent at the waist to my level.

"I prayed for you, you know. We all did," he said. "Are you ready to see what He has done for you?"

After dropping my bag, I followed on, my jaw locked in place. Grenlic took a place in the pew. He seemed pleased to be off his feet. I suppose it was a long march there and back to retrieve me, but instead, I saw the age creeping up on him. He was a hard man, but bodies, no matter how solid, still begin to fail us one day.

The priest led me behind the altar and stopped. Upon the altar lay a crown. One to represent the same crown Ald'Kair left on his throne when he abandoned it. Some seem to think he was injured and needed to heal before he returned. But I wasn't so sure. I stood there stupidly. I had guessed there was a specific room they would use for the priest's exams.

"Are you ready, Bringer?" Father Feirtney spoke as though I were of his flock come to mass. "This may feel a bit...invasive."

I nodded. He nodded back. I wasn't convinced by the surety on his face that I would pass. He held his hands before his face as one would in prayer to The Breath, palms apart and partly facing the invoker as though to catch their breath in their palms. Rather than prayer though, this was a somatic meant to conduct whatever emyon he had prepared. He whispered the soul language into those hands. The also imperceivable weight of the white essence that strained the seams of the cathedral dissipated and concentrated itself into Feirtney's hands, flowing to him like winds. He was using the essence of all those in the sermon just moments ago.

Soon, thereafter, the essence started to take on the form of an emyon, a sun emyon, to be specific. Emyon is the result when a person's essence is made into something tangible, and sun emyon is particularly bright. The priest's eyes were sealed shut against the brightness and soon I was forced to turn away. The moment I did, the light shot through me.

My vision went white and my muscles locked intermittently throughout my body. I didn't have time to panic or decide whether to scream or not before it was over. I found myself breathing heavily on my knees. It had felt as though I had been shocked. I jerked my head around, expecting more.

Feirtney looked as I felt, as though something had gone wrong. "That's odd," he said, hands still extended toward me. "It is as if it were bloc...wait." He was looking nowhere in particular like a man possessed by visions. "Ah." He smiled. "You see, Bringer? You pass." He brought his hands back together and bowed to the altar. "Well done, my son."

"That's it?" I asked. "That was all there was to this?"

He approached me. "Things which are important do not always have to be complicated, my son." He smiled and tried to place his hands on me. I avoided them with a small shake and set off as though there were more important things over near Grenlic than my clean bill of health.

"If that is all, Father Feirtney, I will see Bringer back to his quarters." Grenlic rubbed his head and yawned with a grown, but I could see the relieved lines around his eyes.

"That won't be necessary." Estry seemed to appear out of nowhere. Maybe there had been more of a time-lapse in the test than I thought. I should have noticed her coming in. "Mistress Hydel gave us instructions if you were to pass this test at great disapproval of Lord Eneric."

"And a separate set of orders *if* I were to fail." I glanced pointedly in Grenlic's direction. He had the grace to look away.

Estry ignored that. "You've been promoted, Bringer. She smiled, an odd thing on her. I had the feeling she was trying to be kind. But it didn't belong on that face.

## Grenlic's Confession

They had promoted me to Resin's old position. The alchemy school for new citizens came under my care. I quickly sold it and put the marks toward my coffers. It was a fight with Estry convincing her that a mobile facility would be better suited to teach and rate new arrivals. In the end, she either saw it my way or gave up the fight. I replaced the school with a wheelhouse and two beasts of burden. This was enough to carry all my supplies to and fro from then on. In truth, that's all I cared to ensure. That, and that I could move freely.

Resin had done well hiding how wealthy he was, at least in terms of slavehood. With his being gone, his savings came to me. And his salary was nothing to snub your nose at. His marks were too many to keep on my person. The blue strawberries had been good to him. I hulled the marks to the nearest citizen bank and opened an account, leaving only a few of the silver-colored coins in my purse.

I spent the marks quickly to establish myself. The wheelhouse and beasts were just the start. I purchased Resin's land at a discount. The thought of living in a hole in the ground didn't appeal to most. For me, it was as close as I would get to something akin to the ice caves I grew up in. I commissioned a new outfit. No more drab surf clothing for a leader of the Alchemy Division. It took some bit of searching, but I found a leather worker excited about mocking up a new design. The design consisted of a shendyt for my lower half and a leather and cloth top with compartmentalized pockets to store vials of alchemic products. I discovered too, that one could have a pauldron crafted to replace the one issued to them. The process took far too much time, paperwork, and an annoyed set of guards to swap out, but I was pleased the new one matched my outfit. With the cooling seal emyon in place, I was nearly markless once again.

Finally, from that ramshackle bag I left the woods with, I had another craftsmen fashion me something special: a deer skull mask complete with alchemic sigils burned into the side. The antler stubs were removed and replaced with holes for my horns to fit through. It all was quite expensive, but I refused to be just 'Bringer' anymore. Some mistook me for an essence wielder for some time, but I didn't mind. After a short period and the legends revolving around the Blackwood and its fire, all in Yalor knew of me and the name Bringer was never used as a slur again. Mostly, others wondered what, in fact, I was the *bringer* of.

Alchemy was no longer what the empire had known it as. For the next few years, between teaching new alchemists and other duties I had as a head of the Division, I wrote a book with the second soon to be complete. This was done under the direction of Estry and thus Mistress Hydel, but I was happy to do so whilst keeping the best secrets for myself. Across the fiefs and enclaves, a brand-new science was making waves. And Yalor got all the credit. No doubt a feather in the cap of our illustrious mistress. This, along with the Golden Dawn, were to be her major contributions to the empire.

I had since gathered what the Golden Dawn truly was. And it would be soon. The entire city shifted according to this. There would be no more need to recruit new citizens to bring it about. I picked up the last of the new alchemists on my way to our new purpose.

Conarance did his little speech of orientation just as he did with my group, only this time, no one died. He wasn't looking the best these days. If you didn't know Conarance, he would seem normal as anyone. But the loose hair strands here and there, spoke volumes to the rest of us. The medical facilities couldn't make heads or tails of it and an apothecary in the Alchemy Division was now at work to discover a cure. He never came knocking on my door though. I gathered he didn't want to see me for one reason or another. It was a blessing. He and I hadn't had an interaction for a long time.

"Citrine: Provisioning and Marketing..." Jarce still looked young. I supposed you would want your heralds to be so. "Vermilion: Little Ceth. Head Wielder: Anigob. Emerald: Alchemy Division..." I stepped forward to stand next to Anigob, a distinctly unsettling character with its colored scarring. "...Bringer."

"So, errm, I guess I am with you then?" My newest apprentice was a young Wahyn man, much like those who discovered Korigara when it first washed up on the southern shore of Orecul. I only knew this through careful study and direction from Kyda. All humans looked the same to me when it came down to it. Until very recently, I could only make out differences in their origins based on clothing or ornamental choices. Now, I could tell through their faces easily enough. This was not a thing I did to be any more sort of more conscious or caring of those around me. Rather, it felt good knowing the enemy. Kyda certainly put me at odds with myself in this regard, however. It wasn't easy ignoring the good she had shown me and she continued to do so. Somehow, I managed. I liked her well enough, but her people were the root of all the world's issues I could make out from between the bars of my imprisonment.

I led the boy onto the wheelhouse without saying anything until he came in behind me. "Sit there." I sat opposite him and announced out the front window, "It's tea time." There was a series of chitters and the wheelhouse set into motion.

"Tea time? You know tea, yes?"

I stared at him for a long time. Long enough to make him quite uncomfortable, which may have been shorter than normal, given I was wearing a skull on my face.

"He has grown to enjoy tea a lot, certainly," Kyda interjected. "Forgive him. Bringer has grown accustomed to being...unsettling. I think he enjoys it in his own way. When he has had his fill, he'll speak to you."

When the boy pulled his eyes away from me and met hers, he blushed.

"I'm Kyda. The Alerez who fashioned himself a fiend is Bringer, as I'm sure you know. He's the head of the Alchemy Divison's student distribution center, though that is changing a bit now that you're the last. This is Bik and Holin, the current students and—"

"What is your profession?" I asked.

"Sorry?"

"What is it that you do? Are you new to being a slave?"

"Slavery?" Genuine surprise. "They called us citizens."

I shook my head and let it sink in.

"I suppose that makes more sense." The enthusiasm that had been there melted away.

"Well?" I didn't care to give him time to process.

"Oh, well, my last owner went out of business. There I was a gatherer, though. I was known for making popular teas."

My tail flicked back and forth, irritated. I didn't like Bik or Holin, but they at least had some capacity for alchemy. They had even been able to learn what I had made the standard for alchemy in recent history. I wasn't sure I had any patience to sculpt another. Sometimes, it seemed that Yalor's lords and ladies had no real idea what alchemy had been, let alone what it was now. They just took those who worked with herbs to any degree and threw them at our division hoping they'd prove to be something. I understood why Conarance considered me to be a special find. He had never found an actual alchemist except maybe Resin. The others were barely herbologists in reality.

"Read this." I handed him a copy of the first alchemy book I wrote as the wheelhouse came to a stop. The box at my feet now in hand, I said, "When I return, I will ask you a question. You had better be able to answer it."

"Wait, what happens if I can't?"

The door slammed behind me.

"Sorry we're late, Grenlic." The Olenous sat on the floor of the belfry as he was the day I met him.

"The tea is getting cold. You make me a bad host again." He growled.

I opened the teapot and pinched some grains from one of my pockets into the container. A sigil lit up on my skull mask when I placed a finger on the side of the teapot and the tea steamed again, heated as though fresh.

Grenlic stared down at it disapprovingly. He was very particular about his teas, most of which he now made from his own gardens. Even if the fire salts were no longer part of the tea, he felt I had altered his work.

Taking my seat opposite him, I pulled the box from underneath my arm and took the pieces out. I busied myself setting up the board, hoping the winds wouldn't pick up too much. I've had to retrieve or replace pieces enough times during our games. I fashioned a number of pieces with bits of lead on their underside to help prevent this, but sometimes the winds were belligerent.

Grenlic poured Kyda and myself a cup of tea in the same style he had many times before. His hands practiced, sure, and methodical. He's become quite good at it, even in his armor. His weapon, a very large bow, leaned against a pillar behind him. Technically, we shouldn't be meeting him when he was on duty, but it was a good vantage point for him up here. He could make out disturbances down below without anyone noticing he was up here and if necessary, he could use that great bow of his to end most dangerous exchanges rather quickly. If he was lucky, he didn't kill anyone in the dispute with the first shot since there was no way he could know who was in the wrong. He would always figure it out fully instead when he went to retrieve his rather large arrows. Luckily, since he's begun positioning himself up here, it had become enough of a deterrence for his intervention to be rare. The guards below could handle most else and would come to retrieve him if necessary. This was also rare. After tea with Kyda and myself, he would handle anything brought to him that lacked the emergency qualifier.

I dispatched my ziel on the board alone and drew my hand.

"Why are these considered wars if you only have one piece?" Kyda asked and sipped her tea. "Mmm, Grenlic, this is wonderful. What is it?"

In response, Grenlic passed her a tin where the leaves had been stored, shrugged, and played a card on his own ziel. There was no label, but she smiled and opened it for a sniff. It was as wordy a response as you could expect from Grenlic sometimes.

"It's considered a war because the premise is that the world's population is too limited, at least in the world we're playing in. So limited, in fact, that the loss of one life is all that can be afforded to settle large disputes."

"No diplomacy?"

"Now, what fun would that be, Kyda?" I moved and played a card myself, initiating an attack.

We played in silence then for a long time. Grenlic and I exchanged blows between sips of tea. I lost, as I do most of the time.

"You're distracted," Grenlic said rather than asking.

"How can you tell?" Kyda asked.

"He thinks he beat me too easily."

"Not think." He sat back and looked out unto Yalor for any ruckus

As I thought about setting up another game, I considered the coin he had been fiddling with when we first met. Too afraid to ask after it, I settled for another risky line of questioning. Maybe I would find the answers I didn't want to know and then wouldn't be able to dwell on my foolishness.

"Kyda, would you give us a moment?"

She looked as though she wanted to argue to stay. It became customary for us all to be up here at the same time. It was our little cut of the world to ourselves, safe and away from the anxiety of breaking any rules you may not know about and being on the sharp end of someone's ire. The guards kept the peace, but we all knew that some of the slaves were monitors who reported directly to the nobles. They also had the authority to punish you with the pauldrons. You never did see it coming. One moment, you're doing something careless, you realize you've broken a rule, and the next, you're on the floor in a pool of your own bile. There's nothing to be done about it. No one to accost for their mistreatment of you. You just pick yourself up, and hope to the hells you don't mess up again. The clock tower was the only place we ever let our guard down. We were the closest thing to free up here. Or at least we wouldn't be tortured for minor infractions. The anxiety scraped your back with every move. And I had just asked Kyda to forsake the respite for the week. It wasn't the first time, nor would it be the last. I liked having her around. But I was still very unsure how much I could trust her.

Kyda practically slammed her teacup down, only resisting the urge enough to save the porcelain, and stormed off, knowing there would be no argument. She didn't want to go back to being a house slave, so she wouldn't fight me. Though, I've never threatened her with such an act as sending her away for good. I needed to find better ways to let her know how much I valued her.

"She's still with you?" Grenlic watched her go. "How?"

I took his meaning. "Some in the court were having at her for being so kind to me while I searched for the cure. Though she was sworn to Mistress Hydel, others argued her allegiance was with me. I took that and requested she works for me rather than her succumbing to another, bleaker fate."

Grenlic grunted and let it be. He watched me.

"I wanted to ask you..." *about that coin.* "Why are you here?"

He gestured to the bow and smiled. He was encouraging me to be specific.

"What made you a slave? Olenous are part of the empire, aren't they?"

"Humans as well."

He made a good point, but I didn't fill the silence so he could avoid the question. He glanced over to be sure Kyda was out of earshot. Curious that he wasn't sure he could trust her either. Somehow, I knew what he had to say had to do with his life as a Writ Executioner. During one of our secretive conversations before, he had revealed to me what his life was like before his capture and subsequent enslavement. That conversation was some time ago, but it gave me time to research the subject in the library. Each book I selected carefully as I knew those too would be tracked. Some books I had to order in secret.

What I discovered was that the Writ Executioners were specialized bounty hunters, or assassins in some regards, who were sworn to the empire. They were more than hired dogs, however. Sealed writs would be issued by the Emperor or someone he trusted with the authority to do so. This writ possessed a name and the only course was a brutal, very much in the public eye, execution. No headsmen's axe for them. Often, word would get back to the person in question, and the one to be executed would meet the Writ out on the battlefield. The result was always the same. A lot of dead people for the sake of killing one. In a sense, Writs were the enforcers like the monitors in Yalor. Punishers and a deterrence from certain behaviors. The books were not specific as to the crimes committed against the empire, but from the synopsis, I gathered they just rubbed the empire the wrong way.

Grenlic didn't answer immediately. This was common for him, but this time, I think he knew I had been doing my research. He was gauging how much to give away and how much he could leave out. He spent his turn in our game preparing his character. My character couldn't see his behind the cover he'd placed his ziel behind, so his cards were played face down.

"I would ask you why you needed to know, but then I remembered to whom I spoke. The boy with little more than the question 'why.'"

I smirked at that.

"I disobeyed an order."

"The short answer is never enough. Reasons frame the means and give light to the ends."

"Coming from the Alerez who leaves the light in refute."

Once again, I didn't argue the truth. I removed the skull mask and set it down beside me in a way to hide without hiding. If anyone could read me and tease out any plans I have or will have prior to my conceiving them, Grenlic would be the man to do it. I both liked this about him and it brought me discomfort. For now, at least, I didn't have to wrestle with the idea of killing him. Quietly contradicting this thought, I moved my ziel in for the kill.

"Northwest of Kytgro is where the writ brought me. A small city. Famous for a special wine that only they knew how to make. The bottles are still the most expensive the empire knows. But a geological survey of the land revealed even further fortune in their future. Precious jewels and ore. With this, the empire started to sweat. His enclave was becoming too powerful too quickly. It could offset power rather easily in the near future. Make a king of a common man. I am not sure who sealed my writ, but I suspect someone high up didn't take too kindly to the idea. Effort was made to bring the lord of the land in line. It was successful."

"Then why send a Writ? The man had already come in tow, right?"

Grenlic held a hand up to stop me but took it as an opportunity to wet his mouth with tea. I supposed his tongue had to be dry. This was the most he had ever said to me in one breath since the day he took me from the Blackwood grave.

"The landlord was very ill. He could be passed on for all I know now. Which means his son would inherit his father's wealth and power. This boy...he was my target. Not easily swayed. Not easy to control. Not easily bribed. Not ideal. When I received the writ, they didn't tell me he *was* a boy. I refused to kill him. For this, I had to run. I earned the shackles running in the wrong direction. Soon, I'll earn the grave for my slight. They do not know where I am. But they hunt me still. This, I know."

"A child, eh?" I moved my piece in closer. My next move would bring both pieces into their respective fields of view. "That should have been an easy kill. Had to be better than facing armies." I was more interested in his counter-argument than making a point.

Grenlic kept his piece still for his next turn again. I was starting to get nervous, but I had no other option. My ziel needed to close the distance to deal the most damage it could. If I could get it within two spaces of Grenlic's ziel, I could win with little effort. I moved in again, this time opting to forgo any extra actions during my turn in order to sprint in closer than a typical move. As soon as the characters were within view of each other, I saw my mistake. Grenlic flipped his cards one after another. Three were nothing, red herrings. The first card he played was a modus operandi, a form of very strong emyon. He had been charging it since his first move, and now it was at max strength. His character would lose an eye to cast it, but my character had a tenth of the health it needed to survive the attack. Unless some great luck came my way, the battle was over.

"Children are pure potential. Nothing they are, is what they shall remain. We are our worst selves in adolescence. It cannot be any other way. A man's pride keeps him steady-minded, and change comes at a great cost. Children have nothing to bargain with nor anything the world wants to rip from them. They only have to make a choice and they will be better than their initial circumstances." Grenlic unleashed the modus and threw his dice. The attack connected.

I paused, tea halfway to my lips. "Am I?" Looking down at the tea's pinkish hue, I found it resembled blood diluted in an alchemist's solution. In my mind's eye, a crimson drop, the last drop required for one to hold on to their mortal coil, fell in and spread throughout the liquid. "Lost."

Grenlic smiled. "'Reasons give light to the ends.' I don't know what you're planning to do, Bringer. You will cause something that will change the world forever. This I know. Something horrible."

"The books? I would hardly call that a horrible contribution."

He stared at me, waiting for me to be honest. I knew that wasn't what he meant. He could see I held something close to my chest. I set my tea down and stood up.

"I'll keep the board up here from now on, I think. It is just another thing to carry about. Besides, no one is going to come take it. Even the bell maintainers are afraid to come up here. They won't mess with our things." I returned my skull mask. It set in place perfectly as though it were my own skull, the slots for my horns hooking around them to secure it in place. Through the eye slots, I regarded Grenlic. "Yalor will experience my magnum opus. Then, it will consume her."

I threw the wheelhouse door open.

"Times up." The others startled at my entrance. I took my seat and set the wheelhouse in motion with another word. With a stark finger pointed, "New guy, what does every alchemist require of themselves before pursuing the practice of alchemy?" He sat there stupidly for a time and went to flip the pages of the book. "No, no. Answer only."

"Um, well, the philosopher's stone. They need to set their sights on its creation. The highest goal. Anything less is a waste."

The carriage came to a stop. "Wrong answer. A soul of raw essence, is correct. Unaffiliated with any of the elements." I threw open the door again. "Get out."

I left him there on the side of the road next to the tea shop. I hoped he would be found useful there. But I had no time for herbologists.

## Caged Monsters

Once the wheelhouse settled within the Coliseum walls, I let myself out. I pulled two fish from a bucket that hung on the side of the frame and threw them to the beasts pulling our little building. These lizard-like birds were heinously smelly, but they were intelligent enough to remember locations after sufficient training. All I had to do was say a location's name, and they would take the wheelhouse there, breaking only *some* normal traffic standards. If not for the smell, I was sure Yalor would present them in the Golden Dawn to come. Instead, they made a cheap but effective beast of burden for me. A fish was easy compensation for their efforts.

Before the others struggled out of our tight quarters, I took in the scene. There may as well have been a market happening in the Coliseum. I couldn't imagine what all these people could be doing here. It was a place of blood sport, not mercantile arts. A deep look settled my own dispute. No merchants here. Wares were being presented rather than pushed. But where were the soldiers?

"Estry," Bik said. A warning.

There she was, walking like an out-of-place shadow. It's funny how monsters are less so when you take them out of the territory most suited to them. Instead of a stalker in the moonlight, she was but a black dot in the sunlight, a tall, lanky figure with bad skin.

"Line up."

We each bowed the Yalorian bow implemented sometime back, fingers interlocked like baring a cup to the receiver. It was told to us that it was us presenting our bit of light to the coming dawn, but...

"Bringer. Disciples. Did you not receive the newcomer this morning as instructed?"

"I did, m'lady. I also gauged him to your standards and found him wanting. I have issued the process to have him repurposed, for the benefit of Yalor."

Ego is such an easy string to tug at. Estry smiled at that. Well, she smiled what passed as a smile for her, which was usually a quick twitch of the corner of her mouth.

"What seems to be going on here, m'lady?"

"The first ray of light for the dawn." I never could tell how invested she was with Yalor's direction. Was she truly trying to be a part of something bigger than herself or simply along for the ride. It wasn't like any of us really had a choice. "You will integrate yourselves with the other divisions here. Work together to find how we can best serve them and enhance their presentations. Use that talent of yours, Bringer." She pulled a tome from Breath knows where. A thick bound thing full of loose note pages. "This is something we will be working on independently. You are now the lead of the Alchemy Division's presentation. The others across the Division have already been notified. Send word to them on tasks that they can complete to assist. Do not neglect their use. You may have shown the world something we didn't know, but the other apothecaries and labs do have their specialties."

"Of course, m'lady." I still hated the my lady this and my lady that, but I had learned to play the game as much as I was willing. It was enough to keep me out of trouble, especially since Estry had been granted pauldron privileges after Yalor shifted into higher standards for the Dawn.

Sifting through the tome, my face wrenched down in disgust. I slammed it shut and regarded Estry.

"I have my books too, Bringer."

I wondered why something like the project she set before me wasn't within the *Soul Apothecary* or any other texts that I had read. Any time they mentioned homunculi, it was all theory or conceptualization. To create life. I wasn't sure that was an alchemy I was willing to explore. I have shown that I'm willing to push my chest out to the gods, spit in their faces even, but I am not a god. This was a level of arrogance even I wouldn't explore...did I have a choice now? I've shown them what I can do. Could I skirt around this new responsibility?

I handed the book to Bik. "I shall look into it, m'lady. I will not insult you by asking if you understood what you're asking of me, but why does this need to be?"

"This was something I was researching alone, Bringer. When you changed alchemy forever, it gave the experiments and concepts a new life. It is achievable now. Mistress Hydel wants to become a queen. How do you think that happens? A woman of moderate wealth going from owning no land, to founding an enclave, to founding a fief with the blessing of the Emperor all in one generation even before the wrinkles of age set in? All this, with not a single drop of noble blood. You must make yourself worth something, yes? Mistress Hydel's will is to do just that. In order to achieve this, what must one do? She must bring on a new dawn, a new epoch, a new age entirely."

I heard the others making a fuss about the tome behind me. "Put it away. We'll read over it later. That's not why we are here."

"See that you do."

I watched her eyes for a long moment. "You lot set up shop. I'll be about."

I wondered off then, concerned. Creating a homunculus was not something I was keen on exploring. I wasn't certain the act wasn't a thing to cause The Heart to blush with all his dark dealings. In just the few pages I skimmed over in Estry's tome, my gut turned.

The next few hours were spent drumming up business for me and my team. I saw little we could do for a number of them but asked them to stop by anytime. Mostly, I asked their leadership to explain to me what it was they were trying to accomplish. More than a few of them were apprehensive about divulging their secrets, but once they realized who I was, the skull-wearing Alerez alchemist, they practically begged me to assist them. I made no promises as I went, only beckoned them over to us. I did so because I needed time to think. I could be creative and fit myself into their plans, but I needed time. Eventually, I saw the soldiers running drills and fighting techniques with each other.

When they were referred to as the combatants, the Coliseum Division was easy to visualize as expendable in the eyes of Yalor. Now, there were soldiers which implied their purpose. Yalor's favor was upon them now. They would receive training and discipline rather than strictly adhering to the concept of blood sport. Seeing how their numbers had dwindled, I supposed that was the intention all along. To leave only the strongest or most skilled to become the soldiers Yalor would need if Mistress Hydel was to succeed.

They noticed me much further away than I would have liked. Not much in hiding in the middle of a sunny day when you're dressed in dark colors and wearing someone else's skull on your head. I cursed at myself when I realized it. I must have looked similar to the way Estry did when she approached us. I glanced at the skin of my arm. Instead of looking in on the soldiers like a scared but interested child, I strode up until I was too close for my own comfort to Krolec.

I presented the most Yalorian bow I could manage without taking my eyes off him. "Good day, Master Krolec, Commander of Dawn's Soldiers."

"I must say, I like your new look. Super scary." There were a few laughs from the men behind him. "What do you want, razor? There is nothing here for you. Your friend is no longer with us."

Friend? Where was Leegius? "You misunderstand me. I am here for you. The Alchemy Division wishes to—"

"Alchemy? Scientists have no place on the battlefield, boy."

"No, I—"

"Off with you. Let us not forget that you and I still have a score to settle. And we have an audience this time. Still, you did cut some of the weak from our ranks, and for this, we'll just have to settle later."

Like that, I was dismissed. Not much to be done. Krolec was the equivalent to Estry for his Division. I wasn't keen on discovering if he had been granted authority over our pauldrons as well. I set off back toward my camp, ignoring the eyes of the on-lookers of our exchange. I felt my father's pride attempt to call me back and demand satisfaction. Though I was his son, I never did become as great a warrior as him. I had a few moves here and there, but I caught the soldiers off guard last time. They knew what I was capable of now and would take the fight more seriously. I wouldn't survive another exchange like that.

"Bringer."

Despite myself, I jumped at the voice and took a fighting stance, keenly aware that I had no weapon and Hydel's threat of using my natural-born weapons hanging over me.

Browler stood there, hands up in truce. The new nose I had given him made him look like a hog. "Not that. I'm not here to fight."

Stiffly, I returned to a normal standing position. "Your leader has sent me away. Our business is concluded."

"Aye, but I'm not here about that. Leegius, he's your friend, right?" I said nothing. "Well, he's not dead, razor. He's in the cells with the other creatures."

"What for? Others are not kept in captivity here. That's what the jail is for."

"Yes, but monstrous things are." He pointed to a large portion of the Coliseum I had not noticed before. Up at the top in the stands, a half circle of the Coliseum's structure was just not there. Like it had been blown away with some great force. Reconstruction of the section was well underway. "He did that. Surprised the hell out of all of us. No one died, surprisingly. But he was locked up. Too dangerous. Those...things he wore seemed like they got into his head. He thrashed and raged but didn't kill anyone. It took an essence wielder to calm him down. He's been down there ever since. Thought you should know."

"Why would you give me this?"

"Because, you're a warrior. You beat us pretty bad last time. I think you've earned respect from more than a few of us."

I shook my head. "I got lucky."

He shrugged. "Luck is a warrior's friend too, razor. Just the same as training and skill. It's not always the sword that saves you in a battle. Sometimes, it is just dumb luck."

We parted then and I returned to the wheelhouse. The others had done well in setting up. Tables and chairs were in position for our interviews and basic equipment was already heated and ready for us. Kyda watched me approach, her smile uncertain. When she asked what was the matter, I shook my head and brushed past her.

A line was beginning to form just outside of our camp. Our customers were eager to see what we could do to enhance their divisions. I took a seat at the table just before the first one.

"Let's hear it," I said.

It took too many hours to go through the crowd of people who had come to see us. There were more than a few we were able to assist, but for the most part, there was nothing we could do or nothing I was willing to do. If the concept bored me, I sent them away. Textiles were a good example of this. The gentlemen wanted me to come up with a miracle cure for his creation, a fabric woven from a material he invented. He was so proud of it, but it caused his model no small amount of discomfort. The model scratched at his skin underneath, mercilessly begging the weaver to let him take it off. It has to be said, it was a fine tunic, the finest I had ever seen.

"Have you considered allergy?"

"What? Like pollen?"

"No, y—just take off the tunic." He did so. "You see all that red that's not scratch marks? That's allergies. Try another model and see if it happens again. If it does, come and see me then. If not, chances are this young man has skin that doesn't agree with one of the fabrics you used."

As the men stepped away, Kyda offered me a drink. "Water or wine? Because I'm prepared to numb my brain a bit to crawl down to their levels."

"Not everyone is as much a genius as you, m'lord." This coming from Bik.

I stared at him, the drinking skin poised over my mouth. He blanched. Rumors enough of my ill temper were alive and well. He required no rumors as he's been on the receiving end before. I had to ease myself internally before I could take a drink. *Water, damn.*

When I brought this new form of alchemy into the world, I suppose I expected it would erase the old version entirely. To my disappointment and chagrin, despite my need to be entertained with new or experimental pursuits, this was not the case. Those we could help, the products or services we could offer were of the mundane alchemy. We were to provide the Calvary Division with better feed for their beasts, tonics for the guards to help them keep awake and aware during the long nights, philters to the soldiers for use during combat, and a number of other rather bland creations for various other sections. Perhaps I had been spoiled? The instruction a true master would recommend is to 'stick to the fundamentals', but the fundamentals were...dull.

I let the list of accepted jobs fall from my hands with just enough care to ensure it glided down to one of the other's feet. It bored me, but we still needed it.

"I believe I am going to take a walk around and find someone with a more interesting task for us."

Bik regarded the line. "Don't we have enough? There's enough people here to keep the entire Division busy for months. And we still have to run the shops."

"Bringer!" Holin shouted after me as I departed.

"I'm sure you'll be fine without me. Just don't sign us up for anything stupid like working on clothes or some nonsense."

I wasn't sure how I was going to find Leegius, but I had a good idea where to start. Humans like to keep the considerably lower life forms—lower. I walked into the main compound of the Coliseum like my being there was as normal as the sunrise, ignoring the well-dressed men and women, possibly nobles, discussing events to come with their up-turned wine-tasting faces. How they crowded in at the entrance made it a simple thing to push through under the eye of the guards posted there. As Yalor is like to do, there were countless cultures in just this one room. The only difference was not one of them wore pauldrons, save a few white gems who served the wine and catered the event.

Most in the room were focused on—Conarance, who was rambling on about something pertaining to Yalor's great purpose, so I was able to pass more or less unremarked, with my bravado temporarily snuffed at his presence. Those who did take notice of my passing were so surprised they practically jumped out of the way. Only one resisted this urge. I came to a full stop and looked her in the eye. The skull I was wearing should have been enough to deter her decision to invoke her high-born smugness, but it was instead my eyes that had her rethink her life choices. We came to an understanding and she stepped aside. With small, quick motions, I uncorked one of the many bottles about my person. It didn't much matter what I had just dosed her wine with as I passed; most of the products were septic at one level or another.

When I was through the crowd, I decided I should resist my temptations. I wouldn't get far if I kept poisoning royalty and I still had a long way to go. I checked the bottle to see if I needed to go save the woman's life. I returned it to its pocket, relieved she'd only suffer debilitating diarrhea for a time but would otherwise be fine.

"I'm here to see the prisoner Leegius," I told the guard at the desk before the holding cells' entrance. Once I got through the crowds it was nothing to find the place. A short distance down a hallway or three and passed the barracks. I was grateful the soldiers were outside.

The guard was propped up by one hand, elbow resting on the desk. The other hand held a book level with his nose. "Purpose?" He didn't look up from the literature.

I'll admit I hadn't thought this far. An audible 'uh' was all I could muster. It was then he felt it necessary to hold me in his regard. He turned from his book to the child before him. The skull mask prompted him further than my words.

"Uh," Apparently, it was his turn to lack cognitive phrases.

There is power in fear, in throwing people from their normal lives into a reality unfamiliar and unusual. You start to see who they are, what they are made of. How someone reacts to strange things puts their true self out in the open for all to see, despite their previous resolve.

"I'm here to see the prisoner Leegius," I supplied again.

The guard glanced at my shoulder, trying to understand who I was. Apparently, the green gem meant nothing to him. A scoffing twitch of the eyebrow. Once he had recovered from his initial shock, he eared the corner of a page to save his spot in the book and walked me to the door. No more questions, then.

I grabbed the first lantern from its hook and started to lead my own way. Through the haze of scowling determination, I realized I had no idea where I was going. I hesitated. The guard passed with a sneer as though greatly suppressed. A note of my father's aggression, along with my mother's ability to ignore the inconsequential, ran through my veins, conflicting. I let it alone and followed along.

When he put some distance between us and my lantern wasn't a sufficient light source, the guard snapped his fingers. A small but potent light source sprang to life over his shoulder. A reminder just how deep Hydel's pockets were. The best people bought for every task. I realized then just how incredibly stupid I had been being. Yalor's rule of purchasing the best must extend to Krolec, right? I had been overconfident in the arsenal about my person. I needed to mind myself more lest I get into another situation like the first trip to the Coliseum. I left the lantern behind.

The guard brought me down long flights of stairs. Each level was filled from the entrance to a far wall with cells. Some larger and obviously not meant for any humanoid, I hoped. Pulley systems created lifts in the farther back sections, presumably to deliver the combatants to staging areas just short of the Coliseum's blood fields. I wanted to explore these cells. A grown from a far back cell changed my mind quick enough.

We finally came to a halt in front of a cell three stories down, held at the far end closest to the lift. Before we made our way down the series of cells, I noted that there had been a continuation in the stairs themselves. It seemed to go down forever. Maybe only stopping shy of Disiea.

"You won't have long before this wears out, but it should be long enough." He grabbed the light above his shoulder, caging it with his fingers like you would a moth so as not to damage its wings, and placed it in the air next to me. "I wasn't given orders to watch over visitors to the prisoners, and seeing as you've no weapons about your person, I'm leaving. I don't care how long you stay, but you'll have to find your own way in the dark."

"How do you know I am not armed?" I asked, trying to keep the challenge out of my voice.

He pointed out the ball of light. He smiled and went on his way.

"Thank you, sir." He had had the tone of an ass, but I still realized how generous he had been. If he had been slightly less bored with his duty and slightly less thrown off by the skull, I don't think he would've granted me access.

The light ball watched me, not quite accusingly but still somehow invasive. I sighed in relief and let it be. The thing had searched me for weapons without my knowing. I was lucky my weapons were not the traditional type.

"Leegius?" There was no response.

I was about to speak again when a dimly lit giant came into view from behind the bars.

"What the hell are you doing here?" Leegius's voice still intimidated me in its gravelly state.

"I could ask you the same thing," I said. He stared at me until I complied. I sighed, removing my deer skull. "I'm here on Alchemy Division business."

We continued to glare at each other. It began to appear it wasn't just one of us that possessed the bull's head.

It was his turn to give in. "You realize how much trouble you can get into for being here?" He spoke softer now.

"Not really. But if that is the case, it is probably a sight less than what would happen to the guard," I said. "At any rate, I've made myself quite indispensable since last we spoke." I raised my left shoulder to the light as proof. I took my time getting comfortable on the floor, heedless of how extra small this made me seem in comparison to his standing form. "So, we are both scaring people now?"

He said nothing.

"The disfigured wall, that is why you are down here, is it not?"

He brought his mass down to sit across from me. Leegius may as well have still been standing. It hadn't done much to equalize the size difference. Finally, he nodded, answering my question.

"How did you know?" He asked.

"Browler," I said.

We sat listening to the soft chiming of the light emyon for a time. I hadn't noticed it before over the roar of my own thoughts. You might have thought the thing a pixie at a shallow glance. A little bit of life observing colossuses of various sizes and shapes out of pure curiosity.

"The whole of the city is beyond repair, Bringer." Leegius caught me off guard this time. It wasn't my musings on mythical creature's thoughts that startled me. It was the breaking in

Leegius's voice. Suddenly, I felt like breaking too. "Each small group, division, tasked with its own objectives are innocent enough, each one a small improvement to our meager world. The entirety, however, is nothing less than the atrocities that man has committed since their first breath–gluttony, a quest for power. I am a weapon, Bringer. Conarance thought to control me." He held his hands to his face. A gesture my imagination could have never painted on the man. "I only wanted a normal life," he sobbed. "To work metal. To love my wife and children. To die an old man, happily in my own sled." Coals stoked in his voice. "When I was taken, still all I sought was simplicity. All they saw was an engine for siege and devastation!" He exploded from the ground we sat on, reaching for the heavens and roaring. "Why have you damned me so? Ald'Kair!" The last exhalation could've cracked the walls around us if spoken with just a sight more ferocity. Leegius collapsed back down to his knees, broken iron left to cool; useless and overworked. "What purpose do wretches such as I have?"

I let him have this moment uninterrupted, his voice no longer cognitive but somehow still audible left in the stones. How many other stories take place while we write our own? How many heroes fail their labors and have history forsake them? The gods direct us and force us to place our trust in them until we find ourselves toys, discarded after sufficient play. A tool neglected and easily replaced.

"Even now, I feel The Breath call for me and I'm at a loss. I can feel the white essence mixing with others knocking at my doors, filled with malice. They feel the same. I can't tell the difference anymore." Leegius spoke low. I started to think he had forgotten me. "I don't know what to feel. I am hollow." He said like an afterthought.

I watched him. I had been hoping Leegius would fight for me before, to save my life, but here he was off fighting for his own.

"You said you wanted to work metal?"

Leegius gave a dull, shocked head jerk when I spoke. He had forgotten I was there too, so far into his own mind. It was time to bring him back before I lost him for good.

He smiled ever so slightly and rubbed the accumulating wetness in his eyes away.

"I was never an apprentice or even owned my own shop doing easy work, but at a young age, I discovered I was good at shaping metal. Good, not great. But I enjoyed it. I had designs in my head and my hands were beginning to match my imagination."

"A fine, endeavorous art, Leegius," I said solemnly.

He grunted a laugh. A dream too far.

"And you... Bringer? I don't like that name on you." He shook his head. "It's silly."

"Give it time," I said. "It grows on you. Not dissimilar from a diseased foot."

He smiled slightly. It sank away swiftly. Grief surfaced, not only for himself.

"When I look at you, there's a difference now, but still reminiscent of what you were," Leegius said.

"Did I mention I may have saved the world?" I smiled. I felt I knew what was coming. Leegius seemed to be one of those individuals who could reach in and discover who you are. These maniacal and knowingly clever facial expressions of mine were starting to hurt muscles I couldn't name, but I couldn't seem to stop them breaking the surface.

"No." He shook his head. "You've leapt into the darkness, Bringer."

"Enlightenment can change a boy just the same as a man, Leegius." I almost whispered.

"You've been through more than a boy should." He nodded, agreeing with himself.

"Maybe. But maybe The Breath has a plan, as your like tends to say."

*Maybe I have my own.*

"It's possible. Travel carefully down that path though. Else you will be worse than they are." He gestured up to the rest of Yalor.

I didn't explain how I was worse already. It hurt to know he cared about me. It was a pain I cherished for the time.

"Is that what makes you so dangerous?" I changed the subject, pointing at the ruby around his neck. The ruby itself had been coated in an odd webbing.

"...yes." He grabbed the gem with one large oversized hand.

"What is it?"

"Who he is, I couldn't say. He won't tell me his name."

"He?" *What?*

Leegius nodded. "He is a weapon from ancient times. You may know him as Shields of the Mountain War."

"...You can't be serious." I was a child again listening to my father's stories.

The Shields of the Mountain War, an artifact of the Arks, though which particular Ark could not be said. A powerful warrior wielded them during the Mountain Wars before the first epoch, before the empire was established. They turned a loss into an overwhelming victory. The warrior went missing shortly after the victory was declared. All that remained of him was a necklace he frequently wore in a pool of blood.

Since then, many would-be heroes have attempted to wield the Shields. Each has been...eaten. The Shields were actually bol'ruka class weapons. Large hunks of metal that would cover the entire arm starting above the shoulders, jointed at the elbow, and ending past the fingertips in a large blade, axe head, or blunt shape. The Shields were instead shaped like a monstrous skull. The top of the skull along one arm and the lower jaw snapped off along the other. Each time summoned, the jaws would slam shut. The weapon would vanish back into the necklace, leaving behind one pair of bloody boots and a head, surprise still written in the eyes.

Leegius nodded. "I am."

"And how is it you have yet to be eaten?"

Leegius chuckles as if that was the oddest thing to ask. "He says he likes my smell better than my taste. Something about my essence. But get this—" He waved me in like a madman telling a secret to a bystander and whispered, "He qualifies it as: 'So far.'" He laughed so hard and loud that I jumped back from the cell. "That's right, Bringer. The collar to my fate is also my noose."

This cage was killing him. The would-be scholar I had known was down a deep well, constricted and forsaken.

"Leegius!" I shouted over his pain-filled, wretched laughter.

It reached him. Leegius stopped and composed himself. The look in his eyes was like picking up shards of oneself with no sure way to reconstruct. Delicate, carefully navigating the razor edges.

He snorted out a breath through those Materic nostrils of his. An exhalation of whatever he could be rid of off his heart.

"Brother, tell me, what is the purpose of Yalor?" I asked, feeling as though I should run. Something was building in the air. Dense.

He snorted again, more scoff than release. "We are not brothers," he said.

I smirked, a mask for the hurt.

Leegius sat against the far wall. "What the big picture is, I cannot accurately say. But the Coliseum District..." He breathed deeply. Vision un-focusing, Leegius peered into possible futures. "War. It is as simple as that."

"You're going to have to elaborate on that a little."

"Bringer, the Alerez keep to themselves in their little glacier, so you wouldn't know. There's plenty about Orecul your kind are kept from. Races, cultures, and histories you couldn't even fathom. My people lived in harmony with many. Úlfur, Olenous, and yes humans, alike..."

"If there's so much peace, then why is there a prepping for war?"

"Why is there ever war?"

"No, you know what? I'm going to stop you there because I already see where this is going."

Leegius was taken aback at my intervening. "'You're an Alerez. You couldn't possibly understand what the rest of the world goes through."

"I'm not as ignorant as you think. Peace in this nation of ours is like holding knives to each other's throats while locking to the other with a free hand in friendly greeting...and *you* were supposed to be the knife."

Leegius paused. "The spear."

"And when they found this spear would almost just as well cut the wielder, they locked it up for good." I pointed at the ruby around his neck. "And took it a step further by dulling the blade."

We sat in silence for a while. I reflected on my thoughts while it seemed he just sat thoughtless. The empire was stronger than ever, but the power made them feel more exposed. Yalor's purposes would sell easily to them, and Hydel would sit pretty like the empire's right hand. The empire would attack inward to sure up anything and everything that could threaten its own design. Then...what then? Would they use all the 'spears' acquired through these means to take the rest of the world? The answer was obvious enough to develop the rhetorical question. The light emyon flickered. The thought of traversing back in the darkness didn't appeal to me.

I looked down at Leegius and another thought occurred. "You're a minotaur," I said.

The power that slammed into the bars was staggering. I hadn't even been close to the cell.

Leegius began spitting out an assortment of obscenities with the occasional, 'Didn't I tell you what would happen?' thrown in.

"Shut up, you half-whit," I screamed over his rage. I'd like to think at this point in time, I would have spoken to him thus whether he'd been caged or not, but I cannot be certain. Situations aside, I doubted he would've given me the chance to do so. Amazingly, he heard me shouting back, and he did as I asked. Curious rather than obedient.

"You. Are. A. Minotaur," I spoke each carefully. "You are a beast, a monster to these people. A weapon unfathomed in a generation for that jewel around your neck."

"What is your point, you little bastard?" Leegius snarled.

"Give it to them."

"What?"

"They will never see a peace-desiring Materic, Leegius. So, give them what they already expect. A minotaur. A violent, beastly, instinct-driven, destructive minotaur. Stop holding back. Embrace the image they've painted for you."

"I'm not a killer."

I shrugged. "Then let them kill you. They'll never be able to sell you. You will be a spectacle for the masses to be sure and perpetuate the stereotype of lesser races. You'll lie bleeding out with only the fading standing ovation to accompany you on your way to Disiea...where you'll be made into a machine for war anyway."

He didn't respond. He knew I was right. Nothing was right in life or death. There was no sweet embrace of death nor rest for a weary soul. It didn't work that way anymore.

"Or." I was close enough then that he could have grabbed me if he wanted to. "You can stop being a toy in their games. In case you've forgotten, behind these walls, life is a war, and we are losing, Leegius. My darkness, you pointed out, is just what I've become to survive. What they've made of me. It's not pretty, but it's all I've got." I started out tentative of the light going out but stopped myself short of the cell. I pulled a bottle from one of the many pockets on my person. "That is an emyon on your ruby, isn't it?"

"Yes." His voice was broken now.

When we were chained together and I was whipped for the first time, Leegius had stepped in the way of the guard to dissuade any attempt to continue the beating. This at risk to himself. I never told him, but I did notice his kindness. I tossed the bottle into the cell low enough to keep it from breaking, hoping to return the favor.

"Rub that solvent on the ruby. It will weaken the emyon. Once a day. A little goes a long way." I showed him my back again. "Show them the minotaur, Leegius. They want it, but you're going to give them more than they bargained. Force them down a path they are ill-prepared for." I made my way out toward the staircase. My mood became hotter with each step, turning my mind to a war of my own choosing. "Stop being their plaything!" I screamed loud enough for Leegius to hear, but I was talking to myself. I placed the deer skull back on my face and the light emyon flicked out.

## 13

## Chance at Redemption

Leaving Leegius in the cells felt...wrong, but I wasn't so delusional in my own abilities to have him out of there. Even so, Krolec would promptly suggest I was the culprit once the rounds were made to find him missing. Neither of us would get far wearing these pauldrons on our shoulders. Seeing all the nobles, or whatever they were, coming through our city more and more frequently led me to the understanding of just how deep Mistress Hydel's influence had reached into the empire. She was doing as I had with my talents, making herself indispensable.

Leegius would need to be on his own for a time. Grenlic, on the other hand...

"What are those?" Kyda asked.

I replaced the small scrolls into my pouch back out of sight. Grenlic walking up saved me from avoiding the question.

"What is this then?" Grenlic asked, still fully plated.

I had never beaten him to the tower before. He was usually waiting on us, already preparing the tea when we showed up.

"Keep your armor on, Commander Grenlic," I said. "There's no time for tea today."

"Oh?" Grenlic was clearly displeased. I didn't blame him. This was his time. Even on weeks when my research prevented Kyda and myself from attending, Grenlic had his tea and his peace.

"We've important things to accomplish before the court retires for the evening." I opened a hand toward my wheelhouse. As Grenlic fixed his gaze on it, Avol, my wheelhouse beast closest to us, made an ugly, yet gleeful, squawk. Mules could take lessons from him on unappealing sounds.

Grenlic scowled at me. "Bringer..."

"We are off to meet with Mistress Hydel."

That brought a smile to his face. "Yes? And how did you acquire this audience?"

I feigned embarrassment. "Kyda may or may not have forged your signature on a few documents."

Grenlic shot her a look of clear, aggressive disbelief. "Is this true?" Kyda shrugged, unashamed.

Grenlic shot back around to me, now near the wheelhouse. I opened the door and waved him in. After a long glare for yours truly, he groaned audibly and climbed in. He fixed me with very displeased eyes the whole trip, short as it was.

<hr />

The aristocracy of Mistress Hydel's looked much finer than my last visit. All jewels and luxury I didn't even know existed. I was pleased to see the temperature change from outside to in, with the help of the pauldron cooling emyon, created an ire shroud around us as we stepped through the threshold. I had it in mind I looked like the Spirit of the Grave come to collect his due. I wondered then why I enjoyed shocking others for shock value. The looks gifted to me on my way to the dais had me cast the question aside. I wanted humans to be afraid of me. Particularly these ones. Though, it would be some time before they understood why they should be concerned.

I walked swiftly, leaving Kyda and Grenlic more or less behind. "Lady Hydel," I bowed. "Sir Eneric. How the—"

"Commander Grenlic, why does an underling speak directly to me prior to you when this meeting is your request?" Hydel didn't even look up from the papers Father Feirtney held for her signatures.

Apparently, my new status wasn't enough to allow me as much freedom as I thought. I bowed again and stepped back. Picked my battle, if you will.

"Apologies, Mistress." Grenlic stepped up but did not take my place. We had vexed him enough not to be under his protection for the moment. I couldn't argue the reasons and hid a smirk under my cowl, having left the deer skull behind. "I'm sure his excitement caused him a lapse in procedure. I will remind him of his bearings later."

"The boy lacks more than procedure, Master Grenlic." Ah, Eneric puffed up as ever. "Be sure to teach him well, lest I must. And I am more generous with my lessons."

"Of course, Lord Eneric." Grenlic bowed again.

"What is it then, Commander? I've much to do before the end of the day and have only met with you this soon for the urgency you portrayed in the letters." Hydel let Feirtney flip to the next page.

"Mistress, Bringer would like to..." He looked my way, clearly beginning to falter in his improvisation. "...ask you something?"

I nodded.

"Bringer," Hydel beckoned me to speak with an accompanying eye roll.

I approached with less gusto than before, trying to avoid the disposition I had placed them in.

"Mistress Hydel." I bowed again, this time omitting Eneric for spite. "It has come to my knowledge I could do something to greatly serve the city of Yalor and her prospects."

The quill pen in her hand ceased. Hydel looked my way, leaving Feirtney standing poised and stifling his displeasure. Hydel's eyes told the story, although they didn't have to, a hunger for progression and profits.

"Is this on the same scale as your last project?" She asked wryly.

*Cunt.*

"Larger, I assure you," I said, equally wry.

Hydel placed her quill down in a well on the small table the priest held and shooed him away.

"Go on, Bringer," she said, all sweet like an attentive mother.

Eneric crossed his arms. I wanted him in the arena next time. Maybe Leegius would come around just in time to end him. I was unsure if I could kill him. Not yet.

"There is a small town north of Kytgro." I smirked at Grenlic. His heart appeared to be on the verge of stopping. "Forgive me. What was it called, Commander?"

"Mw...Mwinstead." If Grenlic had been any less the man he was, I believed he'd been slack-jawed at this point.

More heads in the throne room popped up at the name.

"Ah yes, Mwinstead," I continued. "Well, Master Mwin has fallen ill, and I am willing to offer my services."

"Lady." The young man who had attended Conarance's broken hand so long ago came up to Hydel's throne. He wasn't quite as young as myself, but in little need of a razor. He wore a new tunic this time, a greenish blue, golden long locks of hair cascading over his shoulders. "This would cost little more than a trip for us and the possibility of success with Bringer's talents, no matter the percentage, outweighs the expense. I advise you to greatly consider this."

"Back you." Eneric waved him away. "I would not have this."

To his credit, the boy stood fast, blatantly ignoring the big man's order. He wanted to obey. I could see it in the lines of him, but his eyes were only for Hydel.

"Mistress," Eneric beckoned her. "If you do not deny this to Bringer for the fact he is an asset we need here, then deny him for the fact that he's a conniving little shit."

Damn, he didn't even get this red when I broke Conarance's Hand.

"Look at him!" Eneric shouted when it appeared Hydel was considering. "He plans even now. Eyes darting about like vipers."

I had to force myself not to smile. Eneric was more perceptive than I had given him credit for. I forgot he was a hunter of sorts.

"Enough, Lord Eneric." Hydel held a hand up and all argument died there. "Tari, this is the city I remember?"

"Yes, Mistress, the very same." The boy almost bowed with his nod.

I was under the impression I would need Grenlic to argue the final points of our little trip, but here was this boy with the coup de grâce all his own. Hydel's eyes lit up. The convincing phase was over.

"I request, Commander Grenlic, to go with me, Mistress," I said, all humble. "He knows the area."

"Is this true, Commander Grenlic? I thought we acquired you closer to Appon."

"Aye, Mistress. My prior travels have led me there before. I've met the lord of the lands before and can assist in negotiations. I believe Bringer could use my courtliness to his benefit as well. It is no secret he understands little of human etiquette."

Hydel smiled. Loose enough in her own joy of the situation to accept a joke from one of her slaves.

She turned to Tari. "See to it."

Tari's face lit up. I didn't understand why exactly, but didn't inquire. I had gotten what I wanted. Tari was gone through the back doors before I could blink.

"You will be given supplies and a stipend of empire florins for your travels. Get with Tari to shore up the details properly." Mistress Hydel almost looked embarrassed. An odd mix in her delight. "Bringer, could I ask you a personal favor?"

"Oh, but of course, Mistress. How may I serve?"

"That region, it is known for the bitter rose, is it not?" I swear, the blood vessels in my eyes almost burst. "Will you bring me a bouquet when you return?"

I bowed again to hide the smile, quivering. This one full of teeth mauled for the kill. "Yes, m'lady. It would be my honor." It was all I could do to hide the shaking in my voice.

---

"Explain, Bringer." Grenlic stopped me from opening the carriage door on our way to leave the palace with one hand on the door's panes.

I offered him one of the scrolls from my pouch. "Here is a letter about the Lord Mwin. He is still alive, but barely. He's a husk and his advisors have taken control of the city. There's a lot happening over there right now. We are going to join the throngs for the will of Yalor. We are going to make a deal."

He blanched when he read the scroll's contents. "How do you know this?"

"I have a guy." I offered the other scroll. "This one is the real reason we are going."

This scroll Grenlic let fall from his hand when he was finished reading. He grew pale beneath his orange-brown scales. I retrieved it to prevent evidence from blowing into someone else's hands.

I nodded to his unspoken questions. "A writ has been issued yet again for the boy you spared. We are going to stop it.

"It's not all that bad." Kyda's words were aimed to pull me out of my sour mood, but the cupidity written on her face spoke of a more selfish objective.

Unbeknownst to me at the planning of our little journey, Hydel had given us leeway to leave only with Tari accompanying us. Another fact I had somehow missed was apparently, to the human eye, Tari, was—handsome. His being there raised my temper. But with Kyda's gawking, the purpose of my frustrations had been...redirected. I never pictured myself ending up with a human but turned out I was given to jealousy.

"I am truly sorry, Bringer. But you've been amongst Yalor long enough. You know how our mistress can be."

"I already had a babysitter." I thumbed back toward the front of the wheelhouse, where Grenlic steered Avol and Teket along the roads. "And besides, you don't send a youngling to watch other younglings." Avol squawked his agreeance...maybe.

"It wasn't the children aspect that held her concern." Tari had the wit not to direct attention to our shoulders. Good sense, or he felt he wasn't in danger. Also, either way, it really fecked me off.

I racked on the partition and slid it aside. "We need to stop in Kytgro first, Grenlic. Change course at the next crossroads. Eneric's orders. He has some business there and wants to keep us in line of sight for as long as possible."

"Aye."

Avol grunted at Grenlic's steering. He probably wasn't as gentle as Holin in his direction. I slid the partition back. Grenlic would appreciate the solitude more than our background conversations. He would need to reflect. Grenlic would be facing his past and would need to form his resolve.

"Why aren't you riding with Lord Eneric?" Kyda asked.

"I am with Lord Eneric almost every day. He can be stuffy. The man is a great warrior but a bit of a bore. Plus, I'll be continuing on with you to Mwinstead. How marvelous this opportunity to get to know the greatest alchemist Orecul has ever known...or his companions." He offered Kyda a smile. Even if her skin hadn't been so fair, the coloration in her face would have shown through any complexion.

"Did he tell you why we needed to go to the capital?" I asked, trying to change the subject. I wasn't arguing though. Grenlic and I found a way to use the extra stop to our advantage. Apparently, Grenlic needed something from the capital as well.

"Lord Eneric has something on order. Until now, he hasn't had the opportunity to retrieve it. Something about a blacksmith?"

"Won't that make us arrive later than we need to be?" Bik asked, bored and drawn out over a couch in the back.

"The paths of life have far more variables than can be explained or established by ledgers. We make choices every day and the outcome cannot be mapped so easily. Drink from the river in the desert or don't. Decide on the circumstances at hand—"

"You may find the water toxic or a city over the next dune," Tari said.

That shut me up. It wasn't the exact phrase, but I had to give it to him. Damn, of course he would be smart too. He was young, but Hydel trusted him as an advisor. Only the best for Yalor.

"I like that," he said. "But who said it?"

"My father." I bit off a snarl.

"Wise man," Tari agreed with himself.

I dropped the subject. "We need to stop in Kytgro anyway. For ingredients, rare ones."

"Which ones?"

"Apologies, I've not the patience to take on a pupil of my profession."

"Bringer!" Kyda came back, offended for him.

"Try me. I know a thing or two." He smiled that grand smile. All charm to show Kyda she didn't have to intercede on his behalf.

"Tari has familiarized himself with your work, Bringer. He's read your book," Kyda offered.

I studied him a moment, and a lock of that perfect light hair fell in front of his face as if planned. "Tch. Fine. Like Cary Coffer Cap." An ingredient I knew he had never heard of.

"Oh. Grand idea, Bringer. We could use it for its anesthetic properties."

I decided then that I hated the guy.

## 14

### Black Wyvern's Way

The capital was more than I expected, and I had been expecting a lot. I stood outside the wheelhouse as a stable boy attempted to lure Avol away with an old fish head, gawking. None of the others joined in my moment of awe. I paid the snickers at my reaction from the others no mind.

I ate my apple vigorously, attempting to comprehend why such large buildings would exist. Korigara was massive, even more so than Yalor. We even lived in the glacier walls. But we didn't squish our population in such a seemingly sporadic way. The buildings were beautiful, I have to say. White bricks, clean and steadfast, were the city's primary material. I had no idea where they may have obtained it from. It had to be a rare make. The roofs at least broke the sea of white with a red-brown canopy. Beauty aside, no race was meant to cluster like this. From the stables at the gates, I could make out more people than I would have known if I had been permitted to continue my life in the glacier.

We made our way in toward the main gates across the river. A small child passing latched to her mother took a moment from sucking on her fingers to wave at me. Despite my resolve against humanity, it warmed me. I reached out to return the wave, but the mother jerked the child away. I couldn't make out the words, but my pauldron had been remarked upon. I was cold again and any enthusiasm I may have been able to conjure up fell, washed away down to the canal in the center of the city.

"Done already?" Kyda smiled. Maybe I had had some sort of smile. She would be the one to notice it had taken its leave.

I looked at her pauldron and then just watched the horizon to the west. The sun crawled slowly down. This was the first time I felt marked...branded. The true distinguishing feature of us. It wasn't that half our party was exotic in the world of men. I could make out a few of the other races here. It all came down to a piece bound tight to our shoulders.

Kyda understood and said no more.

I wanted to ride the wheelhouse into the city. Let them remark on Avol; he wouldn't care. Hell, maybe it would do his ego some good. He thinks he's far more majestic than he is. He had been turned back before the bridge. Something about not having a permit to ride in the city walls or other. Eneric and Tari were able to get us through the gates easy enough though. Maybe it had been good that they came, after all. I doubt we could have entered on our own. Without getting in, our mission would have had no chance. If I had to forsake going to the apothecary, things could still work out, but Grenlic was anxious to get whatever it was he thought he needed. I never saw him anxious before, so I took him seriously. It didn't seem the others were getting the same feeling from him.

"Right then," Tari continued, oozing enthusiasm. "Let us all meet back here and we'll grab a tavern for the night. Sound good? I could kill for a warm bed after being stuck in those tents."

I looked up at Grenlic to get his take on the boy. A wall like always. I settled for a bow and set off. Three steps in, I felt the void. Kyda was walking in the opposite direction...with Tari.

"You're going with him?" I couldn't stop the question from coming out.

The shock, guilt, and abashment spoke clearly enough for her. I turned and went on my way. I tried to see it as a victory that now Tari would be plenty distracted. But I felt I had just traded my last apple for a damn potato. I must've been allergic to the local flowers; my eyes stung.

Eneric stood there towering over me. "You are with me. I intend to keep an eye on you, boy."

That put a damper on my plans. It was wise to assume that if I were going for ingredients at any given time, I would also obtain rare and unique products for poisons as well. With Eneric nearby, this would be impossible.

He accompanied me to the apothecary just as I feared. He watched every exchange I had with the shop keep. The alchemist was more than a little nervous with the large man standing at the doorway scowling. It had been as I thought too, so many ingredients I would have to obtain another day. Tuft of a lion's mane was the worst loss. I was surprised to see bits of a holy creature on the shelf, but I supposed it could've been offered rather than taken by force. I wondered how Ald'Kair would feel about such things.

After each parchment-wrapped item was checked and rechecked, Eneric handed me back my satchel. I wondered how much he had familiarized himself with my craft. He was making a convincing show of it.

"Come with me to the blacksmith."

No room for argument there. The thought of remaining in the city was accompanied by dread. I didn't want to be a spectacle anymore. Too many heads had been turning, followed by redirecting attention. I heard the word slave more frequently than I would have liked. At least Yalor had the grace to use the word 'citizen.'

The blacksmith's shop was not what I had expected. Usually, their shop is open in the front to allow potential customers to witness their labor and skill. Something to remind those trying to strike up a bargain just how much effort was required to bring each piece into existence. This shop was just as luxurious as the other shops nearby, save for a pillar of smoke frothing from the back of the shop.

The sign outside bore a black wyvern with its talons wrapped tight around a blacksmith's hammer. Today was a day for holy symbols, apparently. The inside was too extravagant for a smith, polished marble and granite, but the walls were covered in arms and armor, each of value tantamount to the building itself. A tiny bell poised over the door announced our arrival.

The sight of the arms gave me a rush. Echoes of my father, perhaps. My enthusiasm was never as grand with a fine-honed blade as with alchemy. Even so, I still liked weapons. I think it discouraged my father from finding 'flowers' interested me to any degree.

I remembered the look on his face after our last training session before he left for his missions. There was remorse and disappointment at my willingness to go to my lessons with my mother after our duels. He, I think, misunderstood. It wasn't me trying to be finished with training as soon as possible, it was me trying to fit in as much learning as I could into the limited hours of the day. My father had lived by the sword, for the sword, and not much else. I think it hurt him to see his only son having other interests, other interests involving a traditionally feminine art.

Swords, hammers, axes, and many other artistically designed weapons flanked our every side, as many different metals and alloys for as many unique nations of Orecul. The craftsman must have trained his entire life with masters scattered across the land.

I hefted an axe, a piece of wicked curves conjoining to an overly sharp bit. The weight surprised me and I attempted to put it back on the rack. It promptly disobeyed, fell from my grip, and took a few more metal works with it on its way down. It didn't help that my wings acted on their own accord, trying to help stop the falling weapons, but instead contributed to the clumsy mistake. Once the deafening echoes had passed, I unpeeled my eyes. Eneric held me in his regard. The scowl the man wore matched his armor: rough, dark, unyielding, and plentiful. I blanched.

I blew out a breath and went to put the weapons back as quick as I could without reliving the failure. Both hands on the axe this time.

"An Alerez, huh. A slave, no less. Not what I expected to waltz into my shop today." I shot around quick-like, a sword in my hand, guiltily. "You know it is illegal for slaves to bear arms." The gruff voice came from a man from behind the counter. He moved with an elder's pangs, but he was solid. Young in the eyes but experienced. He carried a weapon underneath fine cloth, rubbing it profusely to finish the shining process.

"Sorry, sir. I was just—"

"Have it back to the rack, boy. I only jest."

"Where is my weapon?" Eneric asked, irritated at being addressed second.

"Calm down, Lord Eneric." The smith placed the weapon he had been polishing onto the counter and took a long drag off a loose-lipped cigarillo. "I'll not be losing your business any time soon." He spoke through the smoke. "Your sword. I heard you were in town. Figured this would be why."

The haze wrapped him but undercut the dare in his eyes for Eneric to contradict him. Eneric was a man of power, but that stare said the old man knew he was the best in the business and his art would not be rushed.

They seemed to reach an understanding and the blacksmith slid the weapon closer to our edge of the counter. Eneric flipped the cloth back. I couldn't see his face or the weapon, but a tug at the warrior's ears was enough to know there was a grand smile. He covered the weapon back and carried it at his side, concealed beneath the cloth. With his free hand, he snapped his fingers and found his way out. One of the honor guard blue gems that had been waiting at the door produced some bill, left it on the counter, and found his way out too.

I watched them leave.

"You gonna steal something or buy something?" the old man asked, thickening the haze about him.

"Huh?" I said.

"Well, I've never had a slave in my shop before. A pageboy, sure, but nary a slave. Just trying to figure out what to expect."

"Oh, no. I'm not the sneaky type. Stealing is beyond my capabilities." I smiled.

"So, a purchase?"

"I'm afraid currency is beyond me too. All the florins I had in my possession have found other owners." I patted the satchel of ingredients on my side.

"An alchemist then." That threw me off. There were no indications on my person to suggest this to anyone outside of Yalor. "You look surprised, eh? Those pockets around your person, they ain't for coin or other trinkets."

Something in the back of my mind told me the pockets were not what gave me away.

He took another drag and let the smoke fall from his mouth instead of the cloud affect, almost like he was entertaining himself. He was nicely dressed and clean for a blacksmith, but his arms straining the seams of his sleeves told the truth of it. If he moved wrong, the fabric would tear.

"I hope I pissed Eneric off enough." He grabbed a nearby blade and began oiling it to give his hands something to do.

"Why?" I wasn't interested in his answer as much as watching him perfect metal. My art may be in a completely different field, but artists can appreciate another artist's work. I caught a smile from him when he noticed.

"He will be on his way to Yalor soon. What with the whole presentation coming up. Every major player in the empire will be there. Man like that, well, he'll be ranting and raving. But the story he tells will have to include that sword of his. He'll be forced to show it. Hells, he'll show it with pride, despite his anger. It'll drum me up some nice business." He had a chuckle at that.

"That is why he had you make that weapon then?" I asked, retaining my disinterest in the conversation as the old man had passed me the weapon. A simple piece but open to possibilities. With that sword in my hands, Eneric didn't scare me. "I'm from Yalor, actually. Eneric seems to have left without me. Do you make a lot of weapons for the Golden Dawn?"

He nodded. "I make good business doing what I do, but this has been a profitable quarter." He put out his spent cigarillo and lit a new one. "The way you handle that sword...you've handled a blade or two, haven't you? Didn't imagine a being with wings used the same tools as the rest of us. More limbs to lop off and all."

I gave the blade back before I got all creative with my swings. "Yes, my father was a soldier."

"Any favorites?"

"I'm partial to spears and polearms."

"A soldier, huh?" He furrowed his brow. "Did he wear a caliber cape?"

"A what?"

"You know, a cape concealing the left shoulder with an insignia: wraps around their lower back."

"That's what those are?" I looked down at my shoulder. These devices had been designed with the same idea in mind. "I thought it was odd all guards wore them. The ones here too. Eneric and...Conarance."

"It's a mark. The left shoulder is traditional to establish devotion, office, or just all around belonging to something."

"My father didn't wear a caliber cape. Not as far as I have seen."

He crossed his arms, tense. I couldn't pinpoint what I was reading in him. "How did he mark his office?"

"I'm not really sure. He flashed a coin when most outsiders came through."

"A silver coin?"

"Y—yes."

He looked around his shop. "I can't do a spear. Slaves are forbidden from weapons and all."

"Master Smith, I can't offer any—" He waved it off as unimportant and left to the back of the shop.

The old man came back with two armfuls of blades, small ones, linked together. "This is someone I couldn't find a buyer for. I'm thinking this is the reason for that. He's a lamque, of sorts."

"Huh?"

"He was made for you, boy."

"I'm still not on the same page here."

"Just try the metal, son." He held out the gauntleted end of the bladed chains.

I tugged it and the change in weight distribution found the chain slithering very loudly onto the ground.

He laughed. Oddly pleasant. A quick look around and I saw him mentally retract the 'try' statement. "Maybe somewhere where there are less...obstacles."

"Is this part of it?" The metal sliding away revealed another smaller piece. A claw-like weapon with metal that would slide between fingers and support weight across the hand, each talon as long as an assassin's dagger, curved and wicked. The old man held it for me and I slid my hand inside. The whole set felt awkward but, oddly enough, made me feel empowered for the first time in a long time. I wasn't certain this would be a good thing. "I don't understand. Why are you showing me these, let alone letting me hold them? I can't buy it. I can't even own it."

"Call him by his name," he said.

"What?"

"It's Reaver."

I looked at the coil of metal, then back to the blacksmith like he was playing a joke on me.

"No," he responded. "Try."

I thought back to what Leegius had said about his necklace. Two gems had been worked into this weapon in my hands. One in the talon, and another in the wielding end of the tail of daggers.

"Reaver." Nothing happened.

"Listen, boy. You don't like to be spoken to like an object either. Say it like you are talking to a person."

The expressions on my face were starting to exhaust the muscles there. I'm not one given to be completely ignorant and the longer this went on, the dumber I felt.

The blacksmith wasn't lying. His eyes told me as much. They were hopeful. He needed me to make this happen. Whatever this was, it was genuine, but I couldn't grasp it. I rubbed my face, trying to focus whilst almost failing to keep the blades from giving me a new look.

I focused on the orangish gem embedded in the palm of the claw portion.

"Reaver."

The claw snapped back onto my wrist and locked there. The chain flexed and morphed. The fecking thing broke at the handle and actually climbed up my arm. It wrapped around my chest and seemed to shrink. Then it locked onto itself behind my neck. The claws snapped back into a bracelet design.

"It looks like...jewelry," I said, checking myself over.

He crossed his arms, pleased. "No one will know you are armed. Just call him when you need him. He should be able to respond to your whims to make control a little easier until you understand how he works. Lamque are exceedingly difficult to master. This one is more stubborn at that."

"Why?"

"I fashioned him based on a design I did a long time ago—"

"No! Back to my prior inquiry. Why are you doing this?"

He shrugged his arms palms up. Funny, I didn't think palms could scar. He fidgeted a lot. "Hmm." I felt a half-truth coming on. "I knew your father."

"What?"

Or not.

"He was a...loyal customer. Call it a gift from a family friend. I don't buy into chance. Nybe may be throne-less right now, but her gears are still turning."

Half-minded, I noticed how late it was getting through the window. I was going to be late for Tari's hard deadline.

"What is really going on here? There is a lot of information I've gathered, so bear with me." The slave persona was gone now and the blacksmith took note, dropping his arms to his sides. "First, you are lying. Maybe not lying with words, but you are a lie. It hasn't smelled like smoke in here the entire time and you've burned through at least three smokes since I've walked in. You have scars where, by my education, scars do not form well. They may heal faster or more thoroughly, but they don't look like yours, regardless. They represent a much, much deeper wound and your back hands do not possess any damage related to them. There are a lot of gems in this workshop, plus in the weapons, yet you are no jeweler. Your weapons are highly functional, not the gilded filigree of princes. The walls are lined with weapons and you are cleaner than anyone I've ever seen a smith of anything." I had an extra thought. "And what the feck is this thing on my shoulder." I hadn't realized I was basically shouting at him until my words shot back at me.

For a moment, I thought I would either get thrown out or receive a thrashing, but he smiled. A low-throated laugh followed.

"All my time here, no one has caught on so thoroughly. Mostly, the more brutal individuals come through here, so I suppose it is not too surprising. Your father spoke well of your mother. I believe last I saw him, you were about to be hatched. I didn't see him much after that. But all that you just said, that is your mother." He laughed aloud now. "Very good, my boy, very good."

The blacksmith pulled up a stool and sat down. "You want answers? I'll see what I can do." He flipped another stool over the counter and placed it for me. I didn't accept it. I stood my ground, refusing to relax. He didn't remark on it with even a glance.

"Those things on the slave shoulders are mosoleth. I won't go into details because the way you keep looking at the window says you're short on time. Reaver is a mosoleth too, but far more...advanced. I'll tell you one thing about them: you can easily kill one by breaking the gem. Those pauldrons are not sentient, so I don't mind sharing that bit. Reaver though, you better take care of him or I'll come after you."

"...Go on."

"Don't kill yours yet, son. I see you want to, but I know you've enough brain up there like your mother to know you need to plan this out. You can't just be the only Alerez for miles, countries even, and expect to go unremarked. As for the lying." He showed me his palm. There was no scar and the place smelled of ash appropriately.

I started toward the door. There was a sense in the air that instinct told me to run from. I could walk away from this place that, more and more, with each moment, felt like a den of sorts and call it a win. I had another piece of knowledge to fix into my plans and a weapon to reave through the obstacles.

I stopped at the door, something still crawling up my spine. "What are you not telling me about my father?"

He sighed. His voice wasn't the same, but I didn't look. It was too much. Too many voices. A horrifying mix of despair and care.

"The Alerez never had soldiers. They never joined the empire as a cooperative country. They have tribal warriors to be sure, but 'soldier' implies an army governed by a leader. Your kind keeps to itself and protects its own. There's no such thing as an Alerez soldier."

I left then, easing the door shut. Did I start running to my wheelhouse to meet up with Tari on time or to put as much distance between myself and the creature within?

Nybe was indeed moving her gears...or was it Disiea.

<hr/>

I knew I was late getting back, but the old man had given me plenty to think about, including the fact he was no old man. There were questions I needed answers for: To whom did my father devote himself if he wasn't a soldier? Why would he do dealings with that smith shop that delves so much into over powered weapons? What the hell was my next move? Where—

A flash caught my eye. I looked around thinking maybe it had been a flash from some passerby's jewelry or my own. It was too dark for that, I realized. Another green flash. It had come from the gem in my pauldron. When Conarance had used the torture methods installed within the pauldron on mine, it did something similar. But the light had been solid. I kept my pace and the pauldron continued the flashing. Soon, I realized the time between flashes was growing shorter. I started to sprint.

The pauldron's flashes were only a few seconds apart now. I blew past a crowded courtyard, toppling an older woman and a few children in the process. I came into the main road, taking out a fence that I overestimated the sturdiness of. I could see Kyda and the others. The light solidified.

At first, it seemed like nothing happened. I blew out a sigh. The air did not come back. I struggled for it. Nothing. I focused on Tari and ran. Thank you, father, for that obscure training you've put me through. He had cut my breathing off with a belt before as a form of panic control. Today, it proved exactly what I needed to experience.

I pushed through the burning that started first in my lungs then my legs. But then I lost the grasp on my heart beat, against my training, and it went into overdrive. Panic wasn't too far away either. I found myself hoping Tari would cut my breathing back on before the black spots forming became too wide. This thought was accompanied by a steel determination to skewer him with a pike.

My body began to fail me and I fell to a midstride. This was a clumsy gesture that pulled a groin muscle badly. The pain was minimal compared to my lungs. Those felt like a heated stake had been thrust through them. Not one person looked my way in the streets while I slid to the ground against a stone wall. Apparently, a slave's torment was a common enough spectacle for it to merit comment. I watched the sky, believing the stars to be the last beauty I would see in the world and my vision went black.

My body convulsed one more time and sucked in air. It tasted like the sweetest thing I'd ever imagined, better than apples even. I was up to my knees coughing before color bled back into my vision. I wanted to stay down and lay in my misery, but it was time to move. More lessons from my father on pain and war. I didn't fully have the mechanical functions back in my legs yet, but still, I clumsily charged forward. Tari had to die. Now, before he could act again.

A few feet more and my body started to return to life. Air poured in. Legs, arms, and wings lunged me forward.

I wasn't sure how to use the bladed tail of Reaver and wasn't willing to risk a falter. The claw portion, however, was an easy shiv under the ribs. A quick twist to ensure maximum organ rupture. When I noticed Tari was faced away, I pushed forward even faster for the kill. I moved like an assassin who waited too long to take his mark out and it was the critical moment. I shot up a wagon of fruit and time suspended as I flew.

"Just give him a moment." Kyda's sweet voice was beyond the edge of my tunnel vision. "He would have only just recovered. How could he get to us if you won't let him recover?"

The 'old man' instructed me to call his name when I needed him. Obscure and odd-tasting in my mouth, but I went for it.

"Reav–"

The gem on my arm went solid again and something shot me in the gut.

I lost my air in both my lungs and elevation. I slammed into the ground, sliding passed Tari into the circle of the group.

A massive weight stood on my stomach like a large man leaning on a blacksmith's hammer. I could almost hear my veins rising through my skin as I attempted to suck in what air I could.

"He is here. Let him loose," Grenlic demanded.

Tari ignored him and knelt down beside me. No expression was written on him or, at least, it was one I didn't recognize. He held one thumb from his opposite hand onto the ring gifted to him by Hydel as we left. He was somehow worse than Conarance with that kind of power. Conarance at least knew not to cause real harm with the pauldrons. This pain wasn't just instilled. I was taking damage.

"You'll not be late again," he said.

I opened my mouth with the intent to bite his face off when a light started to form in my throat. I didn't understand it, nor did he. He staggered back, dropping his thumb off the ring. The spot of illumination on the ring dwindled down and my suffering stopped. I curled into myself. I just lay there gasping cool breaths out. Cooler than they should be. It was of no interest to me at the time. Instead, I was trying not to lose control of my mind while again trying to regain my body. Every fiber within me wanted to go on the attack, but some small voice in the background prevailed. Just enough.

Grenlic convinced Tari to give us a moment, steering him away back to the wheelhouse. I needed the moment. I was at war with myself.

There was a pause in Kyda's caressing my scalp that scared me, and I sat up quickly. She shot into me.

"I thought you were really hurt," she sobbed. I hugged her back, the jealousy from before nonexistent.

"I thought I lost you," I whispered.

"What?" She pulled away just enough to ask unmuffled.

"Do you have note material on you?" I whipped away the bile and saliva away from my cheek.

"Mmhmm." She smiled, rubbing her face away from the various fluids. She knew I always wanted something to write on when I was feeling an urge for notes, so she was sure to always have something for me on hand.

She handed me the book. It was fresh, unused, and gilded. A very nice book. I gave it back to her.

"Thank you, but I'm not going to be the first one to use your new book. Save it for your diaries. Come on."

Eneric's carriage was nowhere in sight. Apparently, he had his prize and that was enough. He would let Tari take us for the remainder of our journey.

Back in the wheelhouse to find a tavern we could afford for the night, I climbed on top of Tari, making sure my ass was more or less on his head to search the cupboard. Ignoring his protests, I found my seat after retrieving some paper and a coal stick. I drew as best as my hands and memory could produce, which doesn't say much when it is not a picture of a plant or mushroom. When finished, I wasn't sure what was staring back at me.

I held on to it for a couple more hours before I got up the courage.

"Kyda, what is this?" I flashed her the picture.

She examined it longer, smacking my hand so I couldn't take it back.

"I'm not sure," she relented.

I scowled at Tari when he smiled expectantly. I showed it to him regardless.

"Damn, you stumped me," he laughed. "What is it?"

I snatched the page from his hands.

One more chance. This one I feared an answer from the most. I dropped the partition.

"Grenlic."

"Aye."

I passed him the page and moved over to the door. I unlatched it and crawled on the side of the wheelhouse while it was still in motion. Grenlic had passed the reins to one hand. The rest of him was stiff and a cloud passed over his face.

"What is that?"

He cleared his throat and handed it back. At first, I didn't think he would answer.

"It's the eye of a reclaimer god. Ark of Retribution." He sounded grim. "It's the sigil of the Writ Executioner."

Slowly, as though to remind himself that I already knew, Grenlic produced the coin he had held in his hand when I first met him those years ago. Upon the coin, the eye stared back at me.

I slid back into my seat, feeling worse than when Tari had activated my pauldron. I sat in my thoughts, staring into the drawing, coin in the other hand, and my heart darkening. I held them, more brittle by the moment, washed with implication in my hand. The truths of the sigil in my father's coin.

As the wheelhouse crossed the vineyards surrounding Mwinstead, the plants flowed like clotted blood. Eerie, to say the least. The sunlight cresting the horizon on a clear day did little to soften the image and if anything, the red hue caused it to look fresh from the veins.

"The bitter rose," I said in awe.

"You know of it, do you?" Tari asked. "These flowers make the rarest wine in all of Orecul. I've never tasted it myself, but it's not bitter. I've always wondered why the rose got the name."

"I'm sure there are other ingredients," I added and sat back in my seat away from the window. It was all I could do to keep the tremors of excitement at bay.

The others took the opportunity to crowd the window in my absence.

"Why is it so dark? It doesn't look right." Kyda's disappointment was clear to see. She was a girl who enjoyed her flowers.

"They're black-tipped. A beautiful sanguine red of love, finishing up with the black of love lost."

I didn't correct Tari. I wasn't sure where he had heard such a thing. Maybe it was a marketing idea summoned up to add a taboo flavor to the pallet of the sampler.

The partition at the front of the wheelhouse slid open.

"Problem," Grenlic said.

I hung out the door to see what was the matter. As the city grew larger in our sight, it was plain to see we would need to approach on foot. Too many men and women crowded the streets, all on their knees. A long, dull humming, almost singing, rose from them and the city.

Once close enough, the wheelhouse fully disembarked. We stood there stupidly and watched them. The humming had ceased and all the human collective knelt there, heads bowed.

"What the hell is this?" Bik asked.

The people held their hands like when the priest in Yalor did his examination on me.

"This is about the Breathing Church," I said. "A prayer?"

The congregation of kneeling individuals were all angled toward the town square. At first, I had thought maybe everyone had simply died in the position, but then a bell tolled, high and sweet. Each person in succession, beginning from somewhere deep in the city, straightened at the waist toward the morning sky and started a monotoned, deep-throated 'Ah.' I'm not one to boast of the ability to detect the presence of essence, but in that long moment, the area was awash with the stuff. Holy spiritual power is hot, like being too close to the campfire.

Grenlic was unpacking vitals and tending to Avol, disinterested. Kyda had tears in her eyes, almost ready to collapse and join them.

"It's the Breathing Church's strongest prayer, Breathing. Not the most inspiring name, but the effects are staggering, as you can plainly see." Tari supplied. "They breathe in slow and deep and out just as slow toward the heavens." He smiled, showcasing his knowledge as if he hadn't just witnessed it the same as I had.

"What are they praying for?" Kyda dabbed the corners of her eyes.

"We're here to cure an afflicted man. Maybe it is for him. I did some digging and apparently, he is well-loved."

"But not his son," I murmured. "Gather what supplies you can carry. We'll take that small path they left us over there," This time loud enough to be heard over the prayer.

"Are you from Yalor?" A white and gold-robed woman approached us, hood concealing her face.

"We are." Tari stepped forward. Fine, I'll let him play leader. The more I am overlooked, the better.

"Follow me." She turned and started away without another word or motion.

Grenlic shot me a look. He would remain here. Tari didn't seem to mind. I almost nodded my consent but remembered who I was about to respond to as though he were a subordinate. As we set out, I saw Grenlic pull a massive work of wood and metal from the roof of the wheelhouse, a bow taller than Avol.

We took the path I had identified before. The entire city gave me an uneasy feeling, but what I saw in the centered leading the congregation out right scared the hell out of me. The bell tolled again. The people raised for their hymn once more and a form spread its almost glowing white wings as though it were absorbing the prayer in the space in front of it. I couldn't make out who or what it was, but the form stood like a man. Two other uglier, black, crippled-looking things flanked the white form, their wings decrepit and frayed.

I thanked Nybe I was inside and away from those creatures and before the essence pressure built up again. I had enough of that essence before in Father Feirtney's care.

The hooded woman closed the heavy oak door behind us and dropped the latch. When she threw back her hood, I jumped back. I blamed it on the presence of so much of the new and uncomfortable. Odd white markings decorated her face down past her collar bones. The effect was disconcerting. She had those same markings in her eyes, making piercing decorations of her blue-gold irises. She moved on as though Kyda and I weren't gawking.

I made the mistake of leaving Grenlic behind. Now Tari would have to be my guide. He noticed it too. The smug bastard.

"Essence Scarring." Tari looked at where the hooded woman had passed into the adjacent hallway. "That was the most severe case I have ever seen."

"Terrifyingly beautiful," I said.

"She's an essence wielder?" Kyda didn't sound any less stunned than myself.

"Yes—"

"Are you coming?" The woman snapped from the next room.

"—and a terribly powerful one. Best not to ire her if you ask me. Shall we?" Tari led us in.

It was a straight shot down the hall to where the essence wielder waited, hand clasped on the door handle, not peeved but impatient.

She threw open the doors and led us into an antechamber. Tari led on behind her, chest out. I don't think it occurred to him we shouldn't be meeting a dying man in a great hall, yet there on the throne, a dying man sat. Slumped, swollen, and disfigured, Lord Mwin could not even raise his head to his new guests. A well pen lay in between his fingers, lacking any grip to sign the page some old fellow held against the tip.

It finally became obvious to me and I stopped mid-stride. The congregation, our essence-wielding guide, and the Writ Executioner soon to come; all of us here for our cut of the pie. Kyda looked at me oddly. I moved on. I didn't want to talk about my thoughts, about how much harder this was going to be than I expected. We were at war with more than just an illness.

When we came to the throne, I pushed past Tari, who was mid-bow. I shot up the dais as the satisfying thump of Tari hitting the ground filled the silence. Lord Mwin followed me with his eyes and I watched them. Was that all he was capable of?

I shot a glance at the old man holding the slate with the parchment, my skull mask giving him pause. He wasn't dressed like our scarred guide. I guessed him not to be an essence wielder; otherwise, I would not have been able to do what I did next. I snatched the slate and he made to stop me, but I held him at bay with my tail blade to his throat. Lady Hydel said I couldn't use my Alerez armory against any Yalorian. I was certain she didn't mind someone else's loss of a priest. It helped that no guard made to stop me.

The page was gold-leafed and hand written with artistic professionalism. Terribly expensive and would take maybe days to complete. I am no scribe, so I wasn't certain. Either way, I knew it was something they would rather keep undamaged. There were no markings in the signature area. I ripped the parchment to shreds.

"Bastard child," the old man cried, scrambling for the pieces. I walked back over to a stunned Tari as the priest continued with his livid disapproval.

"What the hell, Brin—"

I cut Tari off with a hand on his shoulder and brought him closer. He stiffened, forgetting his little ring. He thought I was going to kill him; I didn't tell him how right he was.

"We can't have him signing or being made to sign anything. Not until we understand what is happening here. You see all the different pieces in play, don't you? The Breathing Church, our guide from the Ceth Isles." I glanced over at the scarred woman. She stared back expectantly. "Everyone is here for their own interests and mean to take anything and everything they can get before the man departs. They are not concerned about saving this man."

"Who else?"

"What?"

"You said 'all, not 'both, then labeled only two. Who else is in play here?"

I locked up for a moment. It was short, but I think he took note, even relaxing in my grip a bit.

"Us, you moron," I said.

Tari hesitated but stepped to the Ceth woman anyway. "My apologies," he took her by the hand. A revulsion ran through her body. "We must insist Lord Mwin does not sign anything in his condition...legality reasons and all, you understand."

The essence wielder took her hand from him as if he were a leper.

"Just do what you came to do." She spoke to me directly.

Ah, smart woman. There had been nothing in the letter preceding us mentioning who I was. Tari was the face. She threw up her hood and left without another word.

Tari didn't let it phase him, all professional-like. Probably rejected regularly. He approached our host and bowed deeply. "Lord Mwin, we have come to help you. Mistress Hydel wishes you good health and has sent us to make sure that comes to pass." Lord Mwin looked on blankly at him, eyes almost inoperable. "M'lord?"

Kyda and I glanced at each other, apparently coming to the same conclusion. I walked back up the dais. "Kyda, find me a lantern, please."

I tested the lord's pulse, his skin contraction, and finally, his pupil dilation with Kyda's lantern. I recorded my findings in a fresh notebook, trying to hide my building glee. His eyes appeared to be calcifying.

"Bringer...Bringer!"

"Hmm?"

"He's trying to speak," Kyda said.

Lord Mwin's eyes borrowed into me. I leaned in.

"What's he—"

"Shh!" I sharply cut off Tari.

Mwin murmured for a time and I pulled away with a sigh. True regret, no intellectual glee remaining. I nodded to him, ignoring the welling in my eyes.

"Get this man to his chambers." I barked at the first soldier I could see. He stared at me blankly for a moment with the slightest 'who the hell is this boy to give me orders' in his eyes. "If Lord Mwin dies on his chair like a common house maiden, I am sure his successor would find it displeasing that the men in his charge allowed his suffering to be paraded for all to witness. It doesn't matter if it is his son or not. The new lord will end the incompetence here like hot iron to infection. He shouldn't have been in the throne room in the first place in this condition. I am absolutely positive this is not the first time this has been implied to you, yet you and your men allow this to happen? For what? The chance to get ahead with whoever could get the lord to sign? Make no mistake, they will remove you and all of your men for being too easy to convince. Has Lord Mwin treated you in any negative way to receive this treatment? Has he harmed you and your family or treated your wife like trash? Or did he welcome you and your worthless soul to his budding town with open arms to save you and yours from the winter's blade?"

I was on a roll and couldn't find a good stopping point, but another guardsman stepped forward.

"Alright!" he practically shouted with the anxiety I had placed there. The guard I had been acknowledging looked relieved. "You're right, boy." He sighed. "You're right. If anyone is to blame, that would be me." His caliber cape was more decorated than the others. Perhaps a commander. "Move him to his chambers."

Hours later, Grenlic, Kyda, Tari, and myself sat or lay in the grasses outside while Bik and Holin collected samples from Lord Mwin. I was beyond relieved and even thanked Nybe that the congregation was concluded with its 'prayer.' There was a sermon now, but the massive amount of essence was gone from the air. They spoke of Ald'Kair and his eventual return. Some nonsense about the rewards to the faithful.

My sense of amazement was on the decline. The man, or whatever, leading the sermon didn't strike me anymore. It was some sort of bird-like man. Beak and all. Maybe an owl? The others flanking him more crow-like. Another race like Materic or Olenous? Kyda seemed to be the only one strongly interested. I let her go investigate and have her time. Some extra information about our situation couldn't hurt.

He didn't ask about the Lord of the land, but I felt the disappointed undercurrents coming from Grenlic.

Tari was the one who gave voice to the looming question. "So, what's our next move?"

I answered Grenlic, "What we've come to do."

Grenlic took one more long look at the bird person and his two uglier attendants, got up, and moved out. I could see in the lines of his face, though we were doing something good, preparing to kill one of his own weighed on him.

"Where's he off to?" Tari asked, nervous. Three people under his command were making him anxious.

"Tari, we don't like each other—"

He sat up. "I like y—"

"But in order to succeed we need each other. Remember that scarred woman?" He nodded. "You know where she's from, right?"

"The Breathing Church."

I sat up abruptly. "What?"

"I didn't correct you earlier because I could see I needed to act on your behalf right then, but she's not a Ceth. She is a church member."

"Fine. Go to her and learn what you can. What exactly do they want. Above all else, keep them busy."

I know Tari wanted to lead us initially when we set out on our little journey but reality had set in well. He could serve us politically but this was my mission. He nodded and set off to let me brood about our situation.

When he was a ways away, I threw a tablet into my mouth and lay back in the grass using my wings to encase me afraid they may be stepped on when I stopped paying attention. I needed time to consider the pieces at play and what to do about them.

I sorted my findings on Lord Mwin's illness. No one had been able to help him these years he's been afflicted. The hope was there was something I could do for him. If we could have saved him, our mission would be clearer. We could get the writ withdrawn and Grenlic wouldn't have to worry about the boy he saved. In moments of meeting Lord Mwin, it was plain this plan was not going to work. Now, Grenlic was scouting the area for a place to hold up. I did my best to trust in his skills and that he would know the direction of approach the Writ would use. The illness was sorted as no value in my mind.

I spent some time sorting our situation out in my head as I lay there in the grass. I sorted Grenlic and the others into their appropriate categories in order to visualize our situation and any direction we could take. My least favorite ending was to have to face the Writ head-on. We needed to have the writ itself revoked, or something, but even after my sorting and playing through different scenarios, I wasn't sure we had enough time. Unfortunately, when I had received the information concerning the issuing of the writ, it had been old already. It wasn't easy for an information broker to obtain the sellable material, let alone one who was a slave. We were lucky to get the information before the deed was done. We were lucky convincing Hydel had gone so well. Even so, time was not on our side.

Writ Executioners move to their target slow in their armors. They were too heavy for any beast or vehicle to carry them to their destination. Their pillars of steam crawled across the land for all to see and it was a clear sign to stay away. The pillar which made its way toward Mwinstead would be visible to us soon. I had by then to make something work. By then, no message to the Writ itself would reach it in time to change its course.

I wondered if I should beg the help of the guard who had his men carry Lord Mwin to his chambers. Was his loyalty to the lord and his son strong enough to stand against the empire? Would he offer the boy up to the Writ to save those who would be bystander casualties, or would he evacuate the city and leave the boy to fend for himself?

Maybe the Ceth woman, who apparently wasn't a Ceth, would be willing to use her most powerful emyon to fight the Writ? That didn't seem likely. The Breathing Church was closely integrated with the empire. A shared goal in resorting Ald'Kair to his throne. It wasn't a bad endeavor, I had to admit, but it would keep us at arm's length for our purpose. Maybe I should have convinced Father Feirtney that Disiea had sent a small army to Mwinstead. Would he have donned the armor of his god to fend them off? The whole image of that exchange gave me a laugh.

The quiet of the moment had me back, and pulled away from my musings. I unwrapped myself from my wings unsure of just how much time had passed. Alcillis was coiled about itself nearby, patiently waiting for me to come back. I had to admire its ability to go without being detected. It hadn't been in or on my carriage the whole trip as far as I could tell. None of the others had made a comment about a snake or a moth.

"I'm going to miss a real snake one of these days because of you. Then—" I slid my finger across my throat. "—it's over for me."

The unexpected silence that brought me from my thoughts made me think of the eerie figures, both the city's people and its visitors. They all had ceased their breathing prayer and now knelt with their hands open to their faces toward the ground. I guessed with to be a normal prayer but there was something like a trance also occurring here. Not a single person reacted to my presence. Nor did anyone adjust themselves the way you do when you're in an uncomfortable position for an extended period of time.

I saw Kyda there weeping and unseeing. She wasn't in the trance as the others but I could see her making the effort to do so. It was less eviscerating than when I felt I had lost her to Tari but I felt the divide between us widen.

Kyda was no longer mine.

I stepped past more people in their unanimated states and even checked the pulse of a man when I found myself concerned for The Breath's crops. I started to view the church in a different light. I couldn't stand the church and was sure they shared their own corruptions within their ranks, as all human establishments did, but they weren't my enemy. This didn't prevent me from the bitterness at losing Kyda to them.

I strode over motionless bodies to the bird-like being leading the congregation. I regarded the two forms flanking the platform. Wretches to the design of this race. A closer look and I was sure that this is how their race saw them too. These crows were part of the priest hood, but more akin to slaves. A thin black choker blended in with their feathers. Another mosoleth, maybe. The priest was a thing of beauty. Majesty incarnate, an owl-esk breed. He was clothed in robes of unimaginable wealth. For all I knew of the Breathing Church, this could have been any level of their leadership.

I jerked my head around the lake of prostrate bodies. I couldn't make out anyone who may be armed. Either this wasn't an important leader of the church, or even their guards were not exempt from participation in prayers. Seemed foolish and, in fact, was very foolish for this instance alone. Give a name like Triurgoath, you'd think there would be a third verity of bird too. Wait...there they were. Two large ones with blood-dyed feathers around their necks. They were also in prayer. A man with more malice than myself to the church would have a fun harvest.

I took one more look at Kyda and the two crows. Taking out a small bottle from under my jacket, I knelt down to the massive owl-thing's beak. I uncorked the bottle and held it up to the bird's nostril.

I replaced the bottle and made to leave the congregation. I may have stepped on a foot or two on my way out.

"What was it that you did?"

The question caught me off guard and I tripped over someone's leg. I had just almost made it through.

I turned my head slowly. I hadn't noticed anyone watching while I did my deed, but I was sure this boy saw everything. I flushed at the thought of him reporting me.

When I looked the boy over, an odd thought flittered across my mind. *Discount Conarance.* The boy wore fine clothes but it was plain enough, no one guided him on how to properly wear the them. Each piece was all too large. The buttons of his jacket were fed through the improper eyelets making him look lopsided. A comb had been run through his coal hair, but no product had been added to keep it in place.

"That was some sort of prank, wasn't it?" His smile spoke of grief, like he'd been asked to grow up too fast. This 'prank' delighted him.

"Uh, yes?"

"Yes?"

"I mean, I suppose you could qualify it as a prank." I wanted to turn this around, but I wasn't exactly familiar with the concept of pranks.

I came in close, debating if I was going to have to kill this boy or not. I called him boy, but the closer I got, the more apparent it became he was a young man and my senior.

I gave him the bottle, and he held it up to a standing torch placed there for the ceremony, where he examined the contents.

"It's empty," he said.

I shook my head. "It's bacteria. If you leave the cap on that bottle on long enough, it will begin to brown ever so slightly." He handed it back to me, losing interest for lack of understanding. "They are little invisible life forms like you or I, and I just released the vast majority of their population into that thing's nasal-cav...its nose."

His face scrunched in growing disgust. "So, it kills them?"

Do I look that monstrous? Well, there may have been a slight reach for a different vial before selecting this one, I admitted to myself. I removed my mask carefully.

"No, it just makes them sick." He visibly relaxed. "A normal immune system–" I observed his glazed eyes. "Sorry. A normal body will fight off the bacteria for about a week, at which point it will spread. They won't die. It will be little more than spewing out both ends for a few agonizing days."

He looked at me, then at the owl. He burst out with laughter, presumably imagining its moment of shame. A few deep inhales later and an agonizing moment when I thought he may wake the dead along with those who are praying, the young man calmed down.

"That...is hilarious." But he wasn't done. His laughter shifted slowly into sobbing.

He did all that he could to play it off and when the boy turned back to me, he was all smiles.

"My apologies." He wiped his nose on a cloth produced from a pocket after catching himself halfway to wiping with his sleeve. "I'm a little...flustered this evening."

"No need."

"Say, would you like to join me?"

"I'm actually–" That little tug. Always trust your gut. Lessons from my father. "Sure. Where are we to?"

"I'm to meet a woman." He started off. It was then I realized what livery he was clad in.

His outfit spoke well above peasant but not quite to nobleman status. He wore the sort of outfit one would to court; the colors brought to mind the bitter roses that surrounded the city.

"You're not going to inquire further about the woman?" He continued on, trying to fill the silence that had fallen on us.

"Didn't figure I needed to. You're helping me out by giving me something to do."

"Ha. I know that's not true."

"Oh?"

"You are a man of science, yes? Hard to believe any one of you would be lacking in questions—" He stopped abruptly and held his caliber cape in hand. "It's not noble born, no, but my family wasn't considered close to noble until recently. It is true we may be so very soon." Apparently, I had been eyeing his outfit rather obviously.

I stood still for a moment. "No, I imagine an extremely hard-to-create wine would not obtain you such a status."

"We do okay. The wine has been a blessing for our family and it is the most popular in all Orecul but, as you say, the challenges we face keep us from mass production. It keeps our quality, in my opinion."

We entered the city's cathedral as respectfully as possible. His decision, not mine. I wanted to respect my host. I closed the door behind us to keep the disturbance as minimal as possible. I had to rush to catch up, not realizing he hadn't slowed his gate.

"What are we doing here?" In the emptiness, my voice echoed back. I felt almost ashamed my voice, though a whisper, came back loud.

We had come into the main worship hall of the town's Breathing Church. Ald'Kair's lion head regarded us crowned in a wicked twist of thorns. Apparently, the city was given more to his tyrant manifestation.

"We are here to see the scarred woman. I told you," he whispered back. Somehow, his voice did not echo back at us so harshly.

"Right..." She's not Ceth, I reminded myself.

Either I resisted accepting this because Tari was the one who told me, or it just seemed too outlandish. I've never heard of an essence-scarred church member. Stories I've been told of essence scarring have more or less only been related to the great essence wielders of the Ceth Isles.

These islands were said to float above the Kaguel Straight to the East Coast and were inaccessible to anyone other than those who were masters of essence. Scarring wasn't a requirement but was a common enough side effect of their craft. A member of the Breathing Church possessing those scares was somehow—unsettling. I wondered how the Ceth would receive that?

We left the main worshipping hall and headed to the back of the cathedral. Lord Mwin led me the whole way, obviously familiar with the building. We started to hear voices closer to the larger set of doors at the end of the hall.

We entered them and my heart sank.

"And here he is!" Tari said, all ecstatic to see me.

I had forgotten I sent him to see the woman.

The room was smaller than the worship area but somehow felt all the more important. There to the left, were Tari and the scarred woman sitting at a table together. To the right was a massive quartz hung by the absolute least needed gold wire to support its weight. Any extra weight added to the structure and the thing would fall and crush...a woman. This one was prostrate on the ground beneath the quartz but not in prayer. She was unconscious.

Tari met the young lord and I halfway. "I was just regaling Miss Ul'tay of the wonders you've conducted in Yalor. The prowess of your skills and talents."

"Deacon Ul'tay," she interjected, approaching us.

Tari tensed, but it was Ul'tay who had been rigid. Something was uneasy in her. It wasn't until I took another step into the room that I discovered she was tense because of me.

"Deacon Ul'tay, be at ease. He is harmless," Young Mwin assured her. She bowed her acquiescence. She didn't want me in this chamber, but Mwin was law here. He looked at me quizzically. "Wonders?"

"Yes!" Tari was excited to boast on my behalf? "Bringer here has solved all of Yalor's biggest problems through sciences. It seems as though he pulls the solutions out of thin air. I've read books relating to his craft. Nothing he has done seems to be proper. Yet, Yalor's woods are re-growing without disease, the Coliseum District are the best warriors Orecul has to offer, and he's improved the entire city in various ways. He has even managed to rid our citizens of near all bodily plights."

Mwin glanced my way, disbelief and confusion written on him. Apparently, my behavior thus far in his presence did little to convince him I was anything too important. I gave him a mirrored look back, even if it didn't quite fit my face the same way it did his, and fixed my mask back into position. I know he's trying to take the mantle of lord serious now, but I was sure he knew everyone had heard the stories of the Mwin son who seemed as though he would never grow up. He got the picture and it was his turn to bow to me.

"This is not why we are here and is unimportant. Bringer will do right by my father," Mwin said. I locked my jaw, grateful he had been looking Tari's way. "Deacon Ul'tay, I would like to know exactly what you are doing here. You've sought fit to bring a saint here, of all things. This speaks of great church importance; however, there has yet to be any treatment of the holy nature to my father."

Ul'tay appeared to note the arrogance Mwin was emitting, but something gentle in her must have let it be. I think she and I both understood what this was. Mwin was forcing himself to wear a face and bravado unnatural to himself. He was trying to be the man his father had always wanted and his people needed. But the boy who always needed to be told what to do and enjoyed pranks was far from gone.

"Truth be told, Lord Mwin, I was sent on a holy mission."

"Oh?" He crossed his arms, attempting a tough demeanor with his displeasure.

"Yes, Lord Mwin." She bowed. "Your father is not long for this world. We wish to join your city and its future. Not to profit from it." I scoffed. She held me in a regard that put Estry to shame. Something about those stained eyes and scarring made her a monster, a beautiful monster of majesty or an angel come to save the souls of her own volition. "Because money is not everything. Is it, Bringer?" The way she said it. The way she stared. This woman of the church knew more about me than I could make out, and it scared the hell out of me.

Mercifully, Mwin interjected. "So that's why the saint is here." He turned and started for the woman lying beneath the large quartz. I started to follow, nervous. I couldn't tell you why.

He stopped what seemed to me as a respectable distance. I and Tari joined him on either side. Mwin bowed but did not speak to the woman. Tari followed suit. I examined her like a project bound to explode.

"To speak to a saint, is to speak directly to Nybe, Bringer," Ul'tay instructed from behind. Mentally, my first reaction was to go on the attack, but when I turned to her, it was obvious; she wasn't expecting me to do as the others. She was playing as a tutor, not an enforcer. When it was apparent to her I had calmed myself, she continued. "The Breathing Church has no written scripture. We rely on saints to commune with Nybe and deacons such as myself to interpret and carry the message to the people."

"Why does she lay here?" I asked.

"This woman gave herself freely to become a saint. Her ability to walk and see among her many sacrifices. The crystal above is using her as a focal point. This allows us to collect the white essence Father Glechin has been requesting from the citizens outside. It is a technology akin to infusion."

"In—what?" I asked.

She held a hand to her neckline.

It took me a moment to understand. Then I flushed. She knew. She knew about Reaver. Would I need to kill her and everyone here to stop this unraveling?

"Deacon Ul'tay, I don't understand." Mwin sounded shaky.

"You will. But now, we've run out of time." She raised a hand to stop him from asking the obvious questions to come. "I believe Bringer will have the answers you need." She turned and started away. "The Writ doesn't have much further to travel."

Tari and Mwin both jerked their heads my way. "Writ?" they asked. Both with a fresh fear rising.

"They want me dead? Why?" Mwin asked, facing his own mortality for the first time.

"Shhh," I hissed. The prayers in the city had reached their conclusion. We hid inside a storehouse down the road from the square and watched the tide of citizens depart through the window. The empire was...well, the empire. They could have any number of spies hidden amongst the people. Sure, the Writ Executioner was a form of legal murder that would arrive regardless, but I wanted to catch the damn thing off guard.

I peered out the window, motioning Mwin to stay quiet. Nothing looked too far from normal. It wasn't that late in the day, but the people looked exhausted. I had it in mind that this was the conclusion of collecting their essence. Citizens should be back to their normal activity soon and the visitors must be on their way. The city should go back to what it should have been upon our arrival.

"How often does this happen here?" I asked.

"Once a month. I don't think I want them back though, after speaking with that...scary woman. If it's not for my father—"

"Good. Starting tomorrow, have the guards arrest anyone they don't recognize."

"Why the hell should I do that? We are a trade hub, you know?"

"Outriders and spies. We have to keep their information network at bay for a time at least. You can't shut down the city

either. May as well start smoke signaling the Writ if you do." I
sighed. "And yes, they want you pretty dead," I said.

"How do you know this, Bringer?" Tari was trying to decide
whether it was more important for him to feel deceived or afraid.

"The pangolin is one."

"Grenlic!"

"SHHH, you twit," I hissed. "You can say nothing, Tari. You
understand me? If word gets out—there's too much at stake. If this
thing knows we know it's coming, it may well kill all of us and
anyone else it has a suspicion about."

Tari sulked then. He slid down the wall on his back and sat
there. Tari had been so sure of how things would go. Now, it was
all out of his control. He was probably considering the light this
would cast him in. There was a good chance Conarance had been
mentoring him for this position. He had high ambitions and the
thought of disappointing anyone in Yalor; he was afraid of being
cast out.

Confident we would go unnoticed, I sat down too.

"I need to get to Kyda. Then we should all go into the fields," I
said.

Mwin looked down at me, still leaning on the door frame.
"What is this, Bringer? What are we doing here?" I stared back at
him, finding my mouth dry. He shook his head. "They want me
dead. The empire of all things. How did I screw this up so bad?"

"The empire does as it sees fit," Tari rubbed his head as he
spoke, messing up that perfect hair of his. "You don't have to be a
screw-up at all for them to do the same."

"Your father is very sick. The mine your family has been
constructing is said to be one of the richest in the fief, maybe the
continent with this response. Your family and their wine made you
wealthy already. This vein could put you in competition with the
empire's nobles."

"That is why all of these people have come? They know nothing
of the empire's intent but to gain my father's favor?"

"To procure as much of your father's wealth as possible before
his passing." I stared at the floor.

"Who would benefit the most if you and your father were to be
out of the picture?" Tari offered.

The young Lord Mwin thought for a moment longer before speaking. "That is why you are here..."

Tari shot a look my way. I supposed, in lies, he wasn't as light on his tongue as any other time.

Tari wasn't going to lie in time to save face, so I offered the truth. "Yes, but no. I used your foretold wealth to convince Hydel to let me come." I grabbed my pauldron. "I may be a slave, but do not mistake that for loyalty. Grenlic, Kyda, and myself have different intentions for being here."

Mwin glared at Tari for a moment, who couldn't break his flabbergasted expression from me.

"Which are?" Mwin prompted.

"Not your money, if that's what you're worried about."

His gaze drifted into the city beyond the window. "I should face him. I should go and see the Writ Executioner...right?" He spoke to no one in particular. I let him continue. "I'm the reason he's coming. If he comes here, he will hurt anyone he must to get to me. He'll destroy large portions of the city."

"A Writ is a trained killer with armor that enhances his abilities. You will die without a chance." I stood up and made to the door. "We'll do it. I just need to look at your roses while there's a bit of spare time. Just don't do anything stupid until it gets here."

"How? He'd kill you too."

"The same reason I know all this off-hand. The big ass Olenous we have, he was the one sent to kill you before."

"Before?!"

## Bitterness

I stared at the bitter rose and she held me in much the same regard. I knew her secret but could not recall it, and the flower was none too willing to remind me.

When preparing a rose for wine, plucking the petals will suffice. The roses were willing to give a few for the sake of being cared for. Most try to take more when creating such a delicacy, but with the bitter rose, it will cost you. Obsidian glass thorns grow from every stem to stave off those who are too greedy. It is said this is the same glass that spires around the Ark-Life Kiln where the titan Ecyila touched the world, and just as sharp.

She allowed me one petal. Just one. I had the distinct feeling it would cost me to gather anymore. This a favor as I was not her caretaker.

When I scryed it, the petal went up in black and red, much like the petal itself. It wasn't common for plants to have more than one essence shown in a scry. Black too, was extremely rare. The usual love plants have at being alive and their inherent connection with Celn, gave them over to greens and yellows, never blacks. Even to alchemists, the rose was warning to stay away.

The sigils burned into the air in front of me. No weakness to fire was a surprise. In fact, it seemed that it would thrive in such conditions. Most of the sigils I didn't recognize, just as they had been from the Wohe sands. A second warning. But there was one I did recognize. A sigil I've never seen coming from plant life, only in animals and beasts, a desire for blood.

I sighed. "What? I'm quite busy." The sigils dissipated, but I didn't take my eyes off my work. The hooded figure had been watching me for too long and he was beginning to bug me.

He approached smoothly. He wasn't moving to attack, but I kept Reaver at the forefront of my mind.

"No need for your friend. I am no threat to you," he said, taking his place behind me but at a respectable distance.

I shot my eyes in his direction but didn't turn. "Do all your people invade minds or just you?"

"Only a few of us, Lord Bringer."

The formality earned my attention and I faced him. The cloak he wore reminded me of the scarred woman back in the city, but darker. This was concerning. Ram horns came out the sides of the hood and he wore a skull mask like my own.

"I'm flattered, but I don't believe I'm worthy of emulation just yet."

He laughed. "As much as it would please me to tell you we emulate you—" He removed his hood and pulled the skull mask away by the eye sockets, "it is our mutual Lady we allude to."

It hit me then. Abomination. What did she want with me now? My body stiffened and I watched his eyes closely.

Removing his mask revealed not a man, but the face of a goat. I had been right to compare him to the scarred lady too; this goat was covered in black scarring in much the same way. Alchemy said nothing about essence scarring. The only thing I knew was that they signified that the person in question was an extremely powerful essence wielder. I was cross with myself for sending Grenlic and the others on various tasks in preparation for the Writ's arrival. I had come to the vineyard alone.

He placed his mask into his flipped-back hood for safekeeping and then bowed deeply at the waist. "My name is Lich-Fex. I am a high-ranking leader in the devotion known as Undergrowth. I am here for you."

"To take me away?" I gave my back to him. The bitter rose, though coy, was plainly jealous of my lack of attention. Her flowers curled up in protest. "Maybe another time, sorry. Far too busy today."

He shook his head and clasped his hands behind his back. "The Abomination, our lady, sends her love and congratulations on your mastery over her gift."

I stopped any other thoughts. This was real. This Hyrocim knew everything. There could be no fabrication.

I used to think that devotions were just glorified clubs. Of late, it has become apparent that it was an inadequate thought process. These were powerful organizations with one single-minded objective, doctrine, or purpose. They were ideals given corporeal form. The Breathing Church was among the most influential I had seen. I had never heard of Undergrowth, and understood that to be likely the point, given the name.

I carved perfectly geometrical shapes into the dirt around the rose bush. With them, and a bit of essence, I pulsated a small vibration into the plant. I used vibrations not to loosen the dirt beneath her but rather an attempt to massage some good graces. I have heard very little about how to handle a bitter rose aside from how dangerous they were. I knew it to be a great product for alchemy, but I had no idea how to harvest one. The gentle approach just seemed to piss her off more.

The goat bore no sigil and I wondered if his was more akin to Writ Executioners' devotion. Unknown and unannounced until the need arises.

"Tell The Abomination I decline her praise. I do this for myself and no one else. Anyone else to benefit is no more than a byproduct."

"Which is the very reason she sends her praise. Every step you take is to her wonder. Oshoku is that of change. You are the...bringer of change."

"What does Undergrowth want with me, Lich?"

He waved his hand as if to dismiss the thought. "You misunderstand me, Bringer. I am not here to take from you. I'm here with a proposition. You wouldn't happen to have a little time to chat, would you?"

I gazed longingly at the bitter rose. I couldn't shake the feeling that it was the final key to everything. As though, maybe if I could harvest it properly without dying, I would finally understand myself. I would know what it was I really wanted.

"Sure."

He smiled a genuine smile and waved his hand. The ground inhaled nearby and small spires of blackened wood sprouted up. Before too long, the wood had twisted and gnarled into two chairs complete with wrought iron supports and crest rail.

"The misconception of The Abomination, as with The Heart, is how evil they must be." He sat in the chair to the left and gestured for me to join him. "Nothing is further from the truth. The titans are titans because they held mantles, not necessarily power. The Heart mantle in recent times, if you can call it that, has been more or less ignoring its duty by those who possess it. Though a titan no longer possesses the mantle of The Heart, the responsibility remains. The Abomination has always remained true and constant in these regards. She is resented because she is the lady of change, for time is her mantle. As much as it is needed for life, change is never a welcome comrade. You, dear Bringer, have attracted her attention." He stroked his goat beard almost as though forming the thoughts on the spot. This was common knowledge to him and he was trying to simplify it for me. "I am both a loyal servant to our lady and the ambassador for Undergrowth. We want to help you use your gift from Oshoku, as our purview is to facilitate her mantle. We want you to join our devotion."

I stared at his devilish eyes for a long moment. "I understand how natural our alliance may seem, but I'm not apt to take another master any time soon." He nodded but said nothing. A man to listen to the whole thought before responding. "I am not even sure what your purpose is, nothing about your people, who or what Undergrowth wants."

"I assumed you'd never ask. Nothing." That raised an eyebrow. "Well, nothing definitive. We simply serve in whichever way our lady desires. Oshoku informed me that there was no way you would suffer another's whims. However,..." He magicked a black pipe into his hand and took a long drag. The smoke dissipated into the air differently than smoke normally would. It seemed almost heavier, perhaps liquid, in a sense. "I've been authorized as ambassador to dissolve Undergrowth, temporarily or otherwise, in order for us to serve in a better compacity. Maybe she'll be your lady too at the end of things, but we can weed that garden when the season is right."

The clock tower bell tolled in my ear, a distant memory, but shook me to my core. I almost felt like I was about to make a deal with a devil, but I was fairly certain one version of hell or another would be my soul's destination regardless.

It was then that Kyda decided to come stumbling out of the woodwork. She looked my way but made no comment. Just a smile. She turned her attention to the bitter rose field before us, taking note that I had not one flower in my possession. She reached for one. She did stuff like that. Little things that, from an outside perspective, seem trivial but are sweet and subtle in their own way.

It dawned on me then.

"No!" I screamed and ran after her.

Before I could reach her, she snatched her hand back with a sharp intake of breath. Her pretty fingers were all still in place and I muttered a silent prayer to whom it may concern.

"That hurt!" She held her bloody hand in the other and I tried to pry her fingers open to get a better look.

The wound was deep, but she would keep the use of her fingers.

I wrapped her hand with cloth from inside my satchel. "You can't just grab at the rose bushes here." She winced when I pulled the cloth tight. "We'll need to get that fixed up better in town."

"Lich..."

"What?" Kyda looked in the same direction as I was, but there was no goat man to speak of.

"Never mind. Let's go. Your hand is bleeding pretty bad..." I stopped short. There at my feet lay a full, lively flower from one of the bushes. Kyda's blood still appeared bright and full of life on its petals.

"Couldn't we take it up by the root then if it's so dangerous?" Kyda asked, ignoring my request.

"The roots are worse." I circled around the bush, careful of her neighbors as only a man can when all he ever desired is before him, but it was denied him still. The flower slipped into my bag smoothly.

"Bringer?" She sunk into herself.

"Hm?" It was getting dark and I was beginning to think I'd need to come back the next day. I also couldn't never mind the Writ.

I pitched the ridge of my nose. I felt like time was slowly becoming my next enemy. I had so much I wanted to accomplish and this journey would soon be over. We'd either all be dead, or

Tari would drag me back to Yalor to face a creative and life-disrupting punishment. I put my skull mask back on and searched over each shoulder for the goat.

"You're still blighted...aren't you?"

The question caught me so off guard I forgot what I had opened my mouth to say to her.

I made to speak again. She held up a hand. "Before you tell that lie on the tip of your tongue, you should know, when Tari used the pauldron's abilities against you, your skin crawled into other colors. You became blotchy in spots all over your body. All black. It was as if you were losing control over something internal. I don't think the others realized." She looked at me then. "But I did. It was the same color your skin was when the disease was in your blood."

"Who else have you told?"

Behind her, I could see Alcillis in its demonic form posing to strike. I moved her to the side out of its reach.

Her eyes started to well up. "So, it's true?"

"Kyda, who?" I snapped at her.

"N...No one."

I relaxed visibly and wrapped my fingers around my wrist. I squeezed hard and let go. The skin I had placed pressure on was as black as the grave and slowly gave way to my natural blue. She gasped, clasping both hands over her mouth.

"I am stained, Kyda. No longer with the blight, just stained." I produced a vial from under my vest. "I have to take one of these pills every day to keep my normal color. You know they never would've believed I was cured unless there was something different externally. Humans have a hard time processing or excepting anything they cannot discern with their very own eyes. How else was I to convince them to let me live?"

She studied my eyes. Truth be told, I never found out how my eyes looked midstride in a lie, but I did my best in the moment. She visibly relaxed and I forced myself to do the same. She didn't trust me anymore and the slightest change in me would send her down any number of paths. I wondered what she had planned to do with the information after she confronted me, but I couldn't ask.

She didn't trust me. That stung more than I could fathom. I wasn't sure how much longer Kyda and I could be acquainted.

Because that's all it was, wasn't it? Acquainted. She didn't love me like I did her. She wanted a human suitor. She wanted a human salvation in the church. No matter how much I loved her, none of that would matter. As much as we like to fool ourselves and believe that 'love conquers all,' it is a line created by a hysterical man. Maybe he was too afraid to lose the love he had when they found out how much they hated each other. The line survived. But she probably ended up with another. He probably murdered them both in a dark alley one night, still spouting 'love conquers all' as he crested her bleeding caved-in skull. It doesn't. Love is fickle. Love is weak. Love is...hope.

My mother's love had probably gotten her killed. My father's love...well, that's why were there, wasn't it?

Kyda offered me a bag, and my heart sank.

"I thought you may need these," she said coldly.

I took the bag and the stones clattered together within. Inside, I knew there were three of the things. Small yellow-orange stones of alchemic creation. A recipe I left out of the books Yalor forced me to write. I didn't have to ask if she looked inside the bag.

"Philosopher Stones," I told her unprompted.

Her eyes widened. There was no need to read the *Soul Apothecary* to be familiar with the stories. They were a great work all alchemists strived to create, and here I was with three in hand.

"What are you planning on doing, Bringer?"

Grenlic didn't take his eyes off her as he approached. Even I almost missed the tremors of his steps.

"It is time," he said, saving me from having to answer.

I stepped around Kyda to go with him. "Keep an eye on the bitter rose for me, Kyda. Don't touch her again. She is in a world that loves her not. She will give us her sweet side in wines and treats but will kill those who become too familiar."

I left her there without looking back, too afraid of what I might see.

"I know."

We had been walking so long without so much as a cough, I wasn't of mind to understand.

"What?" I asked. Then, I stopped in my tracks as the implications became more apparent. He stopped shortly thereafter and held me in his regard, daring me to lie. "How long?"

"Since the day I came to arrest you in that carriage."

"But..." I scrunched my eyebrows. "But that was when I first revealed I was cured."

"Yes, but you were a nasty mix of far too confident and too nervous. I didn't know right away, but I watched you. Something wasn't right. Your behavior was inconsistent. Your finding the cure felt too perfect. I thought maybe it was true at first. The way you breathed with that deathly look in your eye, as though you may have to execute anyone to protect your secret... I knew. Father Feirtney got lucky that day, I think."

"Why didn't you tell them? The safety of the city is your charge, is it not?"

He turned his whole body toward me then, crossing his arms. "I wanted to see what you would do. And here we are."

"Yes...here we are. What now?"

He smiled. "You think I'm about to betray you now? In case you haven't noticed, Bringer, I follow you. Since that day, have I not? Besides, Yalor is my true master as much as it is yours. I was never a man for guardsmen duty. I am a killer." He paused. "Just like you."

"Follow me? I am a child to you. You are a century's worth of experience. What am I but a lizard in the path of your life? You are a Writ. How can I live up to such grandeur?"

"Children can make a larger difference than most men if given the right tools and enough time. Men are too set in their ways. Their minds are solidified, unchanging. Hard found to new ideas. Potential spent. You have had nothing but grandeur in your heart since you came to the belfry soaked to the bone with corruptions and blood."

I hesitated. After a long moment, all of which I couldn't look him in the eye, I threw up my hood.

"You knew," I said.

He grunted. "I cannot say I agree wholeheartedly, but I've seen a lot of this world, Bringer. Nothing changes for the better when a man is comfortable. It takes something...jarring to wake people up.

Yours is not the pretty path for the world, but it may be exactly what they need."

I felt tears well up and I gave myself some time to greet the first stars of the night. Astrology means nothing to me. People think the heavens care enough about our lives to tell us what our future holds. But I saw a constellation, the only one that somewhat resonated with me, The Ender.

"I'm going to kill so many people, Grenlic. Is that something your resolve can withstand?"

## Execution

"Stupid idiot boy!" I cursed under my breath as much as I could manage without giving us away. "He's going to screw this up completely."

"He's taking a chance to change." Grenlic didn't fool me. He was cool, but I knew he was just as anxious. Protecting that boy was, after all, the whole reason he had come.

Grenlic didn't waste time cursing like myself. Instead, he strung his weapon, the piece of well-crafted wood reinforced with metal. It was the biggest bow I had ever seen.

The muscles in Grenlic's arms bunched up hard as he attempted to string it. The bow bowed so slightly at first that I thought if Grenlic pushed any harder, it would throw him into the air and we'd never see him again. One more show of the earth-like strength the pangolin had in his body and the bow was strung. When he pulled it away, it left a large crack in the rock he used to support his effort.

Tari and I had to close our jaws manually.

"What do you fire off from that," Tari asked. "Spears?"

As though on cue, Grenlic pulled out a handful of spears specially designed for the bow out from behind a bush.

I turned my attention back to Mwin, shaking myself from the spectacular. "How did he know where we were intercepting the Writ?"

Tari hesitated. "That was my doing, I think." I shot him a look. "No! I didn't mean to. I told him a direction or something, I don't know. He knows this area better than we do. He likes to play the fool, but he's not dumb."

*Yet you make the same mistake with me?* I almost blurted out. There would be plenty of time to shame Tari later.

Things grew quiet then. I watched Mwin for a time and Grenlic's attention was somewhere far away. I wasn't sure what else to do. We had to ambush the Writ and I wasn't sure if there was any other way to do so now rather than using Mwin as bait. Maybe if I just went for it and got down there, Grenlic could remain undetected.

"Remember, Bringer, we are here to save that boy. Don't get caught up in imagined grandeurs." Grenlic knew I was about to go before I had.

I shoved my pride down. He was right. I swallowed. "You think we'll be here for a while?"

"Not as long as you'd like, I'm sure." He pointed to a pillar of clouds behind the trees. "If you've got any ideas, I suggest you get about them."

I took a breath, grabbed a handful of Tari's tunic, and bolted.

"Don't hit the boy, Grenlic. I'm certain there wouldn't be anything remaining to bring to his father," I shout-whispered as we disappeared into the brush.

"Bring...Bringer, what the hell?" Tari encountered every branch and brush as I pulled him along. He spat out a mouth full of leaves when he was able to shake my grip. "Bringer, stop!"

I turned back and stomped toward him. He didn't expect the fist, and it landed hard on his cheek.

"Shhh!" I hissed to his crumbled form.

He looked shocked. More than shocked, really. I don't think any slave had ever laid a hand on him in his life.

"Okay Tari, fine. We lied." He looked up at me, his hand twitching toward the ring. "We didn't come here to cure a man."

"You never tried?"

"I examined him and I was going to do something, but he stood no chance."

"But...then why did we come?"

I pointed a stark figure toward Mwin. "We came to save him. We came to stop the Writ. And if you don't get off your arse and come with me to fulfill this duty, then you are staying here. I don't have time to make you understand everything."

He glared at me for a moment and steeled himself. He shook the leaves from his trousers and we moved quickly to a closer vantage point to Mwin. We dove underneath some brush.

"What in the world is that?" Tari looked as though he could be shaking, but the tremors that preceded the Writ made it difficult to tell. "Smoke?"

The trees fell at a distance as the smoke stack seemed to push them aside. I watched the devastation closely.

"It's steam, not smoke," I said.

"What? Some kind of emyon of steam?" Tari didn't take his own suggestion seriously.

I shook my head. "It uses steam?"

Tari thought for a moment. "In Yalor, the Engineering District is always covered in steam..."

"It is, isn't it." I slumped.

To his credit, Mwin watched the giant approach and did not move. I couldn't tell if his knees were weak in all that armor, but his shoulders were resolved. He was prepared to die.

I wondered about his reasoning. Was he wanting to die or merely willing to risk death? He must know there was no way for him to survive. Did he think he could come out a hero here and the town would embrace him anew? I found I worried for him for more than my usual self-interests...however, those come first.

We waited a while longer in anticipation. There was no telling how long. Every moment, the dread grew. The tremors grew until there was nothing else in the world. Finally, they stopped. Everything stopped. I wished this meant the threat was gone now, but I knew this wasn't true.

I moved to get a better view, crawling under the brush, cursing each small noise from my wings catching. That soon was no longer a concern. Nothing was. My purposes, Mwin, Tari; nothing mattered.

The steam cleared slowly, counted in heartbeats. The Writ stood still before Mwin and didn't move. It was as though it were analyzing him. It was just as Tari and I were anticipating, but far worse. The Writ was a large frame of mechanical parts. It made the being who wore the armor extremely large compared to their base size. I called it armor; I wasn't sure what else to call it. The size wasn't what caught my attention though. The Writ…was an Alerez.

I stood up from the brush, limbs weak all of a sudden. I no longer cared to stay hidden. The Writ did not look my way. Instead, little panels of its anatomy popped open and the Writ vented a mass cloud of steam as though it were exhaling after a long run. I approached with no purpose other than to keep my eyes on it as the clouds grew.

"You don't scare me, monster," Mwin's lie came obvious and shaky. "I've come to face you…away from my people. You will not harm them to get to me. You realize this, don't you? I am he who you seek. There are no pretenses here. Stay away from my people and we will resolve this here and now. Ask not how I know this. I just do." He drew his sword and hunkered down behind his shield. "Just you and I now. No others involved."

It was then the Writ noticed me, his horned face shifting my way.

Mwin startled. "Bringer, I—"

"It was you, wasn't it," I started. "You, the empire's dog. With your help, they entered the glacier. How else? We knew no one could get to us…unless an Alerez showed them how." I started clapping. "Bravo, m'lord. It almost worked. Turns out, humans are greedy and they made a quick florin off me. They didn't kill us all. I'm sure I wasn't the only survivor. I imagine Alerez women could make plenty of freaks happy." I stepped closer, boiling with anticipated violence. "Why'd you do it? What did they really want? Skjarn? My mother's secrets? What? For the life of me, I can't figure it out."

I stopped to catch my breath and realized I couldn't think of what else to say. This Alerez betrayed his people; that much was plain and simple. But he didn't know me. Truth be told, I wasn't even certain the whole glacier had been attacked. It could have just been my village and stopped there. The Writ could be guilty of nothing more than dual loyalties.

He watched me. I didn't move. I bore into the windows upon his visor, demanding an answer. None came.

We moved all three at once. The Writ threw an arm back, grabbing the hilt of the weapon on his back. Mwin backed off and took his stance. Reaver uncoiled onto the ground and I jumped back, knowing my combat limitations.

The Writ pulled from his back a long hilt at the end of a large metal block, grasped the hilt with both hands and twisted. Something clinked and the weapon whirred. The metal block blew out steam and gears turned. Metal unfolded and unfolded again until a large sword was formed. He one-handed the blade and it created whirls in the surrounding steam. With a motion faster than expected, the Writ swung down on Mwin.

Mwin lurched out of the way, losing his footing but just making it far enough before the sword slammed into the ground. Steam and earth flew everywhere with the force of the attack. Mwin was lifted away and slammed into the ground. The limpness of him told me I was on my own.

A dull roar rose. At first, I thought the Writ was moving again despite how impossible that would seem. Suddenly, a large spear blew through the steam. The cloud swirled the spear as the pressure upon approach shoved it all aside. The spear slammed into the ground at the foot of the Writ. The following explosion of earth rivaled that of the Writ's weapon.

I shielded myself against the flying rocks. When I looked up, the Writ was watching the trees through the gaping hole of his steam shroud. He knew precisely where the massive arrow came from based on the angle of the metal protruding from the ground. The Writ's pause worried me. Did he know that another Writ had shot at him?

I used the distraction to my advantage. I flung my arm and Reaver's spear-tipped chain thudded into a tree past the Writ. I pulled and Reaver flexed like a muscle retracting. I was pulled through the air toward the Writ and snapped Reaver's claws down in my other hand. As I reared back to strike the Writ's head, a metal-cased hand snatched out and grabbed the bladed chain. One hard yank, and my arm popped out of its socket and I was flung into a tree.

On the ground, I clenched my side, cursing myself. I should have attacked a different way. I had opened myself up to that. Any normal opponent I could probably have bested, but not a lifelong trained killer.

The Writ approached and hefted his massive sword in both hands as if to execute me.

"What is it with you Writs and your oversized weapons?" I managed to wheeze out, still on my knees.

The Writ stopped at that, looked at the giant arrow and then back into the tree line where it had come from. As if on cue, a throng of thick strings sounded.

I moved and bit my cheek against the pain. I wrapped the end of Reaver's chain around the Writ's ankle. Then I rounded a tree and dug the chain's blades into the thick trunk and pulled as hard as I could with my one good arm. I braced against the soon-to-come forces. Another dull roar intensified as the arrow bulled its way through the branches.

The Writ jerked to move out of the path of the projectile and the chain's blades bit harder into the trunk. There was a loud crack and the tree was forever disfigured, but it held. The Writ didn't miss a beat. As soon as it was apparent he couldn't move in time, he threw his blade onto his shoulder at an angle. The arrow slammed into the sword and ricocheted. The impact shifted the entire Writ partially into the ground and its metals groaned. The spear hit a tree and practically vaporized it at the point of impact.

I took a note from the Writ and moved myself. I let go of Reaver and pulled two large bottles from my coat with my good hand. Reaver finished retracting and I ran. Flanking the Writ opposite its weapon, I threw the first bottle. The liquid coated the machine's side. I held a hand toward the liquid. The Writ ignited and the explosion threw him to one knee. I was thrown back and hit the ground. I still found it in me to thank Resin for helping me create the last of my essence jars.

The Writ stood up straight, calmer than was comfortable. He skewered his sword into the ground and pat the flames away as though it were trivial.

I just stood there after that, watching him scraping off some soot. It gave me a moment to think just how fucked we were. There was barely a dent behind the faint black mark I had left on him.

Grenlic and I could have planned this better with the time we had. I hadn't known about the Writ's armor and Grenlic didn't know I was armed. Well, maybe he did. Either way, we didn't go about this well. I should've prepared alchemy for non-organic material or at least heavily armored foes. I was useless in this fight.

I thought about Grenlic's approach. He wouldn't have brought that weapon of his unless he was confident he could do something with it against this monster. I hoped this wasn't a suicide mission for him. He may well have purchased us all passage along the same trip. Maybe he couldn't beat the Writ and knew he couldn't, but this was his last-ditch effort at redemption. Seeing the warrior sent by the empire now, I didn't think anything could take him out. Even if I had the power to, there was no way for me to operate. I think I had just broken some ribs and the other pains were getting harder to ignore.

I regarded the craters made by Grenlic's arrows. We had nothing else. Grenlic had one last shot, and that single spear was all the hope we had. Grenlic had missed each and I wasn't confident that a third try's charm would smile upon us.

"Conarance, what are you doing?" A shout from Tari, cowering somewhere in the bushes.

I appreciated Tari for cheering me on, but I didn't think—Wait, Conarance?

I jumped back as hard as I could and prepared Reaver's claw not knowing where he might come from. Funny how a man who smiles gave me more motivation to save my own life than a massive trained killer. Still, the lunge was too much. I couldn't force myself to ignore the pain. Instead of landing on my feet, I crumpled.

A quick branch-snapping sound came from the side and I shielded myself from him, knowing I would be the source of his ire. The beating never came.

I looked up and couldn't find him. That is until my eyes met the original threat. There was no carriage. No man with a round hat upon his head. Just Conarance, the smile more sickly pleasure than it had ever been.

The blade of the Writ's weapon quivered a foot from where I lay. I rolled out of the way to get a better view. Conarance held the Writ's fist which wielded the weapon at bay. Conarance had saved my life. The metal armor gave a yawn at the effort.

Conarance shot a glance my way and then threw the Writ's blade to the side and charged. This seemed to wake the Writ out of his shock and as soon as his blade hit the ground, it quickly bounced off. Conarance hit the Writ in the chest and hugged the machine. The Writ's attack, again at me, was much slower and I simply ducked down, but still made to place as much distance between us as I could.

To my continual surprise, Conarance held the Writ at bay. Metallic joints protested and steam began leaking from crevasses in its chassis.

I didn't waste any more time being the slack jaw fool.

"Grenlic," I screamed. "Kill them both! Shoot, damn you. Shoot."

A moment later the throng came, the arrow wrecked through the canopy, and it slammed into Conarance's back. Shrapnel blew out the other side of the Writ in a screech of metal.

The Writ fell like a building cut from its supports, crushing down loud and stiff. Once he fell completely, I ran into the dust, careless to wait for Grenlic.

I climbed the suit of armor, over a skewered Conarance. I got up to the helm and tugged at it as hard as my broken ribs would allow. It was quickly apparent this wouldn't go anywhere. I walked back, placed a foot on Conarance's back, and pulled the spear out, having to support it against my body as I pulled it with my single arm. It wasn't easy and took too long to do. When it finally came loose, Conarance flopped over the edge in an odd wet sound.

I slammed the pointy end down, damaged as it was, not to kill but to get into the shell. I pried. The Writ tried to shoo me away, but the attempts were weak. The armor must've been malfunctioning.

"I know you're in there," I screamed, dodging another oversized palm. I sweated and groaned at the effort. "Prove me wrong, you bastard."

Suddenly, the Writ stopped trying. Its arms slammed down to the ground on either side of him. The helm released steam and was now loose. I threw the spear aside, pissed. I hadn't even been prying the proper area.

I yanked the helm aside, carful to move it off along his horns as I've done many times before. The steam cleared.

I knelt beside him, defeated. I couldn't keep the tears from flowing and I didn't care who saw. After I reached for my bad arm, I scoffed.

"I know I made a mistake. I did what you taught me not to do. My mind told me this new weapon was the only one I had. And I left myself open. Not a mistake I will repeat, father."

He smiled up at me, head aloft. Keeping his neck straight was too much of an effort. Blood poured down one cheek from his mouth.

He inhaled with effort. "See, I almost got you because of it." A wheeze. "You corrected yourself well. But we both know you weren't armed for this fight. Consider more intelligence gathering next time."

"You should too. You did the same, I think. This metal bin you came in, your tactics suffered. It seems like the Writs come in believing they are immortals. A god leaving a wake of destruction as they make their way to their mark." I looked down at his wound.

"It's pretty bad, huh." He groaned. A statement rather than a question.

I nodded. "I don't have much time to beat the answers out of you, do I?" He said nothing. "This isn't fair, you know," I said. "It isn't fair that I can't take all this anger you gave me out on you. The divines should have granted me retribution."

Something caught my attention in the corner of my eye and I looked away from my father's wounds. To my chagrin, Conarance was trying to pull himself off the ground. Something crawled up my spine and I sought anything nearby to wield.

"Bringer, don't!" Tari made his way around the Writ's heap and helped Conarance. "He still—" It was his turn to feel fear. He jumped back and crawled away.

"What is it, Tari?"

"Som...something's wrong."

Something truly *was* wrong. Conarance stopped trying to get up once I came into view. One eye focused on me like I was the only thing in the world; the other eye flailed about, focusing on me, his wound, Tari, and sought retreat. That wasn't the part that intrigued me, though it merited further observation. Conarance's wounds were already closing. It was slow, but a faintly purple, pearlescent, chitinous flesh was crawling from the open flesh to meet in the middle to close up the wound.

Grenlic came into the clearing with Mwin leaning on his side. "Are you alright, Mwin?" I asked.

He nodded and took in the area. "Is it over then?"

"Unless they send another," I said without thinking.

His eyes grew. "Another? We barely survived this one. My father and his men can't deal with these Writs showing up like plagues."

Conarance didn't object to my investigations, so I lifted his shirt to get a better look at the wound. I stopped midway through the examination. There was no way to feel safe around Conarance, no matter how docile he seemed. The hand I had subconsciously used to keep one of his arms at bay, suddenly beckoned full consciousness.

Conarance's skin was gritty, as though covered in dirt or sand but something wasn't quite right about that either. I had to strain against the failing light and disbelief. It wasn't obvious how the sands of Wohe could have found purchase in his flesh.

"What about your father?" I asked, half listening.

"My father?" Mwin carried himself down to his knees. "Will he help Yalor now and will Yalor help us? I can't keep doing this. I am no warrior. Maybe I should write a letter to the Emperor announcing my allegiance?"

"I wouldn't recommend it," I said. "They've already labeled you an enemy."

"Bringer, I need to think of my father's people." He looked to Grenlic. "I am forever grateful. I can't thank you enough, but I can't expect you to be here."

Tari smiled. "I could try to get Grenlic here added to the manifest of the first citizens sent. Mistress Hydel will be most excited when she here's what Bringer and Grenlic accomplished here."

"What about Bringer?" Mwin asked.

Tari hesitated. "Bringer is too important for Yalor at the moment. The empire and many nobles will be visiting shortly and it's Bringer's job to sell Yalor to them."

Mwin stood up quickly. "So, you are allied with the empire?"

"Hydel will not appreciate what we have done here," Grenlic said. "We have made enemies of Yalor's most desirable prospect. If the empire finds out about this, they will lay siege to Yalor rather than finance it."

Tari looked divided in himself. I don't think he had made the connection until then. He thought we were doing good here but didn't realize 'good' had nothing to do with it. There was no 'good' nor 'bad' side here.

"Never," I cut into the silence. "Mwin, its time you know the truth of the matter. We, save Tari, are allied with no one. Grenlic had a wrong to right and he has done what he set out to do. I myself, I have no such goal. I helped Grenlic because the end result would favor me. Nothing more. I tricked Mistress Hydel to send me here. She thinks we are here obtaining support from you and your father, but it's really for me. Your father has nothing to do with it. You, you are all that matters." Tari looked defeated and betrayed, but said nothing.

"What are you saying, Bringer?" Mwin was becoming exhausted.

"I am saying, your father has left this mortal plane. He passed away soon after we arrived. You are lord of these lands, and this," I gestured to the Writ, "is now in the past. Yalor will send you slaves to work the mines. The income will come quickly once things are underway. Higher competent men. Make sure you have a personal guard who can take out a Writ if necessary. Ally yourself with the scarred woman. You'll need as much power as you can obtain as long as wealth still matters."

Grenlic left Mwin's side, leaving him in his stupor. The former Writ approached my father and looked down at him, sword in hand. He raised the sword in both hands.

"Not this one, Grenlic. We'll leave my father for just a moment longer." He paused and sheathed his sword without another question.

"Father?" Tari and Mwin spoke together.

I rubbed the bridge of my nose. "This is quite the mess, huh?"

"Your father is the Writ Executioner, Bringer?" Mwin asked.

"Purely coincidental, I assure you. Nothing short of divine comedy."

Mwin hesitated. "What will you do?"

"I won't save him, if that's what you are asking. Blood means nothing to me. Not anymore." I stood up from Conarance and came to Mwin's side. "If you ask for the grand scheme of things, I'll show you. Conarance," I demanded.

Both of Conarance's eyes shot to me with anticipation, one eye full of admiration, the other caked in fear.

"Stand up," I said. "I want you to stand if it kills you. Stand because it is my will."

His arms shook as he brought himself up to a sitting position. "Y...yes," all bubbles and pain. He groaned like an old man with a hip dislocation but stood all the same.

"Con...Conarance?" Tari's concern was rising to a level beyond what he could take.

"Look...Lord Mwin." I stood behind him, grabbing one of his shoulders. "Conarance here is an ass who deserved to die more than anyone I know. Practically run through with a spear to the chest and here he stands. From now on, Grenlic and myself are your only friends." I forced him to face me. "Truth be told, this whole ordeal, helping Grenlic is a byproduct. I did this because now you are going to help me. You are now a tool in my hand. When I find out what kind of tool you are, I will send for you and you will do as I ask. If not, the empire will send another. And next time we won't come. Grenlic has redeemed himself. There's nothing else to bring us back."

Mwin stood there, dumb, but ultimately nodded.

From the corner of my eye, I saw Tari lean toward the ring on his hand, but Grenlic quickly grabbed his arm and took it from him. The following punch lay Tari out. I never wanted to be on the receiving end of those boulders Grenlic called fists. I was certain some of that aggression was meant for my father.

I came back to my father's side. He had coughed more blood, this time with bubbles and a clear fluid.

"Leave us," I said. "Go back to the tree line. I'll be about shortly."

Grenlic dragged an unconscious Tari by the arm and shoved Mwin into moving himself. Conarance was already paces before them, disappearing into the underbrush.

My father barely held on to the mortal plain now. His head became increasingly difficult to hold in a comfortable position.

"They made you a slave?" he asked.

I nodded. "After they invaded, they killed that trench hatchling you said I should stop hanging around. I only learned later that these mercenaries acted against the annex orders given. It was much later that I pieced together that you were the one who helped them accomplish the annexation."

He said nothing. It took effort to see he was still breathing. Reaver's bracelet flipped into its blade position. I looked deep into my father's eyes.

"I said I wouldn't save you," I said.

"Rymkin..." I hesitated. "That was to be the name your mother and I chose for you."

I stood there. I couldn't process it for a long moment, nor could I hold back the tears despite the aggression written on my face.

"That name...that name is nothing. That hatchling does not exist. They named me Bringer. Did you know that? No, I suppose not. You probably didn't know I was alive until just now. I was named right, though. I resented the name for a long time. As it turns out, it was perfect, but only half right. You don't know this father, but your son has become rather twisted since you've been gone. I've been looking for a thing; undefined until just now when that hollow of a man ran up and tackled you. You see, hell came and held my hand one night a few years back. I took it as a curse. I've been hiding the curse for some time now. But now, it can be nothing more than a gift. I never thought to research my blood for more than a cure. I've been doing it all wrong. I can't make up for lost time, but I can damn sure see to it that none more is wasted. I won't save you, father, but you will not die. You get to watch your dear son grow up to be the man you can be proud of." I used Reaver to slice my palm. Blood flowed freely from my hand into my father's wound and a large distant bell tolled in my ears. "Today, we learn together what the name 'Bringer' really means. I shall bring forth a blight."

"Lich," I shouted into the bitter rose field. "Fex, where the feck are you?"

"Conarance?" Kyda looked as if ready to jump out of her own skin.

"Never mind him, Kyda. Take Lord Mwin back home and help him into his vestments. He will need to address the people soon."

Mwin, still holding his side, made as to leave. "Will you be along, Bringer?"

"I will. I just need a moment with the others."

"Where's Tari?" Kyda wanted to know.

"He's that heap Grenlic is towing around. He's been hurt pretty bad. Mwin and yourself cannot carry him. Better have the villagers bring a litter for him."

"What about Grenlic?"

"I need Grenlic here."

"But...why?"

"Kyda, the longer you waste everyone's time, the more likely it is that he'll bleed out. Then who is to blame?" I started to shout. "We all just fought a fecking monster, so how about you show some initiative, get the Lord here home in one piece, and get Tari some damn help, or is pulling your weight around here too much to ask? While you were spending your days here finding the gods, we have been busting our hides. For once, do something of value."

She shrank into herself and looked on the verge of tears, but she did as she was told.

As Kyda and Mwin made their distance, I felt heat in my ears. "Fex," I demanded. "I know you are here."

"I am." Lich-Fex grew out of the shadows near the forest in the shade of the trees as though the sun's failing light would harm him. "I just felt as though those two weren't part of your...trusted people."

I turned, the skull mask on my face feeling as though it were melding with my person as I spoke. "Tell your people that Undergrowth no longer exists. You are a part of my devotion now."

He clapped his hands together. "Excellent. Oshoku will be most pleased."

"Grenlic, set him here." I gestured next to the biggest bitter rose bush I could find, the one I had been studying before.

Grenlic set him down with a thud. The others seemed to be picking up well who I cared would be handled gingerly and who I minded not.

"Wake up, damn it." I slapped Tari hard. He dozily came to, but it wasn't fast enough for my taste, so I slapped him again.

He jerked awake then. "Wha—" I punched him in the gut, knocking the wind from him. He tried to curl up against the sudden pain, but I picked him up by the collar, forcing him to kneel at my face level.

Holding him up by the collar of his shirt, I punched him again, this time in the face. "You nearly ruined everything, you know that? You humans took everything from me. Then I finally find something in this world to help me be content—" I head-butted him, horns sending teeth flying. "And you took her away too. But now I got you." He was crying, pissing himself, and trying to hold me at bay, but I held him close, screaming. "No, no, you can't take from me anymore. Never again."

Tari realized his ring was missing, so he searched for another way out. "Conarance—dear Conarance, I am your student. You've guided me. I can be that advisor you believed I could be. I can help Yalor be what she is supposed to be. You've said before how dangerous Bringer is. Help me, please!"

Conarance did not move. He looked my way and realized I would not respond. That single eye wept alone.

"Grenlic, you were one of our most trusted citizens!" Tari pleaded. "How can you let this happen?"

"I was a slave, Tari." Grenlic said no more, eyebrows set.

Tari sagged in my hands.

"I wish you had time to understand that, Tari." I shoved him then, right into the bitter rose.

I blew some chilled air onto my knuckles to ease their pain and walked off.

"What shall we be calling ourselves, Lord Bringer?" Fex had to shout over the screams and wet tearing sounds.

I didn't answer him right away. I could barely hear him with Tari's agony in the air and the bell's toll shaking my bones. But I sat in my own mind, waiting for my prize to have its fill so that I could collect it without harm to myself. I whispered then to myself as the world grew silent once again, "Clock Tower." I touched the rose flower then. She didn't cut me, *she*... was satisfied.

## 18

### Eye for an Eye

There was simply no way I could go to Kytgro one more time before we returned to Yalor. As terrified as I was to see him again, I wanted a word with that odd smith. I had to watch the city disappear behind the trees and imagine what I would have said. My father answered a number of questions, but more formed in their place. These, I could not quench. I had forced myself to not think of home as long as I could manage. Each time my mind had wondered, the pain chased me away. It was a method we slaves of Yalor shared. Even those who still had hope in their hearts kept such considerations far from their minds. In Yalor, there was no hope of being free one day. Even if you retired as a slave, you never left. Yalor was a lie that you eventually lived entirely, your old could-be life forgotten. I wasn't sure I could go back to that line of thinking. I had forgotten home as much as one could. The Writ broke down the wall I had built to protect myself. Now, I hungered in an unhealthy manner about what could have been. I wanted it more than ever. It was difficult to toe that line between my old life and the new one. I had had a taste only to discover I had been starving for years. I had no qualms about what I would do to satisfy it.

Kyda was in about the same mood during the ride back. She nor I said much. We had to leave Tari behind, or so I told her, and be on our way as fast as possible to Yalor. What we set in motion would require some damage control. It would not take long for word to get back to the empire that a Writ had been killed. It was one of those secrets you couldn't hope to keep to yourself. I had refused to give Kyda enough time to check on Tari. She knew something was about but couldn't quite figure it out. I was in a race against time for that too. Kyda was smart. She may not have a mind for alchemy, but there were plenty of brains behind that furrowed brow.

When we stopped to set up camp one night, she finally had enough of the silence. She snatched the box of provisions from my hands and apples rolled through the mud. This angered me more than the disrespect.

"Something on your mind?" I asked.

"We could have gotten him medical attention in Yalor, Bringer."

"He would have died. Tari was bleeding out. He saved us. Let him have his rest. There are plenty of skilled chirurgeons there for his father's sake. Tari will be just fine."

"They weren't able to help his father," she snapped and slapped my recovered apple further. Somewhere in the forming night, a bush ate it.

"Neither could I, Kyda." I walked off around the wheelhouse back to where the others were, to save me from losing my temper. I hoped that getting her away from the rest of the apples could save them from a similar fate as the first. She trudged on behind me. "We will send for him as soon as he is stable."

"Not good enough!" The others stopped what they were doing to watch. "Why did we have to leave so quickly? What happened to Tari, Bringer?"

I stopped then. Not only had she ruined some of my fruit, but her scene would make me look weak to the others. I cracked a hand across her face, knuckles leaving imprints on her cheek. Her eyes grew bigger with the forming tears.

"We were attacked. A damned Writ, Kyda. Tari saved us and was injured. We knew it would be there. Tari knew we knew. This is best anyway, until we can control the information."

"There. Wasn't that liberating? The truth finally comes out. Tari would have told on you and ruined your plans, so you left him behind."

"You're being impossible—"

"You're being deceitful. Bringer, you make it a habit of manipulating others. I'm not even sure you realize you are doing it sometimes. You just do. If you feel it serves you—"

"It was my father, alright!"

She faltered but quickly recovered. "No, you're a liar, Bringer. The worst I've ever kno—"

"It's true." I wasn't loud anymore, but the words still cut through somehow. I had exhausted all the rage with those words. I had killed my father. My eyes stung. "My father was the Writ Executioner. A dog of the empire. I'm almost certain he's the reason you humans were able to get to my village. But he's beyond answers now." Kyda's heat was gone now. The color slowly returned to her face save four red circles that would form bruises later. She was starting to sober up. "Tari got left behind because he would ruin everything. Yes, I manipulate. I control the outcomes. But have you ever wondered why I do these things? Because I get warm and fuzzy from my actions? Kyda, I do these things to save everyone. I'm going to free the slaves."

Kyda shot a glance toward Conarance, now suddenly afraid.

Conarance hadn't spoken since we left the village. His clothes had been completely tattered or worn down in the process of getting to us. Luckily, his money pouch was intact. He bought all new fitted clothes and cleaned himself up. When he peeled his boots off, I thought I saw bone on the sole of his foot. The interesting part, was he didn't make a face until he saw the damage. He painted on a face as though he were in pain, scripted. An afterthought that he should feel something.

When questioned, Conarance wasn't able to give the most basic answers. He would open his mouth full of his typical overbearing charisma, complete with full-bodied livery, and stopped. His face twisted and he closed his mouth.

"Why are you here, Conarance?" I tried again now since Kyda had given me a chance to think of something else.

Conarance straightened himself, the smile still cemented to his face as it ever was. It was still unsettling.

"I walked," he said without further explanation. Maybe he had had enough time to think it over.

I was irritated for a moment, but then I remembered my audience. Conarance wasn't right in the head. That much was plain.

"Why, not how. Why did you come to find us?"

The smile aged. He looked as tired as he should be after such a trip. "I...I don't know," he lied, apparently uneasy with the answer he found. It was a scary thing. Conarance was more human with his brain in a fog than at any other point. Realizing he had no definitive answer, he met my eyes.

Conarance looked like he had had a stroke. One eye wasn't right, wasn't symmetrical to the other. I leaned forward to examine him. The left eye was concentrated, sharp, and focused as though I were the only thing to had ever existed. The other eye was nothing but fear. It shot to and fro seeking asylum.

"Grenlic has Tari's ring. Conarance doesn't have his cane. We could just not go back." Perhaps I was rubbing off on Kyda to a degree.

I rubbed my face with both hands. "We have to go back. These pauldrons mark us slaves. Someone would notice and send us back to Yalor. It's futile. Hydel is building relations with the empire...maybe if we went to Synol?" I shook my head. I wanted to lay my head on her lap the way I had back when I fought back the blight within me. She had been so inviting before Tari showed up. Somehow, that thought hurt worse than the ones about my father.

"How are we supposed to do this, Bringer? With the philosopher stones somehow?"

The others stared. Holin and Bik exchanged looks.

There was no way to put that back in the bag. "I will break all the pauldrons at once. Each slave will become free in that moment." I had expected her to have some look of delight at that, but she had been around me long enough. She knew there would be more. "...with the first stone. With the second, bring down the entire city over the heads of anyone still inside."

Kyda kept an eye on Conarance as I spoke, nervous about being associated with such talk. Apparently the *we* didn't go far enough.

"Never mind him, Kyda. I'll show you." I had a hunch and I was ready to give it a go. "Conarance," I said. His head snapped up. I didn't look at him, but it sounded like his vertebrae were creaking. "Cut out that eye of yours—"

"Bringer!" She tried to stop me.

Conarance magicked a knife from his belt and transposed it above his face. "Which one, sir?"

I turned to him to have one more good look at the eye. The eye still brimming with fear. "The one with what's left of our dear old Conarance we knew and loved. The last living part of him."

The knife plunged. Kyda screamed.

## 19

## Rabid Rabbits

I was upset with myself, but nothing could be done about it. All the work I put into diseases, it never occurred to me to study the disease in my own blood. The damn thing followed me around like a plague, and I never thought to look inward. It could be I was too afraid to. I wasn't sure what I would find. To look death in the eye is something to take hesitation in.

I should have studied my blood, or the moth's if it would have let me. Thanks to Conarance, I could stave off the fear of looking at myself and focus on someone else. Inadvertently, I could study him to figure out what was happening with me.

Under the microscope and a few experimentations during the journey back, it occurred to me. The blight was something beyond my comprehension. I still should've studied the thing in my own blood but I would not be able to solve this puzzle without someone else I had directly infected. The blight was highly contagious. Yes, Conarance was beating me to a pulp when it happened, but arguably the infection itself was simple. After a comparison it was obvious that my blood was the strongest version of the blight. Conarance's was only slightly less potent but lacked a protein that mine possessed. His blood contained a cell that was in my own but also one I was missing. I watched his blood until it dried up, careful to do this only when I was alone.

I tried something while the others were in town for supplies. I trapped two rabbits. One I infected with my blood, the other with Conarance's. The rabbit with my blood was as intensive in watching and listening to me as Conarance himself. The one infected with Conarance's blood was similar after a few days. This one was more delayed in his responses but still looked to me rather than Conarance. It was obvious with the infection rate of the rabbits that the blight was becoming stronger. Conarance had been infected a long time ago and, as far as I could tell, only just recently showed signs. I wondered if anyone at court had noticed.

A group of salesmen stopped our wheelhouse on the road. They felt Conarance would be the best person to approach to peddle their wares. The rest of us were slaves after all. One man said something off handed about how miserable it must be for a human to travel with an inferior race such as myself and Grenlic. A comment I found distasteful. The rabbits broke through their cages hidden under the wheel house, as though them staying behind bars was a courtesy, and killed the men. I laughed too hard as they cut arteries left and right.

Grenlic said nothing and walked away as the men screamed. I think in his own quiet way, he approved. Where Leegius had been beaten down to the point of submission and could not fathom retaliating against humans in such a way, I was slowly learning Grenlic wanted chaos and destruction as much as myself. The empire had taken too much from him for simply wanting to not kill one child. He had seen worse of the empire than I had and grew tired of the corruption. He may have chosen a different way to change things, but I was what the gods had given him, and he wasn't about to say no, no matter how ugly the gift was.

Grenlic and I decided, or Grenlic decided, that the rabbits should stay behind. On a whim, I decided to do the same with Bik and Holin. I set them with the task of retrieving the "very unique" and "rare breeds" of rabbit before returning to Yalor.

The loss of my first true creations should have left a bitter taste in my mouth but my eyes turned to Yalor. The Coliseum was soon to open. All the empire would be there to view the wares and technologies Hydel's...citizens have been researching and creating.

It was curious at first that all would be displayed in the Coliseum. Where were her projects on agriculture, medical treatments, or improving the lives of Orecul's people. The answer was simple. There were none, or none as important. Yalor was a siege factory. Its purpose was war and nothing more. I later found out the perceived war was with keeping control of Orecul's people and the continent Synol at bay. Synol, as it turned out, paid us little to no mind. That's not to say they would not have been ready for our invasion but to them, we were less than worth indulging. This was another example that helped me rationalize my actions against the empire. They wanted war and control over others who just wanted to be left alone.

Conarance led us by chains into Hydel's throne room linked together by the cuffs. Jarce heralded him alone as was customary. You don't announce when the broom comes walking through. I'd at least play it a song, maybe.

Conarance, being back in his element, I was sure the smile wasn't forced. He may have been my pawn now, but he was still the bastard of a man I've come to know.

"Conarance, we've been looking for y..." Lord Eneric cut himself off. "What in blazes happen to your eye?" He stood alone in waiting for the mistress.

Conarance patted the area as though he forgot about it but quickly collected himself. Along with his extravagant clothes, we fitted him with a rather well matching eye-patch.

"Lord Eneric, you are far from the only warrior Mistress Hydel has under her employment." Conarance smirked. "Just because I enjoy the fancier things, doesn't mean I cannot handle a few ne'er-do-wells." He knuckled Eneric's considerably larger shoulder.

Mistress Hydel turned the corner from the hall to her personal apartments. She saw Conarance and rushed over to him.

"Is it...is it gone." She gingerly touched his cheek.

Conarance held her hand. "A worthy sacrifice for my mistress." He gave her the courtliest of bows.

I had never seen this side of them. Conarance was so hated and feared from the slaves, it was hard to consider he may be loved by others.

Conarance stood up straight. "We were attacked by a Writ Executioner in Mwinstead."

I told Conarance before we arrived that it was maybe best to give Yalor the truth, however massaged.

"A Writ!" Hydel held a hand to her chest. A practiced gesture, but I could see the worry on her face, even beneath the makeup.

Makeup? Heavy enough to remark upon. Today was important. Come to think of it, she was dressed rather more eloquently than normal, and she had always been eloquent. A long flowing dress, accompanied by plenty of jewelry, made her look more the queen than ever. I wondered then if the empire had a queen.

Eneric colored. "Where is the boy?" he asked.

The room grew silent as it hit Hydel and the weight settled on her. She looked to Conarance.

Conarance grayed and drew on a grim face.

"If it were not for his efforts, dear Lady, we would not have survived. And I would be lacking far more than just an eye."

"Conarance," Eneric asked the questions knowing Hydel could not shake this news easily. "Why the hell was a Writ involved?" He was concerned about the empire's reaction to having one of their elite of elite warriors killed by Yalor's people.

"This, we do not know. Their devotion rarely shares the objectives behind their actions, but they normally provide a pivotal role for the empire. Someone on high must have signed the writ."

Conarance turned and unhooked Grenlic from our chains and led him forward. I watched the whole way with a pit in my stomach. I couldn't say anything to stop what I knew would be next.

"Maybe ask Grenlic here what the Writ was doing there. He used to be one, you know."

Grenlic's face never changed but his shoulders visibly relaxed. I hadn't realized before. Grenlic had been hiding from the empire for so long. It must've been a relief for it to be out in the open. This must have done wonders for his soul, but I hesitated to think at what this would mean for his physical self.

Hydel jerked her head toward Grenlic. "What?"

"What are you getting at Conarance?" Eneric took a step forward. I wanted to see what he was capable of before the Coliseum event, but not here, not bound and defenseless. That sword of his put me on edge.

"It is true." Grenlic's voice came as earthy as always. Those few words left the throne room still.

Hydel shuttered.

"Take him—"

"No." Hydel cut Eneric off. She stood straight trying to be as intimidating to the boulder as she could. She came up to the bottom of his rib cage in those heels. It was comical if not for the weight her word held. "Take him to the Theater. We'll show our loyalty to the empire by making one of their traitors a spectacle."

And like that, we watched Grenlic being led away. To his credit, he never glanced back.

"Send riders to Kytgro." Lady Hydel seemed to have regained her composure and was back to the Lady we knew her to be. She sat regal and palpable in her presence. "I want to know everything that happened and most specifically why the Writ was there."

"Lady…" I winched as Conarance drew his hand back.

"Speak, Bringer." Lady Hydel cut off his motion and Conarance stepped aside.

"Lady, if I may be so bold, we must send Lord Mwin miners to solidify the deal and his support to Yalor."

Hydel nodded but thought for a moment seemingly about another subject. Men in the back of the throne room were already off to her whims when Father Feirtney came in. He hesitated when his eyes met mine, but like a professional, he pushed through it quickly.

"Oh," Conarance saw him and was instantly reminded. I wanted to trust he knew what he was doing but honestly, I wasn't sure. He had stabbed his eye out on my command but some deep-seated fear told me that had been him putting on a show. Conarance was a predictable man after you got past his smiles. With my influence, I couldn't tell what he was about anymore. "I'm afraid there is more bad news, Lady." Lady Hydel, fully back in command, merely tilted her head his way.

"The church was there in Mwinstead, apparently attempting to gain favor; nobles too. The Lord Mwin passed on under our care but Bringer was able to win the day. He alone won the young Lord's favor for Yalor."

Father Feirtney said nothing.

"Then Bringer," Eneric looked down on me favorably for the first time. "You have done a great service for the city."

Conarance slapped a hand to my back. "Hasn't he? I went to save them from screwing things up, but Bringer had it all under control." I tried to ignore Conarance had let a few hairs fall in front of his face without combing his fingers through, and hoped the others did the same.

"I will see to his compensation. Very good, Bringer. You have served this throne well. Please continue to do so. Estry still needs your assistance."

I bowed. "Mistress, I feel a dismissal coming, but I have one more thing." I gestured for Kyda to come forward. I cleared my throat and shook my shackles pointedly toward Conarance. He joyfully removed them from my wrist. Eneric cocked an eyebrow.

I took the potted plant Kyda held and approached the throne. "Is..is that a bitter rose?"

I nodded and held it to her. A part of me didn't want to stop her, but I quickly jerked it back from her seeking hand.

"Not wise, Mistress. She's beautiful, but not everyone can touch a bitter rose. She always takes something for the honor."

Hydel looked oddly bashful and reached for the pot itself this time. She gazed upon the flower, mesmerized. Speechless. I thought the plant itself would've been enough of a compensation to her for the loss of her dear Tari. I didn't tell her that she was practically holding part of him. The flowers had already been beautiful when I interacted with her before. Still, comparatively, she was now vibrant, gorgeous...sinful.

## 20

## False Idols

Estry's hearth was growing too cold for her liking by the time I brought in the logs. She sat in a rather large chair bundled in more blankets than would be necessary for others. Stress had its fingers wrapped around her wrists while she tried to sip her tea, a compilation of brothed leaves and roots. I didn't care for the stuff but it was effective. Her hands calmed a little more with each sip.

She smiled at me when I passed her, a thing of contempt and admiration mixed poorly.

"Why'd you have to come along, Bringer? You're so damn good at this. The tea itself..." she trailed off. "I think Mistress Hydel is beginning to rethink our deal."

I let her continue uninterrupted while I got the fire going again. "If this thing with the empire goes well, I could be freed. Finally." She looked off into a distant memory. "Free to go home to my people."

I couldn't see her with my back turned but I felt her looking at me. "And then you come along. Who'd you say? Your mother? Yes, she taught you. And then the gods damn me by bringing you here. Making me look like a fool." She sipped her tea. It may as well have been ale the way she was at it. "I'm not usually like this, Bringer. Sure, I'm a hard woman but I don't know why I've become so cruel."

With the fire well on its way back to life, I looked back at her. She was smiling to herself. Despite her crone features, it came across young. Like she was remembering who she was back then.

"It is okay to feel weak sometimes, Estry. Far too often it is considered, well, a weakness, but it is a display of how much you care about a thing. Maybe a chance to recover yourself before rallying and getting back to it. Refusing your moment of reflection is weakness."

"Hmm, weakness. Are you quite alright, Bringer?"

"I'm perfectly fine, why do you ask?"

"You look pale this evening." It felt odd, Estry asking about my health, the right piece of the wrong puzzle.

"Some humans blush when they consume alcohol. Alerez have a different reaction." I had no idea if this were true.

She gazed into the fire as it danced, solemn for a time.

"I've always found immolation to be my least desired way to go."

"Thoughts like stones cast into a pond tonight?"

She smiled. "I suppose. It's the waiting. Everything is in place for the most part. The waiting will be the end of me."

"It's better to focus when your mind wants to run around itself. Less likely to trip and fall onto something you don't expect."

"I'm open to suggestions." She sipped her tea.

"Hmm, we are on the subject of fears; there's a nasty bit of nature I found in a nearby wood. I examined more than a few colonies of ants. One in particular caught my attention. It was fully populated by the dead. These poor creatures walked around blind but somehow knowing where they were going."

She squinted at that. "You just described ants."

"Yes, but no. I opened a few up. Their organs were no longer functional. A new organism had wrapped itself in a lattice work around all their entrails. I examined others to verify this was consistent across the colony." I poured a drink. Something Estry had introduced me to. A potent brew of berries. Ale wasn't the right word, though that was new to me as well. Sipping the sweet brew, I returned to her side. "Delightful," I said letting the sip I had just taken roll down my throat. "I wonder if you could do the same with apples. It's the sugar, right? Sugar and something else that makes a beverage like this possible?"

"You can. Others have already done it." She gestured to the cupboard. "Devil's Gift."

I promptly handed her my glass and set off.

"I watched the progression of this fungus as it went on to infect other colonies nearby. It only seemed to affect ants, thankfully. But it affected them efficiently. The ants would go and invade territories in ones and twos. Never a full-on war."

I found the bottle in question. After uncorking and sniffing the contents, I thought how most of the funds in creating this drink were more concerned with the design of the bottle than the brew. Apples didn't come to mind when I smelled it. Rather, it was the pie Kyda had made me that came to mind. I placed the bottle back with a grumble and returned to Estry's side disappointed. She passed my glass back almost like she knew I would not have been pleased with the apple brew. Apparently, the story of the pie incident had been retold.

I continued as though I wasn't angry at the appalling way people treat apples.

"The specimen would be terminated by the other colonies as invaders, but some found their way to perches. They gripped whatever they could with their mandibles and died...fully died there. After a time, the fungus would then bust out the tops of their heads and spread the disease to the next host and infecting the nearby colony. Thus, completing its life cycle."

Estry thought for a moment about this. "Where did you say you found this?"

I shook my head. "Doesn't matter. The point is it exists. And the even greater point is to prove to you why I'm a better alchemist than you." I sipped the brew taking a long gulp, mustering up my courage. "You are a verdure essence wielder. Always have been. You don't care much more than what kind of veggies you could add to your spiritual garden. I look at everything as an ingredient and its possibilities. And then, through the gift of alchemy, make it mine. Never mind Oshoku. Never mind Undergrowth. I make things mine, to my end, to my will."

I had to stop myself. I hadn't realized just how heated Estry was making me just by being alive and I had just let slip important information. Perhaps I was getting too far into my cups.

"And you had the nerve to dub me Bringer. Pssft. Ingredient gathering indeed."

I went back to my drink.

"You never said anything about your fear with this discovery."

Estry had sunken into her chair a bit more but I think she was more lonely than hurt. She didn't want me to leave in a huff.

I sighed. "Some of the ants weren't actually dead though the fungus had usurped the ant's bodies."

"They were prisoners inside their own bodies," she said.

I nodded. We sat in silence then. She showed no change but the alcohol was taking its toll on me slowly. There's a fine line where intoxication could take you. This line, once you find yours, can make you feel brilliant or strong. You start to let go of notions of yourself and others that hold your potential back. Go a bit too far past this line and you are a weeping child or brutishly violent. But until then, you are a master of cognitive functions. Your creativity levels flourish. You feel like nothing and nobody can hold you back.

This is where I was. I slowed my consumption of the brew to prolong this effect and keep myself from offering up information. If I drank more, I wouldn't be able to hide my smile threatening to break the surface. Everything was just so perfect. It was only then that I remembered she was drinking tea, and that's why she showed no change. I smiled internally again. Maybe I had past my genius line after all.

"Maybe I should've joined the Ceth Isles," she said catching me off guard.

"Given your particular talents and your...brash nature," that earned me a smile, "you would've fit in just fine. I met a Ceth in Mwinstead. You two could've been fast friends. She claimed affiliation with the church but I'm not so sure."

"The only thing that would concern me is what happens to those people sometimes."

"Elemental recoil. Otherwise known as idolization."

She snapped her head toward me. "How the hell do you know that?"

"*Soul Apothecary.*" I shrugged. "Or another book I read. There have been many."

"You've really read such a book?" she asked.

"Oh yes," I stood up leaving the brew behind. "I've recreated it to the best of my knowledge. I published, what two now? If nothing else, Yalor will be remembered for changing how we look at alchemy."

She tried to let go of her glass to no avail. Panic took hold slower than I expected. It was sweeter than my drink.

I rubbed my head. "It has taken a lot of pain to get the memories back. My mother let me read it as part of my training and locked it away with some weird decoction of hers. I've noticed pain seems to unlock it bit by bit. I've gotten back the parts I wanted the most, but there's still so much more to be had." I dropped my hand as I realized something. "I think she knew what was coming to Korigara and wanted to prepare me...I'm not even sure if she made it out."

I walked over to Estry's desk with stinging eyes and started rifling through her drawers.

"They'll find you out, Bringer," Estry said wheezing some now.

"I doubt it. The bitter rose was a gift to Hydel. It is only a matter of time before she touches it despite my warnings. That would be enough. But I'm hoping for something...more spectacular."

I wanted to slap her for calling me Bringer, but I was certain she was suffering enough for my taste. She didn't get to say it, but I knew this would be a close second greatest fear.

"Gifts are a funny thing. As I'm sure you're aware by now, the tea of yours was a special blend of mine. I was almost too drunk to remember bringing it to you, as per my name."

I got irritated and started pulling out drawers to turn them out. Her research scattered the floor.

"Did you know," I continued lecturing her while kicking through her entire life's work. "We have a bacterium in our bodies at all times that is benign as long as our bodies can keep it at bay?"

I looked up at the back of her head while I was crouched down. Obviously, I couldn't see her face.

"Oh good, you don't know about this. Well, if pushed in the right direction it attacks the host and there's just about nothing the body can do to stop it. The host ends up dying a pretty gross death. The same can be said about essence wielding. It doesn't matter whether verdure, gelid, levin or otherwise. When you allow the affinity into your soul, your soul and the element have a nice dance. A dangerous one. Each graceful but both understanding the threat the other one possesses. Do you have a key or something?" The last drawer wasn't budging. I walked over to her and started going through her pockets. "With the right push, idolization begins and the element fuses with your soul and body. There are ways to accelerate the process..." I glanced at her eyes and then to her wooden arm.

"Oh!" I ripped off her necklace ignoring her pleading eyes. "A little cliché to keep a key around your neck but—" I threw my head back letting the last of the brew fill me and took the key back to the desk.

"I...I don't understand. Why?" Estry's voice came out raspy now.

"I brewed your tea, remember? Oh, you said why not how." I found a small hidden key hole and got the drawer open. I grabbed the stick of royal purple wax and seal.

I walked over to her and presented my find to her. "Just this." I pocketed them and her very confused eyes followed them. I shrugged and stood up straight. "I have a package to ship. Without your seal, they may check it. That wouldn't do."

Wood creaked as her flesh converted. The bark reached out from her cheek to encapsulate her eyes. They watered in hopelessness.

"I am sorry about this, Estry. You are a bitch of a woman for the name you gave me, but you don't quite deserve this."

"Then why, Br—," She stopped herself as though sparing my feelings would amount to my being able to save her.

"It's okay. It has grown on me. More of a title now though. I've made some adjustments to it. As to 'why'..." I put the lit, overly-filled lamp on her armrest next to her elbow and fractured the face with Reaver's bracelet. "...I want to kill everyone, and you are in my way. It's nothing personal. Oh." I pulled a book from my satchel. "This, your life's work. No one should play with creating life quite like this."

I tossed the book into the hearth. With a pat on her cheek, I left Estry to her fate.

I returned the next morning carrying supplies that would've been easily misconstrued for another 'Bringer' based errand. Even though I had taken Resin's position, it was still common for Estry to abuse the title. The Alchemy Division manor was a skeleton of what it was hours ago.

Hydro wielders poured water onto the smoldering rubble and managed rogue flames to prevent other buildings from igniting. Estry's bones had fallen from the floor above, where I left her. Her remains lay in the mid-floor's parlor still fused to the broken and burnt bits of chair. No flesh remained. A scatter of leaves and branches lay about her threatening to be uplifted by the breeze. Wood shards clung to the blackened bones like they've lived there all along. I picked up her skull as it glared at me with accusations.

The verdure had infected her well. There were wood-like traits forming in the skull's frame when she had died. I may have pushed the conversion too far. Normally, it is some time before an idol's bones change over. They were usually the last.

I lay her skull down and walked through the ruin that was once Estry. I smiled at a thought that came next. I had given Estry both her worse fears in one night.

The Alchemy Division headquarters was now in ruin. Thirteen total bodies were recovered from the ruins. The Yalorian alchemists were all but dead, save for me and a hand full of others.

I was the obvious candidate to run the Division now. Holin and Bik were still out looking for the rabbits, or dead. I didn't care which. I released any other so-called alchemist to whatever fate Yalor had in store for them. All it took was a simple claim of their incompetence or them getting in my way, and they were gone. Mistress Hydel trusted me completely and she wanted the Alchemy Division to sell Yalor to the empire. Nothing, including a few two-bit alchemists, could be allowed to screw that up. I sold my reasonings too easily. Hydel was becoming desperate with all the catastrophes and setbacks.

After clearing myself of any wrong doing, and being blessed with Estry's pauldron, I returned to my lonely wheelhouse in the charred woods where I met Oshoku. Avol lifted his head in greeting and I made sure he was fed. A large fish from my shopping run.

I knew he was there before I turned. The moth watched me as though he had just constituted himself out of thin air. I turned to greet him. We watched each other for a long time. It was then I couldn't hold it back anymore. My face cracked underneath the skull mask and I began to laugh. I laughed so hard and so brokenly that I began to sob.

I hadn't lied to her. Estry was so many bad things in my life, but I had liked her, at least a little. I was completely alone now. I was sure that I had driven Kyda off. Grenlic was being sold as amusement and fear propaganda. Leegius was destined to die at the colosseum via execution.

I knew what I was doing every day, but I couldn't stop myself. I wanted my mother's embrace, my father's pride in who I had become. But now they were both gone. I killed my own father.

I fell to my knees, unable to bear the weight any longer. I couldn't stop myself.

I prayed for the first time. I'd never before offered such a thing. Ald'Kair and his empty throne, did not respond.

## 21

## Broken Faith

I pat Avol on his flank as I passed. I was leaving him in the stables this time. He had served me well and I decided he deserved a break. It was going to be a long day anyway.

Before I untacked the two of them, I had Avol and Teket deliver the wheelhouse to the Coliseum. I had to walk back up to it now, but it was better than having to carry all the supplies myself.

"Keep them fed," I demanded of the stable hand.

I had grown accustomed to making demands with my new position rather than requests. Estry had had more power and sway than I thought. Maybe she was too focused on leaving Yalor to really throw her weight around. Me? It was just another tool.

The stable hand bowed and got to it. Brush in hand, he approached the first of them to clean him up. As I rounded the corner to leave, the boy expertly dodged Avol's beak. I wondered how long they would combat each other before they were temporary friends. Teket was calm and pleasant, but Avol would have this fight over and over again, even if he liked the stable hand.

My new pauldron was showier than I would have liked. I understand why Estry had kept it hidden away under those robes. Between the burnt patches on the metal pieces, it gleamed in the sun light. I was more worried about it taking away from my image than anything. It would be soon enough that we could be rid of them.

"Come, Kyda. I want to introduce you to a friend. You'll get along well. He hates me too."

Kyda scoffed but came along. I felt she only attended to me now because it was her position rather than any amount of enjoying my company.

I wondered, as we passed, what had become of the guard that let me in the last time we visited. The blue gem who guarded the post now let us through without resistance. She was stern-faced and dutiful in demeanor. Maybe the last guard happened upon a less than desirable fate for his failures and she wasn't a fan of following in his footsteps.

"Bringer," Kyda broke the silence a little ways past the portcullis. "I don't hate you."

She sounded hurt. I didn't wish to, but I believed her and I pushed the thought away. I was beginning to understand, she didn't stay for any sort of loyalty-driven reasons. Especially since our journey to Mwinstead, Kyda had found herself religion. I think she was already a devout follower but something got into her there. When she felt the energy and saw all those people offering themselves to the return of Ald'Kair, Kyda changed. Maybe she stayed in an attempt to save my soul.

I didn't have the heart to tell her that her efforts were in vain. Titans can clash but it wasn't a simple task to 'save' one soul from another. Oshoku owned me. I knew it. I simply misled the Yalor leadership because more people know and fear Disiea over Wohe.

I didn't respond to Kyda.

The sounds of gathering crowds started to prick our ears as we had our way in. These were the days of entertaining the early arrivals until the Emperor arrived.

Mild events. Organizing. Meeting dignitaries who are trying to win over better seating for their masters. Working to get everyone excited for the big crescendo to come.

We made our way through the stands until we were in the VIP section. I had a seat here now. A lead position in Yalor had enough perks to induce sloth and gluttony a plenty. When the show started, I would take my position near the left hand of Mistress Hydel. We would be well taken care of like the Emperor himself. Would I try to take his life since I would be so close? I wasn't sure.

* * *

The guard cast a light emitting emyon over my shoulder as he had before. This time, the guard was very attentive and conducted one too many bows. I unlatched the dungeon door and pushed it open.

The halls seemed darker this time around. I stopped and examined the light emyon feigning I could figure out if anything had been wrong. It looked like...a light. There was no other way for me to describe it. I caught Kyda looking at me with a fixed stair.

"It's a little hard to see," I shrugged.

"I thought, if any one, you would have a mundane source of light."

If I would ever envy anything, it would be how mundane my talent is. One could argue my use of alchemy was tapping into the magic of things, breaking down and reconstituting its essence, but I always hated how little flair there was to it. I could speak of my work for hours but most individuals would have to just take my word for it. There's no flair. If I threw a fire ball it would be nothing to get someone's attention. Unless I have a decoction to set someone on fire from the inside...now, there's an idea.

Kyda clenched a fist out toward me and squeezed her eyes shut. After a moment, she opened her hand and another light floated out. This one was smaller but brighter, stronger.

"How in the hell did you get to do that?" I asked.

We could see clearly now. The emyon she created seemed to push back the dark. It made me feel...exposed.

"It's something I learned recently. Father Feirtney—"

"You shouldn't." The words shot from a sealed mouth.

She seemed surprised and then quickly defensive.

"I mean," I tried again. "You shouldn't trust him, Kyda."

She snatched her hand away. I hadn't realized I had taken it.

"Who are you to say? I don't feel like I've been able to trust you for some time now," she said.

I bit my tongue at that. "I know." I hung my head. "Kyda, I know I haven't been forthright with you as of late. I promise there are reasons for that, but you have to trust me in this. Feirtney is a bad man. I don't hate religion, but there are plenty of men and women of the cloth that betray that position. He is one of them." I couldn't help pleading and she noticed. It made me sound weak and disingenuous.

Kyda walked away then. We kept our distance on the rest of the way down the dungeon path ways.

"Hello, Leegius," I broke the long silence as we approached his cell. I knew he was still there. His smelled more of horse than any other cell down here.

He appeared smaller than before somehow. As if he's been fading away, giving up. A toy left broken and forgotten.

I pulled a vial from a hip pouch.

"You haven't been eating, have you?"

There were no unwashed bowls in the cell with him. No discarded dining ware. The floor was dirty but lacked any scuffs. Leegius hadn't moved from that spot for some time, which meant he hadn't handed the bowls back to the guards. Were they starving him or was he telling them not to bother him?

Leegius didn't respond. I ignored him ignoring the question.

"Miss Kyda, allow me to introduce Leegius the..." I turned to him. "You never mentioned a title or surname, did you?"

I sat in the dirt, crossing my legs and arms.

He didn't respond again. Was the grunt from before my imagination?

Leegius kept his back straight but wasn't leaning on the wall. His eyes were closed. I leaned in against the bars and I thought I could make out a hum of some sort.

"Bringer," Kyda said.

"Hmm? What is it?"

"He's in a trance. He won't acknowledge you."

"A what?"

"It's part of their culture. Something about communion with the eternal heifer."

I looked at Leegius and then back at Kyda.

"You told me you didn't know anything about Materic."

"Bringer, you forget I'm a human. What do we call Materic?"

I hesitated and felt foolish. "Minotaur."

On cue, Leegius's eyes snapped open.

"Ah, gambler of lives."

"Leegius, you wound me. You know I only ever have the best of intentions for all the people of Orecul. Just trying to till the field a bit."

He looked over to Kyda. "Who's your friend?....hostage?"

"You've been getting into your own head, Leegius. I don't do hostages. This is Kyda, my walking, talking, conscience. Now, if you'll be so kind, you've interrupted her attempt to get me to do the right thing. Kyda, you were saying something about the Materic."

She looked uncomfortable now. She looked at Leegius apologetically.

"Materic is not a term we know. I had no idea what you were talking about. We call them min...minotaur."

We both were watching Leegius as though he could reach out and twist our heads off.

He didn't react.

I furrowed my brow underneath my skull mask. What gave her the leeway to say it? Then I thought about our last meeting.

"What of it, Kyda? Speak plainly. He won't do anything, apparently."

She glanced Leegius's way. "This Materic isn't starving. He's fasting. For quite some time, it would seem."

"Why?" I asked Leegius.

He blinked.

"Why?" I asked Kyda this time.

She shrugged. "My books said it has to do with one preparing to break an oath. Though, I am unsure. Begging the eternal heifer for permission or even forgiveness in the acts to come."

"Is this true?" I watched Leegius's eyes but there was no need, he nodded. "Tell me."

"You were right, Bringer. You were and I hate it. The humans aren't going to let me have the life I wanted. I'll never get to see my children's faces again."

"Children?"

"I have to take my fate into my own hands. Which means..." Leegius held the ruby around his neck up to his face. "They haven't checked on me in some time now. I think they want to leave me forgotten until the tournament starts or I starve and they can retrieve the ruby without any problems. Maybe I am to be a sacrifice or practice dummy."

"It's the sacrifice part," I said plainly. They looked at me as though it were too blunt. "What? I have access to the schedule now."

Leegius smirked. "Even so, the ruby is nearly free. I can hear him again."

I hesitated. I didn't want Leegius to be like me. Sure, I wanted him to beggar the whole of the world, but I wanted him to keep his honor. Leegius needed to be more aggressive to the world if he were to save his own life, but I didn't want another me.

"It's very pretty," Kyda said, surprising me.

"I am not too sure if pretty is the description I would assign to him." Leegius released the gem from his withered hand and it fell like a hammer, slamming with all the weight of the world onto his chest.

We followed his finger, afraid all of a sudden. Chills ran up my spine like a predator breathed down my neck. I musted myself and whipped my head around. There, in the dark corner of the hallway, there was nothing but the shadows staring back at us.

Kyda acted as though she could see more than myself. My fear had simmered like when you know something is wrong, but the evidence isn't convincing enough. However, Kyda looked on the verge of shrieking.

"What...what in the hells is that?"

I had never heard Kyda use such language. Her stark finger pointed to the corner in question.

"What do you see?" I asked, incredulous.

"You can't see it?"

"Pretend I can't. Tell me what you see."

"It's...it's, I don't know. It's horrifying." Kyda shrank back.

"What's his name, Leegius?" I didn't turn away from the corner with the shadows when I asked.

"Ah, yours has a name?" He asked. "If he has a name, he has not told me. What he is called though, as I've told you before, is Shields of the Mountain War. He's a bol'ruka though. Two, in fact. I think that those who named him, did not have a word for this."

"Yours?" Kyda shot to me.

Ashamed, I held up my wrist. Reaver stared back at her through a red gem.

"You're telling me that both of these are mosoleth?" Her fury echoed down the corridor. "You can't have weapons here!"

Leegius used a finger to wrench his ear back to working order.

For once, I didn't measure my answers with her. "Yes," I said plainly. "Leegius is here only because he has that damn thing and it won't leave him be."

Leegius pulled at the thong around his neck to prove my point. We knew a small bit of leather wouldn't stop a Materic.

She glanced at me as though I were baring a knife, then began checking the corners of the area.

"You won't see Bringer's, Kyda," Leegius said softly. "His isn't strong enough to project. My friend is another story. Don't worry though...he only has eyes for me."

"How do you release him?" I asked. "He hasn't given you a name. Furthermore, where is the weapon?"

"Yours requires a name?"

I nodded.

Leegius shrugged. He usually comes forth when I lose myself in the bull spirit. If I lose focus on holding him back, he takes the opportunity."

"Then the Coliseum wall?" I asked.

He paused. Part pity, part pleading, mostly regret.

"Everyone," he said. "I wasn't going to leave anyone out."

Kyda looked confused and rigid. I think she understood but didn't want to.

I held out the vile in question past the cell bars. I know Leegius was a man of honor, but Leegius's honor was what made me afraid that this was a mistake. Maybe in that little vial, I was giving the world a chance to stop me. Leegius could've saved me and everyone else if he had just ripped my arm off then.

Leegius looked at the product in my hand, the one last hope to see his family. Then held me in his oh-so-personalized regard. The look he gave me said he knew exactly what I was thinking...and he considered it.

Leegius moved and I wasn't certain what he had chosen, but I stayed my arm. His body cracked while he moved and though he had lost a bit of weight, he was still a minotaur. He placed his hand over the vial, positioning his fingers over my wrist. We locked eyes then. *He* gave me a chance to state my case.

"Leegius, I promise, I am trying to do what is right." My eyes began to sting. "I don't want to kill. I just want to see my mother..."

I couldn't talk for a time. "I just want to get home, same as you. It seems stupid, even to me. There's a fish. That's right, a fish!" I was suddenly angry at no one. "We hatchlings, we go into the ocean underneath the ice. We learn to hunt this way. There was a fish down in the reef. I couldn't kill it and take it home to my family. This little purple thing. I made algae grow for him so that he would always have food. The other hatchling from the trenches I grew alongside...they killed her. She and I used to take care of this fish. No one is there to do it any longer." I smirked. "It's not like I have children, but it's something, right?"

I hadn't realized how much I missed that stupid fish until I said it. It had greeted me on my first trip to the reef, and we had made acquaintances every day since. It would come to check to see who was knocking at its door, and it always swirled when it recognized me.

Leegius watched me for a long time. He eventually took just the bottle with him. He nodded as his grip released from my hand. He was a natural killer. I believed that is why the shields haunted him and hungered for him. They were a stark reminder of who he really was once upon a time. His family and pursuit of happier times hadn't changed that. His sins, same as mine, would not leave him. Though I didn't want him to be like me, it didn't much matter as long as that part of him existed.

Kyda watched the exchange and said nothing for a while.

"You mean to release—" She pointed to the shadow in the corner, "that?"

"Not me, Kyda." I nodded to Leegius. "There are other stories than my own happening here. Leegius is his own, and he will decide what's best for his."

I stood up and made to leave but waited. Kyda wasn't budging.

"Why do you stay, Kyda?" I asked.

"Wha.." She was off guard, but she knew what I meant.

"Why do you still follow me around with this blatant disapproval all the time? It is beginning to beggar me off actually." I turned to her, all mask and none of who she knew before. I was all Blight, not Bringer. "I am going to tear the world in half and laugh as I do it, yet here you are trying to decide whether you can save my soul. I haven't heard one good explanation from you as to why I should consider the god you found in Mwinstead for all his glory. Ald'Kair is fallen, same as Nybe, and though you still contemplate in silence, your judgment could knock a priest on his ass. Your god is dead and I wear the mask of one of his adversaries, yet you stay. Why? Let us be honest with each other for the first and final time in our lives."

"I…" She started but hung her head in defeat. When I thought she would say no more, she finally broke. The sobbing almost made it impossible to hear everything. "I know you think you are lost, Bringer. I feel that way too sometimes. I'm a slave just as much as you, don't forget that! But there are good people out there. I know that's not something you'd like to hear and maybe you think me naive for believing it, but I've met them. I've touched their hands and the ground they walk on, Bringer. They exist! I want to show them to you. I want to prove to you that humans are a beautiful people. Throw a stone into a crowd and every person you'd hit is unique, diverse, and individual. Hopes and dreams and kindness infect each one of them, even those who are a little rougher on the outside. You saw how happy Mistress Hydel was when you gave her that flower. Even though she enslaved us, she is trying to save the world in her own way. She's using her vast wealth to come up with medicines, knowledge, and yes, war machines, but only to protect her people."

Kyda mastered herself, wiping her nose on that pretty white dress of hers, careless of nothing else but this moment. I knew she was right. She looked up at me defiantly as though giving me the next move.

I turned away and left her in the dark.

## 22

## Fiend

As each time before, the breeze beckoned. A love long since absent pleading for release. The mask, Blight's mask, lay propped on a column, letting me rest, however impatiently. I needed to be that nameless Alerez for a time. That young hatchling still capable of dreaming of taking to the sky. The gale spoke of the embrace as it whipped through the clock tower belfry. It and I believed I could take to the sky now. I was ready. It was time for me to earn the name that had never been given. I knew I wouldn't make it more than a hundred yards before one of the monitors would see me fall from grace. I thought about breaking the gem on my pauldron again. Since the blacksmith told me it was something that could be done, the thought came across my mind at least once a day, but the timing never felt right. Everything had to be perfect. My desire to be an Alerez, rather than the slave I was, directly placed all my other plans into conflict. There were more than a few times it occurred to me that I could get away. I could leave everyone here to their fates. But in my heart, I knew that even if I wanted to be selfish, the empire would still be something I could never get away from.

Last I heard, Korigara was still annexed. Their soldiers still patrolled and enforced my homeland's borders. It took the empire a long time to breach our borders thoroughly enough to occupy the lands. Now that they had, it would be even harder to get them out of there. What exactly this meant for my people or how my father had helped facilitate the annexation, I couldn't say. My return home would change little. I would need a damned army to change anything for the better. All my alchemic prowess would be nothing, especially in those frozen wastes.

The bell tolled for the onset of evening. Rymkin. I laughed to myself at the absurdity. One of the frost. That is what was to be my name, according to my father. It was a common enough name for an Alerez, but it felt wrong. Perhaps I had fallen so far from the expectations set before my life that the name just couldn't fit. Perhaps I had forgotten the frosts and their lessons. Blight-Bringer seemed the only name worthy of me now. Two halves broken but fitting to make my whole deplorable self.

"I was a slave once; did you know that?" A mask-less Fex sat with legs dangling, smoke lazily rising from his pipe. Funny that, there was plenty of wind.

"Were you?" I asked. I appreciated him removing his mask in solidarity.

"Not in the same sense of the word, I suppose." He took a long draft from his pipe and let the smoke curl around his face through his nose. He pulled at his beard like a lettered man. "My people use their own kind of rituals. The world scorns my kind for this, but it is not unfounded. Some don't partake, but that is neither here nor there." He waved himself off as though he caught himself trailing off. "Hyrocim children are often offered as sacrifice for these rituals. Though, it isn't a bad deal for a time. The village pampers you; you never go without. You are a king." Fex looked at me and I saw the small child he once was. "They never tell you the cost of being king. The lucky ones lose their lives. Others endure torturous sacrifices. Limbs cut away, no dulling of the senses. Organs harvested. A bit of gray matter taken, leaving you half-witted. The ones with the worst luck, lost parts of their soul."

"Modus Operandi?"

He nodded.

"What was it used for?"

"Does it matter?"

"I suppose not." I grabbed the mask by the eye sockets. "How do you envision the world to come?" Mask on, I was Blight again.

Fex stood up from the ledge, his bone mask on now as well. I was unsure of what creature it had belonged to. A flat face with hateful brows stared back at me. Two crude tusks curled, looking for flesh to rend.

"It will be black for a time, I think. But the land of Orecul will be given another chance. The other races that have been persecuted since the founding of the empire will have a chance to rise and reclaim lands that once belonged to them. The human empire will be brought down to the same level and then all can rise together. That is, if man is willing to share in that experience."

The winds still blew, but they no longer called me. I would call to it when the time came. Would I be able to put down the mask and find my way back to Korigara? Or was the mask the whole me now?

"What have you got for me, Lich? It is time we are on to business."

Lich-Fex summoned a small book to his hand in a burst of black-purple energy.

"The Clock Tower agents have discovered the pangolin is, in fact, in the Theater District Hippodrome. He is chained up for execution, slated for the midway ceremonies of the festival. It begins in five days' time." He flipped the page. "The Emperor arrives in the morning at the rate his caravan travels. They should stop in Pleit. It is the only settlement luxurious enough for such a party."

"Has the shipment arrived?" I said, pushing past the news.

Lich nodded. "Mwin delivered as promised. There is enough bitter rose wine to intoxicate the entire city. She's ecstatic, by the way. Your lady. It will take some will of the gods to keep her from tasting it before the time. She will be looking for you to thank you for earning Yalor such a boon. I don't believe the rest of Orecul will be able to appreciate the flavor of such a fine wine this season."

"See that you don't, Lich." I cut him a look.

"A pity." He looked off as though remembering a lost friend.

"That good, huh?"

"Better than woman flesh, my boy."

"I hope you mean that erotically."

He smiled and moved on. "Bit of news you won't appreciate, I'm afraid. Mwin has arrived in Yalor. I know this wasn't part of the plan, but he couldn't pass up Hydel's invitation. He is slated to become a noble after all."

"And she loves to rub elbows. I didn't think it would be necessary to tell him to stay away. They pulled the writ off of him?"

"It would appear so."

It occurred to me that my lack of knowledge of human politics was going to get a friend killed after we spent so much effort saving him.

"Is there any way to convince him to go home?"

"I'm afraid our options are limited in that regard. You guided him well, it would seem. He's a changed man from last year. His new advisor is the one to blame. It was he who convinced our nobel-to-be Mwin to come. This would solidify his safety from the empire and any further visits from the writs."

"I will go to him, I think."

"It will be difficult, Blight. He surrounds himself with livery and liverous people. You still appear a slave to these people; however, when you are Emperor—"

"I will not be Emperor," I said sternly. "I will not profit from this."

"But Oshoku—"

"Oshoku is our lady of change. Change is what I bring. But I will not replace one tyrant for another."

Fex frowned deeply at that. I had no idea he wanted me to take the throne so badly. Did he want to be my advisor? Take him from rags to riches as it were, or was it something to do with Undergrowth?

"You could change things. You in place would solidify these changes." He was shaking to keep himself under control, expectations collapsing around his head.

I turned to him, hating that I had to look up at him. "No." I shook my head. "I cannot be compensated for the hell that will remain. A far bleaker fate awaits those who would cause such desolation for profit."

I heard a scuff behind me.

"I hope your men held their breath as they passed the threshold," I said.

Swords drawn, the two blue gems who were trying to flank me glanced at each other through their visors.

"Your ghost in the tower story is only partially true." I pointed. "That moss above the doorway is potent. I grew it for just such an occasion. You smelled it, right? An earthy, honey kind of smell. You need to hold your breath while you pass the threshold."

They looked at each other again and decided that nothing was wrong, as I suggested. They advanced on me. I didn't back away.

The guard on the left lost his stride and face planted the stone floor, his sword clattered from his limp hand and flew off the ledge. The remaining guard stopped, suddenly concerned for himself. He took a step back, but his knee betrayed him, buckling.

The guard fell to his knee weakly, dropped his sword, and toppled over the ledge unconscious.

I watched him go. I thought to shout to warn the innocent bystanders below, but there would have been no point. My voice would never reach down there from the tower.

"And who are you?" I turned to face the leader of the band. I assumed the rest were down below the tower for the limited space the belfry offered. There was an audible slap below. "Damn, he hit harder than I expected."

The man snapped his head to me. He had been watching in awe and horror as his man fell.

"I will let you handle this, Blight. I do not have the time to waste if we are to stay on track," Lich-Fex melted into the floor in a cloud of black as he spoke.

"I expect a report on how in the hells we are going to get Grenlic out of there."

The new blue gem foreman released his breath as he passed the threshold, taking my advice offered to the other two.

"What was that?" he asked as he drew his sword, Grenlic's sword.

"Just a friend. Someone who is helping me overthrow Yalor. I've seen you before. Where was it? Ah, you were with Grenlic the day I was to be taken before the priest.

He smirked. "I knew there was more going on with you than we thought. I warned Mistress Hydel you'd be trouble."

"More than you expected, I hope. What brings you up here then? Certainly not a stroll about the city."

"The Writ...it was an Alerez. Wasn't it?"

"So, the report has come in?"

He shook his head. "But it did verify a story I was told." I had nothing to say at that. I couldn't say I was surprised, but still... "I don't suppose there's any way you'd come quietly, Bring—"

"Blight."

"What?"

"It is Blight-Bringer, sir. There's no sense in hiding. So, let's meet each other on even ground, shall we? I've already revealed I have a militia under my command. I am not yours nor Hydel's any longer. I'm not who you believed me to be. So, there you have it. A re-introduction is in order. Blight-Bringer, it is the name."

He straightened his back at that with a smirk. One that says he was considering what I have said and was willing to play along.

"Anet of Lazerisk. Kin of Tulgité of the Mountain War."

"Mountain War? Oh Anet, if you get the chance, I have a friend I would like you to meet."

"I'm aware of that waste of flesh in the blood works. I'm looking forward to winning the shields back from him soon. My ancestor was the first to bear them. To think Conarance just happened upon him." He grew grim as though a connection was just made. "What did you do to him?"

"Who? Conarance?"

"He lost a patch of skin to a rogue nail the other day and had no idea until it was pointed out to him. He laughed as though it were nothing. He's in the infirmary now."

"There you have it. No idea he had been wounded. I've improved him, have I not?"

"What are you really?" He asked with a deepening scowl. "A fiend? Is that why you wear a resemblance to Oshoku?"

"Honestly, I had thought this was original until I met Undergrowth. If I were a fiend, I doubt you'd be willing to stare me down with that sword. I wear it to mark my station. The station Yalor gave me of Bringer."

"You just said you were Blight." He shook his head. "You're coming with me, whoever the hell you say you are."

"Ah, no. You see, I was never given a name, just a title." He paused and began closing in. I strolled, causing us to circle the belfry together, keeping my distance. "That's rather rude, don't you think? You're not going to ask about the title? What it has to do with the disease of the Blackwood from years back? No?"

He stopped then, but this time not to think. Confusion crossed his brow and he looked to see why he couldn't move his foot. The pain had not reached him yet. A set of claws wrapped around one ankle, latching on, nails driven deep. A snarling maw gnawed viciously at the armor on his lower leg.

"Gods!"

"You've met Professor Resin before, haven't you? He's not what he used to be. You see, Conarance got me thinking. Resin has been alive this whole time, but I had to keep him that way. He was in a coma, or so I thought. All it took was me ordering him to rise. That was it. I've been trying to save his life all this time and that was all I had to do."

Anet watched with horror at the creature I claimed to be Professor Resin. The black and greasy look of his fur and the husk crystalizing over his body made him look a far sight from what he had been. There was no professor in those eyes any longer. Anet tried to wrench free. He hesitated to strike the creature down. He must have liked Resin back when he was Resin. Now, he was some creature of Wohe. I couldn't tell you at the time what that was exactly, but it was under my command. Turning Conarance into a creature of my will was one thing, but doing so to my mentor was another. I had been considering ways to end Resin's suffering, but there was little left of the Wohe sand from the cocoon to study.

Ever since I woke him from his coma, Resin had stayed close like a personal bodyguard assassin. This situation is what he had been waiting for. Though it pained me to see him in the state he was, he had just saved my life.

"As you will, Professor." I strowed out of the belfry to the sound of screams, snarls, and wet flesh ripping.

I had gambled someone would find me out eventually. But what I hadn't expected was the adrenaline rush that came with it. My heart raced, trying to find its way out of my chest. Down the clock tower steps, I tried to follow it until it occurred to me that Anet probably came with some backup. He was the foreman of the guard now, which means all of them would be under his command. Why wouldn't he bring others? A group of three hardly sounds proper. I could hear the clanking of arms and armor making its way up the stairwell. The fallen body must have cued them in that something had gone wrong. How much of my arsenal would I need to expend to get out of this? Was it time to kill the mosoleth on my shoulder? Was it time to make my final moves? It was too early. Everything wasn't in place yet.

I hurried back up the tower and almost forgot to hold my breath as I passed the threshold.

"Throw him over," I demanded.

Professor Resin raised no question, just obeyed with lethal quickness. Anet gurgled a final pathetic whimper as he slid off the ledge. Resin stared at me, hulking and gruesome, expecting the next order as though I had any sort of plan. It wouldn't be long before the soldiers made their way up. I was good at lengthy planning, not so much at coming up with ideas on the spot. Whatever I came up with now, would have many flaws. I hesitated, stunned with the what-ifs to come.

I glanced over the ledge at the people below. The wheelhouse was already surrounded by the city guard. Avol was giving them enough hell to bring me a smile, but the thought of the philosopher stones being seized with the rest of my equipment left a pit in my stomach. I would need to forsake them for the time being. Bystanders were already collecting as they do when something new is happening. The control the monitors and leadership of Yalor have over its people left little to be excited about. Internally, we all feel for others going through a hard time, but we watch them fall apart anyhow, snacks in hand.

Few options came to mind to get myself out of this situation. Lich-Fex was somewhere else by now. You'd think Oshoku would have made me his charge. Our disagreement could have convinced him to leave me on my own this time. Pride forced my mouth shut when I made to call for him. I've made it this far without Undergrowth's help. I could see it to the end on my own. Their part would come at the new beginning.

I held Professor Resin in my regard. There was nothing of the man I knew left. He twitched as though his brain and muscles were communicating poorly and his eyes never focused. Pale purple husks reached around his body like the cocoon was trying to form, but each move he made set the process back further, grains of sand falling from him. It had been an effort to help him out of what had formed around him when he first rose after being prostrate for so long.

"Resin." His head snapped to me, and all shaking ceased. "It's time to say goodbye one last time. If you are still in there somehow, I hope you'll forgive what I've let you become. I see no other way out of this, but perhaps this is a good thing and we can finally lay you to rest." My eyes stung. "Thank you, Professor Resin. Thank you for making me who I am today. I would have killed myself long ago if not for you. I couldn't be who I am today without you. Now, go."

To my surprise, Resin hesitated as though he wished also to say something. It was short-lived, however. Before I knew it, the thing that Resin had become scurried toward the edge, dragging that bad leg of his. He leapt onto a column close to the edge of the belfry and crawled onto the roof. It was now or never. I followed and leapt out into space.

As I fell, I suddenly forgot any practice I had conducted in secret for this day. After a short panic and exertion to flip my body in the right direction, my wings caught the air and snapped open. I glided through as much cover as I could, but someone below still shouted in surprise. No doubt the guards below had been alerted to my actions. I prayed no monitor was in the area for just long enough for me to reach the ground. I only flapped to redirect myself and avoid colliding with the local buildings. I had to reach the ground as fast as possible to avoid as many eyes as I could, but not fast enough to be a broken thing when I arrived.

Looking down below, I realized I was the least of people's concerns. I did my best to look back toward the clock tower without losing my form, following the pointing fingers of the populous. Professor Resin had grown more disfigured and monstrous. He shouted over and over as he clung to the top of the tower, sending roof plating fragments over the ledge. I couldn't make out the sound he was making with the wind in my ears. Suddenly, Resin bellowed. He screamed so loud I could almost make out the sound waves visually. There was no way a Fezdt could make such a horrible sound. It was like he was using his own pains to sunder the sky's very fabric.

I hit the main road's flagstones too hard. I may have collided with a group of children; I can't say. I held my side but ignored my pains to get a better look at Resin from the ground. I left whoever I hit and joined the slow collection of people clogging up the streets. Resin was still bellowing that horrible shout. He turned his back to us and slammed his hands down into the structure of the tower as hard as he could. Each fist went deeper than his small form would suggest. The roof tiles shot out like shrapnel. Finally, he let out one last desperate, painful scream. From the back of his head, a large organic spire shot out with great force. Resin went silent.

Studying ants, I knew what I had done in my adjustment to Resin's body. I kept reminding myself that this was not Resin any longer when conducting these experiments and mutations. I had accomplished what I set out to do, but watching it happen was another thing entirely. It is funny how when we imagine doing horrible things, there's no remorse; there's no edge to it. But to see our own horrendous fantasies unfold outside of our minds, we realize just how much of a monster we really are.

I knew enough from watching the effects on the ants with the fungus, it was time I ran. The humans and other races in the street watched as the creature on the clock tower grew still and the cloud forming from him grew and grew. I wasn't sure what the spores would do to me since I was already infected with much the same disease, but I wasn't willing to test it just yet. Just as I got through the crowd and set my direction of travel to the Theater Division, a large wall of steel blocked my path. Eneric did not notice me at first. His eyes were locked to the creature up on the clock tower. My running into him caught his attention, but only enough for a glance. Though when he looked up at the clock tower this time, he was sure to close his mouth.

"Bringer," he said, as though he wanted to ask a question. "Get the Mistress moving," he shouted over his shoulder instead.

Mistress?

Eneric moved back to the convoy he was guarding. Mistress Hydel watched the clock tower with horror from her carriage door.

"Bringer?" she asked.

"Bringer?" Mwin coming from his own carriage approached. I couldn't tell if he was excited to see me or terrified. Based on the way he pulled short from me, I figured it was a bit of both.

It wasn't until Mwin approached did I see how bad the situation was. Mistress Hydel was leading a presession of her visiting nobles. I couldn't see if the Emperor was there, but it didn't matter. The noble men and women were starting to follow Mwin out of their individual carriages. The presession had paused for too long. The others wanted to see what was happening. When my eyes fell on the Emperor himself, I had to act.

"Everyone please return to your carriages. We'll be moving momentarily. Just a block in the road." Eneric's voice went low when he addressed the mistress. "Mistress, please return to your seat. We need to be moving before a panic—"

I rushed to the top of Hydel's carriage only accidentally using her shoulder to step up. "Bringer, what in the blazes—"

"Lords and Ladies! Thank you for your patience," I wasn't sure what I was going to say but we had to get everyone out of here, the spores were getting too close and the people were starting to grow concerned. Though the creature had stopped moving, something wasn't right to them. Instinct often tries to save us where sense could not. "As you can see, our mass pollenizer is a wonderful addition to our city. It is often claimed, we sentient being are losing ourselves by removing ourselves from nature. This creature makes fools of all naysayers to progress. We can fertilize and even sew entire populations of flora within your city walls or your harvest fields. Yalor has bred a number of these fine creatures as...parting gif—" Hydel shook her head vehemently. "As a grand...strand, in the rays of the Golden Dawn." The nobles applauded politely and I gave a slight bow before dismounting. I was careful not to glide down. This was not the time nor the place to be experimental or fun. Coming down from the tower was stupid and only a stroke of luck.

"Bringer, why—"

"No." With a hand held out, it was surprisingly easy to silence the mistress.

"Eneric, I have no idea what that thing is but what it is producing...it can't be good. You need to get Mistress Hydel and the nobles out of here. If they stick around, it won't be long before they and the populous figures I lied."

He stared at me for a long time. Another glance at the mistress and the creature on the tower, and Eneric's shoulders slumped.

"Get them moving!" Eneric shouted to one of the guards. He pulled another nearer to him, "Start evacuating—"

"We can't," I said, perhaps too quickly.

"Hmm?" Eneric seemed like he was on his last bit of patience with me. If it hadn't been for the nobles and Mwin within ear shot, he wouldn't have been so cordial.

"They...they have to stay here. We don't know what that is, or what's coming out of it."

Eneric let go of the guardsmen. When he approached me next, I figured he decided the nobles nearby didn't matter anymore. I suppose, though they were slaves, the prospect of leaving civilians to potentially parish, didn't sit well with him.

One heavy gauntleted hand to my shoulder, I supposed my story would've ended just there. He staired into my eyes and even removed my mask.

"I know this has something to do with you, lizard." Eneric shoved the mask into my chest. "I think you know I can't do anything about this right now and that's why you're doing it. Whatever experiment or work of the devils you are conducting here, if these people come into harm's way, it's on your head. And I'll make you pay for it." Eneric pushed the mask into my chest, hard. He set off with a curt gesture to the guards to keep moving.

Shamefully, my eyes met Mwin's. I could tell he felt awkward in his fine clothes. I made to place the mask back on my face but stopped for a moment.

"It's good to see you, Mwin."

Eneric forced me to lead the quarantine procedures and begin a treatment plan for those who had been near the clock tower that day. It took more time than I had to spare. Before I knew it, there was no time to attempt to rescue Grenlic before the main events. It had to be okay. There was still enough time once everything got underway. Right?

Despite our efforts, the citizens of Yalor spread the word of the monster of the clock tower. Luckily, it rarely made its way to the ears of the nobles. Perhaps the constant state of morbidity we slaves existed in contributed to the name, but colloquially, the district began being referred to as the Lost Zone.

## 23

## A Gift to the Emperor

Mistress Hydel refused to stop. Her ambitions had come too far and there would be no other chance to impress the Emperor. With the constant setbacks and now even an entire district of Yalor was lost, the strain was apparent on her brow, though this was supposed to be her day of victory, the proudest day of her life.

There were no direct lines tying the source of her stress to me, so Hydel and the other leaders were playing with shadows in their minds to figure it out or at least hold the misfortunes at bay.

Eneric wouldn't steer his eyes from me. I often caught him staring at me quizzically as though he knew my secrets but couldn't bring them to light. Too much of the Golden Dawn hinged on my work. The Alchemy Division practically being no more, meant I was their last opportunity to see it to success. Without me, a dawn would not crest the horizon this day. To underscore this, we sat in the cold of the last tendrils of umbra. The moon shone high, but her vision faded as the next day's light chased her away. The smaller of the two moons was absent, as though the failed titan wished to join Ald'Kair wherever he was for this day.

I took my seat close by them in what would have been Estry's seat. A lavish, high-backed design lesser than that of Hydel's and Eneric's but something only those who could afford the finest craftsmen could obtain. Mistress Hydel's chair was almost imperceptibly lesser than that of the Emperor's. A bold move. A statement to be sure. Her dress was also of Yalorian design, with fine silks and textiles brought in from different regions of Avalon. Doubtless she had known how the Emperor takes to as many cultures as possible at any given time. A difficult feat. Hydel took it upon herself to do the same. I could make out at least five different human cultures in her dress. But what *did* surprise me was that most of the ornamentation was associated with that culture's brides. Bolder still. It was a plain enough gesture to make her desires known, or at least her devotion toward her own goals, but not so much that it would be an easy thing to call her out on, if someone had been so inclined.

I tried to keep my eyebrow down when she turned my way to see what it was that I was thinking. I turned back to the collection of people down below. Essence wielders prepared for the opening ceremonies, which were set to begin as the sun blessed the Emperor with its touch. Ah, I could see why this could not be rescheduled for another time then. It was the summer solstice. The sun would appear larger than at any other time of the year, and it was considered a holy day for more than a few human fiefs. If she had pushed it back, there was no guarantee the Emperor would have made time to come again. Even if he had, it would be another year before she had the day of her choosing. This was when she had to present her worth to the empire. This was the only chance she had to sell the empire on the idea of Yalor and its Golden Dawn.

The opening ceremony was a blaze wielder display. With a powder the Alchemy Division helped develop, explosions in a cascade of different colors shone brightly in the dark of the Coliseum's field. All the nobles oohed and aahed at the spectacle, just as we had intended. At once, they were captivated. Not a single soul would count this a waste of time and resources expended to make the journey. The last flame went out as the sun graced us fully. A sun wielder made its beams golden. Not the understood gold of the sun's rays as one would hear in bard's cantos, but true glorious gold. It was too bright to look at but somehow didn't hurt the eyes. As the light dimmed and we could make out down below, a company of Hydel's royal guard stood proud and tall. Somehow, Mistress Hydel was there before them, her garb radiant as though blessed by the sun herself. A work of wielders or something in the fabric, I could not say.

She didn't fool me though. A hair out of place here; an under-polished or scuffed nail on those pretty hands; a broach not in the exact place it belonged. Outwardly, one could see her as a goddess in that moment. Mistress Hydel, though, she was a wreck. The pressure mounted and the possibility of failure grew with each setback. I wondered how much of the show she had to remove from the program with the fall of the clock tower district. It didn't come to mind what projects could have been there. I didn't much care either way. I patted the hip pouch just to verify the stones were there. A nervous twitch of my own, I suppose.

"Lords and Ladies of Avalon, welcome. As the new day comes to greet us, know this: Today will be the first day of a new epoch. The age of man has only just begun, but today, what rises above the horizon is not a normal day. No, we Yalorians have worked day and night to bring you the first-ever Golden Dawn of the myths." Polite claps echoed through the Coliseum. Not everyone was convinced, but they were eager to be entertained either way. "The fruits of our labor will be on display here and throughout the city for the rest of the week. Each piece would be enough to push our great nation forward decades at a time. But we have not brought you one creation, my lords. We have brought you not two or three. Lords, we have brought you them all. Decades multiplied by an endless number. That is what Yalor has brought. A golden age like none we have ever seen. None like we've read in our history." More polite applause and enthusiasm this time as the Emperor himself stood to lead the ovation. Mistress Hydel beamed.

Father Feirtney and his procession approached the Emperor's throne with an earthen bowl upon a pillow. He did not kneel as a man of the cloth does not do so to a mortal man.

"My Emperor, Yalor would like to present to you our very first gift. This ring I present to you in the hide of an enemy of the state…"

I shot up from my seat. That bowl, it wasn't earthenware. It was scales. When…how? I thought I had more time. There was no announcement for an execution to take place in the Theater District. Those were always advertised to the highest degree. One never got a ticket and was rather forced to go as a form of punishment. The executions were drawn out and a spectacle to help keep the other citizens from desiring to earn their place on the stage for going against Yalor. But they were always made a big deal of. We knew when someone was being executed weeks in advance. Did they execute Grenlic in silence?

I couldn't stop shaking as the Emperor pulled the ring from inside the bowl. The bowl itself was put to the side, a forgotten gesture once the prize was retrieved. Still, it held my eye. I knew those cracks. I knew the flow of rock-like features on those scales. My attention was drawn. The audience had settled down and the Yalor nobles watched me. I took my seat again, trying to resist the urge to either weep or fly into a rage.

"A most generous gift, Mistress." The Emperor held an already overly jeweled hand into the air to examine the new addition. "I will remember such kindness."

Hydel bowed deeply and in a flash of more sunlight, she returned to our side halfway up the Coliseum stands. With a flourish of her arms, she said, "Let the Golden Dawn begin."

The terrain below in the Coliseum fields shifted, quaking the entire structure. A small mountain shot up from the earth, complete with platforms to station creatures. Once the mountain hit its peak, it started to rotate around its center axis.

Mistress Hydel's voice was enhanced by some unforeseen source so that all could hear her over the rumbling.

"Yalor has always been a land for all races and cultures. This we do in the spirit of Avalon's ultimate design. We scoured the continent for the best of each culture, fief, kingdom, and sea. Each could boast of their contributions or specialties. We have claimed these, to improve them. With the miracle of essence wielding and Yalor's discoveries in alchemy, we were able to improve even the best of labor and war beasts."

The next hour or so was a presentation of the beasts in question. I had worked on nearly all of them, and I couldn't lie; I was proud of what we had made of them.

The rhinos of Kaguel Eponga were given the tools to traverse mountains. Normally a creature for strict use in the plains and deserts, the rhinos could not naturally keep balance like that of a goat in uneven terrain. Their new hooves solved that issue. When there was too much earth to do even that, or their load prevented them from such feats, the rhinos now possessed essence seals on their flanks and horns to produce terra emyon. The emyon could be used to clear or flatten the path. The trick had been teaching the beasts to do the emyon themselves. I heard the difficulty of their task and did not envy the beast masters. The creatures would have nothing to do with me now though. The process was severely painful for them. It wasn't a matter of giving the beasts over to their essence. All creatures had such energies. But rather, it had been a task in mutating the natural paths their essence took. It was like rearranging their vascular system to suit a new purpose while keeping other body parts from rotting off. In the end, what we wanted the beasts to do required so much energy, we siphoned off a bit from many locations. The largest redirection was taken from the beast's vision.

Vision required much more energy than one would think. Rhinos already had bad vision, but now these were without their farsightedness. The riders did well in keeping that new flaw out of the display. They pulled the rhinos up early from each obstacle rather than let the creature run into anything. It didn't matter what anyone has ever told you about alchemy: There is always a cost of change, even if it's a change you enact. Change has a price, and you will be the one to pay it. Whatever has been suggested of the philosopher stones is also over stated. It is a rare resource to be sure. It has a keen effect on metals and to a degree is able to change a thing's chemical composition, but ultimately, it is an ingredient as any other thing; a means to an end. Everything has a price. My eyes were drawn back to the bowl.

After the rhino mounts, came the tamed riots. I am happy to say I had no reason to participate in this project. Not much scared the hell out of me but a riot in a group was terrifying. On their own, the lizard-like cat was elusive, almost like a coyote that hadn't been stricken by the madness. However, when a fray, or grouping of riots, get hungry or bored, they swarm like unholy sharks given permission to enter the lands. Their long arms had so many joints they were just shy of being labeled tentacles. They were perfect for stalking close to the ground at high speed or swinging and jumping from tree to tree. If you ever heard their unique cough, chances were you were already dead, they were just discussing how best to play with you. These riots were able to be handled by beast masters now. The difficulty to maintain control left the beast master with only five at max. This was impressive enough given the nature of the creature. With a fray under their command and a beast master from Yalor, a platoon of soldiers would have a valuable violent addition to the battlefield, especially wooded areas.

From there, the Golden Dawn focused on what could be added to the forces of Avalon. This made enough since. The bulk of the dawn would be on display in the various districts in Yalor. Barter improvements with anti-cheating scales. A new communication center where we discovered a way to quickly communicate over distances. The nobility, kings, and Emperor would be here for weeks to see everything we had to offer. Some were minor, others may not work practically, but there would be enough yeses to put Yalor on the map once and for all. Credit where credit is due, Yalor made me eat my words about its only goal being war. As for the Coliseum, it would be all about the spectacle.

During an interim in the display of Yalor's offers to Avalon, snacks of fruit, breads, and cheese were passed out to the visitors. Just bread, however, good quality bread, was thrown to those of the citizens lucky enough to be invited to the event. Then they brought forth Mwin's bitter rose wine. Mistress Hydel raised a goblet to the young lord in thanks. It was good to see him. But when he made to take a drink, the dignitaries simply had to express to him how generous he had been in providing such a delicacy. I have to admit, Lich-Fex had been right. The wine was like nothing I had ever tasted. The flavor was difficult to describe in the literal sense. I had heard the tasted described as lust and regret. I could see why. As I sipped, guards started to form around us. Father Feirtney whispered something in the Mistresses ear. She looked my way, but I ignored her and pretended not to notice.

Krolec's soldiers prepared down below with mock fights with each other as part of the show. The crowd cheered as Krolec made easy work of each soldier in turn. It was obviously a show and staged, but it made for an entertaining display. Then it was time to get serious. Warm-up in the form of good fun complete, Krolec called his soldiers together as a unit, individuals forgotten. Krolec at the head, you could watch his mind set change. His shield that had been used as a prop moments before, was now an extension of his body. Though it was down by his side, with his shoulders set and he turned to his side presenting the shield to the opposition, it felt like a statement. 'You, over there, you will not get past me. These men are my charge.'

Mistress Hydel's herald announced the scenario for each situation. Jarce looked better with a bit of gray in his hair. The audience was supposed to believe these men had spent the day training and honing their abilities when the dark cloud of the enemy arrived. The first wave was a group of kobolds. They were accused of stealing the memories of the village children and the 'hero' had had enough and made to face the threat head on. This was part of the show and illusion, we as the audience was supposed to allow to be imposed into our own minds. Suspended disbelief, if you will. But I wouldn't let it infect me. I watched the little creatures pushed into the arena fearful and unsure of the weapons placed in their hands. They realized what was the matter after too long. They were not given a chance to organize before the soldiers charged. Each vaporized in turn as they were cut down leaving only the weapons and primitive clothes they were accustomed to. The crowd cheered them on as the heroes of the story prevailed saving the children from further accosting. As kobolds were want to do, we promptly forgot what the soldiers had been fighting. Luckily, I had written down some notes when I discovered the creatures imprisoned below near Leegius. I succumb to the same memory loss when they were cut down.

The play continued. This time the village was approached by a giant. They did not define which of the eight it was. It didn't much matter though. We didn't have a giant. We had an abomination. Some poor soul designated for the Theater District but had his sentencing pushed back. Instead, he was subject to my hand. Estry's mostly, but now that she was gone, anything the Alchemy Division produced was my responsibility. The disfigured man lumbered into the field in a body not his own. They probably should have written the story of this encounter to be a monster rather than a giant. Giants were perfectly designed beings. Rare as rare can get but we knew enough about them to know this wasn't close.

The man had to stoop to enter through the same gate as the kobolds had. He was clearly weeping, but he did not wait for the herald to bring his storytelling to its natural end, which would signify the beginning of combat. He charged in as fast as his body would let him, limping all the way. The men surrounded him easy enough. Small cuts here and there kept the man swinging his enlarged fist one direction and then the other. Even his screams were disfigured. After a too long a moment of torment, the man fell apart there in the middle of the fight. First, his fist stayed behind on the ground he had just pummeled when he tried to strike a soldier. He looked confused when the fist didn't impact the area he had demanded. He checked the stump he was left with and fell as a leg collapsed underneath him. It seemed a chain reaction took place then and the entire composition of his body collapsed like a tower. Before the soldiers, all that was left was a pile of fat and fluid that resembled a man as much as a slime would.

Krolec, ever the professional turned it to a victory. He flourished to the audience and they bought it. Hydel and the others looked my way knowing this wasn't the plan. I shrugged. I wouldn't waste time defending myself there and then. I was surprised the pseudo homunculus had lasted as long as he did. The pressure and stress of real combat had forced the body to reject itself. He had only lasted this long because he had been forced to be stationary up until then. I tried to pretend I didn't notice guards accumulating nearby and turned my attention back to the field.

Victorious, the soldiers departed until their next bout of entertainment. Krolec eyed me, his scar tattoos furrowed deep, as though demanding the next session go better than this one had.

I hadn't realized until the herald began laying out the next presentation that Eneric was not in his seat. Jarce spoke of the Mountain Wars and what that meant for the history of Orecul. He started to speak of the theft of the Shields and their recent recovery. My blood ran cold. Leegius was carted in kneeling on a wooden frame as it was pulled in by a horse. Once in position in the center of the field, Leegius was unchained from the cart and moved over to another wooden structure that was being hastily thrown together. The crowd cheered as Lord Eneric came through the main gate.

Horror started making me sweat. I wasn't sure how I would manage losing another that day. It was all I could do to resist standing up for my chair. But the closer Eneric came to Leegius, something told me that the sacrifice would be too much. Though I have wept at being alone, I felt that I could be more alone still.

Leegius had decided at some point that I was not the company he would like to maintain. He could see right through me. He could see the rot in my soul better than anyone else. I believe that it told him if he were to get too close, he would never have another day of peace in his life. I wasn't sure he was wrong, but I wasn't ready to give him up. My fingers dug deeper into the frame of my chair with each step Eneric took. Though the crowd grew louder by the moment, and all I could hear was the thudding in my ears.

"Long has it been," the herald continued his story. "since the siege weapon known as Shields of the Mountain War has been in the possession of the empire. On this day, as a gift to Avalon, Mistress Hydel's general, Lord Eneric, will take back what has been stolen and return it to its rightful station. This to show Yalor's devotion and commitment to the success of Avalon's great purpose to unite the realms."

As Jarce spoke, a number of blue gems settled Leegius into the headsman's block and chained his arms down. Leegius gave no resistance. The blue gems maneuvered the necklace to give Eneric as much of the striking surface as possible. The ruby winked at me. There could be no doubt. I've often wondered how one could save another if the person in question wasn't willing to fight for themselves. Would it be all wasted energy or your last good deed before they pulled you under the same waters which threatened them. Watching Leegius, he gave no indication that he would be willing to fight for himself. The crowd grew silent taking in a collective breath as they watched the gleam of Eneric's new sword.

Just as I was about to open my mouth to shout something that would surely get me killed, the world grew dark. The sun still shined and was a mostly cloudless day, but it was as though something started to devour the light. Instinct took hold, and I felt the pull that is an all of us when we don't quite understand but we know it's time to run. Five shades darker, and Eneric dropped the sword to his side. Even its brilliance forgotten. All but myself looked to the sun to see what was the matter. I knew better though, something horrible was about to happen, and whatever was about to occur would be completely my fault. I am the one who had pushed Leegius to be the minotaur, and he had taken my advice to heart.

The world trembled as Leegius began to radiate a blood red aura. Eneric quickly stepped back shielding his eyes to avoid what was presumably heat radiating from Leegius. Brightly colored sweat formed on Leegius's skin. It had become the only untempered source of light in the entire Coliseum. Soon, the sweat flowed like honey down to his feet. The smoking that formed from the ground as the honey touched down had me in mind of a volcano. Sure enough, as the material flowed, it flowed just like lava.

The headsman's block and the chains that bound Leegius' fell apart. He screamed loud and held his head as he did so. Finally, a burst of power sent the lava out in a bubble around Leegius, splattering here and there. After it all had fallen to the ground, Leegius stood there in the maw of a beast. To as near one could say, he stood there between the top and bottom jaw of a great beast, straining. It was all he could do to keep the two from closing in on him. The only sound he made was that of labored breaths as though mastering a heavy weight. In fact, that was the only sound anyone heard over the sizzle of the lava cooling.

Eneric slowly pulled down his guard. Luck had held his hand well enough to save him from any of the lava splattering across his flesh. The stuff pooled around his feet, losing its color. I could see it in his eyes, as soon as it was cool enough to approach, he would strike Leegius down.

The herald did his best to calm the audience as I passed him, smoothly. I had the smallest window. The guards forming around the Yalorian leadership and the Emperor had become too plenty. Eneric was mere paces from Leegius. With his armored boots he could walk on the lava much sooner than he would if he had been wearing leather soles.

The guards took their first steps toward me. I crawled over the audience like a rat trying to escape the river. I punched my shoulder and launched myself. I didn't care anymore. I flew. Reaver in hand, I roared as I bore down on Eneric. A tactic rather than a mistake of the inexperienced. If I hadn't, Leegius would have lost his head there and then.

Easy enough, Eneric parried my attack and I careened off his sword back into the air. We stood there in each other's regard.

From all the claims of Eneric's prowess on the battlefield, I hadn't expected him to hesitate as long as he did. He was still too close to Leegius for my comfort so I decided to bait him.

From my mouth I let a glow of white mist flow down to my feet to freeze the earth. I didn't dare land just yet. Eneric was too fast and it would take me too long to return to flight from a standing position. Alerez were best suited for launching off the cliffs given our heavier bone structure than that of the bird. My trick was to throw enough surprises at lord Eneric to keep his mind stunted. I let the trail of frost follow me and mask the next attack. To his credit, Eneric didn't fall for it. He locked his sword into Reaver's tail blades and used his off hand to pull me to the ground. I hit the ground and slid, frosting over more of the ground as I went.

Finally, Eneric moved away from Leegius. Apparently, the pommel of the sword had been fashioned in such a way to control our pauldrons just as Tari's ring had been, or Conarance's cane. He held the hilt toward me with murder in his eyes, but when nothing happened, I was able to stand up from the ground unaccosted. As I stood, emerald shards fell from my shoulder. It hadn't taken a great deal of effort to punch Reaver's blade through the mosoleth eye. It had left my shoulder bloody but Yalor had lost its hold on me.

Eneric took his sword in both hands and raised it above his head. Split second instinct had me moving before I could think about it. Reaver's tail unraveled and I swung him just anywhere. The spearhead skewered into the ground and his tail flexed, pulling me along with it. Just as I was pulled away Eneric's sword slashed down. Though he was many paces away a burst of light followed the arc of his blade. It burned into the ground where I had been standing. It was then I remembered, too late to do anything about it, that the sword he wielded was crafted by the same blacksmith as my weapon. In any normal fight Reaver would have given me a distance advantage but it would not be so with him. I knew facing off with Eneric I would have little chance. Leegius watched me still laboring and for a moment I thought I had just thrown both our lives away. But past the sweat and deep furrowing of his brow I could see that there's still something left of him. I just had to buy him enough time.

"What honor is there in striking down slaves, Lord Eneric."

"Slaves? No, what I strike down are beasts. The mire and muck of our society. I would say no better than monsters or the creatures that haunt us in the shadows."

We both swung our weapons then. Reaver's tail intersected with the stream of light his sword produced. The light was dispatched but Reaver was shot back. As he fell back to me, I stepped to one side and whipped his tail around at Eneric parallel with the ground. Smooth as anything, Eneric blocked and allowed the tail to spiral around his blade. With his off hand, he grabbed the other end of the tail between the blades to avoid injury. We stood there tugging at the line. Flapping harshly, my wings were all that allowed me to match his strength.

"You didn't think you were the first person I fought using a lamque, did you?"

It was one thing when I used Reaver to pull myself toward the enemy in a controlled fashion, it was another thing entirely when the enemy used that same motion against me. Eneric pulled hard and I found myself having to spit out dirt and ash. An almost too late rolled to the side saved me from becoming either of those things. Before I could get up Eneric was on me. I tried to stab Reaver's claw at him but his size was too great. He forced my arm underneath one knee and through his elbow into my cheek. Dazed, I couldn't fight back against what came next.

Eneric's sword started to glow. He held the sword as though to stab down. Then Eneric pinned my right wing down. Realization came too slowly. My vision gained focus just in time to see the sword boring down. My world became all light. It was not the kind of warmth that told you you were home after a long strenuous journey, it was the kind of warmth that told you something was far beyond wrong. It was the kind of heat that told your body it was broken. It was the kind of scorch that burnt out hope.

"No more, Bringer. No more will you employ these gifts of yours against Yalor," he said, tossing aside a bit of burnt flesh.

My mind started to catch up. I screamed when he stabbed my other wing. It didn't hurt all that much as far as I can remember. But the loss was far greater than any bit of pain could signify.

I breathed through it for a time. When I blinked to clear the tears, Eneric was gone. I had been freed from his weight. I had to force myself to come up from the ground to see what was going on, cursing my weakness and not living up to my father's expectations. It was difficult to ignore the welling up in my chest.

Both Leegius and Eneric also crawled from the ground. Leegius had slammed into Eneric and the two of them sent up clouds of ash in their wake. The weapons Leegius wielded now resembled more to the given name. They had shrunk down to a more manageable size though there was no question that they were of the bol'ruka weapons class. Leegius's fully armored arms led down to solid pieces of bone. Each about as large as a man and resembling a large creature's upper and lower skull. At first glance, I thought it could be a dragon's but the number of eyes and the snout were not quite right. Leegius slammed both shields into the ground to carry himself up against their great weight. It was a marvel when he could stand up straight and wield them effectively.

Lord Eneric took his stance, though his concern was plain. He didn't wait. He charged his sword all a light as he attacked. Leegius blocked but the bulk of his weapon was far more than anything that would let him control the opponent's to any degree. Eneric struck at the wall of Leegius's shield until his sword arm started to get heavy. Though we had all heard the stories of this legendary artifact, it was something else to encounter it. The blacksmith from Kytgro was known all around as the best, but even his custom-made sword wouldn't leave a mark in the Shields. Leegius pushed forward with both weapons poised to shove. After pushing Eneric a distance, he heaved up both shields and slammed them on the ground repeatedly. Each impact caused more lava to pour from the shields. Eneric lurched back out of the splash zone and the droplets sizzled on the ground.

Leegius held both shield's inner side toward each other, creating the illusion that that beast the head had belonged to was staring Eneric down. A burst of light from within jolted the head but Leegius managed to keep the two halves together. Lava flowed like spurting drool down the creature's cheeks. Eneric and I had the same thought, apparently. Leegius wouldn't be able to turn as he prepared whatever it was he was about to do. Eneric could try to get behind him. Instead, though, Reaver's tail wrapped around the large man's knees and he lost balance. The move alone dragged me at least a foot. I leaned back straining to keep Eneric still. He lurched my direction, flipped his body, and rolled. The move unraveled him from Reaver and he avoided tangling himself further.

Leegius launched his attack. A large pillar of lava flew from the open maw of the shields. Eneric avoided getting hit but the same could not be said about his reinforcements. No screams came. The blue gems were simply just not there anymore. Eneric looked on horrified. Leegius took the moment to catch his breath, the shields hanging from his sides.

"I am walking away, Lord Eneric," Leegius panted out. "I am finished with your wars. I am finished being a tool." He stood up and walked over to Eneric. His form towering over the warrior. "I am Leegius of the free and thriving Dusty Hoof Herd, care taker of little sisters and brothers, and herder of the nomadic felt worm. I had dreams and ambitions and a family." He held his voice loud enough to reach the stands where the Emperor and Yalorian leadership sat. "Humans have taken it all away from me. Maybe, I can have it back once I find my herd. Release me, this moment and I will count our accounts balanced. I will seek no revenge. I will leave none accosted. Refuse, and I will show you exactly what it was you feared most I would be. I will kill every single person in this blasted Coliseum, myself included."

Leegius waited there for Eneric daring him to refuse. He did not. A small nod was all he could manage. Leegius watched him for a moment to gauge his sincerity. He let the shields dissipate, the mosoleth returning to where ever it was they stayed when not summoned. Leegius gave me the smallest of bows and a smile. He set off toward the portcullis to begin the journey home. I wondered how far he would have to go and how long it would take him to get there. I wondered if I should go with him there and then. As much as I wanted to, my life was going to take me places he could not go. Regardless, my cooling emyon died with the mosoleth on my shoulder. My Alerez breath could only just keep me cool enough for surviving on my way south where the world grew cooler. Leegius was headed north.

As I mentally made peace with his leaving and said a quiet farewell, Eneric charged the Materic. His sword's glow was less so now that the light was no longer being devoured but it looked like he was taking the sword to its limit. It would be a killing blow that flung from it. I whipped Reaver forward and wrapped him around Eneric's throat. Eneric's sword of light clattered to the ground as he desperately tried to free himself.

"Don't." Leegius had turned to the sounds and now his eyes pleaded with me. He wanted me to do the right thing. I wasn't sure what he meant by that. How many chances was he willing to give them? How often would he allow others to determine what happened around him? I, myself, was through. He knew what I was going to do before I did and he slowly but poignantly shook his head.

With a scream I pulled Reaver's tail and Eneric's throat shredded. Only the top portion of his head was recognizable as it fell to the ground. His body stood there as though surprised for longer than it should have, until it too fell hard.

"Bringer, you—"

He was cut short as both our bodies seized up. My first thought was that I didn't kill the pauldron on my arm as I had thought. But when the essence wielders came into view it was plain enough what had happened.

It took a horde of blue gems and those essence wielders to bring us to the center of the Coliseum's field.

Mistress Hydel met us there in person, doing her best to stave off the shaking of her fury. She ordered Leegius to be taken away and dealt with after me. An essence wielder accompanied him and the guards to ensure the shields would not return today. Then it was just her and I and her royal guards there in the field. The land sizzled around us like an extension of her disdain.

Mistress Hydel couldn't say anything to me, but her face asked, "Why?".

"Because fuck you and your Golden Dawn." It was all I could manage. I hadn't the knack for on-the-spot speeches. If she couldn't piece together why any of us citizens would do the same on her own, no amount of words would convince her now.

She, defeated, waved for me to be taken away. She watched on, forlorn. The nobles were at her ear either offering their condolences or demanding how she could let this happen with the Emperor there. Hydel said nothing, she just knelt in the ashes, ignoring the fact that she was ruining a priceless dress, at the feet of the Eneric.

An odd mix crafted itself in my heart. It took effort, but I found the joy there, and buried the rest as deep as I could. I had taken everything from her now...almost.

Kyda wept to herself just outside of the cell. The way she was going about it, she may as well have been crying for herself. Maybe it would not have appeared that way if she could reach me. Humans seemed to like hugs in such times.

"I had no idea they would do that to you, Bringer. I'm so sorry." Her pretty face was wrenched down in regret. I had the feeling she had been crying for hours. Enough to tip her hydration levels in a poor direction.

"You told them," I said. Not an accusation, just a statement to fact.

She nodded, fighting back more tears, as if she could have produced them any further.

"You approached them?" Reasons have a way of swaying the way actions should be perceived, though I wasn't sure they would make much of a difference in this case.

Again, she nodded.

I flexed my wings out acknowledging the sacrifice I had made, lamenting on what Eneric took from me. There was little else to them now than bone and a thin layer of skin to keep them together. The largest parts of the membrane between each of their long fingers was no more. The gale would never call on them again.

I wondered if it mattered. Did I sell my soul to Oshoku or did she take ownership of it? Did she even want it or was I just her passing entertainment? I had no idea of what was before me in the next life. All I had was the here and now and what to do next.

I wanted to blame Kyda for my situation. The guards were making to arrest me already because of her actions, but my assault and then murder of Lord Eneric placed me there anyway. They would burn me now. I'm sure dear departed Eneric's final wish.

My sins were finally catching up to me. For Tari, Estry, Conarance, and now Eneric. Oh, and that guard or whatever he had been. That first taste.

"Where is Conarance?" I finally turned Kyda's way.

"He's in the infirmary. They are doing what they can to save him."

I relaxed down again. I had been staring at the frames of my wings for some time. It was not an easy reality to accept. It wouldn't matter anyway.

"They mean to execute me soon. I wonder what grandeur they have in store for me."

She cleared her throat in a repulsive way. I supposed she had a lot of build-up in the back of her throat, but still. "They mean to make it a hanging. Then...a burning."

"Well, that's boring. It may not even work. You should tell them I'm too light. I won't strangle properly nor will my neck break. Make sure if they are to use me as a prop of entertainment, they should do it right. There are plenty of essence wielders here. Have one of them lob a fireball at me and be done with it."

"Bringer..." She sounded timid now. "It doesn't have to be this way." She held something in her hands, small enough to hide as she worked to convince herself to do whatever it was she was working through.

"What do you have in mind? I'm plenty comfortable. I even got to hang out with Leegius once more. Isn't that right?" Leegius responded with nothing, of course, but I knew he was in the cell next to mine, the fight lost in him. They had resealed his ruby and taken away his best chance to get out of here. I'm sure he blamed me for his recapture. If he hadn't taken that moment to see what I had done to Eneric, he could have kept going out of the essence wielder's range.

Kyda produced a key.

"You didn't," I said.

"I truly am sorry, Bringer. I was trying to help you. I hated seeing you go down the path that you were. I thought that if I had some help, I could get back the Alerez I knew down in that hole. I didn't know they'd do that to you. They assured me they would just take you in." Somehow, she had worked it in her mind that the Yalorian leadership had removed my wings, rather than it being an injury from combat. She must have not been in the stands when it all happened. "I have this, a way out. We can go, Bringer. You, me, and Leegius. We can be free again. We can go home."

"Dear sweet Kyda." I approached the cell door, hungry. "You'd do that for me? After all that I've put you through?"

She gave me a small smile. "We all deserve a second chance, I think. Don't you?" She held my mask out in the other hand. "I know you've still got your demons, but you can throw this away when you find the strength. I know it will take some time, but I know you have it in you, Bringer. Don't let them define who you are."

She unlocked the gate and I embraced her, slowly. "Careful, they still hurt." It had been hours but my wings were still in a significant amount of pain. She smiled apologetically and we held each other for a long time. "I've missed you, Kyda."

"I've missed you."

"I'm sorry I let so much come between us. I'm sorry I am such a monster." I held her at arm's length to get a good look at her. I took my mask from her. "But it wasn't they who made me that way."

I shoved her, hard, to the ground. Her head fetched up against the mason work of the cell floor. I drove the gate closed and locked it. The echoes rang through the hall and even drew Leegius closer to see what had just happened. I ignored him.

Kyda came up from the pool of her dress, dazed. Blood and muck staining the otherwise perfect fabric Mistress Hydel had demanded her house slaves wear. She turned to me, horrified and unbelieving.

"It's no one's fault but my own, Kyda. I am a monster by choice. I hate everyone. Always have. Humans are a plague. There's no other way to describe them. They should be eradicated, down to the last child." I wasn't shouting toward her but at no one in particular. "You mistake me, Kyda. I let all this happen. Every...single...bit. I knew you would betray me. I hadn't known it would cost me my wings, but it was a sacrifice, Kyda. A sacrifice to make all of your kind pay."

She said nothing. What was there to say? What would have swayed me at that moment to change my mind about...anything.

She couldn't find her voice until I walked away down the dungeon halls. She shouted my name continuously, pleading for me to return.

"I love you, Kyda. You were my hope once. But if I've learned anything..." Fingers in the sockets, I placed the mask upon my face and set off to find the drunkest guards I could. "Hope is poison."

# Blight-Bringer

The crowd's mood had changed since I was last in the Coliseum's field. They were plenty intoxicated enough to forget the trouble Leegius and I brought as something to be horrified at, and instead, they were lively in a hateful sort of way. The way humans are want to be when they know that no harm can possibly come to them for their actions.

They threw vegetables at me as I was carted in from the side. A number of the vegetables were well past their prime and practically exploded on impact. The smell made me want to raise my nose away from its offensive embrace but the riper vegetables they sent my way convinced me to keep my head down. When those met their mark, I felt bruises would be formed later.

The guards had me chained to a slab of wood with wheels, much like the one they had brought Leegius in on but more to scale for my small frame. It was no more than a cart really. It only took one man to haul me in, the others to make sure I had no more tricks since they took Reaver from me. Unlike Leegius's shields, Reaver was mostly a normal weapon. He was not bound to my being as the Shields had been for Leegius.

I felt Mistress Hydel's eyes on me as I was carted into view. Some fool part of me felt shame at being in her presence again. Eneric wasn't a good man so why should *I* feel guilty? Was he a good man, and he was just the way he was to me because he was a good judge of character?...Just like Leegius.

At the gallows they had constructed very much for my sake alone, the guards led me by the shackles and secured me to the framework.

Mistress waited for them to be done and the audience to quiet their jeering before she addressed them.

"We close this first day of the Golden Dawn with one last bit of entertainment. This Alerez before you is named Bringer. He has proven that he is an enemy of the state with no loyalty to Avalon or its people. He has been a liar, a thief, and a murder since the day he was brought from the craigs of Korigara where his heathen kind do dwell.

Bringer, you are sentenced to be hung from the neck until the life you possess is no longer within the confines of Celn. Whether your soul is bound for Nybe or Disiea is not for us to decide. May Ald'Kair find it in his heart to forgive you and take you in his embrace, but your destination is between he and yourself. Do you have any last words?" Mistress Hydel did well to keep the shake from her voice.

I shook my head, resigned to my fate. She nodded to the guardsmen then and he pulled the noose over my head. The drums started while he cinched the thing tighter around my throat, snugger than I liked.

Each beat seemed to drag on. I wasn't familiar with the song they played but I could tell it was a tradition for it to resound such an occasion as a hanging. I was sure they would call for the guard to pull the leaver as soon as it concluded. Before too long, the audience started to chant in rhythm with the drums. In unison they said 'fall' over and over building the anticipation in their own hearts, a desire for retribution. A mob without a clue as to what I had been up to except that their betters have determined I was worthy of a noose. The drums conducted one last rapid beat and went silent.

I opened my mouth.

"Stop." No one dared contradict or interrupt. With one hand and a single word, the Emperor had just saved my life. "Mistress Hydel, please indulge me for a moment." She looked on the verge of bursting a blood vessel but only bowed.

The Emperor himself turned my way and spoke directly to me. "Young Alerez, you are the youngest Alerez slave I've ever seen, but I wonder if you were aware that Avalon has annexed your country?"

I nodded, dumbfounded. I had no idea where this was going. I couldn't decide if I should be bored or belligerent, so I opted for neither. He had such a kind tone so I didn't think he was asking to provoke me. His thick mustache curled further still with a hidden smile.

"Do you know why we did this?" After a pause, he turned to the audience. "Can anyone tell me? To grow in power? I'm sure that is the rumor, is it not? Avalon has had but one goal since it was established by a handful of people in the first epoch year one. That is to bring all its peoples into a unity."

I felt the blood leech from my body as though all circulation had ceased. I didn't like where this was going.

"This idea started with hardly an enclave with Kytgro at its heart. Slowly, over time, we brought others to the idea and they joined our cause. Eventually, the five races of Man were united after long years of conflict, and a few of the other races joined us." He held his fists together. "And we were united across the land. One true nation. We snuffed out rebellions and warred within ourselves until all were under the same law, and the same morals. Then, your glacier washed up unto our shore. For a few hundred years, the Alerez refused to be another part of Avalon. It stands to reason. It's a hard thing to accept new things, no matter how good they may be. I am pleased to say, young Bringer, that it is now officially over. Ladies, gentlemen, as of two weeks ago, Korigara has signed over to join the empire. For the first time in history, Avalon is whole!"

Cheers roared. I did not participate. Korigara's blizzards were nothing compared to the ice in me.

He motioned his hands to quiet everyone down. "It has always been the intention of Avalon to be a sacred land, ready for Ald'Kair's return. How do we achieve this? With peace. Mistress Hydel, you and your people have provided the foundation with your Golden Dawn for the next epoch of Avalon to begin. On this first day of that new dawn, I decree: All slavery will be abolished. It will be phased out one land at a time, and all other races will be granted their freedom! Avalon will be the land of peace it has always meant to be. We start today, this long but necessary process. Today, as a gift to Korigara and her allegiance, the first slave of this decree will be...you."

His finger lanced my heart from paces away. The crowd went wild. Whether for the promise of peace or their intoxication levels, I couldn't say.

The guard removed the noose from around my neck and took my shackles off. I just stood there.

"Look, he is too stunned to speak. Please, Bringer, tell us how you feel."

They all went quiet, each and every person. The wind had even grown silent as though it too, was interested in what I had to say. Mistress Hydel shot daggers at me from her eyes, but she would not object. Her desires were so close she could let nothing, even her vengeance, put it in jeopardy.

"You're a fool."

"What? Boy, speak up. We can't hear you from down there."

I burst out with laughter then. I was pitching deeper into the void with each breath it took to continue. I did not laugh for joy. It had to sound more like a cackle toward the end. I broke. I thought I had been fully broken before.

"I said 'You are a fool'." It reached him that time. "All this talk of peace? It's...it's gone." I shuttered. "Lord Mwin, I have no idea where you are out there. I am sorry."

The Emperor's face grew a bright shade of red. Foam formed at the corners of his mouth as he worked it into various shapes, uncertain what to say.

"How dare...bring me that boy!" The guards next to me pretended not to hear him. When it became apparent to the Emperor they would not act, he ordered others to retrieve me.

A group of soldiers, heavily armored and bearing the Emperor's colors, charged at me in the fields. Some of them pulled up short. The ones that did not disobey their Emperor's wishes, stopped alongside them to see what was the matter.

I am...*sorry*.

"What is this?" I saw Hydel mouth the question rather than heard.

"Mistress." Her eyes met mine. "Estry did not become an idol. Well, she did, but I caused it. You may have heard she sent a package to Lord Mwin the day she died. That was my doing as well. Thanks to Conarance's oh-so-wonderful care of my being, I discovered my blood was a thing of power. Kyda may have told you about the philosopher stones. Those were nothing. They were nothing more than the type of stone used to store essence. Like the ones they use in the church for the saints. My blood was the key to everything, not those stones. I siphoned my blood, Mistress. I nearly bled myself dry and I sent that blood to Mwinstead under Estry's name to prevent it from being searched. And then Mwinstead sent you the finest wine this land has to offer." I let that sink in. A number of wineskins and goblets found their way to the ground. "And you served it to damn near everyone of import here today. Including you, Your Majesty."

"Mist...Hydel, what the hell is he saying?" The Emperor shot her the question, but couldn't find her.

Hydel appeared before me on the gallows, accompanied by two members of Clock Tower, who were holding her by the arms. Their corruption emyon used to transport her faded below their feet as they were pulled to the surface. They offered me my mask and fixed their own to their faces as I did the same.

"Your Majesty, you should have made your plans clear and not kept your people in the dark for so long." My eyes started to burn as I looked down on Hydel, who had been brought to her knees. "Kill them all."

Just like that. Half the Coliseum went about my orders. Chaos. The guards who had pulled up short of the Emperor's orders slew their comrades who hadn't. Friends and family viciously ripped at each other's throats. Mothers bashed their children's skulls on the Coliseum's floor. Husbands strangled their wives. The Emperor himself looked on with horror as he cut eyes from heads using his own crown to do so.

I didn't watch as all my desires came true in an onslaught of innocent lives. I just watched Hydel, and she watched me, wordless. Other members of Clock Tower brought Leegius and my leather jacket once the area had grown quiet, save for the groans of the dying.

"I'm sorry."

With that, I had said all that there was that needed to be said to Hydel. I drew a small needle from one of the pockets in my jacket and stabbed her in the gut. She winced at the injection. Her veins and arteries turned black, radiating from the injection site and she seized up. Still kneeling, Hydel fell away into base components until all that was left of her was a pretty dress and a pile of raw materials.

Leegius watched on and didn't say anything until long after Hydel was disintegrated.

"I think I'll go grab a drink," he said.

I stood there not knowing what to do with myself. I knew this would happen, but I had no idea what it would feel like. I imagined it would have still been horrifying, these things I was capable of, if it had gone as planned. But with the Emperor's decree, there was nothing joyous about it. Revenge was not satisfied. I never thought such a gesture by the Emperor would do such a thing. When he said he would free all the slaves, I hadn't wanted revenge any longer. That one gesture was enough. Peace, that's all I ever wanted. I had single-handedly destroyed any possibility of such a thing.

"Expertly done, Bringer. Yalor will be completely under our control before summer's end." Lich-Fex shook with excitement. "Have we considered a name for it once it is ours?"

"I didn't want this, Lich."

"Oh, but my boy, you did. None of this would have been possible if not for you. Undergrowth was good, expert even, at enacting change on Oshoku's behalf. Never could we have dreamed of accomplishing something like this. Our Lady merely gave you a tool. What you did with it was entirely your choice, Bringer of the Blight. We bow to you now for her sake...Blight-Bringer."

He was right, though I did not want to acknowledge the fact. What I had said to Kyda was not a lie. I was a monster and it was not humans that made me so. Everything I had done since becoming infected was entirely my doing and now no one would stop me. I was too much of a coward to stop myself and no one else could wield this unholy weapon I had been given. The Emperor was right too, though. The dawn may have not been golden, but a new epoch had just begun. Orecul would now be shattered into uncountable pieces. Avalon would fall and disappear into the myths of utopias as ideals like it had before.

I made my way to leave the gallows to figure out where to go from here. I suppose, in a way, I never thought I could actually pull this off, or that I would die in doing so. Now, I had no direction. I thought I might return home. If mother was still alive, could she look at her blackened son with the same love as before after what I had done?

"Leegius, will you come with me? We can go see your family first, maybe. Leegius? Leegius?"

Where did he say he was going again?

# Epilogue

"Olu...Olu, come back to me." I held him by the face. His tears flowed freely and the illusions around us followed, weeping like wet paint. "Olu!"

His eyes snapped open. He was rigid for a moment, but then his body relaxed. His face wrenched back down, however, and the tears continued, the emerald in his eyes glistening. I let his face go, stiffly. He reached up and held his face with his hands, a gesture pilfered from me. I saw myself watching myself then. There was nothing I could do or say. There was never any hero for me at such times, again, there was no hero now. What would I have wished someone would offer me then?

"Iter..." It was difficult to make out his words between sobs.

I sat down in the filth with him. The illusions were gone now, any happy memories in those books which could have been, now, it was just the reality, devastation and loss.

Ruin and rot were all around us. Yalor was nothing but a memory, foul through and through. The buildings and street work were in a disarray reserved for ancient cities. Large fleshy pods, which had burst some time ago, lay wilted and decaying, their remains cascading over the buildings and landscape. Purple web and root-like systems sprouted from each pod's base, defacing the surrounding area and destabilizing structures. I knew enough to understand each pod and root system contained a single skeleton. I tried to overlook the smaller groups. I was certain I saw a school on my way through the city. I considered The Lost and where Clock Tower had led them. Was there anywhere still untouched in all of Orecul?

Olu watched the holes in his hands, sobs spent, eyeliner smeared. It seemed unreasonable he would have the mind for such a detail then. I may have suggested a burial for that little girl, but it wouldn't have made up for Unna not receiving the same treatment.

"There was nothing you could do, Olu. Nothing anyone could have done."

"So, what do we do now?"

The particles in the air drew closer, I returned the mask to my face, checked its filters, and stood up.

"There is no other choice, Olu. We have to go put him down."

Milton Keynes UK
Ingram Content Group UK Ltd.
UKHW020622210824
447080UK00020B/56

9 798218 392789